DAVE DUGGAN

A SUDDEN SUN

A NOVEL

GUILDHALL PRESS

Published in April 2012

Guildhall Press
Unit 15, Ráth Mór Business Park
Bligh's Lane, Derry
Ireland
BT48 0LZ
(028) 7136 4413
info@ghpress.com
www.ghpress.com

 Guildhall Press gratefully acknowledges the financial support of
the Arts Council of Northern Ireland as a principal funder under its
Annual Support for Organisations Programme.

*For Deirdre, Siobhán, Mary, Mairéad and Claire
and to the memory of our mother, Margaret*

As we come marching, marching in the beauty of the day,
A million darkened kitchens, a thousand mill lofts grey
Are touched with all the radiance that a sudden sun discloses
For the women hear us singing:
'Bread and Roses! Bread and Roses!'

James Oppenheim, 1911

CHAPTER ONE

FIRES

My mother says: 'Donna, we could write some stories in this family, if the ones who could write them knew how to spell.'

A fountain of duty springs from her yearning as if there were a line of people behind her, pens poised, sweat pouring off them, all striving to get their lives down on paper.

I can spell now. I have written essays and theses. I have learned the skills and I can plumb the fountain.

But more than that, I can bring order to my own life and to the things that happened to me, so fast they created a fire-storm out of Time. One minute I'm a young bride in a white dress, a flower girl skipping in front of me, the next I'm a graduate in a black robe, a roll of paper bound in a red ribbon clasped in my hand, applause ringing in my ears.

Tony came to the graduation today. I saw him in the crowd before we went into the big marquee, its door-flaps gay as sails in the breeze. I had my mother with me as my guest for the tea and scones. She spotted Tony as we crossed the lawn and nodded in his direction. I put a finger to my lips before she could say anything and I walked over to him. He had his jacket over his arm and was smoking a cigarette. He smiled the same smile – thinner

1

perhaps – he smiled on the day I met him at the top of the aisle.

'Thought I'd come to say congratulations,' he said as he stubbed out the cigarette.

'Thanks, Tony.'

I leaned into him and we hugged like distant cousins, our cheeks barely touching. He remarried. I never did. He has two children now. I have none. No, that's not true. He has three and I have one and she's long dead and buried in the deep, dark ground.

That's what I want to make sense of. 'Stillbirth' they call it, though there's nothing 'still' about it. It rages on in my heart, burning forever. I know it does for Tony, too, in a different way. He didn't get that stoop in his walk, those lines about his eyes, that desolated way of smoking simply from day-to-day living. He's just as consumed as I am, just as burnt out inside. The fires simply took us different ways.

'You look great in the gown.'

'Makes me feel like an old woman.'

'Well, you don't look it.'

You look like an old man, I thought to myself. It was on the tip of my tongue to say that we should talk about it. What I really wanted to say was that he should talk to someone about it, but my mother came up beside us.

'Yes, Mrs McDaid,' said Tony.

'Tony.'

'So, she has her degree now,' he said, pulling another cigarette out of a packet, striking a match and lighting it in one fluid movement. It made him look like the younger Humphrey Bogart in an old black-and-white film I'd seen during my days spent staring at daytime television. It made me smile remembering how I used to feel about him.

'Fair play to her,' he continued, blowing out a long stream of smoke. 'I always knew she had the brains.'

A grimace set on my mother's face and I knew the sort of remark that was building in her mind. Something along the lines of 'aye, that's right, Tony Bradley, but we all knew she had brains when she got rid of you'. I shuffled my feet and coughed, distracting her.

Tony thought it was his smoking.

'Sorry. You never liked the fags, Donna.' He squeezed the top of the cigarette between his thumb and his finger and dropped it to the ground. Then he put on his jacket and prepared to leave. 'I hope yeez have a great day.' Looking up, he added, 'The sun's out anyway. Congratulations, Donna. All the best. You deserve it.' Then he nodded at my mother, 'Mrs McDaid,' and walked off towards the car-park steps.

'He has a cheek,' my mother said.

'Pack it in, Ma,' I chided her gently. 'I'm glad he made the effort.' That's a new thing. Talking back to my mother. I suppose it's because I have the words now. And I know how to spell them.

I watched Tony get to his car. He glanced back and we waved briefly at each other. Then I looked down at my feet, following the folds of my gown, flowing like basalt, to where my sensible black shoes peeked out and the cigarette Tony dropped still smouldered. A single plume of smoke rose up as if charmed from the lone ember that glowed for an instant before consuming itself and becoming dark.

If I am to start anywhere, I know I should start with the fires. I begin an account today. I will not call it a book, because I don't know how it will go, only that I will write it as best I can, whenever I feel I can. If it is to be a record, then a birth is a good place to start, with all the fires that raged and all the embers that still glow and all the smoke that fills my head and stands like a graveyard miasma in front of my eyes.

'Let's get a cup of tea, Ma,' I said and I led my mother back to the marquee, where the hubbub of the celebrating graduates and their families drew us in. I soon fell into conversations with classmates and my mother had two rounds of scones. Then I sent her home in a taxi and followed soon after, walking back to my own place to begin writing this.

I still live in the same house. Tony moved out when we split up and he now lives in a new house with four bedrooms, a garden, a new wife – Mary, I went to school with her sister – and two

3

small children. I am a single woman in the two-bedroom house in Rosemount, the house I moved into when I got married, only now I sleep in one bedroom and I work in another. Instead of a cot or bunk beds, there is a desk, an armchair, shelves of books, and a window with a view over my small yard to other small yards with washing on spinning lines, satellite dishes on walls and back extensions, built on to cope with expanding families.

I am singular, rather than single, as if the whole process of living has tempered and fired me, so that I can sit here and feel almost perfect, finished, ready, not for the shelf, but finally and forcefully, for life itself.

I drain the glass of Beaujolais beside me and smile to myself at my tastes. More changes. The fire in the wine refreshes and cleanses me as I re-read these first sentences, feeling I have done something. Made a start at least. But if I am going to really write this down I have to go right back to the very start. To a birth, yes, but not my own. And to the fires that started it all.

People say that endings are hard, but I say that about beginnings. It's hard to pin them down. The minute you hit on one point and say, 'That's it. That's when it all began,' you find that you are forced backwards in time, to some other more distant point, a Big Bang moment claiming to be the source, the launch of things.

If I start with the birth, then why don't I go back to the conception? And back further then, to the time when I met Tony and back further to the days I was at school and my destiny was being set by the 11-plus exam and the secondary school I went to.

It all started – here I really am taking the plunge – not with a house or a school, but with a hospital, and yes, it started with a birth, but not my own, which my mother told me, in a desire to help me exorcise the ghosts of my labour, was out of the ordinary because I arrived with the cord wrapped around my neck. The midwife had to perform a miracle of contortions to get me free so that I could yelp my first breaths.

Teresa never breathed at all. There. That's her name written down. And if she had lived she might have a brother or sister, maybe two, by now. Tony would probably still be here. Who

4

knows? That's why it's the start and when I write it down, it's obvious.

I remember Tony standing at the end of the bed, thinking I was asleep, but I wasn't. I was totally disorientated and dopey, tired and beaten, my insides feeling like pulp, my bones wrung through a crusher, as if I'd been driven over by a juggernaut. Tony stood there, crying and heaving sigh upon sigh in time with my breathing, saying nothing. The juggernaut had run over him, too.

Nothing ever prepares. Not all the doctors with their earnest consolation, not all the midwives with their gentle hands. They said she would not live. I carried her dead inside me and when my body heaved and convulsed as the midwives exhorted and cajoled, 'That's it, Donna, push on, push on,' it was to push her to the grave, not the cot.

My head swims now, thinking about it. I recognise this nausea, this clammy sense that I won't be able to breathe, that everything will get caught up inside me and I will once more feel those pains, the torment of the flesh and the ravages of the heart. Outside I can see washing spinning in the wind. There are showers now after the day's sun.

Stillbirth, the doctors said. Unexplained. A rare condition, they said. Teresa was one in a thousand. One in a million. I could write a thesis on it now. I read the books. Not immediately. Years after, when I was already studying at the university. I went to the medical section of the library. I took three books on stillbirth back to the desk where I was working on an essay evaluating different methods of disposing of toxic waste. I pushed my notes aside and plunged in. An hour later I made my way to the coffee shop where a cleaner found me crying, tearing my Styrofoam coffee cup into tiny, tiny pieces.

I still feel glad they let us hold Teresa. She looked so peaceful, her pink eyelids closed and her head nestling in the snow-white blanket. Tony sat on the bed beside me and the midwives and doctor left the room. The door sucked closed and we were alone. The family we were trying to be. Something simple and awesome like that. I cherish the memory of those moments as the greatest treasure I have. And when they came back to take her away and the priest came, mumbling and hesitant, I lay back on the pillow, soaked in tears, swimming in tears, burning inside like a great furnace and repeated the question, 'Why? In the name of God, why?'

My mother has a picture of Teresa of Avila on the wall in her living room. An aunt gave it to her on her wedding day. My mother has a special devotion to the saint of spiritual ecstasy. The picture shows the saint in a trance as an angelic figure hovers above her, pointing towards a beam of light. The text beneath the image reads:

Let nothing trouble you.
Let nothing make you afraid.
All things pass away.
God never changes.
Patience obtains everything.
God alone is enough.

We named her Teresa, after the saint in my mother's picture.

People say a little knowledge is a dangerous thing. I disagree. I think you need knowledge and if it means you have to start with a little bit of it and then get more, so be it. Since that time, I have always made sure I knew what I needed to know. I am not going to let that happen to me again, have something I know nothing about creep up and poleaxe me. I am going to know in advance. I suppose that's what has taken me here. That's what has made this room a study and not the child's bedroom it was supposed to be.

I will not write here every day. There will be gaps, as my daily life prevents me from going into the past. But I will go there.

And the future?

There may be other children, I don't know. But I have no will for it at present. That was what made Tony leave, everyone said. My mother believes he deserted me when I needed him most, just when I was coming out of the depression and beginning to get myself back to normal. She can't stand him. But it wasn't like that. He didn't desert me. I drove him out in my search for knowledge.

'What do you want to know?' he'd plead with me, his head in his hands.

'Everything,' I'd reply coldly. 'Everything.'

I searched everywhere. Inside myself, in the lives of my sisters and my mother, in the papers I read, in the actions of politicians, the games of children, the formations of the clouds, the learned ideas of experts in the field, every book I could lay my hands on, every article in women's magazines telling the true life story of some woman who had the same experience as me. I devoured these as truths, because that's really what I wanted. Knowledge was one thing. But the truth was something else. The truth would set me free and I wanted to be free. Free of it all. Free in the way I was as a girl. Free, in a way that Teresa is free. Free to stop crying inside.

CHAPTER TWO

BEGINNINGS

Let me record the day Tony took me home from hospital after Teresa died.

'Altnagelvin' we call the place where the hospital stands, like a great cruiser riding on the top of a hill. It's Irish and it translates as 'the steep glen of the sparrows'. There were no sparrows around that morning. Just rows of cars, stunned by the cold sleety snow, and people dashing about, hunched over in their coats.

Up to that time I'd always felt the hospital was a kind of sanctuary, as special as a cathedral. Even the view you get of it coming home from Belfast, the first big building you see, high and graceful, sailing up there with the clouds and the sparrows, makes it seem venerable. That morning I thought nothing of the sort. It was a deathtrap. It was not a temple for the miracles of life. It was a charnel house for the horrors of death.

I picked a newspaper off the seat and settled in. Tony fussed about me with the seat belt and a blanket from the back seat.

'Get that round ye until the car heats up a bit.'

He closed the doors and started scraping the windscreen, the noise like a machine trying hard not to break down. A swathe of clear windscreen appeared as his hand swept by, then another, and another, arcs of clearness and his face huffing and puffing, then seeing me, smiling bravely. I smiled back, but felt my teeth chatter and my jaws ache.

I glanced down at the newspaper in my lap and read the headline: DU PONT ANNOUNCE INCINERATOR PLANS.

I read that the chemical company intended to build a facility to burn toxic waste at their site on the banks of our river, the Foyle. The first thought that struck me was that, since Tony worked there, that was good news. Anything that made the company bigger, more successful, more likely to stay in the city, was good. But the word 'toxic' simply wouldn't leave me. I almost laugh as I write that the word 'toxic' was new to me. Now I have a degree in Environmental Science and I'm a specialist. I sit here in my study and read books, reports, analyses and accounts as if such an act was as everyday as hanging washing on the line. And if things go well, and there is no reason to think they won't, I am going to be sitting in a room in the City Council's offices overlooking the same river and it is going to be my job to write reports, give accounts and perform studies and analyses of the city's waste, toxic included. Now I'm an expert. That day in the car outside Altnagelvin Hospital, I didn't know what the word 'toxic' meant. But I felt it. I felt like toxic waste. Toxic inside like a cauldron of gunge and slime, pus-yellow and snot-green, rancid and putrid, vile and unclean. A complete waste.

Tony scraped the last section clean and the windscreen was practically clear. He climbed back into the car, stashed the plastic scraper under the dashboard, brrred a few times and rubbed his hands, blew into them and started the engine.

'Do you know anything about this?' I asked.

He looked at the paper on my lap.

'Not really. They were talking about it at work, but I know no more than is in the paper. Still, it should mean they'll stay. Here, you warm enough?'

He leaned across and tucked the rug round me and buzzed the dial on the heater but he had already turned it to maximum and the car was heating up. We turned right at the hospital exit and a bus turned in, outpatients and ancillary staff looking solemn at each window. There were two parallel black lines on each side of the road, traffic marks in a fresh fall of snow. We slid onto our black lines like rollers in an automated process and headed for town. With the snow and the slush, everything seemed closer. Lisnagelvin Shopping Centre was quiet. A yellow school bus lurched up to the traffic lights, then lumbered forward. I saw no children but I knew they were there, huddled behind the steamed-up windows.

The road swept towards the river and, at Dale's Corner, running my eye along the green fence of the army barracks, I saw the river in a line to the clock of the Guildhall, the water like molten lead, heaving and rising in the freeze. I felt like a voyager, a first time visitor to Derry, a tourist in a foreign place. We crossed the lower deck of Craigavon Bridge, almost a tunnel, the huge metal stanchions slicing views of the river.

'We'll go the town way,' said Tony, with a smile. 'There's no rush.'

He was putting it off, too. Wanting to spin out the time before we had to be in our own house. Before we had to cross that threshold. Alone.

We crawled along by the river and the park. The road seemed worse here. That was in the days before the big shopping centre. Before Marks and Spencer came. It seems like pre-history, but it's only yesterday. It might as well be an eternity ago.

Tony took us along the Strand Road. Warwick's had a January sale on selected lines of wallpaper. Now there is a hotel there, and a cinema complex and a shopping centre so ugly people lower their eyes to avoid seeing it.

Even remembering these bits is hard, as if the changes that have come to the city are so complete I will not be able to go back and really remember. How can I be sure anything happened if many of the places, the buildings and the streets where it happened, are not there?

Where we live is still the same. Where I live, I should say. As Tony turned up Park Avenue at the post office, the dread that was lurking inside me gathered itself and rose in my throat as bile. I had to wind my window down for air. Tony glanced at me anxiously as he turned into Epworth Street and we passed between the two facing terraces. By the time Tony parked outside our house, I was heaving and gulping, my breath coming in chunks of solid matter, cold as ice.

He ran to the front door and tried his key, but the door was open. He turned, with a puzzled look on his face, and came back to get me.

The rush of cold air when he opened the door slapped me in the face and I clambered out, a riven girl, bent as a granny. He took my arm.

'The door's open,' he said, sharing his mild surprise.

We made it to the house. I had a sense of neighbours looking out from behind windows. Tony pushed the door wide open and we walked down the short hall. The inner door swung open and my mother stood there. She took me from Tony and led me on. In the living room a fire was lighting and my sisters – Anna, holding a teapot, and Martha, her arms crossed on her chest – stood on either side of it. From where I stood I could see the tears in their eyes. Mine poured out, too, and my mother held me. I felt Tony's hand on my shoulder and I reached back to touch him.

I was home and I collapsed into the bosom of my family. Wasted.

Family. Thankfully I've only got one of them! As I get older, and all of us get older, relationships between us don't get more simple. They get more layered and overgrown. And pressures that were held down by fear and common sense press out in the most unlikely places.

I remember how my mother became defensive after I first came home from the hospital. She performed her acts of love and mothering with wonderful care and attention, but an edge came to her tongue as if she was impatient to have that time pass. I don't blame her. We all felt that way.

Actually, when I try to look back on it now, I remember I felt a confusion of emotions that oscillated between extreme heat and furious cold. So perhaps it's the case that I can't remember what I felt, as if all memories have been destroyed in the fires that raged in my heart and soul. And fires there were, because if I have one memory, it is of ashes, bearing the taste of the blackness on burnt toast, a mouthful of incinerated bread, polluting my insides through and through.

Loss tastes like burnt toast. Black and crunchy, teeth-grating and grim, loss is life overdone. You can scrape it with a knife, a blade honed by your best intentions, your plans for a new life, your commitment to making a future for yourself and, though you will manage to scrape off the outer flakes of the burnt bread of life, you will never totally remove the sordid taste of it. Loss is an indigestible burnt offering. A charcoal crust. Accompanied by countless cups of tea and numberless visits from kindly people as the great blanket of community that holds us all together in this city wrapped itself around me. I felt the fabric of it, warm, coarse and kind, multi-layered and various in its weave. Secure. And stifling.

I remember ... God, I hoped it would be like this. I hoped the act of writing would bring it all back ... I remember sitting in the living room, feeling totally tea-ed out, women's voices all around me, a plate of toast on the table, my mother standing in the doorway of the back kitchen. Her face seemed to distort, expand and then melt as she looked across at me. She'd seen something in my eyes, something I had not even known was there. At that moment I dropped my mug. It seemed to take ages – maybe I just remember it that way – but it finally crashed against the tiles in front of the fire, going off like a bomb. A great spurt of tea and shards leapt from it, splashing Anna and Martha in a crazed benediction.

No-one spoke for an instant. There was the hush of the grave in the room and I got up and walked to the stairs, my slippered feet flip-flopping across the floor. Anna bent over and started to pick up the pieces. Martha held her face in her hands. My mother quivered in the doorway, little spills of tea slurping out of the teapot's spout as her shoulders heaved and she gulped back tears.

The truth is none of us knew how to react. People used to say to me, 'Ach, Donna, you must be numb inside.' They couldn't have been further from the truth. I wasn't numb. I was raging. I was consumed. There were flames of every colour coursing through me, so that I felt I would combust at any time. I had fevers the health visitors could find no cause for. My skin became flushed

12

and then bronzed as if I had been taking sun-bed sessions. I had an unnatural colour. I was incinerated.

I don't know when I made the connection between what was happening to me and what the newspapers said Du Pont was planning. I'm not even sure I ever really made a connection and I wonder if that is the way life works at all. Do people do things because something happens to them or do we trundle along, coping with what is thrown at us, hoping we will survive? Then, if we're lucky, we grow into a nervous old age as we realise we haven't managed to trick death? It is time for me to check with myself once more. Do I really want to do this? Do I really want to record all that happened by writing in this book, however intermittently? Do I really want to get it all down? What if my mother or my sisters should read it?

I have two older sisters, Anna and Martha. I've always felt closer to Anna, even though we're not a bit like sisters. Martha and me look more alike. We both have the large open eyes we got from our mother, eyes that made us look sensuous and desirable when we were younger, but that now make us look dopey and lost. Anna must have my father's eyes, I suppose. She is alive and jumpy. She is a woman who makes the job of coping with a husband and three children look like a doddle except that everyone close to her knows how hard she works at it, how much energy she expends. Martha blunders through, though you could say she is the most successful in some ways. She married well. Damien Ferry, her husband, owns a plastics factory in Springtown. There was talk of a job for me there, in the months after Teresa. I wouldn't have minded that, because Damien is one of those decent sorts who thinks everything can be fixed with money and, up to a very far point, he's right. It's just that the things I needed sorted out couldn't be paid for with cash, credit card or cheque.

They can perhaps be eked out in ink, a form of blood seeping out of me, through the pen and onto the page. That is why I am here, today, years later, trying to make sense of it all as I look back. That fire-storm of Time, when Teresa didn't come to us, when Du Pont announced the plan to build a toxic-waste incinerator. That's the start of it, because my father was long since dead and my two sisters, older than me and married, were 'settled' in their lives and my mother had already begun the last phase for hers, her golden period perhaps. That time was indeed the start because it was the year that the story of my life ignited and scorched all around it in one great blaze.

CHAPTER THREE

THE NUT

I haven't written here for a while. It's not that I felt that I had written all I had to write. It's more to do with how living now makes it harder to write about times past. But I'm always drawn back to those days.

I went into work today. That's a laugh. What I really mean is that I went into the office, drank three cups of tea, shuffled a few papers and came home early. It's part of my induction. A series of days at the office, a seminar in Belfast, a conference here in Derry and then I start full time in two weeks. It is like I have been charmed into it. I couldn't have written the job description better myself, though in a sense I did write it.

I can reflect here on how focused and clever I have become. Now I really hope no-one reads this. They'll think I'm a right fool. But I know I organised that the sandwich part of my university course would include a placement at the City Engineer's Office and I gave my specialism as waste management, making myself indispensable at the end of the year. I convinced my boss, Paddy Robinson, by my presence and my hard work, that what the city needed was an environmental scientist (me!) to assist his unit in its waste management responsibilities. Who better to do that than Donna Bradley, the woman who had more or less created the job out of nothing?

Waste is something I have a talent for. I carried it inside me. I was a receptacle for wasted life. A human wheelie bin. A landfill site. My womb connected to a pipe down which, to the exhortations of midwives, I discharged and I discharged, until my whole world was polluted. I honestly used to feel like that. Now I look back and I like to think I have a healthier view of what happened to me. Now I see it as part of the cycle of life. Birth and death hand in hand. The cycle as a null point, the two poles so close together as to be inseparable, as a storyteller once laid it out before me.

I remember being in the library in school when she came. A large, elegant woman, who moved smoothly behind her swirling scarf, which she used as cloak, drape, flag, waves and sails in different stories. I remember a roomful of students, maybe two or three classes, in our green uniforms and our white knee-socks. It must have been GCSE year, because I remember being big, grown-up and dismissive of the idea of listening to stories. But I soon got swept up in the words and actions of the teller. They were funny and entertaining. The pictures she painted were vivid and close. She finished by telling a story about death and it was all we could talk about for the rest of the day. We stood in huddles and shivered together, daring ourselves to relive the story and to understand. This is how I remember her telling the story of Jack and the nut.

The Story of Jack and the Nut

Jack lived with his mother in a small cottage by the sea. One day his mother said to Jack that, as she was very old and had lived a full and enjoyable life, Death would soon be coming to call for her. Jack told her that would never happen. Later that day, he was walking down the path from the cottage to the sea when he met Death, coming for his mother. He swept Death up and carried him under his arm and rushed towards the sea. As he stood on the pebbled beach, he noticed the shell of a hazelnut at his feet and he picked it up, and stuffed Death into it. Then he tossed the shell as far away into the waves as he could.

When he went back to his cottage he heard his mother singing and found her working about the house, sprightly and gay. He had never seen her look so straight-backed and happy. She told him to go into the village to get some meat for dinner, but when he got there he found the butcher's shop closed and a sign on it saying that there was no meat because no animals could be killed. He tried to get some fruit but was told that nothing was ripening, that no fruit could be taken from the trees. There was no bread in the bakery because the wheat could not be harvested from the fields and no flour was made.

Jack went home and told his mother how all the people of the village were near to starvation. Then they heard that old people who lived near them were in great pain and anguish, because they were tired and could get no rest. They learned of young people with terrible illnesses who could get no relief. Jack's mother began to complain that she could not stand it any longer and Jack realised it was all his fault. He went back to the pebbled beach and looked out over the sea, confused and tormented. The waves rolled in, one after another. Great white horses charged at him, to rest, spent and thin, at his feet. Then he noticed one wave had brought back the shell of the hazelnut. He pounced on it before the sea could reclaim it and opened it, freeing Death into the world once more.

Very soon the sounds of harvesting filled the air and the butcher's shop had meat and the cycle of life and death was complete. Death came for Jack's mother and she left him peacefully, and though Jack was very sad, he knew it was better this way, since Death is a part of life and living.

Now that I have written it down I can appreciate how important that story has been for me. If I do nothing else in this book except record stories like that, I will be happy. Stories that are embedded in my own story, glistening barnacles on the side of a great whale, cruising the dark ocean. Will I go crazy recording such morbid tales? I'm still young and I'm sounding like Jack's mother, an old woman. I know that I have aged more in these recent years, more than I could ever have imagined. In fact there was a period, in my depression, when it seemed as if I was ageing too fast, as if my whole life had speeded up and was tending to become like Teresa's, where the line between life and death was non-existent. But now I am putting distance between them again, by writing in this book. That's what I'm doing. I'm cheating death. Cheating Time. I am confounding the Second Law of Thermodynamics, which has Time moving in one direction, generating ever mounting piles of waste out of my life. I am clawing my way back through this waste to face my past, as in my day job you could say, where I will perform civic acts of waste management. I am picking up the shell of the hazelnut before it lands on the shore. I am tossing it out again, knowing full well that it will return on the surf and that I will have to face it, again and again and again.

I want to get down how I first got into the campaign to oppose the incinerator and I've been thinking hard about it for a few days now and realise that it took quite a few months for the whole affair to really have an impact on me. In one way that is not surprising. That period is stuck in my mind as the time of grief and anguish, the time of the wee white coffin, the beaten crowd of mourners, the Valium-induced haze. The sense of aimlessness that took me onto the rain-sodden streets is so much a part of that time that I am finding it hard to have a sense of anything else. Then there are the tricks of memory, the failings, the omissions, the things I want to block out and I know I won't bring up. I comfort myself here that I am now distant enough from that time and that I have the words and the methods, so I should be able to do this. I am a scientist after all. I have my methods. Thesis, hypothesis, experiment, review. New hypothesis, experiment, review. On and on and at the end of it all? Truth?

When the spring came that year I began to meander down the town. Firstly, Anna and Martha or my mother would come with me, or they would try to stop me, but eventually they realised I was so crazed I wanted to be meandering all the time and they couldn't keep up with that. They also realised that it was harmless enough; that I wasn't going to break down in the Richmond

Centre; that I wasn't going to break into Ferguson's and steal a whole pile of pretty baby-girl dresses. God knows I wanted to. I stood in front of that shop window and looked at the frilly infant dresses as if they were the most prized items in the world. I would imagine myself buying them and taking them home. I would imagine myself taking them out of the tissue paper and showing them to Teresa lying on her back, just a nappy on, her pink legs kicking the air. Then I would snap open the clasp at the back of the dress but when I turned to the baby she was gone. There was nothing there, though the image of the small white coffin shimmered somewhere just behind my eyes.

I always had to sit down after a bout like that. I used to stumble along William Street and sit on one of the metal seats in Waterloo Square, among the emigration statues, in front of Wellworth's. This is no trick of memory; it was always raining then. What my mother refers to as 'wild wet rain' and though we all know how silly that is, we also all understand exactly what she means.

Sodden, sullen and hunched, I sat on the bench watching people come and go from the supermarket, cars pulling up to drop people off, though it was a pedestrianised area even then; sticker sellers rattling their tins; dogs sniffing about, pin-pointing any hope of meat. I became one of the statues. A young woman in a grey coat, her hair plastered down on her head, resting, as if she, too, like the statues, was on a long despairing journey, away from the bleakness of famine and death.

CHAPTER FOUR

ACTING

I don't know exactly when I first noticed the performers using the statues and the space in front of Wellworth's. I became aware that they came there on Saturdays and gathered a crowd and that it all had something to do with the Du Pont announcement. There seemed to be three or four of them. Sometimes different ones. Mainly men, but some women, too, and they would be dressed up in white coats and silly glasses and they would start into a performance and a crowd would gather and have a laugh or shout things up at them. Then an argument would start and people in the crowd would get talking and everyone would get involved. More people would join the crowd. And then, just as suddenly as it had started, it would be over and the men would dismantle the things they had brought: a bockety card table, rusty garden seats, the inner cylinder of a carpet roll. They would stroll off towards William Street. I followed them one day, after they'd completed their act. They still wore their white coats, their silly hats and other funny clothes as they sat in Frankie Ramsey's café drinking tea.

I was drawn to this Saturday spectacle in a way I can't explain. I never spoke to them or asked them what they were about. I stood on the edge of the crowd when they were performing. Often they pretended to be scientists. One of them, a thin man wearing glasses, who hardly ever spoke, was called Doctor Angstrom and he had the cardboard cylinder set up as the chimney stack of the new incinerator which they said was going to be perfectly safe and that we didn't need to worry, that everything would be all right. Another man wore a white coat and read from a clipboard. He kept going on about how we had nothing to worry about, how Du Pont had all the expertise in the world to do this and that there would be no pollution or toxic emissions. Then the thin one climbed a stool and inspected the top of the chimney stack. He leaned over and peered in and a puff of black soot shot up. When he looked up again his face was covered in soot and his eyes peered white out of a mask like Al Jolson's.

Everyone laughed and even I smiled. Maybe that was what drew me to them. It was the one thing that made me laugh then. They did other mad things. One day they turned up in white coats pushing a pram with a small plastic barrel on it. The one with the clipboard went round the square asking for directions to Du Pont, saying they had a consignment of toxic waste for the new incinerator. He had a big map which he kept flapping about. There was a woman with them that day. She had a brown coat like you see on school caretakers and she wielded a big yard brush.

When they got to the statues, the one with the clipboard drew a chalk circle on the ground and kept telling people to keep back, that this was an 'exclusion zone'. I realise that their acts brought new language to the city. I wonder how many people knew the words 'exclusion zone' or 'toxic' before the whole affair happened. You could even say the job I have now grew out of that time.

People came up to the edge of the 'exclusion zone' and laughed at the mock seriousness of the 'scientists'. I'm just stopping to wonder here how do I feel about that, now that I am a scientist? They were very definitely mocking my profession. Maybe we deserve it. I'm on the side of the scientists who are trying to do something about waste. I take my public responsibilities seriously and I have morals. In a different time and place, would I have worked on the Manhattan Project and helped to develop the atom bomb? No, I don't think I would. What I do know is that 'time and place' play a big part in all these decisions.

You've got to be at the right place at the right time for so many things and those Saturdays when the actors did those stunts, it felt like that was the right place for me.

When they knocked the barrel off the pram and a river of dirty suds flowed out, crossing the chalk line, rushing up to the feet of the onlookers who instinctively backed off as the one with the clipboard kept running about shouting, 'It's all under control, it's all under control,' and the woman in the brown coat tried to sweep it back with the yard brush, I knew that among this playfulness there was something important, not just for the city, but for me, Donna Bradley, the woman with toxic insides, the woman who had given birth to death.

I was so hard on myself then that I weep now, remembering. I had no hope. That was it. I was utterly without hope. Yet I heard a calling in the antics of those actors and the campaign they were supporting, so that when I found my usual bench and they didn't come I felt more alone than ever. I felt I had even less than nothing, which, I realise now, is pathetic. I had Tony, my mother and my sisters. I was healthy enough, given the circumstances. And I would be fine. I knew that, deep inside me. I was young and I've always been optimistic. In the playing of the actors I sensed hope, and clarity in the laughter, at a time when the whole city was confused. In the middle of all of that, I was in a whirlwind of grief and uncertainty.

The Saturday I remember best was when they held the mock TV debate. There were three of them, two on upturned milk crates making speeches, the other holding a long pole with a fake microphone dangling from it. He swung this back and forth and the two speakers delivered their arguments. They were dressed in modified everyday clothes. Nothing too outlandish, but something not quite right, as if they were clowns pretending to be real people. One of them was in favour of the incinerator and spoke about the jobs it would bring and the safety record of Du Pont and the need for a responsible society to properly dispose of its toxic waste. The other was against it and spoke of the dangers and the need for what he called 'clean production'. That phrase is a commonplace for me now. Then it was the oddest thing in the world and here we all were on the streets on a Saturday talking about it.

The actors were trying to get the crowd going. It was obvious that I wasn't the only person who had seen them before. Some-one from the crowd shouted up at them, 'What happened? You were in favour of it last week.' You could see the actors grinning slightly but then carrying on in their roles for the day.

The one in favour of the incinerator kept talking about the need to think about the future and a man in the audience began to argue with him. He was red-faced and stout, with beefy fore-arms resting on his barrel belly and a shovel full of gravel in his deep voice.

'What kind of future are you on about? What future will we have when we're all poisoned?'

It was obvious that most of the crowd agreed with him and the argument passed back and forth, until the actor appealed to him saying, 'I'm only trying to put across a point of view here. It's not easy up here on this soapbox. It's all right for you down there on the ground. Come up here and say it.'

And the man did. The actor stepped off the milk crate and the man stood up and spoke to us.

'I worked in factories all my life. I have a brother dying with emphysema from the same factories. You're telling me that every factory in the country is going to bring its waste here and we're going to burn it. Is that the kind of future we want?'

There was a murmur of dissent from the crowd and he got down. The actor got up again and seemed to be smiling as a rip-ple of applause died down in the crowd.

'That's all very well,' he intoned in a condescending manner, 'but we have to be realistic here. Industry is here to stay and we can't be wishy-washy about the future.'

He shook his head and looked about the crowd, catching the eye of the man who had spoken. Suddenly the actor got down again and the stout man strode forward. It all happened in an in-stant. As he came towards the soapbox, he passed a woman with her child, a girl of about three. The stout man lifted the child and climbed onto the upturned milk crate. He held the child up to the crowd and declaimed, 'This is the future. What do yeez want? The child or the incinerator?'

A torch lit up in me, a great flaming sunburst flared and I called out, 'The child. The child.'

I wanted the child so much. And in a way I still do. The fire doesn't rage inside me quite like it used to, but there are enough glowing embers there that it doesn't take much to rake them over and set them blazing.

There comes a time when you have to do something. That's what I've found. The act of writing this comes from an impulse to action that grew out of all the years between then and now, all the events and people running through my life, all meaning something and having an impact on me, all pressing and demanding on me until I have to act. I have to get it down on paper. I realise now what I'm doing. I'm making a story out of my life. Not a once-upon-a-time story, but a story all the same. A narrative to document it, as I might in a scientific experiment, except here it is remembering as much as observing, imagining as much as recording, that I am engaged in.

I've settled into the new job now. The induction fortnight went smoothly and I'm onto my probationary period. It's like I was doing it all my life, as if I was meant to be at this from the very start. I have a corner desk in the City Engineer's open-plan office. A workstation, with a phone, computer, desk space, filing drawers, a cupboard for my coat and large items of stationery. There is a drawing table, angled to the window, that gives a view of the river, curving towards the red-brick shopping centre and the heart of the city. Other desks and workstations belonging to my colleagues fill the room. In a far corner sits a small coffee and water point for the use of staff on this floor. When I set myself up on my first official day I turned things around so that I was facing the big windows that look out over the river across to the green trees in the park and the open sky above. I made myself a mug of coffee and I sat at the desk. The clean surface shimmered in front of me. The screen saver on the computer twirled and spun beautiful, irregular geometrical patterns. There was a low murmur of voices over the soft humming of the heating system. I pressed my arms against my sides, hugging myself. The longest deepest sigh I ever produced eased out of me. I was finally in the right place at the right time and I was the right 'me'.

That first real day, I took a framed photograph out of my bag and put it on the desk in front of me. It is the one item that always stays on the desk, beaming amid the piles of papers, the coffee mug, the occasional vase of flowers, the mountain of reports and files. And that day, when I put it on the clean desk, I almost cried.

It is a landscape view of a beach in Donegal, near Culdaff, in Inishowen. *Cúlaphúca* the locals call it. There's a long beach and in the distance a headland on which the sun is shining, as if it had burst suddenly from behind the white clouds stacked above it. There is no-one on the beach. No-one in the water. There are some small boats near a concrete jetty. The view is nondescript and magnificent at the same time. It is where my mother comes from and, in that sense, where I come from, too. Putting the photo on my desk made the desk home.

I've blurred the edges between home and work so much now that I take the disc from my computer in my study and put it in the computer at work so I can add to my journal there. I have become fascinated with myself and my past, the fascination of a child playing with sand and buckets of water, creating something magical out of the very substances in her hands.

The job itself is straightforward. As I said, I practically created it so I know what it's all about. I'm home safe in the world of work. Who would have thought it? All those years ago when I walked up the aisle to meet Tony and the only thoughts I had in my head was that we would be happy together and make a lovely home together and have lovely children. Did losing Teresa mean so much?

When exactly did the turn happen? When did I start doing things that meant I would end up here?

I cast my mind back again, to the sodden months of an early spring all those years ago and the Saturday afternoon antics of the actors. Images of the day when they tied strings between the statues and the lampposts stand out in my memory. They had pens and markers and they were inviting people to write messages on yellow sheets they set on two old card tables. Messages to Richard Needham, the minister in Belfast responsible for the incinerator decision. They had clothes pegs and they hung the sheets on the strings so that they became washing lines. Even in my Valium haze I realised it was funny in a small way. People stopped and wrote messages. Then they read what other people had written. I circled around the spectacle and took up my usual seat. I don't know how long they kept it up, maybe an hour or more. The actors kept calling out and inviting people to write their messages, saying they were going to send them to the minister and that you could write anything you wanted.

'Anything you'd like to say to Mr Needham, you can write it here. You don't have to sign it. We'll post it to him for you,' they shouted. I saw people laughing and you knew they were writing all sorts of mad things.

There was one of the washing lines near where I was sitting and I got up and walked over to it. I read some of the sheets. A group of wee lads had written 'fuck' a few times. Two people, signed Liam and Maura, wrote 'We Don't Want Your Toxic Waste'. Someone else had made a big headline out of 'No Incinerator In Derry'. I read on, moving around the display. A gust of wind whipped across the square and a scatter of sheets flew off the line. The actors ran after the sheets and one of them landed at my feet. I picked it up. It said: 'You will not waste our children. We will not be your dumping ground. This is not toxic city.' And there was the squiggle of a signature.

One of the actors approached me and I handed him the sheet. He said thanks and offered me a fat marker.

'Do you want to send a message?'

I took the marker from him and he pulled a sheet of yellow paper out of his pocket and handed it to me. Then he worked his way along the lines lifting off the messages and the pegs.

A surge of panic rushed through me. No-one had asked me to write anything, apart from filling and signing forms, since I'd left school. I stood in the square and the wind swirled up. The sheet flapped in my hand. I held the chubby marker awkwardly, like an infant in nursery school, and I started to sweat. All I could see in front of me was the small white coffin and Teresa inside it. So I wrote one word. Big and firm: 'Teresa'.

Droplets of wet began to appear on the yellow sheet around the word. Rain and tears. The actors began to hurry, taking down the last messages and gathering up the washing lines. I walked over to the card table where they had piled the yellow sheets and were beginning to put them in a big padded envelope. I handed in mine and the actor said, 'Thanks. We'll make sure the minister gets it.' He read it and looked at me and smiled, then put it with the others.

I went back to my seat and soon the square cleared. For a little while I felt agitated inside, but it was okay. I felt good that the minister would get my message. I felt good that the actor had smiled and not said anything. I felt good that I had written Teresa's name like that, in a public way. I had connected us with the biggest challenge facing the city. I had acted.

When I recall that incident now I realise that it was the first act of writing in my adult life. I know I shouldn't read too much into just one word, but I also know that it marked the quickening of my journey. I wouldn't be writing these words if I had not written 'Teresa' that day. I was beginning to see how she could have a 'life' in me, even after her death. I was beginning to see it wasn't all waste and that I was not toxic. Yes, I was still burning inside, but perhaps I could make the flames heat and console me, not burn and consume me.

CHAPTER FIVE

CALDRAGH

I don't blame Tony for leaving me. There, I've written it down so I have to hold to it. Writing an idea makes it firmer, less easy to dodge. I've known how I felt about Tony for a long time and the day I saw him at my graduation in the millennium year made me realise how far I've come. So far that I can sit in my room now and type those words into my computer and stare at them on the screen and, through them, draw up all the hard days that grew between us before he finally left, nearly ten years ago. It was winter by then, not long after Christmas. I would wake up and find the bed empty but warm beside me, the clothes folded back neatly, all impression of him vanished. I'd lie there alone, listening to the wind whistle in the telephone wires and a lone dog barking from somewhere over by the Glen, an aimless, tired bark that seared the heart in me. I got up most nights and went downstairs and found Tony, sitting on the sofa in the dull light of the table lamp, smoking a cigarette.

He looked like a condemned man, waiting for the morning and the firing squad. I can still draw that image to me and shudder. I joined him on the sofa and sat in his smoke haze for a while. We didn't speak, just sat there until I finally went back to bed, climbing the stairs as the dog let out one more mournful howl.

Tony came up later or sometimes he went straight to work. It was the only place he could hide.

We had such plans. We looked so good together. We had laughs and good times. We loved each other and managed to be together in all the right ways. We could talk and make love and plan and go out or just sit in with a video and a few drinks. We could party. He could paint, I could paper. We liked the same films. He did a bit of fishing. I did aerobics. And when we lay together in bed we knew when to reach for each other and when not to, so that, when we did, it was all consuming, whether fast or slow, great roaring fires between us, him calling out, me urging us on and on and on.

That has to be part of our troubles of course. I gave up on sex. I know he understood why at the time, but I think it went deeper than the physical shock I had. I wanted nothing to do with my body or anybody else's. I detested myself to such a degree that everything I did was dirty, wasteful and poisonous to me. But it would be too easy to put it all down to sex. Fundamentally, I changed. When I finally came out of the Valium haze I wanted something else. I wasn't going to let the world go on as before. I wasn't going to slide back into life as if nothing had happened. I wanted to 'do' something and that's really what drove Tony away.

'Maybe if we take a break, Donna. Give each other a bit of a breather.'

That was how he said it to me and I realised he couldn't catch his breath in the house any more. He had taken to smoking out in the yard, standing at the back door if it was raining, puffing plumes of smoke into the grey sky.

'We need to give each other a rest. A bit of a break. It might help us.'

I knew he was going for good even though he only took two small bags. I thought he was going to his mother's but he wasn't. He went to stay with one of his friends from fishing. I admired him for that. It was saying to everyone that he was his own man and that he had made his own bed and that if he couldn't lie in it, he wasn't going to dash back to Mammy.

* *

My own mother called him all the names under the sun and got the priest to me. I'm not sure whether the priest was meant to console or chastise me. I don't think the poor man had any real idea himself, but my mother bullied the priests at the Cathedral and they sent up the young one to keep her quiet. She made us tea and left us in the living room. I sat in the armchair and the priest sat forward on the sofa, the cup and saucer perched on his knees, precarious and formal.

'Your mother says you're getting better. Coming back to your old self a bit,' he said.

I shouldn't laugh, but even now his earnest helplessness makes me smile. He managed to miss the whole point. I might have been getting better, but I certainly wasn't getting back to my old self. No matter what else I was uncertain about, by the time Tony left I knew one thing for sure. I was becoming a different person.

'It's been very hard on ye. Both of ye. But, you know, Donna, you can always turn to God for help. Especially in your darkest times.'

Oh, and we had been through dark times, Tony and me. We held each other in the hospital as the nurse took Teresa away. We stood side by side as the white coffin disappeared into the stony brown clay. We lay beside each other in the bed, frozen and stunned, pretending to be asleep, so as not to frighten each other, too pummelled by life to find comfort in each other's presence, not to mind touch. Those were the nights when he pushed my hand away when I laid it across his thigh. Those were the nights when I turned away from him and shrugged into myself. Those were the nights when, if we tried to kiss, our mouths filled with ashes and we separated, embarrassed and awkward, hurt and distressed, to continue lying there like lumps of sheared metal, frozen to the core.

'Perhaps if Tony and yourself came to meet me to have a chat. And pray. We could pray together.'

I nodded a few times but made no commitment. It's not that I didn't want consolation. It's just that I didn't think the priest could offer it. I didn't think he knew anything about what Tony and me had been through.

'Excuse me, Father. I have to ...'

I made it sound like something intimate, womanly, unknowable to him. Our eyes met, the cup slid from the saucer on his knee, then rattled and spilled. He blushed. He knew that this would be our last meeting. He nodded and said, 'God bless you, Donna,' and I went upstairs.

When I came back the priest had left and my mother was upset but I told her not to worry, that everything would be fine, that Tony was gone for good, that I was getting better, that life would have to go on and that as far as I was concerned it was bloody well going to. Besides I had a meeting to attend and I was late.

It's when you start talking back to your mother, telling her what you're planning to do, that you really feel you've started to grow up. And it's scary.

I have a very good relationship with my mother now. It's one of the better outcomes of the changes that came into my life. We treat each other like adult women now. She's immensely proud of me, I know that. Her only daughter to go to university. And now this daughter, her youngest, has a 'big' job in the council. She was heartbroken about Teresa, too, and like me she aged through it all. But now the fires have diminished somewhat for both of us and we can talk.

I remember I took her to lunch to mark the start of the job. I said I would as soon as I got settled in. She likes Austin's, the big department store, with the café on the top floor. She likes the name, to be able to say, 'Oh, me and our Donna had lunch up the town the day. In Austin's.'

We were lucky to get one of the seats in the bay window so we enjoyed the view of the rooftops, the Diamond and the river sweeping towards the Foyle Bridge that joins the two sides of the city like a great reach of whalebone. She had lasagne and salad and I had a baked potato. I made some remark about her not having much chance to eat lasagne when she was growing up. Something along the lines of 'it's far from lasagne you were reared' and it got her started into memories of her childhood. She retold me the story of her Granny McLaughlin and her Auntie

Eileen. This is how I remember her telling the story that day in Austin's, her lasagne steaming in front of her, my baked potato open as an oyster.

The Story of Auntie Eileen

Granny McLaughlin already had six children and she was excited and anxious that she was going to have another. They lived in a small cottage by the shore. Granda McLaughlin put out lobster pots in a small boat and kept a cow on a wee bit of land. There was enough to eat if everyone worked hard. The night the baby came it was cold and windy. A northeast gale blew over Inishtrahull Island and whipped into the small cottage. The birth was difficult and the women who were helping had it hard. Granny McLaughlin had it hardest of all and she knew something was wrong when a powerful gust of wind blew the door open and, though her husband managed to shut it again quickly, a black bird swept in and landed among the rafters. It stood there cawing and cleaning its feathers until Granda McLaughlin took a stick to it and drove it out again, with Seamus, the eldest, holding the door open. But it was no use because when the baby came in the morning she was dead and Granny McLaughlin lay exhausted and beaten in the bed.

Granda McLaughlin wrapped the baby in a sheet and placed her by the fire. The rest of the family gathered around and the women who had helped left for their own houses nearby. Granny McLaughlin sat up in the bed in the room and looked out at the scene around the fire. The first light of day was coming in the windows and they all said prayers for the baby they named Eileen. Then Granda McLaughlin bundled her under his arm and went with Seamus to the yard where they lifted a pick and a spade. The rest of the children followed them to the shore. There was no-one else about, except some gulls standing headstrong into the wind.

They dug a grave for Eileen among the rocks above the small beach and buried her there. It is a holy place to the people of that locality, known as a caldragh. *It is where they buried the children that didn't stay very long with them.*

Telling the story upset my mother's appetite. I told her to leave the lasagne and I bought her a big cream bun and another cup of tea. She wolfed those down. She's built like a bird – a seagull – strong, bony and light – and she has the appetite of a honey bear.

I know why she often comes back to the story. It's her way of talking about Teresa. It's her way of trying to make sense of what happened by linking it to something in the past, by connecting it to our family story and giving our incidents and troubles a form of lineage. She wants to see the death of children as an echo down the generations, carried by the messengers of the old ways, the big black birds. And even though I know, as a scientist, that it was the randomness of medical conditions that took Teresa and not the overwhelming, consistent brutality of rural poverty, I always find a sad comfort in the story as it confirms a truth deep inside me. I am not alone.

I reminded my mother of the day I made her take me to the *caldragh*. It was the month or two after she first told me Auntie Eileen's story. I think it was the year I completed the Access Course, before I took the Science Foundation Course at the university. It was the summer so I said we could take a run to the beach. We could get Anna to take us in her car. When we got to the beach, I drew my mother away from Anna's children playing in the sand, saying she and I were going for a walk. I led my mother off the beach – the usual way was to go the length of the beach as far as the river, bathe our feet and then return – but this time I made her cut across to the path on the dunes, treading carefully so as not to squash the coloured spirals of the dune snails. We came to the narrow road that runs behind the beach and she knew I was taking her to the old home and for a moment her step quickened. But as we came near the old house, broken and battered by years of weathering and neglect, she said, 'Maybe we should go back to Anna and the weans.'

But I pushed on past the ruined house when the road swung left and down towards the little harbour. I stopped then to look at the small boats jostling each other beside the jetty. I was sweating and I took off my cardigan and dangled it over my shoulder and let my mother catch up.

'Here is peace,' I thought to myself. 'This is where I'm from. Here is sanctuary and calm.'

When my mother came up to me I saw the sweat on her brow, too, but I also saw the smile in her eyes, looking at the boats and the craggy rocks opposite and the way the water lapped in and out ceaselessly.

'Show me where your Auntie Eileen is buried. Show me the *caldragh*,' I said.

She looked at me and, without answering, stepped behind me off the road onto a path between the rocks. I had stopped in exactly the right place. I followed and stumbled behind her surefooted tread. She picked her way over the rocks until we came to a flattened place, nestling in a ring of outcrops. There was a large stone standing in a leaning position on one side and I rubbed my hand on it, feeling its coarse texture and the heat buried deep within it. I looked around and I could see the jetty and the small boats. I could see the back of the dunes in the distance. My mother said nothing but her lips moved and I knew she was praying. I stood in the heat and the light and rested my hand on the rock and thought of all the babies buried in the ground and I wept the greatest relieving tears I ever wept. For my daughter Teresa and my mother's Auntie Eileen.

CHAPTER SIX

GOING PUBLIC

Martha, Anna and my mother took me to an anti-incinerator campaign meeting, perhaps four months after Teresa. The whole city was consumed by the issue of the incinerator then. Tony and I were still together, but only just. He was smoking more, as we were talking less.

I grew stronger. I walked in Brooke Park, right across from where I live, marvelling at the greenness of the lime trees. The sight of young children playing in the fountain, dashing in and out of the spurts, didn't upset me as much. Instead of a devastating depression, I was enveloped in a bittersweet melancholy that tasted like sherbet gone off.

Everyone was saying how well I was looking and I think they meant it. I always tan in the summer. Something to do with the dark swarthy skin I got from my mother's people. Family lore has it that we're descended from shipwrecked Spanish sailors from the Armada and that's why we have brown eyes and silky black hair. All four of us, sitting side by side at the meeting. Me next to my mother and then Martha and Anna.

Posters had appeared in the shops and pubs around where I live saying there would be a public meeting about the anti-incinerator campaign in the leisure centre in Brooke Park and Anna said that we should go. I knew she had a hidden agenda. I knew it was all part of a family plan to 'get me out of myself'. That's not to say she wasn't interested in the campaign. Everyone was. Everyone was concerned by that stage. Even Martha, who is usually too busy redecorating her house or keeping up the tan she got on holiday in Greece.

'I'm just not having it. Du Pont can say what they want, but there is no way I'm going to see Derry be the dumping ground for the whole of Ireland,' she said.

When I think back now, I realise that everyone was becoming informed about the issues. Everyone became an expert on dioxins and chimney stack temperatures and dangerous cocktails of emission gases.

'The town is bad enough already without adding to it. Sure look at the many weans in this area alone has asthma. Do they want to poison us completely?' Martha continued.

Hearing things like that made me think about Teresa. I had moved to the questioning stage, the stage that would finally drive Tony away. I had begun to ask why. I also remember being able to smirk to myself as Martha complained about Du Pont and what they planned to do while she sported a pair of Lycra ski pants. Martha couldn't survive without the chemical industry. None of us could.

That's the point Tony used to make, though he was very cautious about expressing his fears. He wasn't going to sink himself into a row with his in-laws, but privately he would reiterate our dependency on the plant.

'You think this house came out of thin air? You think we can afford the suite because we're rich and famous? No way. This is all out of Du Pont and there's plenty of men in this town would be glad to be able to say they're earning the good money I'm bringing home.'

And he was right. But he didn't stop me from going to the meetings. That's not the kind of man he is. He did feel I was wrong, that we all were and, in my case, he gave the impression of feeling that I was being disloyal, though he didn't use those words.

'Look, Donna, we have to think of our future. If things go bad and Du Pont decides to go elsewhere, then where would we be? We have to be careful and think about that.'

I did think about it, in an addled way, but what Tony and the others didn't understand was that I was already involved in the campaign, even before I went to my first public meeting. I had joined in the activities of the actors beside the emigration statues and seen the public debate get under way. I was already a campaigner.

At that first public meeting in Brooke Park Leisure Centre, I remember we sat in a row, the McDaid sisters and their mother, an impressive foursome, well known in the area, my mother preening slightly at the thought of everyone seeing her out with her fine daughters. A wee man from Grafton Street came up behind my mother and leaned into her saying, 'Fine bunch of dolly birds yeez are and you, Annie, are the best of the lot of them.'

My mother laughed and he moved off, then she turned towards us and mouthed her distaste of the man, but secretly grinned in the pleasure brought on by what he'd said.

She knew everybody.

'That's your man Bailey lives down Park Avenue. He's a teacher. He must be behind it. And that's Sean McCorriston. Look, he's bringing in a video. I don't know who the other fella is. He has a bit of a brogue, hasn't he?'

She swivelled round and spoke to a woman behind her. Then she swivelled back and said, 'Nancy doesn't know what you call him, but he's on the radio. That's how I recognised the voice.'

When the meeting started there were about sixty people in the hall. I knew most of them to see. We were in the small hall in the leisure centre, sitting on stackable plastic chairs, the breeze-block walls grey and cold around us. Now that room is filled with exercise equipment: bench presses, cycling machines, rowing machines, dumbbells, weights and mirrors, and I work out there twice a week. I hardly recognise it from that time.

I hardly recognise myself for that matter. I have had ... no, I have given myself ... a complete makeover. I'm years older but

I'm fitter and stronger, more confident and calm. I feel like I belong in my life and I'm really happy with myself.

Today at work I put the finishing touches to my first internal report. I had been asked to comment on a document circulated from the Department of the Environment on noise pollution in cities. I wrote over a thousand words with ease. I lifted material from a discussion group on the Internet and included it. I made reference to a relevant study completed in France. I applied all this knowledge to local circumstances. When I printed the text off and read through it for accuracy I had a sense that I had come a long way from that meeting in Brooke Park. Then I had concerns and fears. I was on the edge of the whole thing. Now I have knowledge and power and I'm stuck right in the middle of it, where I want to be. Now, of course, I'm working for an institution. Power manifest. A height from which decisions are made. Incineration is back on the agenda again. We think we know everything. Burn it all! Arrogance, totally. Maybe I'll be standing at the barricades again. Have I crossed over? Am I on the other side now? What do I do if the City Council asks for options?

I can confidently say that I will give them options and that I will draw those options from my own learning and experiences. They will be open and dependable, but also humane and broken, as earth is when it is reclaimed from landfill. I will link my own processes of reclamation – and if this account is anything, it is evidence of that – with the need for reclamation and recovery in our city. But before I can look at such options I must face the time when I had no option but to stand, abandoned and bereft of hope as a victim of torture, beside my daughter's grave.

I want to write about Teresa's funeral. I convince myself I am strong enough to enter a key record here. It has taken all these days of typing at this screen, all these months of remembering, to get to this. I note that it is 'recording' things I want to do now, as if I am making a documentary of my life, in a series of entries. I'm constructing a story out of my past that will act as a foundation for my future.

I remember the hole in the ground and the wind ripping into us on that January day in the cemetery. There was such a greyness in the air that I wasn't sure I could breathe. I leaned into Tony but could find no ballast in him. He had become a wasted shell, too, all strength gone. I held my mother's hand for warmth and comfort and it felt like a frozen rag, a piece of cloth left to freeze on a washing line overnight. Martha and Anna stood beside me but their faces, clenched in agony and pain, offered me no shelter. I was alone. I tasted the gritty brown soil that lined the hole into which we put my baby.

My Teresa.

I remember. I am a living memory bank, dredging it all up, years later, now that I feel strong enough.

The coffin was as white as a wedding cake, decorated and iced. Teresa lay inside it. I thought of her swaddled form, wrapped in a pink blanket, someone, maybe Martha or Anna, had given to me. I remember wondering would she be warm enough, my maternal instincts kicking in with all the chemicals and hormones racing through my system, my breasts large and solid under my coat. Hugging myself. I remember hugging myself. Against the cold and the disbelief.

The priest mumbled or else he said it all clearly and my ears were stuffed with cotton wool, to block things out. He had a wispy head of hair, not even a head, just some strands that lay across his bald scalp, that flew up in the wind like thin streamers of smoke from a dying fire.

My own fires raged inside me then. Sharp and searing. Violent as flames from Hell's coals spitting inside me, but making me more and more cold.

Tony carried the coffin under his arm, rare, yet familiar. I remember that and I remember thinking that it was a present he had for her. We were only after Christmas and I had seen men walking the streets with little bundles under their arms. Dolls in boxes. Talking dolls. Dolls that walked. Dolls with long plaits and squidgy faces. Dolls that went to the toilet, that sang when you pressed their belly buttons. Dolls that opened and closed their eyes as if they were alive. And now my man was carrying not a black plastic bin-liner to hide a doll's box but a white confection of a crate to bury our doll, our living doll that never made it. Birth was the death of her.

The Cathedral had been packed. The statues of saints and angels, perched on their columns, stared down at us with their blank eyes. There was a choir. I don't know who organised that. I remember the voices, tiny and remote. The building so big. The vaulted ceiling so far away. Me so small. I remember feeling so small, my chin resting on the wooden railing, Tony's hand on my back, trying to ease me up, the priest mumbling into my cotton-wool ears, then my teeth biting into the wood, hard enough to make me feel pain. When I sat back I saw the marks I left, tiny fresh slits in the wood, the grotesque shape of my mouth.

Even as I write this I realise how frail a faculty memory is. I can't even be sure if there was snow. Cold I can remember, but was there snow? I see no whiteness except the coffin. Brown is the colour I see most of. Ash-brown. Grey-brown, like turf fire embers in a great black hole of a hearth where there is no warmth or welcome. Nothing but bitterness and cold wind. I must have had a black coat on me and yet I see myself in brown. And the sky an ugly brown, like the inside of a tin bucket left too long in the rain.

There is a noise rain makes falling on mourners in a cemetery. I remember that noise. Like the exhalations of ghosts, a clammy noise you don't really hear but which drowns everything else out.

So there was rain then. I shouldn't depend on memory for this. My training tells me I should turn to research. Look into meteorological records, check the newspapers of the day for weather reports, talk to someone who would know.

But it is not only the remembering of facts I am engaged in. I am recalling the emotions and I must be doing it well for I feel my fingers tremble on the keys. I'll have hours of work with the spellchecker to make sense of this. Memory mixes with current sensations so that I alert myself to the danger of falling back into the depression of those times. In remembering, I scare myself.

* *

40

There was a crowd at the house afterwards, making my grief public. Just tea and sandwiches. No drink. Nothing like a wake or a send-off you would have for an old person. No telling of tales, no recounting of funny incidents. No stories. No memories. We have no memories of Teresa. She was born over a grave. There was nothing to be said. People hushed one another with 'wild sad' and 'ach, God love her' and 'dear knows how they'll cope' and 'but God is good and they're young' and 'wild hard blow' and 'they're not ours, they're only loaned to us'.

Decent people trying to make sense of it. I was senseless by then. Valium saw to that.

Someone put a cup of tea in my hand and I looked at the brown sludge floating in front of my eyes. I was in shock of course. I remember the pitted centre and the concentric circles where my tears splashed into that liquid. I remember now, as plain as anything I remember from any time in my life, the question that hammered in my head.

'How do you walk away from a child's grave?'

Slowly. Falteringly. In bowed and beaten procession through the sodden headstones, looking over the city. There, the city Walls circling and enfolding. There, the spires insolent and tremulous. There, the river, ominous and leaden. There, the chimney stacks of the factories and the plants, pluming and grey.

And here am I, tumbling inside myself, being led away, powerless and amazed.

There is no way to walk away from a child's grave. You stand there forever.

CHAPTER SEVEN

CAMPAIGNING

I remember the great public meeting, in the Guildhall Square, which I also attended with my family, later that spring. It was bright and sunny then, trying to be warm. Just like me. I used to stand in front of the mirror and practice smiling at myself. The first few times I did it I ended up in tears, stumbling onto the edge of the bath, my head in my hands. But eventually I managed to crease my cheeks and show my teeth in something that didn't look too much like a vampire's grimace.

I was off the Valium by then, I think. Memory is so unreliable. I tell myself I should keep a diary of events now but I can't get the energy for it. It is as if I'm blocked by the events of that past time and until I get them down on paper I won't be able to really live now.

An incident happened at work today, for example. A man almost asked me out. I didn't realise what was happening until it was over and he got embarrassed – I think he took my confusion for disdain – and we sat there like eejits, twirling spoons in our coffee cups, he going clockwise, me going counter-clockwise. It happened in the canteen. Gerry is his name. He works in the same office, but on the engineering side. He has nice eyes. I suppose he is the sort of man I could go out with. If it happens again.

'You don't take sugar?' he said. 'No sweet tooth?'

'Oh, I've got a sweet tooth all right. Cream buns, yes. Sugar in tea, no.'

'Do you ever go out for coffee ... or lunch?'

I shook my head and lowered my eyes. We were sitting side by side looking out over the river. We were alone in the canteen, both of us on a late tea break. The river was stock-still in front of us. Solid and stable.

He returned the conversation to work matters and the weather. I felt relaxed sitting beside him. He's about my age, maybe a bit older. I didn't find the conversation boring. Why, I wonder?

Here I am searching for explanations again. That's not surprising, given that I'm a scientist now. But which came first? The rationalism? Or Teresa's death, making me want to rationalise?

As I look back on it all from this distance I can see the charred beginnings of my searching, the ash and clinker of my observations. I blamed everything and anything for her death. I blamed myself. I blamed Tony. I blamed Tony and me for making love when I was pregnant. I blamed the British army helicopter chattering overhead. I blamed my father for dying when I was young. I blamed the rain that falls on the city. I blamed Du Pont when I became involved in the anti-incinerator campaign, not just going along to things but actively taking part.

I can wonder now if it was the act of taking charge of my life that finally drove Tony away as much as my depression. He said I had become obsessive. But I couldn't let the questions remain unanswered. I wanted to know.

The best way I can describe my process of becoming involved in the anti-incinerator campaign is to say it was a process of osmosis. I remembered that from basic science at school, when I came across it again at university many years later. It appeared like an old friend among the newness I was experiencing.

Basically there are particles in a solution on either side of a semi-permeable membrane, a skin or a layer that certain particles can pass through freely. The concentrations are different on either side and the side with the lower concentration will tend to attract or pull particles across to equalise the concentrations.

Or is it that the side where the concentration is higher will push the particles across? I'm not sure I remember now. So much of what I want to write down is dependent on memory. In this case, I could always look at the shelves behind me and check a basic chemistry book. But for now I am really interested only in the process whereby I crossed that semi-permeable membrane and whether it was push or pull is not really relevant. In a sense it had already begun through watching the actors' performances. I was already involved, but only in a form of Brownian Motion. There, I have to laugh, my basic science coming in handy again. Robert Browning made observations in a smoke box which led him to the conclusion that, in systems in equilibrium, atoms and molecules move in random paths. That was me. I was in Brownian Motion. I was in a smoke box, smoke generated by the fires dampening down inside but still frighteningly there, never fully extinguished, smouldering like a log someone lit beneath a pile of sodden leaves in a dense dark wood.

Thousands of us in the city in Brownian Motion on random paths and then the sobering threshold was presented to us, Du Pont's plan to build a toxic-waste incinerator, the semi-permeable membrane that could be crossed in order to become 'active', in order to achieve a path that was not simply random, but was designed and developed by myself. Something I could say I was definitely in charge of.

It was at that first meeting in the Brooke Park Leisure Centre that I really became aware of the push/pull involved. I remember the pleasure and the comfort of being with my sisters and my mother. I was at a point where I could rely on family. I was no longer totally lost to them. I remember sitting next to my mother and our eyes met. The lines and creases around her eyes and mouth – worry lines, weariness creases – miraculously realigned and transformed themselves into a smile of love and tenderness.

Her eyes glistened as she spoke softly. 'Shur you'll be grand, love.'

And I took her hand in mine and squeezed. Child and Woman. Daughter and Mother.

The meeting began with the man with the brogue welcoming us and telling us what would happen. Someone turned off the lights, the screen cleared and a video began. I couldn't see very well because we were at the back, but the sound was good and I paid attention to it as best I could. It was from America and it was about toxic-waste incineration and the effects on a community. People came on the screen and told their stories. Ordinary people. I remember thinking that. Ordinary people. Like us.

I looked around the room. My sisters and my mother. Mrs Donnelly and her husband in front of us, little scratches on his bald patch. Two teenagers with long hair and scraggly beards, awkwardly gaping down at their trainers. The wee man from Grafton Street who had an eye for the women. Tommy Bardon and a man he knocked about with. Mrs O'Kane, Ida McDowell and Ruby McNaught from my street, in their good coats. Charlie Doherty and Mickey McGuinness. I was surprised to see them there because they worked in Du Pont. Mickey had his work boots on. Your man Bailey, the teacher. Harry Giller who owned the shop. Marian Farrelly I went to school with. All these and more, ranged round the hall, watching the video. At the end, there was a shuffling of chairs and a few coughs. Then the man with the brogue asked if there were any questions or any points people wanted to make. I remember voices coming from all over the hall, instruments sounding random notes.

'They're never going to get away with it.'

'You have to think about the jobs.'

'Are we going to form a group? My sister is in one in Shanta-llow.'

'Will we have a committee?'

'Is anybody doing anything in schools about it?'

'It'll never get built, never you worry. And if it does get built, the Provos will blow it up anyway.'

Nervous laughter at that.

'What will we do if Du Pont pull out? The town'll be devastated.'

'Can someone explain to me why they want to do it anyway?'

'My brother worked in it and only lasted six months after he retired. I want nothing to do with it.'

'We have to stop Mickey Mousing around and put pressure on the company and on the government. We have to let them know we mean business.'

There were murmurs of assent to this and the man with the brogue said there were plans to have a major rally in the Guildhall Square and asked if we should take part.

I remember a silence then, a hesitation, a moment when all the random movement in the system paused, skipped a beat, when Time hesitated and hung in the balance of my life. I don't know how long it lasted. An instant in all likelihood. It was the moment when the semi-permeable barrier came into the solution and the osmotic push and pull became strongest.

And in that instant, at stasis, I moved. I took charge of myself, with an urgent assertion, driving Time forward once more.

'We should be at the rally. I'll make a banner.'

My mother turned to me, her mouth open. I smiled at her, her eyes flickered and she grinned back. All around me people were grinning and smiling. They knew me. They knew I was married to a man who worked in Du Pont. They knew about Teresa. They knew what had happened to me and they welcomed my strengthening. They heard my voice and the resolve in it and it gave them strength so that decisions were made and plans for action were taken.

'Fair play to you, Donna,' Martha said to me as Anna smiled. 'I'll help with the banner.'

And that's how a picture appeared in the *Derry Journal* after the big rally in the Guildhall Square. Me, Martha, Anna and my mother – all smiles and laughs in the bright spring sunshine – holding a big banner in front of us that read: ROSEMOUNT GIRLS AGAINST TOXIC WASTE.

What a day that was! I can conjure up the warmth of it as I sit here in my room, watching starlings alight and lift off from my whirligig clothesline. Isn't it always the case that we remember the sun shining? What is it about memory that it plays tricks like that on us? Perhaps it is a colour we lay on our memories. A latter day makeover. I wore a red top. Cotton and long sleeved. I have it in the press and I'm pleased to say I can still get into it. That's how they spotted me on telly.

'There's Donna. Our Donna. 'Mere, our Donna's on telly.'

And I was. Among the thousands in the Guildhall Square that day, I stood out. I didn't video-tape my appearance on television. I wish I had now. But it was only a news item and it was over in an instant, but it was my instant. In that brief flickering of a TV image I became the anti-incinerator campaign. The number of people who came up to me or one of the family afterwards saying they had seen it!

I was with my mother and sisters, standing behind the banner: ROSEMOUNT GIRLS AGAINST TOXIC WASTE. We were listening to the speakers, all eyes on the platform. The TV showed the four of us, then it zoomed in on me in my red top, my features in profile, my gaze focussed and my concentration intense.

It was really me. Strong. Calm. Capable. Ordinary. For that brief moment of TV, I was a woman in a crowd. One of many. Numberless and unique. It gave me such a lift. Such a great lift.

Making the banner was a howl. First came the complaints from Martha.

'Typical. Donna opens her big mouth and we all fall in.'

She's the only one who can sew or make anything. I'm useless with my hands, especially with anything that might be called 'the feminine arts'. It was the same doing the science degree. Theory; terrific. Experiments; challenging.

It was really Martha who got the banner together. She's forever running up curtains, sofa covers and wee dresses for her girls. So there was a whole session round in my house, when Tony was on an evening shift. The four of us, like a coven. Endless cups of tea. Martha brought a portable sewing machine with her, crimping scissors, a sewing box you could have sat a child in. My mother and I laid on a cream sponge and biscuits. Did we laugh? Buckets. Stupid laughter. Laughter about nothing. Laughter that went so deep into ourselves and who we were that there was no knowing what the reason was. We were skittery and giggly. We spilled tea. We said we couldn't possibly have another slice of cream sponge and then we said, 'Ah! Go on. Here. Give it to me. Shur you're only young once.'

But that's not true. We were young again. All four of us. That night we rediscovered our youth and the laughs we used to have growing up. Reminiscing began.

Martha said, 'Remember the time I was going with that McFeely fella and yeez locked me in the bathroom and told him I'd be down in a minute and kept the poor fella sitting with me daddy for nearly half an hour?'

Anna added, 'You'd be still in it only me daddy came up to go to the toilet.'

Roars of laughter and the look on my mother's face, forlorn and delicate, that told us we should move off reminiscing about my father. Then the way Martha handed her the scissors and asked her to cut out two letter 'o's from the black cloth.

''Bout the size of a dinner plate.'

Then the three of us catching each other's eyes, colluding. Sisters.

The banner was big and bold and red with black letters across it and everyone thought it was brilliant. Everyone wanted to get behind it, even the men!

And when we appeared on television the whole town knew about us.

'That's wee Annie McDaid and her daughters on the telly.'

'I know. Shur they were on the front of the paper and all.'

Was it Andy Warhol who said everybody should be famous at least once in their lives? Me and Tony, when we were running around together, used to be into ska music and I remember The Selecter had a hit with a song called *Three Minute Hero*. It's probably up in the attic somewhere, in a box. All our records ended up there. I suppose they're really Tony's, but he left them here. There is other stuff of his up there. Old football boots. Some boxes of clothes. I think he took all his fishing gear, but there might be a few broken rods and spun-out reels piled in the corner.

I don't mind that stuff being there. It's only in the attic and I have no need for the space. The house is big enough for one person and that's no lie. It is funny to think what he's left behind though. Things he doesn't value any more, you might say. Me among them?

He didn't like the banner. He grew tense and confused. When he came in from his shift, after midnight, we were still there and the banner was draped over the sofa. The atmosphere in the room was warm and relaxed, filled with a sense of real achievement. He came in and stood before us, his face drawn and tired, his bulky lunch box under his arm.

Martha was bubbly.

'Yes, Tony. What do you think?'

He waited a long time before he said anything. Composing something, or perhaps too tired to think fast.

'Great. Will ye make one for me when I'm campaigning to keep me job?'

Then he walked into the kitchen, dumped his lunch box and his coat, came back out and went up the stairs without another word.

That was the beginning of the end with Tony. I know that now. Life was coming between us, rather than bringing us closer. It's a growth thing I suppose. Two branches of the same tree, joined but separate and growing in different directions. I was growing towards the light. Tony had stopped growing, I feel. Yes, he's changed over the years, that's obvious, but I'm not sure he's grown. I'm not being harsh on him, but that's what I think happened. I have to go back to it time and time again. He never really talked about how he felt about Teresa.

He did say that maybe we should try again, try to have another child.

'I don't mean to replace Teresa. We can never do that.'

Oh, how his eyes melted when he said that. And the tremble I knew so well rippled across his lower lip. But he bit it back and continued.

'Maybe it would be good for us. We're still young. We have to go on.'

I pity him now, thinking back. He was trying to do his best, but he picked the wrong time. I was ashen and smouldering, my brain addled, my body lumpy as a sack of wet slack. I detested the very air I breathed in and choked on the air I breathed out. There was no starting all over for me. At that time I was a burnt-out kiln, nothing more could be fired in me, all possibility of combustion gone. I was spent. Maybe he and I began to operate to different clocks then. Developed a different sense of time. For Tony there was the chance to reset the clock, to turn the hands back. To redial. For me there was only the inexorable forward journey of Time's arrow. From waste to waste. From ashes to ashes.

He brought it up again at the time of the banner. He was chirpy in the morning and brought me a cup of tea in bed. I sat up and flounced the duvet and pillows around me and he sat at the side of the bed.

'I put the heating on for a bit. It's a bit chilly out. But nice and fine. Going to be a good day.'

He took a slurp of his tea.

'Sorry about last night,' he continued. 'I was just tired.'

I liked him for saying that, but I made no reply. Should I have thanked him more, acknowledged the goodness in him more often?

'You seem to be getting stronger. Better,' he said.

I nodded. I was off the Valium by then. I must have been.

'We have to move on, you know.'

The way he said it I knew it was something he was working up to for quite some time. He kept his head down as he spoke, and began to gently smooth and caress the cover over my feet.

'Maybe, maybe, when you're strong. Not now, I know. But in a while, we could try again. We're young, like. Our whole lives before us. We can start again.'

His voice was so gentle and calm. It was like the way a priest might speak, a good priest, one who had real sanctity, one who really knew pain and pity. A part of me welled up inside, a great yearning coursing through me so that I wanted to look into his eyes and say, 'Yes, Tony, yes, we are young and yes, we will start again and yes, it will be good and yes, we will be happy once more and yes, we will do it, yes, we will, yes.'

He put the cup on the bedside table and leaned across and kissed me. I kissed him back, gentle and soft and my arms circled his neck and drew him down to me, so that he shuffled back under the covers.

For a moment we lay there, half embracing, breathing into each other's face. I don't know what he saw in mine but Tony sighed and said, 'Too soon, eh?' and he closed his eyes. In a few minutes he was asleep, or pretending to be and I rolled out of his arms. Tears formed and hung in my eyes, my breathing deepened and I fell asleep, lost to myself and to Tony. When I woke with a start ten minutes later, he was gone. I knew he would be downstairs, smoking with his bathrobe open about him, a long length of ash dangling off his cigarette as if he didn't have the energy to get rid of it. And I lay in the bed isolated and alone, feverishly alone.

None of us was alone at the rally in the Guildhall Square, underneath the city's timepiece, its hands shuddering towards three o'clock. I was with my sisters and my mother but more than that I was with thousands of other people from all over the city and beyond. Shantallow, Coshquin, Waterside, Culmore, Campsie. And: ROSEMOUNT GIRLS AGAINST TOXIC WASTE.

There was a stage set up in front of the Guildhall. The red brick of the building glowed in the sunshine and soon after the clock struck three times, people came on to the platform and the speeches began. Words poured out and got swept up by the breezes. I heard, or remember, hardly anything. There was a band then, thumping and banging in a discordant mix. They got us swaying a bit. Then more speakers. A man with a guitar singing Bob Dylan – *Blowing In The Wind*. Then a woman came on and spoke and though I couldn't hear her any clearer, I liked the way she kept her head up and never got distracted by her hair blowing across her face. She didn't snuffle into the microphone. She stood there, very straight and direct, fervent as an oracle.

I applauded along with everyone else.

My mother said, 'It must be good. All the ones up the front are going crazy.'

The rally ended with more music and there was a sense that no-one wanted to leave the Square. The sun was hot and the breeze died down. We were all in the right place, the centre of the city, our place, right and centred.

I had great pride in my city that day. I felt a warmth inside me for the place and the people. I carry that warmth in me today, as I go to work. It is pride and well-being I feel as I go through the revolving door of the City Council offices. I genuinely feel a sense of that odd commodity: civic pride. I know now it's because this is the scale of my world, the extent of the world I inhabit. I have never travelled (when Tony and I got married, we went for three days to Sligo), and I know that someday I probably will, but growing from that day in the Guildhall Square I recognised a sense of place in me. The notion developed in me that I was of this place and that I would take charge and do something about it. That this was my city as much as anybody else's and that I was going to let my voice be heard, now and into the future. I was going to make a difference. It was up to me. The city – Derry – was up to me.

CHAPTER EIGHT

COURAGE

The first day I stood outside the office of Derry Development Education Centre, the headquarters of the campaign, intending to 'do my bit', I was shaking and full of misgivings. This was probably months after the rally and the banner. I looked in the window and saw a room that should have been a shop but had been converted into an office. There were displays and posters, a desk and a phone, two women sitting and talking intently, notebooks and papers on their laps. I stood for ages, pretending to be reading the notices on the window: UNICEF Water Campaign In Nepal. Boycott Nestlé Goods. An awful photo of a severed limb for the campaign against the arms trade. It was all very foreign, very distant. Very 'educational' in a way that reminded me of bad experiences at school, where everyone seemed to know what they were talking about except me.

So I turned away from the window and walked back down Pump Street, keeping my eyes on the pavement as I went. There was a small café at the end of the street then. I went in and ordered a cup of tea, which I took over to the window and watched the activity on the street. A man in a wheelchair going into the PHAB Disability Services office; workmen fixing something to the front of the convent building; a woman passing, pushing a pram with a baby, in summery clothes, fast asleep. That really hit me. It should have been me. Teresa would have been about the right age for that. God, what I wouldn't give to have been able to do that. Just put my baby in the pram and head out the town. My figure back to its slim form, but now rounded out with motherly depth. The baby cooing and gurgling and then sleeping happily and content, soaking up the warmth of the sun, simply growing in the heat.

The tea tasted like acid, no fault of the café. The light of the day splintered through the window. The sugar in the bowl shimmered like ice. The milk curdled in the jug and my mouth filled with ashes, a feeling I thought I was beginning to lose. I realise I'll never really lose it. Here I sit, typing into this computer and I feel the bile mounting inside me now, coagulating into an ashen lump across my tongue. Even the burly draught of Burgundy I swig doesn't quite clear it out. That day, the loss was so thorough and so searing, I almost vomited.

I sometimes wonder how stable and confident a person I really am. Inside myself I feel a certain strength and assurance, but I know it's something I have achieved and worked for. It is not something I have been gifted. My sisters say I am very confident now and they date the growth of that confidence from the time of the anti-incinerator campaign. But I didn't feel so confident that first day.

Two older women came into the café. One, large and loud, smiled at me. They went to the counter and ordered, then they came over beside me.

'Sorry, love. Have to squeeze myself in,' said the large one, a frown of concern on her face as she nudged past me, taking her seat.

'Milk, Joanie? I only took a wee scone, a wheaten one. I'm trying to cut down.'

Big laugh, which made the folds of flesh on the back of her neck jiggle. I couldn't make out what the other woman was saying, but I heard everything the big woman said and it still stirs me today.

'I just had to get out of the house, Joanie. God knows I'm doing me best, but sometimes it just drives me demented. Ach, I know.

I don't blame him. The poor man. He's not looking one bit well, Joanie. We had the doctor to him again yesterday. And more bottles of oxygen. I'm afeared the house will blow up around us. The poor man's lungs are bate and that's the end of it. He's never been right, not since he left that place. Worked all his life in it and what good did it do him? Well, I know that, Joanie, but at the end of the day all you really have is your health. Gordon is good enough about it. He comes to visit his father as often as he can and, God knows, he's good to me, but he has his own family to think on now. You know what, Joanie? Sometimes I can't be sure if the whole thing was a great mistake. I know that's a funny thing for me to be saying at this time in my life. But you look back on it. He was out working all the time and I know the money was good but what enjoyment did he ever get out of it? I shouldn't complain, I know. There's many a family around us would have been glad to have a man in work like Sidney. Once a year to Portrush, that's the height of holidays for him. He never even walked on the Twelfth. He had no interest in that he said. Never had. He took a wee glass of beer up in the Mem of a weekend and the odd night out, but he was never really mad on that either. He was always good to me, I know that, Joanie, but like, he's lying there in the bed and the breath is coming out of him like out of a bicycle pump when you put your finger over the hole. Squeezed. And I know be the way the doctor looks at me that it won't be long before they're bringing Sidney into the hospital and telling me to prepare for the worst. The worst! What could be worse than watching a man breathe the last bit of life out of himself?'

I don't know if I am remembering this or if I'm making it up. I have such a strong impression of that day and of the sound of that woman's voice that her words, or my memory of her words, flow out of me. I am back to my mother's assertion about the stories we have to tell and now that I can spell and compose and write I can take my memories and express them.

I recognise this process of creation and re-creation. It is what my life has been about since that time. I came into the world with an imprint and I lived by it. I had a given template and though I could vary it, it was always going to be simply 'variations on a theme'. So I grew up and married Tony and we made plans. But with Teresa the template shattered. The theme vanished in the flames around her death. I'm not surprised that I ran around like a headless chicken for a while after that. I had nothing to hold onto. I knew absolutely nothing and lost total control. But gradually other templates and themes began to emerge, hastened by circumstances outside me: the love of my mother and my sisters, the arrival of spring, Tony desperately trying to help though he was lashed to his own stake and burning himself. The energy and excitement around the campaign. The voices of women like the one in the café. Out of all of this, I began to create a new template for myself. I took charge once more, re-created and re-covered my life. Let me drink to that.

I've been taking charge all my adult life. I entered adulthood neutrally enough, right up to having Teresa. Extra charges massed about me then. I attracted an opposite: the anti-incinerator campaign. I arced across and sparked into new life. I still hold a charge, but I'm not as volatile. I don't thunder and bolt across my own and other people's lives in quite the same way.

I ask myself now, 'Where does courage come from?' Are we born brave or do we learn bravery?'

Here's the usual answer to that old nature/nurture debate: a bit of both. Certainly I drew strength from my mother and father, but on that day in the café, it was from the woman's voice and the story that she told that I mined the courage to get a grip on myself.

I realised she had the same template as I had been given, but that didn't apply to me any longer. I had been gifted with new life, given to me by the death of my daughter. I write this with pain wringing my heart. Teresa redeemed me. She offered herself that I might live. She said to me, 'Donna, live your life. Do everything you can. Make every day count.'

In my case courage came from desperation. It's not surprising. We all know of the heroics people perform in war or when they're attacked, adrenalin pumping in the system. I was full of it that day and it took me out of the café and back up the street.

In that woman's voice, talking to her friend Joanie, I heard the woman I might become, the life Tony and I might have together, the waste it would be, how circumscribed it would be, how painfully, slowly we would simply watch each other work our ways to death. Breathlessly.

And so I got up and squeezed past the two women, smiled at them and went out into the sun. I stood there for a moment and raised my face to the warm rays. I felt the adrenalin pump through me. Fear? Of course. But also courage and a desire to make my life count.

I know a lot about courage now. I have the courage to write this and, in itself, it may not seem like much, but by simply counting the scars on my heart as you would the rings on a section of a tree to tell its age, so in these scars are numbered the blows I have taken and risen from. As Chumbawamba's hit song says: *I get knocked down, but I get up again, You're never gonna keep me down.*

Genetics must play a part. My mother was … is … a strong woman, strands of corded steel running up her back and into the sinews of her thin arms. A small woman who looks like a breeze would blow her over until you notice the way she stands. Her feet root her to the ground and then splay outwards as if she is always ready to fend off an attack or dive into the whirlwind. Genetics, in her case, too, I suppose, coming from Donegal fishing-village stock. The elements fused into her down the centuries. Furies of hail and sleet. Rain blasts that would skin a sow. Wave roars to waken the dead. She has all of them deep inside her and it shows in the blaze in her eyes, even as she moves through her final years, arthritis bending her like a stunted oak on a sea cliff, still clinging to its roots in a dry-stone wall.

But for all that nature, as a scientist I know, there is always nurture, too. The environment you live in and things that happen to you shape you. In her case living with my father formed her, too.

This is the first time I have written about him. Takes courage. I feel like a real writer now, bringing a character, an actor, on stage!

And what an actor! My father played the leading man, the vaudeville singer adored by his daughters, the Corinthian, the breadwinner. So many parts that even now I find it hard to draw up the truth of him. He was a baker, married my mother when he was serving his time, they had three daughters, he played a lot of football and he died young. When you say it like that it seems so worthless and yet so complete I'm not sure what else to write. He made my mother stronger and after that I don't know what else to say.

There are photographs of him about my mother's house. On their wedding day he had a quiff you could ski on. There he is, front row of his football team, kneeling on one knee and grinning beside the trophy they had won, the quiff still in place but less steep. They found him dead at his work one morning, crumpled in front of the oven, a tray of baps scattered away from him, like roly-poly pebbles tumbling along a beach. A heart attack switched him off like a light going out. I remember the men he worked with coming to the wake, smelling of baps and flour, even in their suits and ties.

He always smelled of baps. That's what I remember most. Me getting ready to go out to primary school and him coming in with a bag of baps and a laugh like sunshine and sitting with us smoking a cigarette and drinking tea. He hadn't a care in the world. That's it. Not a care in the world. And in my mother he found someone who would make sure he never had any. He sailed through his short life with a grin on his face and his football kit permanently clean and food always ready for him and a few pound in his pocket and never a question about him coming or going or what anybody else in the house might be doing. In that way he was able to never grow up. He wasn't foolish or nasty. He was resolutely immature. I don't know how she put up with him.

Me and my sisters adored him and danced to his every word. When we came home from school he would be about the house and one by one he would dandle us on his knee and sing his personalised songs.

There were three lovely lassies from Derry, Derry, Derry,
There were three lovely lassies from Derry,
And they all loved their daddy like mad.

He had a treasure of songs like that.

I'll tell me da when I go home,
The boys won't leave the girls alone.
They pulled me hair, they stole me comb,
But that's all right, cos me da's at home.

I don't know if I can say I loved him. I was in awe of him, amazed by him. Even as a girl I could see the play-acting he got up to. Working all night, sleeping most of the day meant he never had to face anything. A bit of playfulness, a sup of tea and, if it was the summer, he was off playing an evening match and in winter there were weekend games, training or meetings and then we were in bed and he was away to work, soaking up the heat of the ovens.

It may not be courage I'm considering anyway. It may be some form of wilfulness that runs through me and that made me do the things I did at the time I did them. Some of that came from my father I suppose. He got away with living the way he did because he willed it like that and my mother colluded. He was competitive, with a reputation for being keen in the challenges on the football pitch. I realise now that I never saw him play. I was young when he died, barely ten years old, but surely I should have seen even one game. If I did, I can't remember, though he seemed to be playing all the time. Football has taken over now. I hear Anna complaining that all her Tomás ever talks about now is football. He got that from the granda he never knew!

I never knew him either. He is a phantom, a shadow that was there for a period but not very strong or very real. My mother on the other hand is fixed and firm in my mind and in my memory. She runs though my life, with the energy of an electric current. She is where I locate the core of the courage and the confidence my sisters say I have.

CHAPTER NINE

THE OFFICE

After overhearing the women talking in the café that day and going outside into the sunlight, I had a sense that unless I took my life in my hands and made something of it I would simply fizzle out. That made me go back up the street. I wanted to do more than exist in a life not willed and I took it into myself that it was up to me to make sure I didn't turn out like that.

I marched, yes, I recall it like that, I marched up that street and swept into the office so brazenly that the people there turned around, gobsmacked, as I blurted out, 'I want to do something.'

I must have been some sight, standing in that doorway, the light behind me giving me a charged look, my face as intense as a saint's. A woman came towards me and laughed lightly.

'You've come to the right place then,' she said and gently eased me further into the room.

This was Frances and in the months that followed, though I could never say I got to know her or that she became my friend, I grew to admire her and I saw in her a woman who was living a life that I could live.

I know that's crazy now. I didn't know anything about her life. Who she loved, what she did for a laugh, although we had plenty of laughs during that time. What she really felt. And I never told her anything about myself in all those months that she came and went, bringing her energy and her passion to the city and to the campaign.

'Do you want a cup of tea?'

That was Olivia. And there was Jack and Bill and others huddled together in a meeting. I was guided through them and found my way to the back kitchen.

'Milk and sugar?'

'Milk, just.'

I was handed a mug and the circle widened out so I could sit in. I hugged the tea in my two hands and kept my nose in the vapour rising from it. I was now on stage, myself an actor, no longer watching, but performing, though I wasn't sure what my role was.

The first thing they got me doing was stuffing and sticking envelopes. I lick my lips now and I can taste the sticky threads of gum. I lashed away at the envelopes while Frances and Jack talked strategy, Olivia cajoled a politician on the phone and Bill scribbled out a press release. Then Olivia spotted me and the way my lips were beginning to stick together and she laughed and handed me the wee wet sponge.

'Here, use this. We don't want you going home with your tongue glued to the roof of your mouth.'

I laughed and blushed and took the sponge in its little round dish and carried on. I think now that was the reason why I worked for the campaign. No-one asked me about myself. No-one assumed anything other than that I wanted to be part of it. And then I was given something to do.

Of course there was mild consternation among my family. My mother worried that I would make a fool of myself, maybe even go off the rails completely.

'You don't want to be putting yourself under pressure now. You're not really in the full of your health.'

'I'm fine, Ma. It'll do me good to get out of the house. To be doing something.'

'What does Tony think?'

I'm not sure if I ever really told him how involved I became. He thought the banners and the meetings were a distraction.

He was afraid for his job. Lots of men were. But he didn't really believe it would be serious. I never actually sat him down and laid it out for him.

'Tony, see the anti-incinerator campaign? I'm stuck in it. I go up to the wee office and I put flyers in envelopes. I even answer the phone and take messages if no-one else is around. I'm helping organise a meeting in the Waterside next week. You might think I'm out with Martha and Anna, but I'm with Jack and Frances and Olivia.'

I was being unfaithful, a woman hitching her skirts for another lover, her husband cuckolded by science and the search for knowledge. I was taking action that came out of me and me alone. This was beyond the fires raging inside me.

Those were the days when I wouldn't light the coal fire at home. I brought an old electric heater down from the attic. Tony eyed it sharply, but said nothing. He lit and cleaned out the coal fire himself for a while. I hate the sound of the shovel scraping against the grate. I looked at his hunched form in front of the fireplace, cleaning it out, the scraping sound going right through me and I would have screamed at him to stop but I hesitated because I knew we were growing apart then and what right did I have to stop him dealing with fires in any way he could? I was standing at the door, poised on tiptoes to run to the arms of my new lover. The anti-incinerator campaign.

No-one took me aside and trained me. No-one handed me a manual and said read this, follow these steps and you'll know what to do. I was rebuilding my life and that's a task for which there are no instructor's guidelines. I immersed myself in the campaign and made that my manual. The campaign office would fill and empty with people I mainly knew by first names only. We had no need to dig deep into our pasts. We shared a common purpose in the present and that kept us stuffing envelopes, answering phone calls, organising meetings, drawing up press releases, reading reports and articles. Of course we chatted. Olivia was always good for a chat.

'You know, Donna, when my family ask me why I'm doing this, I tell them to look at my boys. Look at them, I say. I don't want their world polluted with any more toxic emissions and if that means I have to get out and sort it meself, then so be it.'

We never became close, so when we meet now in supermarkets or on the street we have a brief chat and a laugh. One of her boys is doing really well at football. Last time I spoke to her she told me he was going to Liverpool on trial. She never really asks about me. I think I scared her off all those years ago.

'And what about you, Donna? Do you explain the campaign in terms of your kids?'

I looked down into the sludge of my tea.

'I don't have any kids, Olivia. I just have the fires and the need to put them out.'

I must have come across as a right headcase, going on like that. I couldn't have told you where all that stuff came from. But Olivia was gentle and kind with me. And that's what I needed most then. Pass me the sponge for the stamps. Show me how to layout the chairs for the meeting. Give me the mop and bucket and I'll do the kitchen floor. Hand me the Blu-Tack and I'll put the new posters up. Let me stay on here so I don't have to go home. If she only knew the role the campaign was playing in the unravelling of my marriage! Me and Tony had plans and then our first child died and I went a wee bit loopy and our marriage began to break up, then finally fell apart when I started an affair with the anti-incinerator campaign. Sticking envelopes. SWALK. Sealed With A Loving Kiss.

Tony phoned me at the City Council office today.

'Yes, Donna. Sorry for calling you at work. You settling in all right?'

'Aye. Grand.'

'Look, I was wondering. You know, it's coming the anniversary and ... I was wondering if we should do something. I don't know. Maybe something with the stone.'

I felt the air rush out of me and whistle down the mouthpiece.

'You still there, Donna?'

'Aye. Still here. Just ... you caught me on the hop, that's all.'

'Always a first time for that.'

63

We agreed to meet. Nothing in that, is there? A former married couple on good terms in recent years dealing with a piece of history in a sensible, adult way. Straightforward enough. Then, why was I shaking, shuffling sheets of paper in a blur across my office desk as two shags skimmed the river and headed for the bridge?

My mother's opinion is that I shouldn't meet him. The electricity fizzed in her when I spoke to her tonight.

'If he wasn't man enough to stick with you when you had your bother, I don't see why you should even give him the time of day now. He ran out on you when you—'

'He didn't run out on me. There was always two of us in it.'

My mother went silent then and I wondered if I'll ever tell her about the sense I had of being unfaithful. I tell myself she would never understand. She came from a time when beds were made and you lay in them. A time when most women considered it the pinnacle of achievement to find and hold on to a good man and, if God willed it, the arrival of healthy children. She has her own forceful idea of the blight we suffered and the pain it brought.

'I never liked him. Not one bit. He was never right. Not from the start. And shur didn't it turn out like that? Teresa and all.'

There would be no point in telling her that she used to really like Tony. The night he came to the house for the first time my mother remarked on the polite way he said, 'No thanks, Mrs McDaid,' when she offered him another biscuit. All you have to do is look at the wedding photos to see how happy she was with him, grinning away beside him, her spanking new son-in-law. All the girls married off and her family complete. Her turn against him after Teresa died was bitter and final.

'What does he want with you now? Hasn't he his own life to get on with? And you only starting the new job and all. He's not looking for money is he?'

'Stop it, Ma. I mean it. Stop it.'

That shut her up. She covered her cup with her hand and looked out the window when I tried to pour her another cup of tea. We sat in silence for a while until I got up and cleared the table. Moving about broke the spell.

'He wants to talk about Teresa. The grave maybe. It's the anniversary,' I called in from the kitchen, the clattering of dishes into the sink covering the jolt in my voice. I stayed in the kitchen a while. I knew she would be crying to herself at the table and I wanted to give her a few minutes to compose herself.

Sometimes I wonder at the timing of events. I wonder if there's a big clock out there turning and ticking away and that events occur when the time is right, even when we don't know it. I feel this about the job. I was at a meeting today, after speaking to Tony. The full unit. A major review of the council waste-management policy is to be launched. Everything from wheelie bins to toxic emissions and pipes spewing effluent into the river. The whole grubby underbelly of the city's life. And I sat there and made my contributions. Spoke my piece confidently. One of only two women at the meeting. People listening to me, making notes on the pages I'd circulated. Asking me questions.

'Donna, these projections, do they factor in the new developments at the Skeoge lands?'

'You say these figures are conservative. I wouldn't like to see them when you're being extravagant. Can you take us through the second scenario again, please?'

The City Engineer thanking me by name at the end. This all happening now. I am writing about it now, the clock has turned and whenever I sit down to write about times past, I can hardly believe it. It is another place. I am another person. But the clock turns and brings the past with it, amplifying the present.

CHAPTER TEN

MEETINGS

I wasn't long in the anti-incinerator campaign when Olivia started taking me to meetings. The leaves were bronze on the trees in Brooke Park by then. 'Back-up', she called me. A pile of leaflets, a video cassette about anti-incinerator campaigns in America, a video player, a small TV, notebooks, maps, all piled into the back of her car. I waited for the doorbell to ring in the same excited way I used to wait for Tony to come calling.

'You away out again tonight, Donna?' he'd say, torn between the pleasure at seeing me go out, maybe getting better, and the confusion he felt about what I was doing. 'Make sure you tell them your husband works in the factory and the dinner you had tonight came from it.'

He sat on the sofa staring into the empty fire. I sat at the table with my coat on. We weren't looking at each other. He sucked on a cigarette. I jousted with the words and phrases dashing through my brain. I wanted to answer him, but I didn't want a row. I wanted to explain to him that I was doing it for him. For us. For the whole town. Maybe if Teresa had lived I wouldn't have been doing it. I would have been tucking her up in bed and then coming down to Tony saying 'she's asleep' and he would be smiling and saying 'I'll make us a wee cup a tay'. But that's not how it was and I can only deal with what happened. Write it down. Read it back to myself. 'That's it. That's how it was.' Maybe I should tell Tony I'm doing this. Even let him read it. Would he be able to see me and him sitting in the room, not looking at each other, the fire dead in the grate, the light bulb flickering? And the doorbell rings and I rush out with a mumbled 'see you later'.

Escaping from the silence of the house to the frenetic gabbling of Olivia was a relief. I didn't have to talk. She did enough for us both.

'Yes, Donna, sorry I'm a bit late, but I had to pick up Michelle after dancing. Michael said he'd do it, but then his van broke down outside Dungiven and he was stuck there for an hour. He's grand. Something to do with a wheel. Don't ask me. But he's back now and they're all settled, thank God ...'

I glanced sideways at her, letting her words wash over me. She is about ten years older than me. Her husband, Michael, had a roofing business that took him all over the country. She had two children. She never stopped. And yet now she looked like she'd walked out of a beauty parlour. Her hair shone like honey. Her face glowed and when she smiled she lit up. She was not much bigger than me but she seemed more solid. More there. I looked like a shrunken prune beside her. I had barely washed my face. My coat hung about me like a shroud. I was someone you'd take pity on and you'd wonder as you passed where my hat or wee cardboard box was so you could leave me fifty pence.

Tonight we were doing one of a number of meetings we did at community centres. We had it off to a T. We arrived. Olivia went inside and said hello to whoever was organising things. I hung about the car. Then she came out and, in a whirlwind, we unloaded the boot and carried our equipment in, to be greeted by a clutch of people, members of a local committee. The sight of garishly lit breeze-block walls is one I'll always associate with the anti-incinerator campaign.

I knew the drill. I found a small table or improvised with a couple of stackable plastic chairs, set up the TV and video, arranged arcs of chairs facing the TV and put leaflets on them.

Olivia bustled about, fixing here and there, but mainly talking to the committee members; shaking hands, 'pressing the flesh' as I know it now.

Someone always gave me a hand. A wee boy whose mammy had dragged him along laid out chairs. A caretaker with a limp wheeled a trolley load over and said he'd leave a stack by the door, in case a big crowd came. He smiled as if he didn't think it likely. A woman came up to me and said she was in charge of the tea and asked when we wanted to serve it. I had decisions to make. How were the chairs to be arranged? How many would we need? Who would turn off the lights?

'Yes, we'll have the tea at the end, say in about an hour's time. If you had a boiler, you could have it ready and I'll give you hand with it.'

I was the assistant but people looked to me. I was with the expert. I had knowledge and a role.

When the committee reckoned everybody was in, Olivia introduced us and made a brief speech, then nodded at me. This was the scary bit. The crowd in arcs in front of me. The caretaker with the limp over by the door ready to turn off the lights on my signal. The remote control in my hand. All I had to do was press PLAY. I had checked everything. Everything was fine, but a bubble of panic swelled inside me. Then I thought of Teresa. An image of her filled my mind. My own image, a special one only I had. And I calmed. I'm doing this for you, Teresa. I am doing this for both of us. I pressed PLAY. And the crowd hushed as the caretaker switched off the light. The screen flickered for a moment, then cleared and the titles appeared. I relaxed. I knew how it would go now. I had made it happen.

There were many meetings like that. A fervour hit the town. An explosion of activity and meetings. Everyone had an opinion. And mostly people felt there was no way they would put up with an incinerator. It seemed so obvious to me. Why burn off rubbish to make more rubbish? Of course there were concerns about jobs. Would Du Pont stay if they didn't get their way? And if the biggest manufacturer in the town left, where would we be then?

That was Tony's line most of the time.

'Donna, I know you think you're doing a good thing, but what about us? I mean if I lose me job, how can we ever make a life for ourselves? How can we have a wean, even?'

It all came back to that after a while. He was crazy to have a child. He saw it as the most natural thing in the world. And I don't blame him. It is, after all. Two people getting together and enjoying each other, combining their gene pool and a new member of the species comes along. Straightforward science. The stuff of my day-to-day life now.

But then, it was a minefield of pain and grief, a tearing wrench in my heart every time I looked at a child.

Sometimes people brought babies and children to the meetings. Once a young woman breastfed an infant in the front row. I almost fainted. The easy smile on the woman's face. The baby's head nuzzled to her chest, lying in the crook of her bare arm. Seeing a mother like that drove a spear through my heart.

I didn't faint. Sure my speared heart skipped a beat. Something like that. But no more than that. I was in charge of the whole evening then. That was on a night when I was going solo. We had so many meetings to deal with. Olivia was in Carnhill. I was in Nelson Drive. Fifty people, including the nursing mother. And me, the woman who came in a taxi with the videos and the leaflets and the talk. And the twitching eye brought on by the pain in my heart.

I was the expert by then. It's no wonder I went on to study Environmental Science. I knew so much from the videos, the leaflets, the books. I immersed myself in study. I nursed knowledge and I clasped the anti-incinerator campaign to my aching breast and I fed it the good inside me.

The funny thing about the 'jobs' argument is that Tony didn't stay at Du Pont. Soon after we broke up, he changed jobs. He simply left his job in the factory and started working with his brother, laying carpets. He always did a bit of that, even when he worked in Du Pont, pulling his brother out when he was busy. His brother envied him his good, steady, well-paid factory job. He said Tony was mad to give it up. Everybody did. But it seemed like a package deal with him. Give up wife, home, job. Major changes. Of course it's all worked out well in the end. The carpet business took off, his brother took him on as a partner, they went into property, buying up terrace houses, renovating them and selling them on. Then they bought a warehouse and started selling, as well as fitting, carpets. Now the carpet business is no more than the shop window for what they do. The real business is in property deals.

I often wonder would he have left the factory if we had stayed together. If Teresa had lived. His life is better now, isn't it? Is that what people mean when they talk about an 'ill wind'? My life is better, too, isn't it? Am I bad for thinking that?

I met Tony for lunch in the Sandwich Company today. Neutral territory. I was there first and he hurried in as I took a mouthful of my chicken tikka sandwich. The place was packed with office workers and lecturers from the technical college. Tony grinned at me and joined the queue. When he sat opposite me I saw he had a salad sandwich.

I want to get all the details of this meeting down. I want to have everything on record. The way the queue jostled and moved along: the flurry of spreading, folding and cutting as the staff made the sandwiches to order; the hum of conversation; the angle that woman hung her coat over the back of her chair; the way that man picked food from his teeth while staring out of the window.

'Sorry I'm late, Donna. I was out pricing a job. Some people don't know if they want carpet or wooden floors. Tough choices.'

Tony's exasperation and nervousness beamed in his face. I never remembered him as a flusterer. He always seemed on top of things. I looked at the lines on his face and saw the years since the divorce. How do you maintain friendly relations with your former husband? Not easy. It helps if he's not a bastard. No, Tony is not a bastard. I never thought that. Just someone badly hurt, like me.

'How's the job going?' he asked breathlessly.

'Grand. Settling in nicely.'

I was waiting for the pleasantries to end. There was something he wanted to talk about and we both knew that what we had in common was Teresa.

I waited. Tony munched on his sandwich. A piece of lettuce clung to the side of his mouth. When he didn't notice it, I made a sign across my mouth.

'You've got lettuce on your chin. There.'

'Thanks,' he said as he picked it off.

That broke the ice. The restaurant receded around me. The voices eased down to a low hum, people on neighbouring seats became removed and distant. We were held in a cocoon with our dead baby, waiting to emerge as if born again. Looking on you would have thought we were a lucky husband and wife managing to snatch a bit of time together over lunch. I even allowed myself the briefest imagining that that's how it was. Then Tony pushed his half-finished sandwich away, swallowed a last mouthful and spoke.

'I got a letter from the hospital.'

What was he doing telling me this? Was he seriously sick?

'It's from the Pathology Department. It's about Teresa.'

He reached into his pocket and took out the letter. I recognised the hospital logo. He slid the letter across to me. It lay there folded over between us, for a long heart beat.

'About Teresa?' I croaked.

He nodded and I knew he wasn't going to say any more. He had gone as far as he could. I picked up the letter and opened it out. The page shook in my hand. A foolish thought raced in my brain that they were writing to say it had all been a mistake. That she was alive and well and that they were very sorry for causing us all the bother.

They were sorry all right. The letter said that. Sorry to be writing to us. Sorry to be bringing it all back to us. Sorry to be advising us that the department had retained some of Teresa's organs after her death and they were sorry to be asking us what we wanted to do now.

'What does this mean?' I stuttered.

I think Tony was glad I managed to say anything, because he sighed and said, 'I don't know really. I just got the letter the other day. After I phoned you about meeting up to talk about ... They have some of Teresa's organs. They kept them for research.'

'But I don't remember that.'

How could I remember that? I was lost in the black fog at the time.

'When did they take them out?' I asked.

'Must have been at the post-mortem.'

The fog descended over my eyes as Tony continued.

'You remember they did a post-mortem. They said it would help with other kids. Other families.'

'I don't remember that.'

'I handled it. I signed a form. That's maybe why they wrote to me. They have my new address and all.'

'You signed a form? You agreed to this?'

'I ... I don't think so. I don't know.'

He lifted the letter.

'Look, it says they're reviewing procedures. People who agreed to have post-mortems may not have agreed to ... organ ... organ retention.'

'So what did we bury?'

It was the hardest question welling up among the torrent of questions in my mind. It burst out of me and stung Tony.

He hung his head and mumbled. 'Teresa.'

Years rushed by me. The white coffin. The cold day. The empty fireplace. The ash pit in my stomach. My mother weeping. My sisters bawling. The hole in my heart. The pain in my shoulder from lugging a bag full of books. The panic attack the night before an exam. The sweep of my desk at the office. The years since I'd first stood at her grave. All rushing before me, so that I was right back there again.

I didn't return to work. I fled to the beach at *Cúlaphúca*. Tears streamed down my face as I drove. They were trying to poleaxe me again.

Small waves rolled in. Two gulls flew round each other. There was a whispering in the dune grass. Streaky clouds strayed across the blue sky.

I don't even know if I said goodbye to Tony. I lifted the letter and walked out of the Sandwich Company. He didn't try to follow me. Why should he? Where was I going to go?

Only to the beach. And the *caldragh*. To steady myself.

I held the letter and read it out loud. Read it for the ghosts of the children buried beneath my feet. I could face them easier than facing Teresa. And once again the question rose up. Why? If I expected an answer, there was none. No measured advice boomed from the sky or whispered from the dunes. I stood there alone and the great wide sea rolled gently towards me.

The sand at my feet crunched up around the edges of my flat work shoes. The bottoms of my business suit gathered grains of sand as I moved over the dunes. I was far away from any thoughts of work. All that gleaming metal and glass that was my new office. All those blinking cursors and swift words racing along the screen as my fingers typed briskly and accurately. All the neat formulations of reports and meetings that strove to stay on top of the mess that rumbles underneath everything. The great mess of waste and offal, clay and sludge that we make. And once more Teresa rose out of the mess and stood beside me.

I know she is always with me but today, as the two gulls swirled about one another, I wished sorely that she would leave. Tears ran down my face as thoughts I couldn't bear raced through my mind. When will this be over? When will I be able?

I read the letter once more, quietly this time. I directed most of my anger against Tony. Why did he let them do that? What was he thinking? When he carried the small white coffin, what was he carrying? The thoughts drove a knife into me. And I crumpled onto the sand, burying my face in my hands, stuffing the sobs back into my mouth so that, unable to escape from me, they convulsed my whole body. If I had taken my hands from my mouth screams would have left me and I would have woken the dead around me.

Even the delicate shells of the snails slowly climbing the blades of grass could not still me. The delicate shells, curled in orange and ochre and dun to blend with the sand, the tiny bodies, fragile and strong, unique and universal. So many delicate whorls of living amid the dead. The sobs convulsed and then subsided, as a tide ebbs out of a cleft in rocks by the shore. Eventually, I became calm, almost distracted, and raised my eyes above the grass and the edge of the dune, out over the beach to the sea and the waves curling there. The two gulls had landed. One was bigger than the other. One followed, the other led. Where one pecked and dipped the other rushed over and mimicked. The big one was showing the smaller one. The smaller one was learning.

I stood up and dusted off my knees. Grains stuck to the fabric no matter how much I brushed. The dunes and the *caldragh* were part of me.

When I got home there was a message on my phone. My mother checking up on me. I phoned her back.

'I tried your work,' she said. 'You know I don't like doing that, but they said you went out for lunch and didn't come back. They said you must have had meetings but there was nothing in the diary. They're wild nice there at your work. I could have tried your mobile but you have that switched off most of the time anyway, especially if you're at meetings. So I left the message on your phone. You're still coming round for the dinner on Wednesday?'

The twin drives of gossip and concern were full-on for my mother in that message. And I would have to compose myself, have a good story ready to tell her when I went round.

'I'm still all right for Wednesday. I'll see you Wednesday.'

Then I hung up and phoned Tony on his mobile.

'Can you talk?'

'Yes. You all right?'

'Yes. Sorry for walking out on you today.'

'It's okay. Your mother would say you owed me that much.'

I didn't quite understand what he meant and so I didn't respond. Then slowly it dawned on me. He meant the way my mother blamed him for walking out on me. I smiled to myself and let him hear the smile when I finally spoke. 'You're not afraid of her still, Tony?'

'Terrified. Have you told her?'

'No. Have you told Mary? Any of your lot?'

'No. I ... wanted ... I wasn't sure what to say, not until we had a chat.'

'It's better if we get a line figured out. The letter says we can make an appointment to see someone.'

'I'll do that if you want.'

That stopped me. Did I want him to follow it up? He got the letter. He signed the papers. He could handle it. These were the thoughts that first ran through my head. But very quickly an image of a figure in a white coat came to me, a figure from a TV programme, a phantom medical person, turning away from me.

'No, we'll go together. Let's just say we got a letter from the hospital and that we're going to a meeting. Tell Mary tonight. I'll tell my mother on Wednesday. We'll give them more details after the meeting.'

I dread that meeting with my mother. The sophisticated emotional arguments she will throw up. The high-voltage uneasiness I will feel, making my head and my heart throb, when I face her with the letter we got from the hospital, to tell her parts of her granddaughter remain unburied.

CHAPTER ELEVEN

THE SCIENTIFIC METHOD

I remember I grew in ease running meetings for the anti-incinerator campaign. I was on my own soon enough, doing a series of talks. I had my leaflets, posters and the video. I remember one in the community centre in Strathfoyle, because that was the night I decided to go back to school. A woman called Alice was our contact there and when I arrived she propelled me into the room and blasted me with a torrent of questions. Is that enough chairs? When do you want the tea? Are you on your own? Will we take a list of names and addresses? And a dozen more besides. When I think back now I'm pleased to recall how calm I was. I reassured Alice that the chairs and the hall were fine, that I was on my own, but that I had everything we needed. I almost said I was in charge, but I think Alice got the message anyway.

They had a video player and a TV already set up. I tried the tape and it worked perfectly. I put some leaflets on the chairs. Two teenage girls, Alice's daughters, Blu-Tacked posters to the white breeze-block walls. BAN THE BURN. NO TO INCINERATION. Alice made final arrangements in the kitchen.

'I'm in charge.' That's how it felt. And it felt so very good. Of course, I was always nervous before the people came in, but what more could I do except gather my thoughts, settle myself and wait?

I stepped outside the hall and looked across the car park to the green patch where local children were playing. A group of girls had a rope tied round a lamppost. They were taking turns to swing on the pole. There were four of them, all about eight years old. Hair tied back to show ruddy faces. The ones waiting, legs crossed and arms folded. The one on the rope, leaning back and swinging in a wide arc so her ponytail trailed on the ground. I was struck by how 'right' the scene was and I ached to think that Teresa would never swing with them.

I took that ache back into the community centre where people had gathered. Looking back now I recall how different all the people were and yet how much the same, they – we – were. We all wanted to know what the chemical plant, not a mile away, was planning. We wanted to know what it all meant and what we could do about it. Faces grinned up at me. A mother with her young son beside her, holding a book. Two elderly men, each with caps on their knees. A young couple passing a restless infant between them. A group of women in a row, passing a bag of sweets up and down and laughing. Individual men and women nervously looking around them. Alice sitting near the teenage girls. All looking at me.

I amaze myself remembering the calm I brought to running those public meetings. Now, if I am asked to run a meeting like that, in my professional life, I can certainly do it, power-point presentation and all. But I become nervous and tense. Then I seemed to be resolute. I had a new purpose. I had a focus. I was no longer deep in depression. I had purged that by joining the campaign. I was on a crusade and I was standing tall. For Teresa and the girls swinging on the pole.

'Good evening, everybody, and thanks for inviting me here. My name is Donna and I'm from the Anti-incinerator Campaign and I know everybody here is worried about Du Pont's plans to build a toxic-waste incinerator down the road, so I've brought some leaflets – you'll see them on the seats – and I have a video we can watch.'

Can I hear my voice? I'm not sure if those are the words I said, but certainly something like that. Was I clear and loud enough?

Or did I stutter and trail off, sounding like someone who didn't really want to be there?

People shuffled, reached for the leaflets and settled. I checked the video and pressed PLAY.

Late spring light came through the high windows around the room and it was a strain to see the pictures on the TV screen, but people leaned forward as the images told the story of emissions and illnesses, campaigns and concerns.

There then followed the tricky bit when, at the end of the video, I asked, 'Any questions?' Silence. Some shuffling. More silence. What was there to say? The video had dealt with it all.

The young man with the restless baby coughed and said, 'I don't know, but like, I'm ... well ... put it this way, if I got a job in it, I'd take it.'

I remember thinking that it was good he said that. I remember thinking that if we're honest that's what we have to deal with. Then one of the young women with Alice said, 'I don't think anyone should take a job in it. That's what they want us to do. We'd only be poisoning ourselves. And the children.'

I was about to say something when a man stood up at the back. He was tall and thin, about the same age as my mother. His voice was low and raspy and people had to turn and shush each other to hear him. I strained my ears to catch what he was saying.

'It's all very well saying we should do this and we should do that. The fact of the matter is we don't know what we're talking about. Can you tell us what volume of toxic waste Du Pont plan to bring to the incinerator in a year? Can you tell us if they plan to import stuff from across the water? Do you know the constituents of the waste they're bringing in?'

He fired the questions at me and I felt my mouth go dry.

We don't know what we're talking about echoed inside me.

Faces turned up at me and waited for the answers. My mouth grew even drier. Now, if I was in a similar situation, I would be able to dissemble at least. I might even know the answers but, if I didn't, I would be able to direct him to reports, urge him to visit websites and wax lyrical on the complexity of the matter, having thanked him profusely for his question. Then I was raw. Naked and exposed.

I didn't know what we were talking about.

I wished Frances or Olivia were there. They'd know how to handle the questions.

I floundered. I can't remember if I actually said anything. I have an image of me standing there with my mouth open and nothing coming out. I certainly hope that's not what happened but I'm afraid that might be exactly how it was. The man spoke again. I remember that.

'How are we going to deal with Du Pont if the ones in charge of the campaign don't know the facts? Do you have any idea what you're talking about, wee girl? Are you ignorant or what?'

I was stunned. I froze completely. The man wasn't angry. He was almost sad.

One of the young women with Alice stood up and spoke then. She spoke about how we all had to get the facts and how could anyone really know what was going on when Du Pont weren't giving us the full information. We had to go and get the knowledge ourselves and not be waiting around for other people to get it for us. We were all in this together.

When she sat down, there was a brief round of applause and a woman said they wanted to form a committee. The line of women with her, the ones who had been passing the sweets, said they would all get involved. Some spoke, others nodded agreement. All the while the man who asked me the questions stayed on his feet, a weak smile crossing his lips. The energy rose in the room, as if his remarks had spurred people on.

Alice got up and came to the front of the room beside me. She effectively took over the meeting, steering the comments and questions. I remember standing beside her, the colour draining from my face, my palms damp and tepid by my side, my tongue huge and stuck to the roof of my mouth. I couldn't take my eyes off the man at the back of the hall, who stood just as he had when he challenged me, still smiling weakly.

I remember that he stood for most of the rest of the meeting. Perhaps that's untrue. I know that Alice ran the meeting to the end, that I came out of my embarrassment eventually and took some questions, adding information and regaining my composure. I know that through it all I kept my eyes on the man at the back, even when he eventually sat down, his weak smile hardening into a smirk.

By the meeting's end, I felt a vow harden in me, a vow that I would wipe the smirk off that man's face.

Alice gave me a lift home at the end of the meeting. She'd had no chance to properly talk to me as the meeting wrapped up, being busy getting the tea served. But, as I loaded the video player into the boot of her car, she stood next to me and sighed.

'Don't mind him,' she said. 'That man who was a bit, well ... arrogant, he's not really like that. Only, he lost his wife about two months ago and well, he's struggling.'

I picture him lowering himself into his bed, his joints creaking, the bedsprings whining under his weight. I see him lie back exhausted, the weak smile still on his face, the man straining to keep it in place but then his lower lip quivers, the lines on his forehead crimp together in a deep frown and tears fill his eyes as he relives his exchange with me. Tears flow faster as he wishes he hadn't said what he'd said, then he turns on his side to face the empty space beside him.

Nonetheless the resolve I gathered because of that incident stood to me. I would go back to school. I would get the knowledge and the qualifications. The man had a point and I thank him for making it.

Alice continued. 'Shur that's men for you,' trying to laugh it off, but I stopped her.

'That's not good enough,' I said. 'He had a point. We have to know the science. But he didn't need to get on to me like that.'

I was sorry I spoke so harshly, because I saw Alice's smile fade and a frown deepen across her brow. She was saddened by the sour note at the end of a successful event. I quickly added, to reassure her, 'It's not your fault. You're not responsible for what he said.'

* *

Recovering, I placed my trust in the scientific method. The reliance on verifiable facts. The notion that evidence was needed to prove arguments and that the way you got evidence was by observation and the way you tested theories was by experiment. I sought salvation in that. In the anti-incinerator campaign, it was the scientists I most admired. The ones on our side. The ones who took the evidence and looked hard at it. Critically and independently. The ones who were prepared to question. The ones who said the dioxins and furans, the toxic emissions, wouldn't be good for us. The ones who were able to quote from studies on toxic chemical concentrations in the breast milk of women who lived near incinerators. I trusted them and their science. Of course I knew they were biased. That was never a problem for me. I was biased. Everyone is biased. I relied on subjective science, rigorous and analytical, but humane and connected to people's lives.

CHAPTER TWELVE

THE TECH

I remember when I told Tony that I was going to the Tech. He was on night shift and had just got up. It was about four o'clock in the afternoon and he was half-heartedly watching horse racing on the television.

Telling Tony made it real. Up to then, I had been pretending to myself. If I could tell Tony, I could tell anyone. 'I'm going to the Tech, Tony. To do a course.'

'Yeh? Is Anna going with you?'

'No. On my own. Well, there'll be other people there. It's GCSEs.'

A race ended in a flurry of horses thundering past a finish post to the exulting voice of the commentator. Tony hit the button on the remote control and the screen went blank.

'GCSEs?'

'Yeh. I think I'll have a go at English and Maths. And Science.'

Then, I remember it clearly now as I write it, a great smile lit up his face and he stood up.

'English. Maths. And Science. Fair play to you, Donna. Are you sure you'll be, you know, able for it?'

'I don't know.'

'What brought this on then?'

'Well, I ... It won't do any harm and if I can't ... you know ... I'll just pack it in.'

He paused then and winked at me.

'Oh, you'll manage it all right. You'll be good at it. Just ... make sure you're doing it for the right reasons. It's no substitute, you know.'

'What do you mean?'

'Make sure you're doing it for yourself. Not for Teresa.'

He was still smiling, if less warmly, as he passed me, carrying his tea mug into the kitchen.

If I had him in front of me now I could say things. I could quote scientists and philosophers at him. I could give him a lecture on the role of education in the progress of the individual and society. And it would all be impressive and sensible, but it would come back to one thing. I wanted to study science because I wanted to know. I wanted to know so that I would not be poleaxed again. I wanted the benefits of scientific progress and its increased ability to make predictions. I could say that to him now. Then, I said nothing. I heard him rinse his mug, call to me that he was going out for a walk in Brooke Park – 'I'll get some fresh air,' he called – when what he really wanted to do was have a cigarette in comfort. I heard the back door slam shut. I can picture him walking down the back lane, scuffing his feet, sighing and reaching into his pocket for his cigarette box, tapping his trouser pockets for matches, the smile fading on his face, shuffling a cigarette from the box, sticking it in his mouth and lighting it as he reaches the end of the lane, watching the traffic go by as he inhales deeply, holding it, then blowing out a great white stream of smoke, as he crosses the road, shrugging his shoulders, and enters the park. I see him, an ordinary, honest man, doing his best, wrestling with his own pain.

He must have talked about it with men at work. Confided in someone. He's close to his brother, Larry.

'She's going back to the Tech now. She's doing GCSEs.'

'You're not serious?'

'It's the incinerator thing. Her head's turned with it.'

'Fair play to her. Shur what harm can it do?'

'None. Maybe.'

'Just look on the bright side, Tony. When Du Pont closes down, your Donna'll be all educated and she can go out and get a big job. She might even be a teacher.'

If I'm honest, Tony never opposed my plans. In a way, his silent acquiescence was a form of support. I look back now and recognise that we had grown apart. An earthquake had happened and split us right down the middle, so that he was across a gulf from me. I could see him there, his shoulders hunched into his jacket, a cigarette leaking a curl of smoke into the still air. I stood on my ground and looked away from him. We never even waved. I simply turned into the great space behind me and walked into my past. I became the student I should have been when I was a teenager.

Telling Tony was one challenge. Telling my family was a challenge of a totally different order. But I was avid for knowledge and going to the Tech was to be my salvation.

'Are you sure that's a good idea, Donna?'

'But you're too old for that, Donna.'

'Who put that idea into your head?'

The hard thing for them to accept was that the idea was mine. Yes, Olivia at the anti-incinerator campaign said I should go about getting some qualifications. She said I should think about the Tech and night classes and maybe a secretarial course. She saw me filing and stuffing envelopes and by then she knew what little I told her about Teresa and Tony and my life. She could see me making something of myself and finding a place for myself as an office junior.

The great dark that had enveloped me after Teresa's death was lifting. There was a summer of meetings and rallies, advances and retreats as the campaign against Du Pont's plans took off. By that stage the political leaders in the city had woken up to the fact that something was happening. They were bringing their influence to bear, trying to keep Du Pont happy while mindful of the feelings among the electorate. And the thin man asked me if I was ignorant and I admitted to myself that in a way he was right. I was ignorant. But I was not to going to let him or anyone else put me down because of it.

All I had to do was convince my mother and my sisters that going to the Tech was a good idea. Yes, I remember that's how I felt. It wasn't a case of simply telling them. I had to convince them that I could make decisions and plan a course of action for myself. I had to prove I could take charge of my life once more now that Teresa's death had knocked the stuffing out of me.

'What would you want to go to the Tech for?' my mother asked.

I know that she was being solicitous, trying to protect me. But there was also a degree of holding me back. An element of preventing me. And I resented that. I laugh now when I recall the way I huffed and flounced out the door, tetchy as a teenager.

'Look,' I said. 'I'm going to the Tech and I'm going to do some GCSEs. After the summer. Just because ye don't have any doesn't mean that I shouldn't go about it.'

I tossed that last remark at my sisters.

A silence followed me, then my mother flung a question after me as I slammed the front door.

'What do you think Tony'll make of all of this?'

I realise now, after all these years, how much of a competition life in a family is. How much explaining you have to do. How the fears that other people have for themselves and for you can inhibit you from doing the things you want to do. I know that now and I write it plain. If I ever have a child again I'll make sure that they have all the love and all the support they need to be everything they want to be.

Tony didn't object to the 'return to school' idea in principle. He's not one of those men who think women shouldn't use their brains. I admire the way he came to the graduation and all. But, at that time, he felt it was another part of the unravelling of the ties between us. I never meant it to threaten him. I craved the knowledge. I was avid for it. I wanted to know. What problems could GCSEs in English, Maths and Science cause?

I see him standing in front of the empty fireplace, wearing his work clothes, ready to go out on a night shift. I said I intended to go to classes in the following September. He listened and said that was fine, but I knew by the way he looked at me that he was confused. No-one really knew how to behave around me when I was 'delicate'. Maybe I did play on that at times. Maybe I did hold that over him. Maybe I left it in the air that if he didn't buy into what I was saying that I would freak out and become the madwoman he feared lurked beneath my depression.

Only I wasn't depressed. Not in the deep way I had been. I was pecking at the shell around me and I was almost at the point of pushing my tiny beak through.

Going back to school was a kind of substitute. So is work. I know that. Not only a kind of substitute for Teresa, but for family life, for men, for a social life even. But school and work are so much more. They are the means by which I recover my life, the extinguishers I use to quell the fires in me and the bricks from which I build a future. I totter upon them every day.

CHAPTER THIRTEEN

RETENTION

I've always had trouble breaking difficult news to my mother. It's not that she's an ogre. It's because of my desire to please her, in the face of the electrical discharge that frequently threatens to bounce between us. Our relationship is better than ever it was, but, going round to the house after meeting with Tony, I knew that I'd struggle to tell her about Teresa and the letter from the hospital. I suppose I was trying to protect her. Of course, being the youngest of three sisters is part of it, too.

Martha and Anna were there. I was still reeling from the letter and everything that Tony told me. The past had caught up with the present. Things I thought were long buried had resurfaced.

Martha and Anna were rushing as usual. And full of banter.

'Oh, here's the working woman now, Mam. Have you got her dinner ready for her?'

'Doesn't she look lovely in her wee suit? Straight out of *Sex and the City.*'

'Just leave your briefcase in the hall. Your martini will be ready in a moment. Mother is in the kitchen, selecting the olives.'

They made me smile because I knew there was no malice in it. I know there's some yearning in it. Both of them are busy full-time mothers with young children, their lives determined by their children in a way their husbands' lives are not. And I know they have good families and good relationships and good men to be with. But I also know they secretly envy me. They envy my independence. When I notice that in them, I hold to it and use it to bolster my courage to go on.

My mother came in from the kitchen, bustling with tea things on a tray. I joked that I hoped my sisters hadn't eaten my dinner. Mother said it was in the oven and Anna and Martha went into another round of slagging.

'She got you the fillet of pork you like. And a few roast parsnips.'

'Nothing but the best for our Donna. Sure she has to keep her strength up, and she running the City Council and all.'

'Don't mind us. We'll just go home and buy chips on the way, same as we always do. Ach, shur we have no life at all.'

'Oh, and our poor children, starving for a nice bit of pork fillet.'

The smell of the roast meat wafted from the kitchen. My mother does special meals for me. After Teresa, I became 'delicate', someone who had to be watched, looked after, someone who had to have a special diet, treats to keep her happy. I became a medical case. And even though time has passed, I'm still treated with kid gloves by my mother. We're still circling round each other with Teresa spinning between us.

As usual, I was stuck for words when Anna and Martha got going like that. I have no wit to compete with theirs. I can't come back at them because every piece of banter I compose seems like more than slagging. It sounds like I'm putting them down.

So I sipped my tea and grinned and mother sat beside me on the sofa and in that instant we were a family again and I knew that I should tell them about meeting Tony and the letter he showed me.

'I met Tony for lunch the other day.'

They stared at me, willing me to tell them more. I realised Anna and Martha were there because my mother asked them to be. When I thought about it, I was glad.

'He got a letter from the hospital. I don't know why it came out now. Some kind of investigation I suppose. There's a problem with post-mortems.'

'Post-mortems?'

'Who gave permission for a post-mortem?'

'Mary, Mother of God, protect us!'

Martha blessed herself. Anna wanted more information. My mother gasped her surprise and confusion. I focused on Anna.

'Tony says he sort of remembers signing a letter, but he couldn't really say what he signed. They just put it in front of him.'

My mother sneered.

'I knew that bastard was no good.'

Martha asked, 'But why did they do a post-mortem?'

Anna sat forward.

'Medical research. I read about it in the *Telegraph*. It's only all coming out now. Oh, Donna, you must be devastated by this. And poor Tony.'

But my mother was having none of that.

'Poor Tony! Didn't you hear Donna saying he agreed to it?'

The past caught up with the present and drove me deep into the sofa. I was back to the dark months following Teresa's death, in the midst of my family, as they struggled to cope with another catastrophe I'd brought to our door. Why was I visiting this upon them once more? Hadn't I done enough?

I heard their voices around me as I nestled into a fog that felt familiar and dangerous. The image of the thin man at the meeting in Strathfoyle all those years before blended with the image of a man in a white coat, sneering the same weak smile, looking down his nose as he passed a letter that I could not reach. It was the sneering smile that did it for me. I rose through the fog. The voices around me grew more distinct and I heard Anna explain to the other two.

'The paper said that letters were going out to a number of people. It's because they never got the right permission.'

My mother asked, 'Why are they bringing it up now?'

She spoke as if I wasn't there. I can't blame her. They had lots of experience of that. There in body, slumped on the sofa, eyes glazed over, face ash-grey and closed. Now I leaned towards her, wrestling with the images in my head and the burnt crust in my mouth. I spoke with all the bile that the meeting with Tony had given rise to.

'The letter is about Teresa.'

Images in my head. Pink eyelids closed. A puckered face in a blanket. A white coffin.

Martha grew upset and put her face in her hands.

'Pity the little child. Oh, God, have mercy.'

I don't know where Martha gets the religion from. None of the rest of us has it. I sometimes wonder would I have coped better if I believed. But then, as Martha prayed and Anna and my mother stared at me, I knew that there was no appeal I could make to anyone or anything higher. There was us, me on the sofa, my mother beside me, my sisters in armchairs before us, tea things on the low table, grains of sugar scattered across the glass surface, like throwaway rhinestones. I wished there was some telepathy that would take everything I had in my head and transfer it to theirs, every thought, dream, fear and plan, so that I would never have to explain or justify again. It would be all known, for all time, in all of us. Here I am, an irreligious scientist, taking the character of God to myself.

'Look, I don't really know any more details than what I've told you. Tony got the letter. There's going to be a public meeting. He's going to reply and say, "Yes, we would like to attend."'

'Let him go himself,' my mother threw in. 'He brought it on us.'

'No, Ma,' I said. 'I'll be there with him.'

Tony was at the Everglades Hotel car park before me. He flashed his lights at me as I pulled up in a bay opposite. It made me smile to remember how I'd flashed my eyes at him all those years before. Now I think about how grown-up we are and still so frail. Battered by the years crashing in. Tony locked his car, shrugged into his coat and walked over to me.

'That the new motor? Going well is it?'

'Fine.'

I was too nervous for small talk. Looking over his shoulders I saw the clouds streaked over the river, pink and salmon chevrons cutting through the grey clouds of early evening.

Tony rubbed his palms together.

'Bit of a nip in the air. No sign of spring yet.'

There was no sign of a thaw. My frozen heart ached and the winter of my past, the burning ice of those memories, chimed inside me.

A blast from the overhead heater as we entered the hotel lobby surprised me. Muzak played something syrupy. The bright lights and the gay carpets, the nests of large sofas in an alcove round a fake coal fire welcomed us. We could have been attending a dinner dance. A works do. Friends and acquaintances in the bar, some already red-cheeked and loud. Women in bright dresses and brash jewellery. Men preening themselves in their new shirts, drinking too fast. Me and Tony, a couple, welcomed, warmed, drawn into the company.

We weren't a couple. We were a pair. Together right enough but not joined. Linked only by memories that chased behind us and caught up with the present.

'It's the Avonmore Suite,' Tony said, pointing at a display board that had the names of various rooms and suites in gold letters. Grand names. Avonmore. Glenmore. Lisdoon. Ballinderry. And underneath, most of them in smaller letters, the titles of meetings and conferences. Under Avonmore, the letters read 'Human Organ Retention'.

The Avonmore Suite was one of the minor ones, but there was plenty of space for the fifty or so people scattered among the rows of seats facing front. I didn't know anyone at the top table. There were four of them, men and women, obviously professionals. I pressed my palms together in my lap and let out a great sigh.

'You all right?' Tony asked. And when I nodded, he continued, 'We had John Mullan's do here. Remember?'

So there was an event we attended here, with Tony's workmates from Du Pont. John Mullan, a much older man, about to begin his retirement. It was a special night. Not the whole plant, just Tony's section. The fitters and the engineers. Presentations. A gold watch. A bouquet of flowers for Mrs Mullan; a stout woman in a blue floral dress. One of their sons taking photos, gathering groups of family and work colleagues to be snapped as memories of the night. I remembered all right, but I couldn't put a year on it.

'It was before Teresa. The year before.'

I admired his memory. It struck me how much his life is divided by Teresa, too.

'It was a good night,' I said and I smiled. He smiled back, weakly, rubbing his palms together, wanting nothing more than to be out in the car park, shuffling in the chilly air, lighting up a cigarette.

Someone coughed and there was a call to order. The four people on the panel settled in their seats. Then the woman at the end of the table stood and spoke.

'Good evening, ladies and gentlemen. I think we'll start.'

At that moment, the door opened and two women came in. Two sisters, I could see that immediately. Women in their sixties, with good hair, clear complexions, smart clothes. Women used to foreign holidays, having money in the bank. Women who have everything, I quickly made my summary. There they stood, all of us watching, held by our attention, but only for a beat before the chairwoman spoke again.

'That's okay. Do please come in. We're just making a start.'

I saw the women bump together, a small jostle of support and embarrassment running between them, one gestured, the other nodded, they bumped lightly together again, then lurched out of the glare of our attention and into the nearest seats.

Like the rest of the crowd, I turned my gaze forward to look at the panel of speakers. My eyes focussed on one man. He was later introduced as a pathologist, a scientist of deviations from the normal healthy state. I noticed the way he sat, the way he stared at the ceiling, then gazed about the room. His face then turned upwards so that I noticed his shining chin. Above that, thin lips clenched tightly together. Then his fine nose led me to his eyes, closing serenely.

As the chairwoman began again, his face lowered and his eyes opened. Tony and I weren't far back and I could see the dull green glow of his eyes. He hunched forward, resting his forearms on the table in front of him, blinking two or three times. His gaze met mine, stalled briefly then looked down at his upturned palms. And he yawned, making no attempt to stifle or hold it. A thorough-going yawn that brought water to his eyes and made me realise that either this man is very tired – he works long hours, he must do – or he's completely bored. Of course, I can't know for sure what brought the yawn on, but as I looked at him, I was sure it was boredom and not tiredness.

Somehow his mood affected me and I switched off. I could be clever and say that it was a defence on my part. I didn't want to cope with the details of the organs retained. A story starting to come out. A public informed. Yes, for years now we have – the hospital authorities have – been retaining – keeping – organs of your loved ones. In labs. In storerooms. In jars. A story coming out. News just breaking, except that it's not something new. It's something revealed.

The chairwoman spoke and introduced the panellists – a clinician, detailed, soft-spoken, warm; a hospital administrator, garbled, jargon-filled, cold; the pathologist, bored, distant, arrogant.

He stood up. All the others had sat. A restless man, I could see that. A man used to moving. A man who acted, who took decisions and made things happen. He accepted the chairwoman's assertion that there would be public consultations. He explained certain 'unwelcome' practices as being historical, as being part of the way we did things then, more a case of 'custom and practice' than of policy. And then one of the two women who had come in late stood up and interrupted him.

'But nobody asked,' she said. Clear as day. A trumpet blast remark that stilled the room. One of those moments when the heartbeat of the world skips because something resonant has been said. And I recognised her then. It was Miss Jennings, my old science teacher from the Tech. Seeing her reminded me of her classes.

'Remember, everyone. There is no such thing as a stupid question.' That was one of her big phrases. She had a number of them. 'If someone tells you something, a little bit of doubt does no harm. Never forget: no evidence, no proof, no truth.'

The chairwoman came in quickly saying, 'If we could just allow our panellists to make their contributions, there'll be plenty of time for comments and questions afterwards.'

But Miss Jennings was not going to be put off.

'Nobody asked. If somebody had asked, simply explained what was involved, well, we could have considered it. Our family wanted to help.'

My family wanted to help, too. Always. I remember when I was a girl, about three years old, Anna was nine and Martha was twelve. There was sunshine like gold lamé on our street. There were bicycles, scooters and tricycles, prams, tennis racquets, a paddling pool and footballs. Children laughing, calling, skipping, singing.

Anna and Martha went to the top of the street, to the junction with Park Avenue, the main road. I was edging along behind them on a tricycle, propelling myself with my feet.

'Mammy says you're not to go past Mrs Lynch's.'

'Stay you there, Donna. Go back. Go back, Donna.'

'Mammy'll kill you if you go down the street.'

'You're too young. It's too dangerous for you.'

My sisters remain wonderfully solicitous. Protective. Mindful. Inhibiting.

I remember I pushed on past them, to the end of our street. Sharp glints of sunlight blazed off the windscreens of cars, vans and lorries. A bus blared its horn and swung out and around a parked car that was dropping a woman at the chemist opposite.

'Go back, Donna.'

'Mammy'll kill you.'

'You're only a wean.'

'You can't come down here.'

My sisters screeched at me, horror on their faces. Then I felt a hand on my collar, gentle enough, but firm. My mother looked down at me, lifted me off the tricycle, swung me through 360 degrees, lifted my tricycle with her other hand and began to frog-march me back down the street.

She didn't say anything. My sisters scooted behind us, gloating and fearful in equal measure. When we got to Mrs Lynch's, my mother pointed to the ground, then to our house, then at me, her crooked finger a stern admonition. Then she went back into our house.

'There, Donna. I told you Mammy'd kill you.'

'You should've listened to us, Donna.'

But Mammy didn't kill me. Between the helping and the inhibiting, I had made it to the top of the street. And I knew I
would go there again, to face whatever dangers careered past.

CHAPTER FOURTEEN

THE HUMAN FACTOR

Miss Jennings did not sit down at the hotel meeting. I remember that. She stood, continuing to speak quietly but firmly, until the pathologist flapped his hands as if to end his remarks and sat down. Miss Jennings said, 'He was our brother and we lost him to suicide. But when your letter came, it brought it all back again. You see, we're not sure he's settled now.'

Miss Jennings stood there, a magnetic pole, drawing us to her. The chairwoman thanked the panel and said this seemed like an appropriate moment to move on and take questions. The panel was ready to answer our questions as best they could, but, the chairwoman explained, they couldn't respond to queries about specific cases. When she smiled at her, Miss Jennings asked, 'Is he settled? That's what's worrying us. The way this left him.'

Then she sat down.

I understood exactly what she meant. How could her brother, not whole when they buried him, be at rest? I understood that. It shocked me how unscientific it was. I expected her to ask about organs and tissues, periods of time, research and training purposes. Hard facts. Details of medical science. I was shocked that she asked a question so obviously emotional. Spiritual even.

She'd never struck me as a spiritual person when she taught me at the Tech.

'You know, Donna, you have a natural ability for science,' she said to me on the last day before a Christmas break. 'You're really good at it. And you work hard.'

We were in one of the labs. I had gone back to redo a simple filtration experiment. I wanted to check my results again and I was copying them onto a new sheet of paper. The fact that the second set matched the first set thrilled me. The fact that I could replicate things amazed me. That science was so dependable was reassuring.

Miss Jennings came up to me.

'You're working late, Donna. You must have all your Christmas shopping done.'

I smiled at that. Two boxes of Dairy Milk for my sisters, a card and a couple of pounds each for my nephew and nieces. Martha, Anna and me chipping in for the new fireguard our mother wanted. A carton of cigarettes for Tony. People didn't expect anything from me anyway. We had no tree or decorations in the house. No crib or fairy lights. We didn't do Christmas. We went round for dinner to Tony's mother's house, then spent the evening at my mother's. Other people did Christmas for us. They knew. It was the end of another bad year for us.

I smiled at Miss Jennings and said I only had a few small presents to get.

'You're on top of matters as ever, Donna. How's the experiment going? I thought you'd completed this filtration and handed in your results.'

'I did, but it's just that ... well, I enjoyed it. I thought it was good and I wanted to do it again. And look, the results came out nearly the same.'

Miss Jennings scanned the two sheets I pushed in front of her, one with typed columns of figures – volumes of liquid, weight of filtrate, rate of filtration. The other, the second set, with handwritten figures.

'Excellent, Donna. Excellent. You've obviously followed the method accurately. The figures make perfect sense.'

'And they're near enough the same.'

That's what excited me. A week apart. A totally different day, but a process repeated, giving almost the same results.

'Yes, that's true,' said Miss Jennings. 'There's just a small difference there, in the middle of the series.'

A small difference. A slight disparity between the typed and the handwritten columns.

'Why is that?' I asked.

'Could be any number of reasons. A breeze through the window gives a temperature drop. An impurity in the material. Different apparatus reacting differently to heat. You being different from the last time you did it. Small variations. There will always be small variations, due to any number of considerations, including the human factor.'

Watching Miss Jennings at the Human Organ Retention meeting, I knew I was witnessing the human factor.

'Is he settled?'

Two sisters who lost their brother to suicide. Two sisters supporting each other. The human factor. She set the tone for the whole meeting. Person after person who stood up and asked a question referred to Miss Jennings.

'As that lady over there said—'

'That lady, she put it in words for my family.'

'I'm like her. I only want to know what we buried and if, you know, it was all right.'

The chairwoman of the panel directed questions at various members.

The pathologist took most of them, appealing to an idea of historical time to explain things.

'What we're talking about is a practice that grew up over years. Customs that were adhered to without being fully endorsed. All done for the best reasons. For sound medical and scientific reasons.'

Miss Jennings was on her feet again. Her sister looked up at her, a mixture of bemusement and concern in her eyes, as she stared at the tall woman whose lean, perfectly-powdered cheeks blew out a sharp sigh.

'I think we should note that while the scientific and medical reasons may have been sound – and that is debatable – they certainly were not adequate. There was a professional disregard for the concept of informed consent. No-one took account of the people involved.'

All eyes were on Miss Jennings. She stood near the door; clear, obvious and direct. We all felt drawn to her as she spoke for us. Then I heard a whimper beside me, a small gulping sound a child would make at the end of a long bout of sobbing. I turned quickly to look at Tony.

'Are you all right?' I whispered.

He snuffled and nodded as he pulled a handkerchief out of his pocket and began to blow his nose as quietly as he could. But before he could hide his face in his handkerchief, I saw tears glistening in his eyes and running down his cheeks.

'I'm grand,' he said, as he put his handkerchief away. 'Grand.'

Then I did something I hadn't done for a long time. I'm still not sure it was the right thing to do, but it felt like the only thing I could do. I reached across and took Tony's hand. Alarm flared briefly in his eyes and then softened, so that he squeezed my palm and smiled. I squeezed his in reply and let go, feeling the years spin round me, my whole world rush by me in an upheaval. The only stable point was the beacon that was Miss Jennings, standing tall in our midst, making the human factor manifest.

I went up to her in the foyer after the meeting. She was talking to a man in the alcove by the false fire.

'Excuse me,' I said. 'I don't mean to barge in, but—'

'My, my. Donna Bradley. It's great to see you. All grown-up,' she laughed. 'I don't mean that. You were all grown-up when I taught you. John, this is Donna Bradley, one of my mature students. One of my former mature students.'

And she laughed once more, a tinkling laugh with a slight strain in it, as if she was still wound up after the meeting.

The introductions made, the man turned and moved away after politely saying 'hello' and Miss Jennings took my arm and turned towards me.

'I didn't expect to see you here. I suppose I should have realised I'd know people. So many families are affected by this.'

'I'm sorry about your brother, Miss Jennings. I didn't know.'

'Thank you, Donna,' she said. 'It was so sad. Still is. Now this has brought it all up again. You ... I don't mean to ...'

'I lost a baby. Teresa. I ... we ... before I went to the Tech.'

Miss Jennings' grip on my arm tightened gently, but it was the warm gaze in her eyes that stemmed the flow of tears welling up behind my eyes.

'I'm sorry, Donna. I never knew. All those years in those classrooms and labs. I saw so many young people. So many lives I knew nothing about.'

As she spoke, I had an image of her standing beside me in her immaculate white coat, a pair of safety goggles peeking out of her breast pocket, a nurse's watch pinned below it, as she scanned my filtration experiment results.

'If only all human life could be summarised in a neat column of figures. Still, science is one of the best approximations we've got, never forget that, Donna.'

That night in the hotel, she was as authoritative as ever. I felt secure being with her, so I continued.

'I lost Teresa. And I went into a depression. A long and deep one. Starting the Tech was the beginning of my way out of it.'

'And what are you doing now?'

'I'm working for the City Council. I'm a Waste Management Officer.'

'Well, aren't you ... Isn't that great? You did a degree, then?'

'The GCSEs got me onto an Access Course, then I did the Foundation Science Programme and then the degree in Environmental Science, sandwich year and all. It took me ages,' I laughed.

'Whatever it takes, Donna. Whatever it takes.'

Tony came up then. He'd been outside having a cigarette.

'This is Tony,' I said. 'My ... he's Teresa's dad. This is Miss Jennings. She used to teach me Science at the Tech.'

Tony nodded hello and Miss Jennings took his hand and said 'pleased to meet you' and we stood in an awkward silence for what seemed an age until Miss Jennings sighed grandly and said, 'Well, I suppose we should be moving on. I wonder where my sister has gone. Ah, there she is. Good luck, Donna. All the best with everything.'

Then she moved across the foyer to join her sister as Tony shuffled beside me and I wondered to myself how time could vanish so completely.

I turned towards Tony after Miss Jennings left and asked him if he was all right. He knew what I meant.

'Never better. Never better. I'm glad we came. Together, like.'

That's what my mother and my sisters can't understand. How me and Tony can be so civil with each other. I asked him once what his wife Mary thought of our relationship and the way he answered made me realise that if things had been different maybe we could have survived the past and created a future.

'I just tell her,' he said. 'I just tell her that you and me had Teresa and that we'll have things to sort out from time to time, things we need to talk about. She understands.'

My mother doesn't. She doesn't know that me and Tony meet on Teresa's anniversary to put flowers on the grave. Just me and him. He suggested it. He comes back separately with Mary and their children.

'I make sure the kids know they have a sister up in the cemetery.'

I like that. The clear way he has made Teresa part of his new family.

Tony looked around the hotel lobby. It was nearly empty. A man was settling himself at the piano. Some people laughed in the cluster of chairs behind him.

'Do you fancy ... would you like a drink?' he asked. 'Just the one. Before we go.'

I said 'yes' and we moved past the piano – the man was running his fingers along the keys, playing trills and scales, warming up – and we found two armchairs and a small round table. Tony bought the drinks. A glass of red wine for me. A bottle of beer for himself. As I settled into my chair and took my first sip of the wine, I realised there was a small crowd at the bar. Residents of the hotel, locals and people like us who'd stayed on after the meeting. It was normal, pleasant and unreal. Tony felt it, too.

'We haven't done this for a while.'

'It's good to do it now,' I replied.

He smiled and eased into his chair.

'Do you want to go on with it? I mean, that chairwoman said we could just leave it, that they would sort it out.'

'She didn't say we couldn't go on with it.'

'No, she didn't say that.'

We were dancing round each other, feeling one another out. Something of the resolve I felt emanate from Miss Jennings came back to me and I said, 'Look, Tony. It's Teresa they're talking about. They kept parts of her and we don't know what we buried.'

'We buried Teresa.'

'We didn't ask for this. Yes, we buried Teresa. But it's not finished.'

'I must have signed something.'

'Maybe you did, but I'm pretty sure you didn't know what you were doing. How could you?'

Tony gulped on his beer and looked away. Tears glistened in his eyes.

'It'll never be over, so it won't, Donna. I mean, no matter what we do.'

I felt it inside me, too, like pressure in an empty tunnel. Somewhere way back down that tunnel, pressure was building. I could sense it. A rumbling in my ears, a press of air in my chest.

'I see her, Donna,' Tony continued. 'I see Teresa. Not like she was. Like she is now. A girl walking about. I see her and I'm scared.'

'Don't, Tony,' I said. 'Don't.'

* *

Writing this now, I have to stop. The picture is clear in my head. We are an ordinary couple having a drink, glad to be clear of the stresses of family and work, having some welcome adult respite from our daily lives. Anyone watching us would have been heartened to see us. Except that the man had said he sees a ghost and the woman feels pressure in a tunnel come rushing in a torrent through her, so she clasps her hands to her eyes, trying to hold in the torrent, and lowers her face into her lap.

CHAPTER FIFTEEN

AMRA

My sister Anna phones me at least once a week. Sometimes she asks me to go to the pictures. I'm not saying she has a routine, but she is an organised person, so I wouldn't be surprised if 'phone Donna Tuesday teatime' is on a list somewhere.

She phoned the day after the hotel meeting. I remember I was still shaky.

'Did you go with Tony?'

When I told her that I did, she said that was good. But I didn't tell her about the silence between us at the end, about the unfinished drinks or the piano player crooning *Mack The Knife* as we left the bar, how we stood in the car park, our breath enveloping us in the sharp air, the headlights going by on the road, the river silent and dark further on. How do you pick up a conversation that has not so much died as been swept away?

'Will there be another meeting?' Anna asked.

'I don't think so, not like that one. You can have private meetings if you want, to go into your own, you know ...'

'Will ye do that?'

'Yes,' I said firmly. I was speaking for both of us, me and Tony, as if we'd made a joint decision. We'd made no such thing, standing in the cold night, nodding to one another as we moved to our separate cars and drove off to our separate lives.

Anna finished by asking me to meet her for coffee and I said I couldn't because I was with the Nigerians.

The Nigerians, one of them at least, became very important in my life. Now, as I write this, I see things that weren't obvious at the time.

I only remember one of their names. Amra, the woman. She explained to me that there were twelve of them, but only three had come to Derry. The others were in England, Scotland and Wales. She said she couldn't get over how green everything was. She said she was originally from Kano, in northern Nigeria.

'The desert keeps coming our way,' she said. 'Every year more of the desert is coming our way.' She now works as a Waste Manager for the city of Lagos.

They wanted to see how we handled waste in our city. I was the junior in the office so after the official reception with the mayor and the city councillors – speeches, vol-au-vents, the exchange of civic plaques – I was put in charge of them.

I remember getting to my desk early on their first morning. I had prepared three folders – information papers and leaflets, maps and itineraries, contact addresses and phone numbers. One of the men was going out with the engineers to visit a recycling plant. The other man was staying in the office to work with the IT department on the computer systems used in waste management. I was making a visit to one of the city's dumps and I brought Amra with me.

Amra filled the passenger seat of my Fiat. Her blue gown spread in folds around her, then tucked neatly under her arms. Her headdress was squashed as she settled in her seat with a short 'oof'.

'Are you okay?' I asked.

'Fine. Next time I come, I'll get a suit like yours.'

'No, don't do that. Your dress is lovely.'

Then I had a thought. 'But if you'd like to, I'm sure we could find time to go shopping.'

She smiled and nodded.

'Yes, I want to get something for my children and for my husband.'

It dawned on me that we were chatting like friends, two women who worked together but who could hang out together. Go shopping. Have a coffee. Sit and talk. I wondered when I last had an easy conversation with a friend. A chill went through me as I pulled out of the council office's car park and onto the Strand Road roundabout, realising that I didn't have any friends any more. I had my sisters and they were good to me and we talked, but mainly about their families, their holiday plans, their house moves and our mother. I've never kept up with my friends from school and from when I was first married. My neighbours are good. We talk when we pass in the street and if I need anything they're there for me. But I don't have a friend. Someone to seek out, phone and chase to do things together.

I looked at Amra out of the corner of my eye as I negotiated the roundabout. A statuesque Nigerian woman keenly taking in the sights around her. We would make small talk until we arrived at the dump. Later we would go to the shopping centre and have coffee, before cruising the shops. We would be pleasant and polite. Is this how I would make friends again?

'How many children do you have?' I asked, pleasant and polite.

'I have two,' she replied. 'A boy and a girl.' Then she paused, turned away from me and looked out of the window. A huge crane swung over the construction site of a new apartment block and we had a glimpse of the river amidst the steel and concrete skeleton of the building.

'I lost another baby. A boy. Early this year.'

'I'm sorry,' I said.

She turned towards me and smiled.

'It is Allah's will. The living boy and girl are strong. I will show you a photograph if you want. Do you have any children?'

'No,' I answered.

We pulled up at traffic lights. The red light shone fiercely. It pierced my eyes, saying that I should tell her when the lights went green. But still the red burned fiercely. Let it go green and I'll tell her. When the lights went green, I pushed the accelerator, released the clutch and the car moved forward across the junction, traffic flowing and merging around us and the moment was lost.

I wonder if I do that often. Deny Teresa. Is it simply convenient to say 'no, no children' as a way of fending off any further personal questions? I'd love to review those moments, to be able to look at video clips, to watch myself closely. It's a bit harsh to say I deny Teresa. I protect myself perhaps. I am hiding her from myself, as much as I am hiding her from other people.

'You have no husband?' Amra asked.

'No,' I said. 'Divorced.'

She nodded and was silent. Something in my tone let her know I would not say any more. I had no reason to. Polite and pleasant. Civil. I was learning how to be 'normal'.

'It's not far,' I told her. 'On the edge of the city, down where the river opens out into the lough.'

Amra nodded and looked out at the traffic. 'Lots of people,' she said. 'No so many like Lagos.'

'Lots of waste, though.'

'Yes, like Lagos.'

When we got to the dump – technically we call it a landfill site, but the land is actually well filled and the waste is piling up – I became worried about Amra's dress and shoes. I usually put on a pair of wellies I keep in the boot of the car, but this time I stuck with my town shoes and hoped the ground would be dry. I parked beside the entrance gates and I introduced Amra to Colm, the attendant. He shook her hand and smiled, saying, 'Welcome to the back yard of Hell.'

Amra laughed and I grinned. I'd heard Colm use that phrase before.

We climbed a few steps and walked along the decking surrounding Colm's Portakabin, so we had a better, more elevated, view of the dump in front of us. A bulldozer was piling recently arrived rubbish up an incline of older rubbish and earth. A refuse collection dumper truck, now empty, was making its way towards us, grinding gears and belching smoke. Seagulls called and swooped between the two vehicles, a decent flock of them, before deciding the pickings were better in front of the bulldozer. I opened a clipboard to launch into a rundown of the landfill. How many hectares it covered. How many metric tonnes of waste per day, week, month, year were delivered. How the council dealt with the smell, the runoff, the noise. What local residents made of all this. I was briefed. Ready. On top of things. Until Amra let out a sharp cry and said, 'There are no children.'

For a moment, I was thrown. I was staring into an empty cot. I was folding baby clothes I bought – little lemon sleep suits, pastel-coloured Babygros – in the mad months following Teresa's death.

'There are no children,' she repeated. 'With us, there would be children here, not only sea birds.'

Her tone brightened and I sensed that she saw her discovery as a positive thing. One of the ways our world was different from hers was that there were no children scavenging at the dump. When I write it down now, I ask myself 'for how long?'

'Sometimes they get lost. They fall down the holes. Or rubbish tips over them and their bigger brothers and sisters cannot find them. The families come but they cannot find them. Then the bulldozers move the waste and the children are lost forever.'

I remember wanting to tell her to shut up. I must have coals inside me marked 'light now' that bring Teresa back to the front of my mind. Bile slithered up my throat and the red beam of the traffic light burned the back of my eyes. I should have said something about Teresa when the lights went green. I shouldn't have let that moment pass.

'I lost a child,' I blurted out, through a mouthful of bile. 'A girl. I lost her.'

'Oh, my God. You lost your child ...'

'No, not here. Not in this waste. In the waste that was me.'

I want to move beyond that way of thinking about myself, but even now these coals still glow inside me and it doesn't take much to make them flare up. That day, looking over the landfill with Amra, the coals tumbled one upon another and the steely wind off the lough, chasing over the dump and making the seagulls swirl above the bulldozer, fanned those coals into flames of deep pain.

'I'm sorry. I don't understand.'

Amra's look of puzzlement brought me round.

'I had a baby girl – Teresa – but she died at birth. She was dead beforehand really. So yes, I have had a child,' I corrected myself, 'but I lost her.'

I'll never forget what Amra did then. This is really what sticks with me. The memories I commit to these pages, they're all vivid. Some closer than others, yes, but all vivid. That time Amra and her colleagues visited to learn about waste management and local government, that day I stood looking over the mounds of waste that our city produces, gulls screeching as the bulldozer ploughed through another load and tossed some fresh morsels in the air, that day Amra reached her hand to touch my elbow and gently calm the fires raging within me.

'You did not lose her,' Amra said. 'Your baby. You didn't lose her. She left because it is Allah's will for her. And we must live with Allah's will.'

Looking back on it now, we must have made a strange sight. The white woman in her business suit, her clipboard flapping papers in the breeze. The black woman holding her headdress in place with one hand, while stroking the white woman's arm with the other, her blue gown flying round both of them like the sail of an Arab dhow.

I wonder what Colm made of the scene, as he saw it through the window of his Portakabin. He was inside, making tea, surveying his visitors and his kingdom, proud of an opportunity to show it off. For him the dump was the most natural place in the world. He meant it when he called it the back yard of Hell. He was saying it was awful, but as much a part of the city as the great park that ran down to the river's east bank.

'I worked in St Columb's Park, I did. Ach, they near enough named it after me,' he told me once. 'But I got fed up of it. You can get too much of a good thing, you know. Now this,' he said, his arm sweeping grandly over the whole dump. 'This is different. You can never get enough of a bad thing like this.'

Amra and I gazed over it. Colm's kingdom of waste, laid out before us. Mounds of kitchen waste, food waste, packaging, cartons, boxes, broken things you couldn't recognise, dinners not finished, tin cans with streaks of cat food still in them, busted toys, bicycles, clothes no longer needed, pizza boxes and furniture – who put that wardrobe there? – a place indeed to lose a child.

I am closer to Colm than to Amra when it comes to explaining the world. I saw this dump as part of my life, a vital part of my personal and professional life. And Teresa is the same. I could charge no God for what happened to her. Maybe I did at the start, but not then, when I stood with Amra and not now as I sit alone in my room, an autumn dusk settling over the back yards and gardens of my neighbours' houses, voices calling children home before dark, street lights going on in a staggered sequence. There is – was – no God in the trembling days of my life.

Colm interrupted our thoughts with a hearty call.

'There must be better views of the city to show your visitor, Donna. But at least here ye can have a decent cup of tea while you're enjoying it.'

He passed us two mugs and offered sugar, but we declined.

'I drink so much tea in Ireland,' Amra said.

'It's good for you,' Colm said. 'Keeps the dust down.' Then he went back inside leaving us to savour the view. The tea did what it promises to do. It revived us.

'Can we walk here?' Amra said, pointing to the route into the dump.

'What about your shoes?'

'They will be fine. I always wear these. Will we go?'

I nodded and we finished our tea, leaving our empty mugs on the wide wooden rail around the decking. We climbed down, Amra hitching up the folds of her gown to show her tiny feet.

I remember it as summer. The rutted tracks were dry. The air tasted mildly acidic and our nostrils filled with a sickly sweet odour of refuse and lough water. We walked along the main route used by the dumper trucks and the bulldozers. Some seagulls spotted us and screeched overhead but soon realised we were no benefit to them and moved off. There was a series of side routes off the main one and we took one that curved towards the lough. Still the earth beneath our feet was dry and compacted, while beside us banks of rotted rubbish, mixed with earth, rose above us. Whenever I visit these dumps they remind me of crude archaeological digs, especially the older areas. The fresher areas look like what they are; rubbish tips. The older sections seem like the leavings of a mighty archaeologist, digging up our lives with a huge spade, searching for the truth of us.

We were both quiet, walking in step beside one another. At that stage the smell turned neutral, I would say, no real smell, perhaps a sour tang on the wind coming off the lough.

The sight of the doll's leg sticking out of the mound stopped us both. Amra moved towards it and peered closer. I stayed where I was, in the middle of the path. From there I could see plastic bags, something that looked like an oil drum, earth, broken plates or dishes, plastic bottles – there's always plastic bottles – and the doll's leg sticking out, toes pointing to the sky.

'It's a doll,' Amra said. 'A doll.'

'Children grow up and dump their toys,' I said.

Except for Teresa. She never grew up, never had toys to dump. Martha and Anna cleared every baby item from the house the morning Tony brought me home. Every knitted bootie and wee cardigan. Every coloured rattle. Every jingling teething ring. Unbidden, these thoughts came to me. I struggled to repress them as they contested with my will. What finally saw them off was asserting to myself that Amra was the same as me. She had a child that never grew up.

'Do you want to go on?' I asked.

'Yes. Can we get to the water?' she wondered.

I led her along the curving route and then pointed to a narrow path that took us away from the dump, into flat, rush-covered land that bordered the water. It soon got boggy underfoot and we stopped. The dump was now behind us, high reeds standing taller than us on either side, a gentle shushing coming towards us.

'It's the same lough you can see from the office. I mean, that's the river, the Foyle, but just about here it opens out into a sea lough and then it joins the Atlantic. There's a wee boat does cruises. We might go on one.'

Amra was crying. Her shoulders heaved and her face crumpled as she bent her head and dabbed her cheek with a handkerchief she pulled from the folds of her gown.

I couldn't speak and I couldn't cry either. The image I have of us today is of me standing forever watching Amra cry, her blue headdress bobbing, her black cheeks shining. The reeds above her head swaying gently. It all only lasted a few minutes because I remember moving towards her and putting my arm round her shoulders. It was an awkward move. She's a big woman, Amra, and I'm not that tall and people will tell you I'm not really a hugging kind of person. I'm not even sure if I could call it a hug. I put my arm around her and she gave a sigh, dabbed her cheeks a few times and grinned.

'We go back now.'

'Of course,' I said and we separated.

Looking back lets you see things and you wonder if they were really there in the first place, but that moment marked the start of the friendship between me and Amra that lasts until this day. I'm sure lots of things happen in my working days that are important, that have an impact on my life then and now, but the ones connected in some way to Teresa really stand out. My whole life to this point has been connected to Teresa. Tony is right. It'll never be over.

Amra and I walked back to the Portakabin. Colm stood on the decking.

'I thought I'd have to send out a search party. My fault. I should have given ye flares or something.'

'We're grand, Colm. I know my way round this place pretty well,' I answered.

'You do, surely. Though what two fine women would be doing tramping round the back yard of Hell when they could be sitting in front of computers in nice offices beats me.'

'It is our job,' said Amra kindly, letting him know she was not going to be put in a box. She smiled so Colm could see she liked his banter and neither of us minded his 'two fine women' crack either.

'Fair play to yeez. Fair play to yeez. Well, here's one for ye then, yeez 'waste managers' that ye are. Yousuns back in the office think I do nothing all day but drink tay. However, the fruits of my labours are everywhere to be seen. EU directive. Car batteries and toxicity. I pulled loads of them out of that dump, or as many of them as I could get. Now what did ye do with them?'

The car batteries were – and still are – one of the big bugbears for my unit. Colm loved throwing it at me every now and then. With Amra beside me he had the perfect audience.

'Oh, wiser heads than me have spoken, saying, "No more dumping of car batteries. Poisons the land, the water and the air." All very true, I suppose. But we're going to end up with an Everest of them if we don't figure something out soon.'

Amra was smiling broadly by now. Colm was making a big impression on her, and sensing that, he opened up again.

'It's not like the old days. In the old days, everyone looked after their own. Course there was a hell of a lot less of it. Every wee house had its own midden. Just a wee heap in the yard with a few chicken bones, a bit of a cracked plate, a rag or two, the odd spud skin, though the pigs sorted them out. That's some midden here.'

Amra laughed out loud.

'You remind me of Ibrahim. Ibrahim works at one of the dumps outside Lagos. He always has a lecture for us when we visit from head office. But don't worry, I know where your batteries went. They came to us, in Nigeria. Or to some other country like us. We get all the batteries now. Someone will salvage them.'

'But they're poisonous. There's lead in them,' Colm exclaimed.

'We know. Everyone knows. With us, somebody will be making a living out of them. Don't worry, Mr Colm, your batteries are with us in Nigeria.'

When Colm said, 'Maybe I'll go see them, nothing to keep me here, get a blast of sun at least,' Amra laughed out loud.

I added to the banter.

'Ach, don't go, Colm. We'd all miss you. The whole City Council waste management strategy would grind to a halt.'

I didn't know what happened to the batteries. I know that a deal was done with a company to handle them. I'd have to check the files, but I think they went to Holland or Sweden for incineration.

We said our goodbyes to Colm and went back to my car. Before I pulled off I turned to Amra and asked if she was feeling okay. When she said she was fine, I smiled and said, 'Shopping?' at which she laughed, so I drove into the city centre and we had a couple of hours off.

CHAPTER SIXTEEN

ARE YOU ALL RIGHT?

Having an exotic guest made me feel good. The programme for the three days sorted itself out after the initial receptions, briefings and meetings. The two men were friends anyway and made friends with male colleagues. I think they even went to a football match. I 'adopted' Amra. I'm trying to find the right words for what it felt like. I know me and Amra became friends. It seems crazy for me to say this, but she's the first real friend I made. She's thousands of miles away and we only connect by email and Skype, but maybe that's the way it has to be. Yes, when she visited I took her under my wing. I know that she has also taken me under hers.

My mother was fascinated by her, slightly frightened at first, but by the end of the tea party I organised in my house, she was mad about her.

I invited my mother, Anna and her three children, Martha and her two. The house was full, but it was a sunny day so the bigger ones played in the street. Eithne, Anna's youngest, stayed with the adults and ended up on laps, mainly Amra's.

'Does she have weans herself?' my mother asked as she helped me take food out of the oven. I kept it simple. Lots of precooked samosas and sausage rolls. Sandwiches. Some salads, rice and an eye-catching chocolate gateau. I cleared the top of my big table and put the food on it with paper napkins and paper plates and a home-made 'help yourself' sign. There was tea for the adults and juice for the children.

'She has two,' I said. 'And she lost one this year.'

My mother held a tray of sausage rolls in her hand. She had a tea towel under it, but held it for too long and the heat got to her fingers, so she squealed and put the tray down on the cooker top with a crash.

Anna looked in.

'What happened?'

'Nothing. Too busy gossiping and not minding me own business,' my mother laughed it off.

Anna returned to the living room and my mother said, 'Did you tell her about Teresa?'

'Let's get the food out before it gets cold.'

I lifted two plates of food and some kitchen roll and took them into the living room. My mother followed me. Martha brought the children in from the street and they got stuck in, their voices warming the room like a summer dawn.

'Tomás said there was chips. There's no chips, Tomás.'

'Is there no red sauce, Auntie Donna?'

'I don't like cheese.'

'It's not cheese. It's thick cream.'

'I don't like it.'

'I only want a bit of cake. I'm not hungry for dinner.'

My mother fussed about them, Anna and Martha helped them fill their plates and I watched, content to have my family around me. My mother hurried the children along.

'Come on now, for God's sake. Leave some for the rest of us. The guest didn't even get a bite yet.'

Amra sat serenely in my armchair by the fireplace. As the children got their food, the younger ones gravitated towards her and perched on the arm beside her or on the ground at her feet. She was wearing a gold-coloured gown, embroidered with whorls and spirals. Martha's youngest girl, Claire, was full of questions. 'Where did you buy that dress? Did someone sew those white bits on?'

116

My mother hushed her as she passed a plate to Amra.

'Never mind bothering the woman, Claire. She must be starving. Let her have some food.'

But Amra put her arm around Claire and said, 'She can sit here. I miss my own girl and this good girl can make me feel better.'

I miss my own girl. That's what set it off. I was standing on the threshold between the kitchen and the living room. I had a jug of diluted orange drink in my hand. If I had stepped forward into the living room the jug would have spilled over the carpet but not broken. As it was, I stepped back onto the hard ceramic tiles of the kitchen, the jug slipped from my hand and fell in slow motion to shatter in a chaos of shards at my feet.

The girl stood in a beam of light, like St Teresa in my mother's painting. I called her name out loud. 'Teresa.'

Martha, always quick, reacted first. 'Oh, look. Silly Auntie Donna. You should have dried your hands.' She came to me and led me back into the kitchen, closing the door behind us. She parked me on a stool at the edge of the worktop and asked me, 'Are you all right? You look like you've seen a ghost.'

'Did you not see her?' I mumbled.

Anna came in and before she could speak, Martha directed her briskly. 'Keep that door closed. Clean up that juice and the glass. I'll get her a cup of tea.'

'What happened? What did she say? What did you call out, Donna? Claire said she called Teresa.'

Martha ordered her again.

'It was an accident. Her hand was wet and the jug slipped. Just get the juice and the glass cleaned up, will ya? Then go back out there and keep an eye.'

I've spoken to Martha about this – and other incidents – recently. That was a big one. I have an understanding now of the anxiety my sisters feel about me. They are ever vigilant.

Martha passed me a cup of sweet milky tea. Anna finished mopping the floor, swept up the last pieces of broken glass, put them in a plastic bag, tied a tight knot in it and dumped it in the bin under the sink.

'Are you all right?' Martha asked, her brow creased in worry. I am always the delicate sister.

'Grand, yes, grand. Just a wee turn.'

'A wee turn?' Anna butted in.

'Nothing to worry about,' Martha hurried on. 'All the excitement of the party. And you must be working wild hard with your visitor here and all. Drink that tea 'til we get you a plate of grub. Have you been eating at all? Go you back and tell me mammy that it's all sorted out and cleaned up.'

Anna went. Martha ran her hand over her face and let out a big sigh. I sipped the tea and felt the colour come back into my cheeks.

I told Tony later that night, when everything was over. Martha and Anna cleaned up after the party. Anna took my mother home. Martha dropped Amra back at her hotel. I lay down on the sofa and dozed for a couple of hours, half-watching the television. When I came round properly, the contestants in the *Big Brother* house were turning hoses on each other. I zapped the television off and phoned Tony.

'Are you all right?' was his first question to me, the automatic one.

I apologised for phoning him so late, for phoning him at all, but he said it was no bother.

'I saw her,' I said. 'I saw Teresa.'

There was a silence on the other end of the phone, so I continued.

'Just like you said after the meeting at the Everglades Hotel. I saw Teresa as she is now.'

Tony's soft breathing came over the phone, but he said nothing.

'Are you all right?' It was my turn to ask the question.

'Yeh, fine. Grand. When was this?'

I told him about Amra and the Nigerian delegation and the tea party. I told him my nieces and nephew were all there. How I came into the room and saw the extra child. A girl of about eleven with brown eyes and long brown hair and a tomboy look on her face. She was wearing a clean tracksuit top and bottom, as if she'd agreed to 'dress up' for the occasion, but that this was as far as she was prepared to go. No dresses, no ribbons, no flouncy blouses.

'That's funny. I see her more like you. Small and fine, with something dressy on her. I couldn't tell you exactly. And her hair's black and short. Just like yours.'

His voice had a slight laugh in it. He was pleased to be talking about this. And so was I.

'It's your eyes she has,' I said. 'Your brown eyes.'

I feel a chill now as I write this. Even today, a frost of guilt covers my intimacy on the phone with another woman's husband. But who else could I talk to about seeing Teresa?

'Is that the first time you saw her?'

'Yes,' I answered. 'What does it mean?'

'I don't know. Do you think ... is it good or bad?'

'I don't know. It felt okay. I dropped a jug, but I wasn't scared. Just a bit taken aback, but not worried.'

He laughed a small laugh and said, 'I'm worried. A wee bit. I ... I've started talking to her. I asked her about school. About her homework.'

'Jesus, Tony. Does she answer you?'

'No, it's not like that. She's just there. And I'm talking to her – not for long now – just talking, like to myself, but to her, too. Do you know what I mean?'

I did know what he meant. I talked to Teresa all the time. I acted out imaginary scenes with dialogue in my head. But Teresa never had substance or a voice in any of these images. It was only me, wrestling with the build-up of Teresa inside of me.

'Good job you didn't say anything,' he continued. 'Your sisters would have put you in a straitjacket right away.'

'They were fine about it. Only Martha really twigged. Anna knows something was going on but didn't really get it. Martha'll fill her in later. And the kids, I don't know what they thought. Just a wee accident I suppose. Happens all the time at parties. Probably glad they weren't involved.'

'And what about the Nigerian woman? Did she see?'

'No, she was too busy with the weans. She was great with the weans. But Martha filled her in – told her bloody everything – when she dropped her back to the City Hotel.'

I didn't get angry with Martha for doing that. In fact, when I told Tony, there was almost a half-laughing tone in my voice, mocking myself. There I was worrying about hiding things, worrying if I was denying Teresa by trying to keep the lid on everything when Martha told Amra, a complete stranger, the whole story.

I'd love to have been in the back seat of the car for that trip. Or on the dashboard, miniaturised, for the miniature version of the tale of Donna and Teresa that Martha told. Birth and death. Depression and illness. Pain and hope. Study and work. Marriage and divorce. The whole heap. In five brisk minutes.

However she managed to tell it, Amra now knew the whole story. And I guess it did Martha some good to get it off her chest. We've talked about it, me, Anna and Martha, and that's been good. Back then, in the far past, I was still only climbing out of the fire-hole, so I couldn't see clearly. And later, at the time of the organ retention meetings, in the near past, I was still climbing, scaling ice cliffs of dread.

The day following Teresa's appearance in front of me, Amra said, 'The dead are always with us, even when we cannot see them. If you can see your daughter now, it means you are getting closer to her. And that's good.'

There was something sinister and yet comforting about her view of things. Chilling and warm at the same time.

I wasn't frightened by seeing Teresa at the tea party. I willed her to appear again and I conjured images of her in my mind, but I knew these were made up and not real. That's an unusual idea, for a scientist. I'm debating with myself the difference between ghosts and imaginings and I'm saying the ghost was more real. I really did see Teresa that time. She came as if to ask the question everyone asks: 'Are you all right?' Of course I'm not all right. Nothing is all right and never will be all right. But Teresa's coming helped calm me.

Amra said the dead look after us. Even the children. Even her baby, still young in death. She said that Teresa had given me a picture that I could hold on to. I hold on to it all right.

I lie in my bed in the dark. Voices call to one another outside. Young men and women on their way home from pubs in town. I know every corner of the room I lie in. I know the sheets and the firmness of the bed. I know that beside me is a small cabinet with a glass of water and science books – *Chemistry and Chaos Today*; *Heavens Above: Maps, Histories and Futures*; *The Quest for Zero Waste* – also a lamp and the clock that will wake me for work in the morning. Except I am awake at three. And Teresa is with me in the room. The memory of that visitation gives me an image I can draw upon. The clean tracksuit. The hair tied back. Tony's brown eyes. I lie in the dark, my own eyes wide open and I speak to the ghost I bore.

CHAPTER SEVENTEEN

CONSOLATION

It must have been a week or more after the tea party when I
saw Tony to discuss having a private meeting with the organ
retention people. We were to meet in the Sandwich Company
at half twelve, ahead of the lunchtime rush. I was preoccupied
with work. A build-up had developed during the visit of the Nigerian delegation. Nothing critical, but returns and reports to be
compiled and written to deadlines that were right on top of me.
I'd taken to coming in forty-five minutes early in the morning,
before anybody else, to get a head start on work, right after the
day that Amra left.

Seeing her off at Eglinton Airport really hit me. She kept re-
peating, 'Thank you, thank you,' and added, 'you must visit me
at home and I'll show you the desert in the north and you will
meet my mother just like I met yours.'

Amra's bags were at her feet, her passport and confirmation
slip in her hand. Her colleagues were ready. About six of us from
the Waste Management Unit were there to see them off and
there was a bantering mix of sadness and excitement in the air. I
had the intoxicating sense that I was travelling, that those were
my bags at our feet, that inside my jacket were my passport and
my flight confirmation and that I would embark, like Amra, on a

journey to Stansted Airport and from there to an exotic location to begin the rest of my life.

I didn't even have a passport, never mind a flight or a destination.

A call came over the Public Address system saying Amra's flight was on time and that anyone who hadn't already gone through should do so immediately. Amra's two male colleagues lifted their bags and began their final goodbyes, all handshakes and smiles. Amra stood there, tears in her eyes, so I went to her and we hugged. I was lost for a moment in the expansive folds of her blue gown. She snuffled and whispered in my ear, 'Thank you, Donna. You helped with the boy who I lost. He is with your Teresa now. And they are always with us.'

Then she pulled away and we held each other at arm's length. I nodded and she squeezed my forearms.

'I believe that, too,' I said.

Someone called her name and we hurried to grab her bags and take her to the end of queue. As soon as she went through to the final departure lounge, my colleagues made noises about wanting to get back. I offered to stay until the plane left, in case some last minute hitch occurred. In reality, I simply wanted to be there. I wanted the next flight out to be mine.

By the time Amra's plane taxied into position, I was almost alone in the main hall of the airport. Check-in and other staff were on a break. The building was quiet. Even the Muzak was low. I looked out across the tarmac as the harp on the tailplane of the jet swung round, facing west along the runway. It was a bright, clear day and the hills across the lough flashed in purple and green patches. The engines revved up and the plane moved off. I crossed the main hall to get another view in time to see the jet ease off the runway and bank as it rose over the lough. How I wished I was on it, sitting with my friend and our dead children always with us.

In the days following Amra's departure, I immersed myself in the paperwork that had piled up on my desk. Only when my phone sounded in my handbag and I read the text message from Tony did I remember our meeting. I texted him back an apology, asked him to get me a cheese salad sandwich on brown bread and a cup of tea, saying I'd be with him in ten minutes.

Being late was embarrassing but not the end of the world. Tony and I are long past that.

'Thanks for the sandwich.'

'No bother. Must be hectic at your place.'

'It is. Always hectic. Ach, just a build-up after the Nigerians went back. We had a delegation for nearly a week. Took up a lot of time. But it was good. How's your place?'

'Flying. Larry has me going non-stop. We're bidding for part of a big development out past your offices. Apartments and retail. I don't know how I do it. I just follow Larry.'

'You do more than that. I'd say you keep him from going off at the deep end.'

If Tony and his brother Larry were pushing their property portfolio into apartment and retail developments then things were going well for them. I looked round the Sandwich Company and that thought spread out from me. Clerks, accountants and lawyers from the offices on Clarendon Street. Students and lecturers from the Tech along the Strand Road. Maybe police officers from the barracks beside the Tech. Since the ceasefires and the peace process, that was possible. People doing well, apartments and hotels going up, soldiers off the streets. You could almost say it was a new era. Round where I live things are more patchy. Many people not doing well.

Anna says that I should move to one of the new apartment blocks near my office. Great views of the river. A more fitting home given my professional position and new status. Always implied in her suggestion was the idea that, as a single woman, an apartment would be more suitable. But I like where I live and I have no intention of leaving. It's near where I grew up, so I can nip round to my mother any time I want. I go in and out of the Spar for groceries and the people there know me by my name. My neighbours look out for me, even though some of the old ones moved out as students moved in. No, I'll never – and I should be careful about using that word – but I'll never leave this house. I won't be a customer for the new apartments Tony and his brother are developing.

After the initial chat about work, we were silent as we ate our sandwiches. Companionable. That's how it is between me and Tony most of the time, as if we've done all our fighting. Not that we did much actual fighting. More drifting. We were on a great blazing ice floe, burning cold and hard, held solidly together by the intense cold of my depression. Until the thaw came. I can look back and recognise it now. Me in the campaign, especially when I started to run meetings myself. Me going to the Tech. Cracks in the ice floe. Meltings moving and rustling within the deep cold sheet that was our marriage at that time. Him thawing out, too. Going to his brother Larry for support while he helped him with carpet-fitting jobs until the day came when he left me, left Du Pont, left his old life and broke the ice floe clean in two, all the better for both of us. Cold and hard, we drifted apart in the icy sea of the world, with the waters getting warmer all around us, until the day we reached the distant islands we now stand upon. Me, the Waste Management Officer in the City Council, single. Tony, the property developer, married with two children. Our child, Teresa, the bridge between us still. But we didn't go there right then. I asked about Mary and their children first.

'Grand,' he said. 'Growing up. The toddler's tearing up the place at the minute. Sinéad's loving primary school. They're grand. Mary's grand, too. I'll tell her you were asking for her.'

Do that, Tony. Do that. Whisper it to her when you turn to her in bed at night, when you snake your arm across her belly and you draw close into each other. Images like that come to me every now and then. They're not bitter or angry, but I push them away quickly.

Who needs to be jealous of their ex-husband's wife? I suppose it's about what I'm missing – what I've missed – over the years since we separated. But I don't blame Tony for that. Or Teresa. I don't even blame myself. I'm hardened to it all now, I think. Hardened and sad.

'We'd have Teresa in secondary school,' he continued. 'I ... when I see her, sometimes ... I ask her things. What she did at school, those sorts of things. It's crazy.'

I was better able to cope with this kind of conversation than when I was at the hotel, because I'd seen her, too.

'It's not crazy,' I said. 'I told you I saw her myself.'

'You saw her again?'

'No. Only that once, thank God.'

Our sandwiches were finished. There was nothing left on my plate but a few crumbs of cheese and three pieces of the hard white flesh of the iceberg lettuce. There were pieces of brown bread, crusty bits amid a smear of Cajun chicken sauce, on Tony's plate. We both drank tea in silence until Tony asked, 'Why did you say that?'

'What?'

'"Thank God." Why did you say that? You don't usually say it. My mother says it all the time. "Lovely day, thank God. Tony and Mary and the kids are back from Lanzarote, thank God. I got in and out of the hairdressers in good time, thank God."'

'My mother's the same.'

'I never heard you say it before.'

I tried to make light of it.

'Are you saying I'm beginning to sound like your mother? An auld wan?'

He was smiling now but wary.

'Why did you say it about Teresa? "Only that once, thank God."'

He was scraping a nerve with his interest in the 'thank God'. He didn't know he was testing something in me, raking over embers I had allowed to cool down. It was a habit, saying 'thank God', evidence that I was growing older and picking up idioms from our mothers' generation. But did I really want to thank God? And if I did, for what? I'd spent years quietly damning him. It wasn't that I asked the question why an almighty and all-merciful God would allow what happened to us, to Teresa, Tony and me, to happen. I didn't ask that question. I went straight beyond it in the early months and took it as evidence that God was a vengeful, murderous man and we were his playthings. When my science education took off, especially in the second year of the degree, I gathered evidence that there was no God to damn or thank. I suppose as I've grown older I've softened even that view. Maybe I'm agnostic now. Maybe there is a God. Maybe there isn't. Either way my daughter died in my womb, my husband left the furnace of the days that followed before they went completely up in smoke, so that now I've come to the belief that there is no God for me to thank, but if Tony's mother wants to thank him, I won't stop her.

Tony waited for an answer and the only two explanations I could give him were habit and fear.

'I probably picked it up from my mother. "Great day for drying, thank God. Bit of a stretch in the evening, thank God." Just like your mother. I'm learning the auld wans' ways. Or maybe I was afraid. Isn't that why we usually turn to prayer, turn to God? Fear?'

'It's not the only reason.'

'My God, Tony, you've found religion! You're not born again are you? Is it Mary? Is she gone that way?'

'It's got nothing to do with Mary. She doesn't make a big deal out of it. It's just that … have you never needed it, Donna? Something to turn to?'

'Don't push it, Tony. Don't push it.'

I wanted to end this conversation. I could feel the anger rising inside me. What would he know about my need for consolation? And what business of his was it where I sought it?

Tony backed off and paused before asking, 'Do you want more tea?'

I shook my head and he went to get a fresh pot for himself. As he turned towards the counter with the empty teapot in his hand I gazed down upon my plate, where the crumbs of cheese lay scattered. The pieces of hard white iceberg lettuce lay crossed one upon another. Another piece lay on its side at a right angle to them, with cheese crumbs spraying out from it as if they'd scattered off it, an asteroid shower at a glancing angle to a planet. I turned the plate and watched this configuration of lettuce pieces and cheese crumbs swing round, changing and staying the same.

Not for the first time I wondered who or what produced such random patterns in the world.

When Tony came back with the tea, he poured himself a cup and we sat in silence. The queue shuffled forward at the sandwich counter. Orders were given and the staff moved briskly, flashing knives, scooping fillings – tomato and bacon, Thai chicken, curried prawns, roast beef, ham, mixed salad, humus – as they miraculously avoided bumping into one another. The silence between us grew as the hum of voices rose around us.

It is at such times that I see us carrying something heavy and unwieldy. Every now and then it defeats us and we lay it down to our mutual relief. Except that whatever it is that linked us is now gone and we are lost to one another. There is no agreed protocol between us for those moments, but always one of us will reach down to heft the burden again and the other will follow. I often wonder if there will come a time when both of us are too tired to make that lift, a time when our backs will be too bent and raw from carrying, so that once we put the burden down, we are not capable of lifting it again. I hear my sisters musing and yearning for the time when their children are grown, how they'll be 'free' of them. In their case they carry a joyous burden, fraught and fragile but strengthening to the day the children will carry themselves, upright and independent. For Tony and me that day will never come. We are not carrying a child. We are carrying a corpse, one we will not lay down until we join her in the ground.

In the aftermath of the public meeting on the retention of human organs we were left to wonder how much of Teresa we buried and what the hospital had done with the rest of her. It was that chilling burden that I picked up in the Sandwich Company. Tony saw me bend to it and he bent quickly with me.

'We should talk about the private meeting. Are you still on for it?' I said.

He sighed and rested his elbows on the table between us, leaning towards me.

'I'm not sure. I was ripping after that meeting in the Everglades. If I could have got close to someone who was involved at the time, I don't know what I would have done. But then, after a few days, I became worn out. I thought I was coming down with a flu or something. I was fit for nothing. Larry told me to take a couple of days off. Mary said I should go to the doctor. I never bothered. Them fellas only fill you full of pills. Anyway, I knew we'd have to talk, so I phoned you.'

The bridge between us had swung into place once more. The umbilical bridge through which we pass information, nourishment, anger, solace, pain and hope. The single span that links us. Teresa.

'What do we do now, then?' I asked.

Tony pulled a new letter from his pocket.

'They give you two options. Basically, someone will come to you or you can go and talk to them.'

'I don't want them in my house.'

'I know. And I don't want to bring them into mine. To Mary's. We could meet in an office or a house. I could get somewhere.'

'Who will it be?'

Tony passed me the letter and continued, 'It just says "a representative". It'll have to be someone who knows about the case.'

'Teresa is not a case, Tony.'

'I'm sorry. I know. I mean it would have to be someone who knew about Teresa and what happened.'

I think what ratcheted up the tension within me was reading the word 'Trust' in the letter. Not in the body of the letter, but in the address of the sender. The letter came from the Hospital Trust. I couldn't put those words together as the two parts of my brain – the rational and the irrational – clashed furiously. I caught Tony in the crossfire again.

'I'm not meeting some wee clerk with a file who won't know anything that really matters.'

'The letter came to me. They have my details, but they keep mentioning mothers' – he leaned across and put his finger on the page in front of me – 'so I think they'll want to talk to you. But if you don't fancy it, I'll do it.'

'Of course I don't fancy it. And don't tell me you fancy it either.' I paused to take a breath. I was almost hyperventilating as I added, 'But I do want to do it. Just don't expect me to like it.'

'Look, Donna, your problem is not with me. It's with the hospital. No, maybe it is with me. Maybe after all this time you've finally found something specific to blame me for. To hang everything on. Aye, I signed a form. I must have. I don't know what I signed. You think you're the only one blown away in all of this?'

At that moment, with the lunchtime crowd beginning to thin out, my thoughts were purely on self-preservation. No matter what happened I couldn't go back into the deep hole again. I couldn't plummet like the lost child in the dump, down a ravine of rubbish and waste, to lie cloaked and smothered under the debris of my life and the world, hearing voices above me – Tony, my mother, my sisters, medical personnel, Miss Jennings – muffled and remote. Miss Jennings' voice sounded in my head: 'We just want to know if he's settled. Is he settled?'

'We'll both go, then. To the hospital. But tell them we want someone senior. Someone who knows. Someone who won't have to ask someone else for the answer. I get enough of that at work.'

I was angry with Tony then. I'm not saying we were coasting along before that. No matter how much I tried, I was blaming him and that was coming through.

The anger sloshed around my whole family. Anna and Martha are both older than me and, together with my mother, they boss me around sometimes.

I remember I came home from school one day, fear and anger surging through me. I was about eleven, my first year in secondary school. I stormed into the house. Martha and Anna were sitting with my mother. She was dabbing her eyes with a tea towel. I raged up and down the kitchen floor, too wound up to fully register what was happening.

Martha tried to hush me. Anna told me to wise up. Both of them wore their working clothes: Martha, an office receptionist's suit; Anna, the black smock of an apprentice hairdresser.

'Just a wee minute there, Donna. Mammy is not ...'

'Can you not shut your face for one minute?'

They only further enraged me.

'That Bennett one pushed me and Kerry Doherty on the ground. Can ye not see me knee?'

Blood coagulated in a brown stain below my right knee and into the fabric of my white stocking.

'Mammy'll never get that stain out in time for school tomorrow.'

'We'll get something sorted,' offered Martha.

'It'd do you no harm to go to school in your bare feet for a while. So shut up,' shouted Anna.

I was livid. 'Do you want one, too?' I said, squaring up to Anna, bunching my right fist and pulling back my right arm, preparing it to swing.

The room stilled, then my mother stifled a sniffle and asked, 'What did you say?'

'I told you. Ages ago. This second year, Christine Bennett, is pushing me and Kerry Doherty around since we started and to-day she just ...'

'I know that. What did you say, but? Just now, to Anna?'

I quietened, then repeated, 'Do you want one, too?'

Anna made to speak, but my mother raised her hand and silenced her.

'You shouldn't say that. Especially not to your sister. Even if you do sound just like your father.'

Then she laughed, a shuddering, cackling laugh initially, that grew heartier and heartier, until it drew her three daughters in, each of us not sure what it was we were laughing about.

My mother continued. '"Do you want one, too?" I seen him face up to a referee like that once and he only a midget compared to him. Not to mention the big lump of a fella, rolling on the ground, he was after flattening. The referee sent your father off. And rightly so. "Do you want one, too?"'

She laughed again and put her hand on my shoulder.

'Now, Rocky, tell us what happened.'

I told her how things came to a head when the second year girl pushed me and my friend to the ground, how I got up and punched her squarely on the jaw and sent her tottering backwards.

131

Martha exploded in laughter.

'You did what?'

Anna said, 'Show us. I'll do the second year.'

We acted it out. Anna as the bully. Martha as Kerry Doherty. Our mother's stern look of disapproval struggled to suppress a smile. I didn't actually hit Anna, though she managed to land a sneaky clip on my right ear. My mother intervened.

'That's enough, now. That's enough. No more hitting, now. And you, Donna McDaid, you might sound like your father, but that doesn't give you the right to go round punching people.'

'But, Mammy, I only hit her when—'

'And you won't hit her – or anybody else – again. Now get upstairs and get them socks off. A good steep in salty water'll fix them. I'll go over to that school and get this sorted. You and Kerry Doherty needn't worry about that.'

I huffed up the stairs, clunking my schoolbag behind me. I can still hear my sisters and my mother laughing, then settling into easy conversation.

The steeping in salty water only partially removed the blood from the sock. The brown stain persisted. Martha and Anna bought me a pack of three new pairs when they got paid on Friday. My mother went to the school and spoke to the head teacher. Christine Bennett left me and Kerry alone. Martha and Anna called me Rocky for a while, but I didn't mind.

There's a tension, even to this day, when I do something they think I shouldn't do. Over the years I've come to realise that at the bottom of their protectiveness is a fear of insanity. They're worried I'm going mad. Even when I got myself up on my feet again, at each threshold of recovery, their worried eyes followed me and then they sighed in a mixture of relief and foreboding.

'You have to mind yourself, Donna. You're after getting yourself back on your feet and, you know, you don't want to put yourself under pressure,' Anna said.

'We can't go back to them days, Donna. None of us can. Yourself, obviously. But me mammy, too,' Martha added.

My mother sat there, listening to this, happy to let Anna and

Martha handle things. Up to a point. 'Don't worry about me. I've been through plenty in my day, with your father and all. It's whatever you want, Donna. It's up to you, Donna.'

'And Teresa,' I said.

Anna and Martha looked at me as if their worst fears had been confirmed. How could it be up to a dead-born baby, buried in the deep ground years before? In all the pages of this story so far, it's the words to explain moments like this I find hardest to reach. I can recollect the incidents and the conversations well enough, as truthfully as I can, but to describe the continuing presence of Teresa and the way she works in our lives, I struggle with that.

'It's whatever is best for Teresa. That's what'll guide me,' I asserted.

The open and amazed faces before me made me continue.

'It looks like parts of Teresa's body were taken out and kept after a post-mortem.'

'Saints preserve us,' my mother exclaimed as she crossed herself, but I kept on.

'Obviously, they couldn't go into the details at the public meeting and they're offering us a one-to-one on Teresa. Just her ...' I nearly said 'case', but I caught myself in time. 'Just her ... story.'

'What parts of her body? Shur she was only a wee mite.'

Anger flared in Martha's face.

'We don't know. That's why we're going to have the meeting with them.'

'With who? A doctor?'

'I'm not sure. Maybe. The letter just said "a representative".'

'Where's the letter?'

'Tony has it. It went to him.'

'Of course it did. It always comes back to him.' My mother's anger against Tony was never far below the surface.

'The hospital kept in touch with Tony over the years. His name is on the bottom of the forms. I just, you know, cut away everything when I went into the depression.'

A soundless gasp reverberated in the room at the word. The word that should never be spoken. The word that, in their fears, puts me on the brink of madness. Saying it makes them back off and gives me more power. 'Watch out,' they seem to exclaim. 'She's ticking and could go off at any minute. Only she can defuse it.'

'We'll go and meet them and see what they have to say,' I continued.

Martha's brow creased in worry. She voiced the thought that was in all our heads.

'Will they be able to tell us what we buried?'

I'm not one for reincarnation. Or the afterlife. I'm not one for angels or good and bad karma. I do wonder about the world, probably a little more than the average person, but I do so through the rational lens of science. I'm not even sure I have much of an imagination. I see things as I see them.

One image stays with me and holds me firm. Teresa in the coffin in the ground. By now she has returned to the earth that gave her to me. I know that. That's the scientific truth and whatever else I hold on to, that's an anchor for me. I haven't put Teresa in Heaven or Hell, despite the exhortations of everyone around me.

'Don't worry, Donna. God called her home. She's in Heaven now.'

'Teresa's in Heaven, Donna, with all the other angels.'

As far as I am concerned, Teresa is not in Heaven or in Hell or in any such place. Teresa is in my world, this world, the only world I know. Her remains are in the ground in the City Cemetery, overlooking the city, where even on the sunniest of days a chilling wind comes up the Foyle valley and swirls among the headstones.

Teresa is buried with my father and her name is in gold writing on his simple black stone. Teresa Bradley.

Tony was very good about it. It was the most straightforward way of organising the burial. We were too young to have our own grave so Teresa is buried with my father, the sunny easy-going baker who wanted nothing more than to be talking and playing football, who, though he became an adult, married and had a family, never really grew up.

'Your father,' my mother said once, 'never got past being seventeen. He never saw the point. It was his attitude. They should
have called him Oisín, because he never left *Tír na nÓg.*'

My father never left *Tír na nÓg.* The Land of Youth. That's
where Teresa and himself are. That's where I put them. In the
cold ground of *Tír na nÓg.*

Martha's question was the clincher. Will they be able to tell us
what we buried?

The family meeting broke up soon after that. It's hard to sup
tea and eat cake with images in your mind of maggots crawling
through sodden clay and rotting flesh. Anna and Martha left in
their cars. I walked to the corner with my mother before she
headed up the road to her own house. Weak sunlight faded and
the streetlights pinged on above us.

'The nights are starting to close in, thank God,' she said. 'Have
you enough oil for the heating?'

'Plenty,' I said.

'I don't know why you took that fireplace out. No matter how
much oil you burn, a house is never right warm until you see
flames in the hearth.'

'It was the flames I couldn't stand, Ma. Anyway, the oil is
handier, especially with me out working all day.'

A neighbour passed, a bent old man, with a plastic bag of groceries in his hand.

'I hope that poor creature has enough heat in. The winter will
be hard on the elderly.'

I love the fact that she doesn't include herself among the elderly. She sees herself as ageless. She is in *Tír na nÓg,* too. But
that day, as we stood in the street, in the fading sunlight, the
orange glow of the streetlamps revealed the lines in her face and
the thinning grey wisps amidst her fair hair and I thought about
Teresa buried with my father and all the dead people buried in
the ground and I almost prayed for them.

CHAPTER EIGHTEEN

LISTENING

I want to write about the private meeting at the hospital. A one-to-one they called it, but there were four of us. Me, Tony, a patient advocate and a pathologist. Two facing two across a desk. A small office in one of the new wings of the hospital. It was probably a consulting room. There were charts about blood pressure on the wall. A curtain was pushed in close to the wall so that its rail swung out into the room like an idle crane. There was a big window on the back wall, high above our heads and I could see clouds, the edge of the main hospital building and a tangle of twigs and leaves, sprouting the start of spring.

Tony picked me up from work. We hardly spoke on the way to the hospital as we drove, in reverse, the route we'd taken when we came out of the hospital, without Teresa. I had never been back there since. Tony has, a few times. For the births of his other children and when his wee boy had a sudden high temperature.

I let Tony lead. He got the letter. He set up the time and place. He checked the room number and negotiated the corridors to get us there. My insistence that there be someone senior present had brought a pathologist. Now we sat together, ex-husband and ex-wife, facing our pasts and the two people who would take us there.

For days I had agonised with myself how I would handle this meeting. I eventually resolved not to speak. Tony could ask all the questions. But what if he forgot something? Overlooked something? I said to myself that we should sit down together and work out our questions, what we knew and what we needed to know. Have a strategy. But there was no time. We were both busy. And cordial as relations are between me and Tony (most of the time!), it just wasn't possible to meet one evening in his house or mine to prepare a joint approach.

So we never got together to strategise. And not talking in the car meant we had no plan. We had never faced a situation like this before.

The advocate and the pathologist were already in the room behind the desk. Tony knocked and a man's voice called, 'Come in.' They both stood up and the man said, 'Ah, Mr and Mrs Bradley. I hope you had no trouble finding the room. I'm Tom Fairleigh, one of the patient advocates here in the hospital and this is Doctor Lennon, a member of our Pathology Department.'

I was shaking as I sat down. I didn't know what to do about the Mr and Mrs thing but I said nothing. Neither did Tony. It wasn't a great start. I floundered, confused by how young the pathologist was. She couldn't have been on duty the day Teresa was born. How could she answer our questions?

I took a spiral-bound notebook from my handbag. I rummaged for a pen. I needed props to stop me shaking. I resolved to write everything down. If I couldn't unglue my mouth to say anything, at least I'd make a record of the meeting. I could do that. I'd taken notes in classes and lectures. I'd kept journals and record books of experiments and studies. I'd sat at meetings and made notes of questions asked, points clarified, evidence presented and opinions voiced. I gripped the pen as hard as I could.

'We're pleased to have this opportunity to review this case, your daughter, Teresa Bradley,' the advocate began. 'We appreciate that these are very sensitive matters.'

I wrote down the words 'Teresa' and 'case'. The man shuffled some papers in a file. Teresa's file.

'You will know from the public meeting, which I understand you attended, that the Hospital Trusts across Northern Ireland are contacting people in cases where post-mortems have occurred and where organs from those cases have been retained by the hospital.'

I wrote the words 'cases', 'post-mortems' and 'retained'. Already, it looked like gibberish on the page. I gripped my pen tighter and turned to look at Tony as he rose out of his seat.

Tony towered above me that day, though I'm taller than him by a couple of inches. I'm below average for a woman. We're not really tall people. Genes, I suppose. He's slim. Slight rather than wiry. Never had a belly. He doesn't drink much. Never did. The smoking would keep him that way, too.

'Hey! No flesh on a thoroughbred,' he'd say.

Not even the paunch men get when they're married and settled. Maybe I'm saying he never settled. Kept agitated, a pilot light burning at all times so that when the fuel kicked in, he ignited. I'd seen that a few times, when we were courting. Boys with too much drink taken moving in on me. There was Tony, slim, slight, but serious, like a wildcat that would tear you to pieces. The boys swayed and bobbed, then backed off as I leaned in closer to Tony. Maybe I've bounced off him, collided and echoed away, so that when he rose out of his seat in front of the advocate and the pathologist, I was more observer than partner, more witness than participant.

'Stop calling her a case. She's not a case. She's my ... our daughter.'

He didn't shout, but there was steel in his words. And pain. That's the part my mother can never understand and accept. Losing Teresa hurts Tony, too, so when he rose out of his seat, it was years of pain that drove him.

'And we're not Mr and Mrs Bradley. I'm Tony Bradley and this is Donna ... Bradley. Donna McDaid. Teresa's our daughter. Not your case.'

The vein pulsing in his left temple looked like it would blow there and then. I think I put my hand out to touch his side, but I never made contact. I reached my hand towards him as I would to the tank in the hot-press. I sensed him fill with lava. Tony was a volcano beside me and my palm grew warm as it hovered by his side.

'Just tell us what we want to know. Just get this thing sorted, so we can go home and have nothing more to do with ye.'

It could have been me talking. Tony chiselled words out of the air and ranged them in blocks of historical time we could never go back to, or get away from.

When the patient advocate coughed and lifted a page from the file open in front of him, Tony stayed standing. When the pathologist shifted in her chair and flicked her blond hair further behind her ears, Tony stayed standing. He was standing at Teresa's grave once more, the stony clay sodden at his feet, the beaten wreaths and flowers dripping rain onto each other, his shoes sinking in the ooze. Tony has never walked from that grave. I see him there, a small man, standing to his full height, wishing he could pat his pockets for the reassuring clunk of his cigarette box and lighter, then slip away to inhale the long luxurious stream of smoke that quenches the flames within. He always fought fire with fire.

'What did ye take from her? Just tell us that.'

He never sat down again. The pathologist and the advocate continued the meeting, gestured with their eyes and their hands that Tony should sit down, that the meeting should continue in a calm and civilised manner. But Tony was having none of that. He was not going to be civilised. Or seated. He stood. He stood for Teresa.

I wrote the words 'what did you take from her?' in my notebook, which seemed to be covered in Egyptian hieroglyphs, the scribblings of an inattentive note-taker at a meeting of fools.

The patient advocate pushed a single sheet of paper across to Tony. I could see the logo of the Hospital Trust. The advocate swivelled the paper round so it faced Tony, but said nothing. Something chimed somewhere. A church bell rang out across the city and I noticed a smell for the first time. The hospital smell. Formaldehyde. Bleach. Flowers wilting. Starched bed sheets. Death. I lifted the sheet of paper and read Teresa's details, then a list. Whole brain. Lungs. Kidneys. Tissue samples: pancreas, spleen. Dates were noted and the phrase 'Retained Pathology Department'.

'There is a form. A signature,' the patient advocate said. Tony dismissed this with a grunt and a slight wave of his hand. The pathologist pushed her hair more firmly behind her ears and leaned forward.

'There are a number of ... Teresa is one of a number of ca ... children whose organs were retained. For medical and scientific purposes. Like the others, Teresa has helped our diagnostic work over the years.'

This broke my vow of silence.

'We have no problem with that. But you should have told us. You should have asked us.'

'But we did. We have the signature.'

The patient advocate swivelled the file once more so that another document was facing Tony and me. A small slip of paper with Tony's scrawl and a date. And Teresa's name. Teresa made lungless. Brainless. Teresa eviscerated. Cut to pieces.

I still haven't worked out what hurt me most. The news that this had happened or the sense that Tony had betrayed us. Or – and I think this may really be it – the sense that I was being blind-sided again. That's what hurts me most. Something so intimately me, something that grew inside me and came out of my body was treated in so offhand a manner. Liberties taken with my flesh and blood.

In the years since Teresa's death I have been striving to reclaim those liberties. And, that day, with Tony standing beside me, standing up for Teresa, his eyes filling with tears because he felt he should have stood up for her when they put the little slip of paper in front of him the first time, when knowledge as arrogance trampled on knowledge as love, that day when we relived the time they took Teresa apart without our permission, a charge coursed through me. I would have to redeem this part of my life, myself, these dead tissues and organs that grew out of me. Once more, Teresa was saying, 'I'll never leave you.' And brutal though it seems, I took this new waste onto myself and did what I have been trying to do all along. I took charge.

'We want her. All of her. She's our daughter. Brains. Lungs. Kidneys. Tissues. Liver. Pancreas. All of her.'

I could have gone on. I could have gone on listing organs, then I could have gone on to character traits. Intelligent, bright, vivacious, lively, fun to be with, generous. I could have gone on with physical attributes. Lithe, willowy, brown-haired, brown-eyed, smooth-skinned, light-olive coloured. Slightly knock-kneed like her father. A scattering of freckles – from our side – across her nose. I could have gone on to list achievements. First tooth, crawling, then bumping unsteadily around the furniture to find her first steps. Wobbling but upright at thirteen months. Tentative but game by fifteen months. Throwing the odd tantrum at thirty months. My lists are many, long and deep. They are embedded in me. Part of my make-up. And now I had a new one. A new list. Brain. Lungs. Kidney. Tissue. Pancreas. Spleen.

In work, I go to meetings where we stay on the surface of life. This meeting took us into the very blood of it. Had us wading through the slimy viscera of it. Tony standing, leaning forwards, his nicotine-stained fingers whitening on the desk. Me, perching on my seat, running lists through my head like a woman at a guillotine running stitches through her fingers.

'There are procedures … many families want … you may wish to consider …'

As the patient advocate stumbled to bring us to the lip of the grave, I saw myself there. With Tony. And my sisters and my mother and everyone else in my world, everyone who ever knew me or heard of me or had even the slightest connection with me. Everyone that could have known Teresa would now stand with me as we buried her again.

I don't remember getting out of the hospital. I think Tony shook hands. I know they handed him some papers which he tossed on to the back seat of the car. I know he said 'I'll take care of it' in a firm voice, as we eased forward at the lights at the Waterside end of the Craigavon Bridge. The papers slid out of the folder, when Tony turned the car onto the bridge. I put my hand back, without looking, and forced the papers back into the folder.

And the fires roared inside me again. Tony said something as I got out of the car but by then the roaring was in my head as if the meeting in the hospital had pulled out the damper on the furnace of my memories, so that a great gush of wind oxygenated them and sucked them up the chimney of my vulnerable self. Turning the key in my own front door meant entering a world I thought I'd left.

My living room was ablaze with memories. There stood Tony in his Du Pont jacket, ready for a night shift, his face gleaming from the bath he'd climbed out of an hour earlier. There sat my mother chirruping about the daughters of her neighbours who were pregnant or getting married or taking their children on holidays. And there I sat, a mug of muddy tea on my lap, staring at the empty grate, too roasted inside to need a fire.

That day, when I came back from the hospital meeting, I went to the chair where my former self sat. I dropped my briefcase onto the sofa opposite and tossed my suit jacket after it. I eased myself into the chair, curled myself effortlessly into the shape of my former self, cupped my palms together to mime the mug of tea I permanently held before me and became, once more, the woman I was in the weeks after we buried Teresa for the first time.

A tapping on the window brought me round. There was also a hammering on the door and the ding-dong of the bell. But it was the window-tapping that lifted me. Something a bird might do, pecking in a frightened manner. I turned in my chair and saw two mouths shaping my name. Don-na. O-pen up. O-pen the do-ar. Don-na. Everything coming through cotton wool. Two faces pressed to the glass. Fingers and knuckles tapping. My sisters, urgent now, they beat upon the window until I got up and let them in.

Martha went straight to the kitchen and put on the kettle. Anna led me to the sofa. She took my briefcase and my jacket and threw them onto the chair. I was not to be allowed to sit in the armchair again. Anna sat beside me and held my hand. Martha returned – 'the kettle's on' – and stood in front of us and we all went quiet. They didn't have to say anything. Tony had contacted one of them and she'd contacted the other.

'Yeez need to get around to her. We're only back from the hospital. I ... Yeez need to ... She's not talking again.'

That's what he would have said. That's what would have galvanised them. She's not talking again. Their greatest fear about me. That I would go silent, lose myself to the old fires. Don't rake over old coals, my mother says. Here I was, raking and burrowing, tossing and stirring the fires of yesterday so that Anna, caressing my palms in her hands could say, 'Her hand's wild warm.' And touching the back of her hand to my forehead, she could add, 'She's roasting. A fever she has.'

Oh, it's a fever I have all right. The plague lights its way through me, coursing feverishly up my arteries and down my veins, a scourge lighting me up.

'There's the kettle,' Martha said and she was away to the kitchen. There's healing in tea. We believe that. Just tea. Tay we call it. A strong deep vowel with a rasp in it. Tay.

Martha appeared with three mugs. No tray. No ceremony. No saucers, doilies, tea cosies, milk jugs, china, delft or silver. Good solid junky mugs. Derry City Football Club. Three of them. One for each sister. Each mug exactly as each of us liked it. No milk, no sugar for Anna. Milk and two sugars for Martha herself. Just milk for Donna. I heard my father's voice. 'Yeez are all sweet enough and wee Donna's the sweetest of the lot.' His own Derry City mug steaming in his fist, in his other a floury bap he'd baked himself. Our faces like geisha girls', powdered with white flour from the baps we'd stuffed into our mouths. 'Wee Donna's the sweetest of the lot.' Anna and Martha didn't mind. Or if they did, they hid it well.

My sisters hide everything well. Usually. But that day, their worry and the panic, grounded in a deep family history, were plain to see. They heated the room in a way that no coal fire or burbling radiator ever could.

Before I learned how to jump into a skipping rope, I used to hunch nervously as the rope lay limply on the ground. Martha would call 'ready', then she and Anna would lift it over my head. I remember cowering and jumping at the same time, managing two or three loops before the rope snagged around my ankles. Martha would urge me to try again, but I would always run back home, defeated.

But I kept watching the other children on our street, jumping in and skipping. One August day, I joined the queue to jump in. Martha and Anna were twirling the rope for the younger ones. When my turn came, I dashed forward in perfect time with the rope, held myself upright and bounced on my toes – once, twice, three, four, five ... so many times! – as the rope swung round and down, slapping lightly on the tarmac beneath me. Then, I dashed out, breathless, and the next girl ran in.

Rooms for rent,
Inquire within.
As I move out,
Let Rachel come in.

Everyone cheered.

As sisters, we have many shared memories in our brains. But our lives, our knowledge, are different. The little brain Teresa had was cut out of her and put in a jar. Then on a slide. A thin sliver only a few angstroms thick yet deep and wide enough to hold eternity.

My sisters could not let me relapse. Tony's phone call had warned them.

'She's gone into herself again. I'm not saying it's like before. Christ, it couldn't be like that again, could it?'

My sisters would have to keep things cheery.

'You're roasting, Donna. Take a wee sup a tay. Ach, we never even brought a biscuit or a bun or nothing. Mind the baps me daddy always brought us for the breakfast? The big floury ones. We loved them.'

Wee Donna, the sweetest of the lot, was going to crash and burn once more, falling into the furnace of her own insides. But I knew it couldn't be like that again. I knew that, staring into the tea. My God! How many cups of tea have I had? Tay, a milky, fawn sludge that threatened to drown me.

I put the mug on the floor and I stood up. Anna and Martha readied themselves to pick me up when I fell. But I didn't fall. I licked my parched lips and flexed my fingers. I would fight fire with fire. I looked at my sisters and said, 'I need a drink.'

Martha gasped. Anna laughed. I smiled and went to the kitchen where I knew there was a good bottle of Rioja on the worktop. I called back, 'Either of you want a glass?' and got two muffled 'no's' in reply. We're not drinkers, our family. One of my father's brothers, Uncle Tommy, is a bit of an alcoholic. We never saw him much, even when my father was alive.

The cork gave a reassuring pop as I pulled it out of the bottle and the wine made a hearty glug-glug when I poured it into the glass. I saluted my sisters when I rejoined them and we clinked cheers together. Anna said *sláinte*. Her children are at the *Bunscoil*.

'A toast,' I said. 'Here's to the fucking medical profession.'

And we clinked again. When I took a deep swallow of the wine I felt the fiery-red liquid rush into me and bellow in my stomach. 'There, now,' it said. 'There's fire for you.'

'You all right?' Martha asked.

'Grand. Yeh. Grand.'

'Only, Tony said ye were at the hospital ...'

So I was right. Tony had phoned Martha and Martha had texted Anna and they'd both rushed round to see their sister in the hope of stopping her from going mad.

Anna pointed at the wine glass. 'You'd want to take it easy. This time of day and all.'

I let it go. She meant well. Her mad sister who went from being deeply depressed to being obsessed in her science studies and now, in frustration and anger, was taking to the drink.

I remember a wedding. Not mine and Tony's. I was dancing with my mother. She loves the *Hucklebuck*. We were in the middle of the floor, laughing and moving. And Daddy joined us to make a small circle, our own dance, the three of us linked. I must have been very young. Only a girl. The sweetest of the lot, dancing with my mother and my father. Then Uncle Tommy barged in and grabbed my father round the shoulders, out of rhythm with the music, out of rhythm with our dance. I know now there was no harm in him, but I was a little frightened. Amazed that this man and my father could be brothers. My mother took my hand

and led me back to our table. The song continued as I watched Uncle Tommy bowl my father about, an uncomfortable grin on his face.

'That man's always drunk,' my mother hissed. 'One thing you can promise me, Donna. Never get involved with a man who drinks.'

I was too young to understand what she meant. When I got serious with Tony, it was one of his good points, in her view, that he took a drink, but wasn't a serious drinker. Neither am I, but I relished the second mouthful of that red wine. I felt it course round my tongue and behind my teeth. I ran it round like a mouthwash until Martha admonished, 'Don-na!' and then I swallowed it in a great quenching gulp. That's how it could be. How the fire in the wine would fight the fire in my memories. Never too much fire. Never too much wine. Fire is always dangerous. Consuming. To be wary of. I swirled the last of the wine in the glass. Sipped it this time, sat down beside Anna again and told my sisters about the hospital, told it in a calm voice, only breaking slightly when I came to the part about having a second funeral for Teresa.

Libraries NI

Derry Central Library
35 Foyle Street
Londonderry
BT48 6AL
Tel 028 71229990
Your Library Doesn't End Here
Get free eBooks and eMagazines
www.librariesni.org.uk/pages/.niebooksand
emagazines.aspx
Or ask Staff for details

Borrowed Items 05/06/2018 17:04
XXXXXX4259

Item Title	Due Date
A sudden sun	26/06/2018

Thankyou for using this unit

Email:
derrycentral.library@librariesni.org.uk
www.librariesni.org.uk

CHAPTER NINETEEN

NEAR MISSES

Little things frazzled me at work at that time. I accidentally deleted a document on my computer and spent a morning harrumphing about it, slamming drawers and sharpening pencils until Gerry retrieved it for me.

'There's nothing lost and gone forever,' he said, when I told him what had happened. We were in the canteen, looking over the river to the park. The trees blended shades of light green together as spring gradually arrived.

'You're wrong there,' I said.

I would have left it at that only he added, 'I mean about the computer. I didn't mean really important things.'

That's when I realised he knew my story. Or the public version of it. Everyone knew my story. We live in a small city, growing out of itself these days, still with enough of a grapevine to make sure a story like mine would be known. Besides, the job in the City Council plugs me into a great and vibrant gossip mill.

'You might have heard,' I said. 'I mean, you probably know I was married to Tony Bradley. His brother has the carpet place. They buy and sell property now.'

Gerry nodded.

'Anyway, me and Tony had a wee girl. Teresa. And we lost her.'

I paused and looked out of the window. Nothing moved on the river. Nothing moved in the air. The trees in the park held their breath.

'She died. She was never really born. And, well, me and Tony, that was the end of us.'

Gerry nodded again. I felt tears rise under my eyelids.

'That's all gone and lost forever.'

Once more he nodded and looked warmly at me. I'll always remember that. He never said anything. Never tried to make it all right by saying 'she's in Heaven now and you'll all meet up again' or 'that's wild sad, but yeez have to be strong' or 'she's not gone really. You'll always have the memories.'

I haven't even got a photograph. That's how thoroughly 'lost and gone forever' Teresa is. I have a grave and a mound of smouldering charcoal nestled somewhere inside me, but it hardly adds up to a daughter.

If Gerry had nodded one more time, I think I might have burst out laughing. That's how fragile I was. On the edge, but at least not over it. Instead, Gerry turned to the view and said, 'There's a path that runs near the water's edge. Right beside the railway line. There'll be bluebells soon. Maybe we might take a walk over there.'

Later, he came to my desk and with a few clicks of the mouse, a little humming under his breath and a couple of muttered 'there nows' and 'just one more wee thing', he retrieved my lost document. *Key Learning in Recycled Bin Uptake.* A policy-development paper for the council's Waste Management Sub-Committee. We're a small city but we produce mountains of waste. It's what makes us truly human, our ability to produce and cast off waste. So we recycle what we can't cut back on. One of my jobs is to promote and monitor the Recycle Bin programme. I'm the Blue Bins Lady and the Blue Bins are a hot issue for the council. The sort of thing that makes councillors squirm in the local radio station as ratepayers phone in complaints and the presenter asks the awkward questions: Has the council met this year's targets? Will the European Commission levy a fine on us if we don't? Will the rates have to go up to pay for that?

It was reassuring to be beside Gerry. He sat in my chair, in front of the computer. I perched on the edge of my desk. I watched him become absorbed in unravelling the set of Russian dolls that my document lay within, his brow creasing, his lips mouthing instructions and exhortations to himself. I noticed I felt okay about being helped in that way. Usually you couldn't get near me. No-one could. I was obsessively independent. I remember Miss Jennings in the lab in the Tech saying, 'You don't have to do it all by yourself, Donna. There's three of you in the group. Emma and Charlene can do some of the work, too.' But I wasn't going to wait around for Emma and Charlene. Or for anybody else. They were younger than me and they thought I was bossy. Later, at university, the other students considered me odd. I cut no corners. I craved no easy routes. I attended every lecture, seminar and lab session. If I was part of a group, I stayed on the edge of it, semi-detached. I needed and wanted to know everything. That's what would get me through. That's what would hold the smouldering charcoal in check.

With Gerry at the computer that day, I didn't feel any sense of pressure. He gave me a quick review of what he'd done, mentioning 'undo functions', 'preferences' and 'dump files'. I understood enough to be comfortable with it. If I needed help for something I couldn't manage, I could call someone. Gerry, even.

'Get that saved onto a memory stick straight away,' he said, pulling one from his pocket and passing it to me. I took it, not saying I already had a couple and I pushed off the edge of my desk, just as he stood up out of my chair. For a brief moment, as he rose up, we were chest to chest. I could feel his breath on my cheek. A button on my jacket skimmed his belt. Then there was an awkward shuffle as he slipped past me and I turned to take my seat once more. I watched him walk between the desks on his way back to the City Engineer's offices. I fingered the memory stick he'd given me and wondered how I might be as a woman with a man once again.

My greatest fear is that I will be pregnant and that Teresa will happen to me as before. Of course it affects how I deal with men now. Tony and all that is in the past, but I have nothing in the present or building into the future. It's not that I don't want to. I have urges. Course I do. But I haven't really done anything about them. There were a few drunken fumblings when I was at the university. I look back on them now and I cringe. I regret that I never managed a mature relationship with a man. And that doesn't necessarily include sleeping with him.

I remember one big bony technician, from the computer labs. I groped him at a rowdy Christmas do. I was drinking like a teenager. Shots and loud talk, letting off steam and throwing myself about. The evening developed as farce rather than passion play. Tongues and hands flaying, I'm sure I terrified the man. I'd practically torn the shirt off his back, before he came to and disengaged. I don't blame him. We were locked together outside the Students Union disco bar, behind the science block. There was a gale blowing around our ankles. Sleety rain mashed our hair to our heads. I think I must have dragged him outside. I blame Pernod. Wicked stuff. The cloudy tempest in a glass. I glued my lips and my body to his. I could feel his ribs against my breasts. I tore at his shirt and sank my tongue as deep as his tonsils. He sprang back at me and my head clunked off the grainy surface of the building. His hand reached between my thighs and I readjusted my balance and a piece of his shirt came away in my hand. He reared back, startled, glazed eyes gaping and intense, showing a mixture of pain and passion. Then two black plastic bags full of computer printer waste blew out of a nearby skip, ripped apart on a jagged metal edge and scattered a confetti of shredded paper across us.

'What the fuck?' he roared.

I laughed and slithered. I remember I was wearing purple high-heels and a light party dress. The shock of the paper shower brought us to our senses and I ran off, back into the disco where the music thumped and the press of people swallowed me up, my teeth chattering and my chest heaving. I don't remember seeing the computer technician afterwards. I probably puked up the Pernod. I remember a couple of nights like that. Enough to give me a chill now.

When term restarted after the Christmas break I went to the IT labs and asked the technician how his shirt was. He laughed and said he had a tough time explaining the rips to his wife. I liked him, but that was the end of that.

There were a few other near misses like that, but since Tony left, I've been celibate. It's become fashionable in that time. That doesn't mean that I like it. But I have to be honest and say that I'm not really fussed either. My energies have gone elsewhere. Campaigning, returning to study, academic work. Finding my brain and not my gonads. It can't always go on like this. I'm still young. Juices flow in me. I toss and turn in bed at night sometimes and wake up wet between the legs after hauling Brad Pitt under the sheets.

Intimacy is one thing. Sex is another. Pregnancy is another one yet. I suppose if Tony and myself hadn't split up, we'd have other children by now.

CHAPTER TWENTY

THE THIN MAN

It was around the time of the one-on-one meeting that the incident in the food court with the thin man happened. I remembered him the moment I saw him. He was older of course, more crumpled into himself, but I was sure it was him when he spoke to the teenage girl who was with him. She was about eighteen or nineteen and acted like his carer. I took her to be one of the girls I'd seen swinging on the rope tied to the pole outside the community centre in Strathfoyle that evening when the thin man had said: 'Do you have any idea what you're talking about, wee girl? Are you ignorant or what?'

I've always held on to that. I've replayed that scene in my mind many, many times and in each replay instead of freezing with my mouth open, I eloquently and comprehensively reply with facts and figures. Dioxin content analysis. Volumes of toxic and other waste planned to arrive at the incinerator on a daily basis. Rates of burn and ratios of residue to load. Everything at my fingertips.

I remember the teenager asked the thin man if he wanted to finish his soup. The man's low, gravelly voice was barely audible above the Muzak.

'I have enough. Can we go now?'

I'd come from a meeting at the Community Network. Suit,

briefcase, two bags of shopping (toiletries and underwear). It took me a while to get used to the money in the new job, but I've managed it. I bought black, low-heeled dress shoes with a satin strap for a party Martha was planning.

'We'll get the red wine in for you, Donna. We know you like that.' A brittle enough smile. Always checking to make sure I didn't go over the edge.

Basic cotton pants. You can never have enough of them. Moisturiser and a camomile shampoo I like. The light spangling through the glass dome above the food court in the shopping centre. People around me supping lattes, eating soup, mopping up sandwich sauces, crunching lettuce leaves. I sat easily among them. The woman who knew things. The businesswoman catching some shopping. The professional on a lunch break.

I wonder am I the sort of person who carries a hurt a long time? I didn't do it with Tony, but I suppose he didn't hurt me. Or maybe I didn't feel it because we simply hurt each other. I can't think of other instances. I certainly carry something about this thin man. Hurt I suppose I'd have to call it. Pain even. Certainly a welling of anger stirred in my breast when I saw him with the teenage girl. A welling that calmed and drew back when I heard him meekly ask, 'Can we go now?'

That's how it will be for all of us, I've learned. We'll all grow to weakness. Some of us will do so from arrogance and the lack of consideration. Some of us from goodness and the care of others. But all of us grow to weakness.

I got out of my seat, gathered my bags and went to the table where the thin man and the teenage girl sat. She looked up at me and smiled, a little confused, the question 'do I know you?' creasing her brow. I nodded at her and faced the man. I saw the thinning brown hair on top of his skull, flecks of scalp whitening the strands. My voice made him raise his eyes to mine.

'I've always wanted to say thank you.'

'Thank you,' he repeated.

'You don't know me, but we met years ago. At a meeting in the community centre in Strathfoyle.'

'Strathfoyle's where I live.'

'That's right. And I ran a meeting there. About the incinerator and Du Pont. You were at it.'

'They should never have let them build that thing.'

'They didn't. They … we stopped them. It'll never be built.'

'Oh, they'll build it all right.'

'No, they won't. We know too much now. We can stop it.'

'Have you a gun?'

'Granda!' the teenager said.

'No, I haven't,' I laughed.

'You'll need a gun,' he said. 'That's the only way to stop them now.'

His eyes watered so I was looking into two green pools, opaque and translucent at the same time.

'Anyway, I want to say thanks, because after that meeting, I went to the Tech and university and now I work for the council on waste management and I'm not ignorant anymore.'

'You are. You don't have a gun.'

'Come on, Granda,' the teenager said. 'You said you had enough.' And to me she added, 'We have to catch the bus.'

Then she shuffled the thin man out of his seat, placed two walking sticks in his cramped paws and led him towards the escalators. She'd tell her pals later. Maybe phone them from the bus as her grandfather nodded off beside her, a snail-trail of drool running from his lower lip.

'This madwoman came up to us in Foyleside and started talking to me granda. She looked all right. Had a nice suit on and all. But the minute she started talking you just knew she was not right in the head. Her and me granda going on about guns and Du Pont. If anyone heard them, we'd have all been locked up.'

There was a time when my sisters and my mother thought I would be locked up. I'm sure they sat together, maybe even with me in the room, stupefied by Valium and tea, and talked about what they'd have to do. My mother would have excluded Tony.

'There's no point talking to that fella. He doesn't care anymore.'

'He's still her husband,' Martha always trying to keep things right.

'What I don't understand is why she just doesn't get over it. I mean, it happens to loads of women,' Anna puzzled as usual.

'We're not talking about loads of women. We're talking about our Donna,' Martha being reasonable.

'She bought two more Babygros today. A pink one and a blue one,' my mother producing the evidence.

Small snatches of cloth you'd hardly wrap around a loaf of bread. I must have bought a dozen of them. I only have one left. I think my mother gave the rest to the St Vincent de Paul shop. I can smile about that now. Some child somewhere, maybe in a poor family, benefited from my madness.

I imagine Martha and Anna taking a Babygro each and fingering the soft cottony fleece. They've both had babies. They know what it's like. They know the way madness lurks within joy, the way exertions and commitments of the flesh play upon the mind. They would claw their way through barbed wire to save their children and think nothing of the frenzy and the pain. But these empty Babygros, these gentle cloths billowing with absence, they recognised them as pathways to madness.

'What does she do with them?' asked Martha.

'She puts them on the bed and she looks at them. Sometimes she moves them around and talks under her breath at them,' my mother told them. 'Maybe if we got her a doll. There must be one lying around one of your houses. She could dress up the doll in these.'

I picture my sisters looking at their mother in amazement. What she'd said was sensible and crazy at the same time. They were left wondering if they were all going mad, talking like this. I was a sad case back then. Like loads of women. Different degrees of it. Shocking even to remember it now.

And that day, in Foyleside Shopping Centre, when I watched the thin man stagger along on two sticks beside his granddaughter, who kept looking back at me, a look of awe and pity in her eyes, I heard an echo of my Babygro-buying weeks, an echo only, a bell still chiming inside me, but that I had managed to dampen and soften. By work. By shopping. By the odd glass of red wine. By being with my sisters and their families. By living.

This has been my project since I lost Teresa. I know that now. Since the fires began inside me I have been trying to recover my life by living it. Buying the Babygros was part of that. After a couple of days playing with them – playing is the right word to describe what I was doing – I would leave them and continue my wanderings round the town. I had thrown a bag of wet slack on my burning insides, not putting the fire out, simply banking it up so that it would be less vicious and I could move once more.

Now I can see I oscillated between buying Babygros, walking the streets and sitting in a stupor in my chair while Tony watched horse racing on the telly. Until I was saved by sticking envelopes and licking stamps for the anti-incinerator campaign.

The thin man was right about one thing. They want to build it again. It's not clear who this time. Not only Du Pont, but the City Council, other industries. The whole city even. See all that waste? Just burn it to fuck. And I don't have a gun. Never had any time for them. When the incinerator comes back on my agenda, I'm going to have to face it down like before. Except this time I'll be doing it from inside the City Council. It'll be my job.

When I was in the campaign with Olivia, Frances, Jack and Bill, I was a girl, like that teenager with the thin man. No, not as strong as her. Just someone tagging along most of the time, even at the end when I was running meetings. Now I'm right at the centre of it at my desk in the Waste Management Unit of the City Engineer's Office.

I'd like to bring the thin man in to see it someday. Come and look at this I'd say. Come and look at me is what I'd really be saying. See, I'm not ignorant. See, I can spell and write and answer questions. I have the facts, the knowledge. I would show him my filing cabinet and my files bulging with reports and analyses. I would show him my computer and how the graphics and charts I display on my screen answer all his questions.

Then he would grapple his two walking sticks into his gnarled paws again and lean awkwardly forward under the watchful gaze of his granddaughter, who would look accusingly at me.

'Why did you bring him here?' she'd ask. 'Can't you see he's dying?'

Of course I could see he was dying. More than that I could see we all were. Even you my fresh-faced girl. And even me, the near madwoman with the shopping and the briefcase. I see his grey pallor. I see his bent back. I see his watery eyes and I know it all comes down to this, to the slow creep to the grave and the steady climb into the hole in the ground. The relentless return to earth.

I knew I'd have to face Teresa's grave again. No ordinary visit. Not just an anniversary. I'd have to reopen it. Something deeper than a wound. And in doing that I knew I'd be beginning my own slow creep. Once again I was grateful to the thin man. I never knew his name. He's probably dead and buried now. But he showed me the future and how living took us there.

CHAPTER TWENTY-ONE

CHEESECAKE

Out of my fragility came the strength not to say a complete 'no' to Gerry the evening we both arrived in the car park at the same time. I remember there was a warm pink glow on the hills outside the city, telling us there'd be daylight for at least another couple of hours. Gerry swung his briefcase into the boot of his car and closed it with a deep clunk.

'Tough day?' I asked as I approached.

'Tough day indeed.' He clapped his hands briefly in front of him. 'But the bluebells are out across the river. Fancy taking a look?'

I shook my head and staggered an answer.

'Maybe ... eh ... Not today. I ... my sister ...'

He simply nodded, smiled and got into his car. I got into mine and shook silently for a few minutes before phoning Martha.

'I've just turned down a date.'

'You have not! Who with?'

'A fella at work. I didn't say no outright.'

'Good. What's he like?'

'Nice. I don't really know.'

'Sounds like you should find out.'

I knew she was right and I knew I would find out. But I wondered if I could manage it. Being fragile like I was, how could I get into something with Gerry? I was wise enough to know that being fragile was what living was really about. I can write this now, looking into the near past. That's what I call it. The time when I started work and I went with Tony to the hospital and they told us about the organs they'd retained and how it meant that if they returned them to us we would have to have another funeral.

Tony said he'd take care of it and he did. He must have gotten a report from Martha because a couple of days after the hospital visit he phoned me and told me what he'd arranged. We had two options the hospital said. We could ask them to dispose of the organs – his voice cracking when he told me this – and they would write to us and let us know. Or they would return the organs to us via an undertaker we named and we could inter them with Teresa.

'They didn't ask me to make a decision there and then. They said we should talk and think about it. They're trying very hard.'

'I wouldn't award them any medals for that.'

'I said we'd take her. I'm sorry, Donna. I know I should have talked to you first but I thought … I think I know how you feel. I mean, by the way you spoke at the meeting.'

'It's okay, Tony. She's our daughter. No-one's going to dispose of any part of her.'

It's become my profession, the handling of waste. I act professionally and, personally, that means I take responsibility for my own waste. I write this now and wonder at myself. At my sanity. At my hard bitter core, that can talk that way about Teresa. What kind of woman am I? The more I look back on those first months – the far past, I call it, the time when I was stripped down to the rusted bare bones I'm built from – the more I see myself as a mechanical process. I met a man, a boy really. Loved him, made a baby with him which grew to death inside me, came out of me a breathless rag doll, that left me dazed, broken and burned out. I incinerated myself.

Tony had made the right decision. I would not let anyone incinerate my Teresa. I sat looking out of the window after speaking with him and thanked him for saying, 'I'll take care of it.' At that moment, I couldn't have said that directly to him. I couldn't say how I'd be in future weeks but at that very moment when I personally faced words I faced every day at work – incinerate, landfill, bury – I was glad Tony was first to pick up the burden.

He told me he felt responsible.

'I signed it, Donna,' he said. 'I signed the form.'

'You didn't really know what you were doing,' I argued.

'Matter a damn if I did or didn't. I signed it, so I want to see it through. I have to stop running away from it. This is my chance.'

I never saw Tony as someone who would want to make amends. I saw him, in the early days of the far past, as a good man with an even temper, an easy-going, simple man who loved me and who would make me happy. I never granted him complications. But he was telling me he had run away from things. From what? From me? From us? I didn't push him on it, but maybe someday in the future I might ask: Did you run away from me, Tony?

That's always been my mother's view. She'll take it to the grave with her I suppose. What happens such thoughts when we die? Do they pass onto someone else? Me or my sisters? Do they skip a generation and will they lodge in the lives of one of Martha or Anna's children? Or will they be lost forever?

'That's my signature. Yes.'

He said it squarely to them, one-on-one at the hospital, his finger stabbing the blue biro scrawl. The pathologist raised her palms to face him and then brought them forward and down as if the air pressure might make Tony retake his seat.

'But let's just see what I signed.'

He pulled the file closer to him.

'There. That's me all right. My signature that says I agreed to a post-mortem. That's all. A post-mortem. Do you know what that is? I'll tell you what it is. It's a chance for someone in a white coat to make someone like me feel like a fool. Oh, maybe not nowadays. Maybe it's all 'patient charter this' and 'patient charter that' now, but back then, back when we had Teresa, and that's not too long ago, I didn't have a clue what a post-mortem was and nobody in a white coat explained it to me.'

I wish my mother had seen him like that. He was like the Tony I knew, but amplified.

'Oh, I know it wasn't either one of you two, but let me tell you that whoever it was should be ashamed of themselves. I'm not saying they hoodwinked me, but that 'doctor knows best' way of going on wouldn't work now.'

'But if ...' the pathologist tried, but Tony wasn't going to let her in. He drove on.

'And I tell you another thing. I might have signed for a post-mortem, whatever that is, but I didn't sign anything to say ye could hold on to Teresa's organs or any part of her. I've read the newspapers like everybody else. Me and Donna were at the meeting in the Everglades. I know you've been caught out. And it's just not good enough. Ye – I know it wasn't you two person-ally – but ye – doctors, hospitals, managers, experts – didn't have permission and now ye're caught. We're caught, too, and we're here to sort the mess out all over again.'

Once more his finger stabbed the scrawled signature. Once more.

I bought my mother a cheesecake the day I told her about the organs. She jokes that she should avoid sweet things, but that cheesecakes are not really sweets. They're more a savoury item and if it's a lemon or a raspberry one – her favourites – she can get one of her five-a-day portions of fruit. It was a lemon one that day. Sharp and clean. Moist and firm. The light falling from it, a golden glaze on our plates and forks, set my mother 'oohing' and 'aahing'.

'Where'd you get it? The Lep? They always have lovely stuff. Looks fresh, too. We'll only have a wee slice each. I had me tea already. Did you have anything? Do you want a fry?'

There's a capacity for excitement in my mother, even in her late years, that I admire and envy. Could I have that energy? See everything as a slice of cake to be enjoyed or fought for? That's it. My mother is either laughing or struggling, fighting her way through life. I can't really compare myself to her. She's done much more living than me. Felt much more. Had three children. Buried a husband. She doesn't go to his grave much now. Once a

161

year, around Teresa's anniversary. But that's for Teresa, not for my father. Martha puts his anniversary notice in the paper, not my ma. She said it was maybe time to stop it. I wonder if burying Teresa marked the end of her grieving for her husband. We both lost our husbands to death. Her to his own. Me to my baby's.

My mother knew I had some special reason for calling round with the cheesecake, so after bantering about the weather, my job, her prescription for aspirin, Martha's new car and the way students up the street were giving Mrs Holloway a hard time, she settled back into her chair, resolutely refused a second slice of the cake and stared me into stating my business. I'd made a start on a second slice. I'd need it.

'Me and Tony had a private meeting at the hospital.'

'You went with him, then.'

'Course I did. We're in this together.'

'Make sure that's all you're in to with him.'

This was going all wrong.

'What do you mean, Ma?'

'Well, he is a married man, you know.'

'Catch yourself on, Ma. It's about Teresa.'

'That poor wee girl is long gone. What business has he or the hospital bothering you now and you only getting going in the new job?'

'Oh, she's long gone all right. But not completely. Look, Ma, at the hospital we met a pathologist, a doctor who does post-mortems. She showed us a file. Tony signed a paper when I had Teresa that said they could do a post-mortem on her.'

'What did he want to do that for? Shur there was hardly anything in the poor wee creature.'

She was right. The white box under Tony's arm was as light as air and empty of all Time.

'The pathologist told us that ...'

I was going as slow as I could, as much for myself as for my mother.

'Well, that after the post-mortem the hospital held on to Teresa's organs ... parts of Teresa ...'

'What do you mean 'parts of Teresa'?'

162

'Samples, Ma, like tissues. You know, the way doctors take samples for tests.'

'Shur what were they testing and she dead?'

I was beginning to wish I had Martha or Anna with me. My mother was right. What use would all their testing be? No use to Teresa.

'They wanted to see if they might learn something that might help other babies.'

'So they held on to bits of Teresa? And Tony agreed to it?'

'It all happened—'

'The bastard. God forgive me. Where are they now? The bits?'

'I don't know. In the hospital. Tony is dealing with it.'

'You can be sure he is. Just like he dealt with you and us and everyone else after Teresa was born. He'll only look after number one, that fella. I've learned that about him.'

I wanted out of that room fast. My sisters have described similar feelings to me several times. How they love being with our mother for short periods, yes, but how they often feel like fools in terms of rearing their children, dealing with their husbands, living their lives. I felt incompetent then, as if I was in a meeting where the agenda was slipping away from me.

My sisters always love and protect me. They bought me the Buck's Fizz single for Christmas. I was eleven. Our father was dead over a year. I'd spent months singing the song *Making Your Mind Up*. I was such a child then.

I lifted a thin platter wrapped in flimsy Christmas paper. I recognised Anna's scribbled name and Martha's florid handwriting: Keep on dancing, Donna. Happy Christmas from Martha and Anna. I opened the present and four fresh, blond-haired faces smiled up at me. I couldn't believe it. My first record ever! Martha let me play it on the turntable in her room.

Anna said, 'I'll put a blond bleach in your hair if you want.'

My mother snapped 'no', but Anna did anyway, just before I went back to school. It washed and grew out quickly. I grew out of Bucks Fizz and grew up. Martha and Anna saw me right. So did Frances.

* *

I remember, during the anti-incinerator campaign, how Frances was always a stickler for setting the agenda in advance of meetings. The others would simply turn up and cobble together a list of things to be done. But Frances would get the agenda straight beforehand and then worked through in a clear way. My mother was even more focussed. She had her teeth into Tony now and she wasn't going to let go.

'I bet you if it was one of his other kids, the ones he had with Mary Stuck-Up, he wouldn't sign over anything. Too cute for that now. Going round like a cowboy Onassis buying up wee women's houses and knocking flats out of them and sticking students into them. That's all he ever was, that fella. A homewrecker. That's all he did with you after Teresa.'

She was full on. There are lines I won't let her cross, but I knew there was no point getting into an argument with her then. I wished she had been at the meeting with the pathologist and the patient advocate and had seen the way Tony stood up for Teresa.

CHAPTER TWENTY-TWO

FOX

I have samples of Tony's signature on our marriage certificate and on our divorce papers. His scrawl next to mine. Could I trace a life through such signatures? His schoolboy near-print version on the card for my eighteenth birthday. The young man's leaning letters, racing forward, on our wedding day. The older man's weary slants, when we divorced. My own signature would follow a similar trajectory, right up to now, when, at work, I sign myself with a confident flourish. I put pen to paper now with aplomb.

I remember the first time Olivia asked me to sign a document for the anti-incinerator campaign. I nearly passed out.

'Frances wants us to do it this way. It's not really a crisis meeting. Just an important one. You typed up the agenda. Put your name at the bottom. Why not? You're in the office, too. You can send it out to all the contacts. We have to get a way forward or the campaign will run out of steam.'

That must have been late in the summer of the year Teresa died. The far past. I was still married to Tony then, so I signed – I almost printed capitals – Donna Bradley. I rehearsed it a few times. Mrs Donna Bradley. Missus Donna Bradley. Mrs D Bradley. I finally settled on Donna Bradley, tried it a few more times, then committed it to the agenda page. I know why I keep Tony's name. My sisters changed to their husband's names when they got married and so did I. I see Tony's letters leaning forward into our future. Mine upright and alert. Donna McDaid, soon to be Bradley. I keep his name because that's who I am. And because I want to have the same name as Teresa. That's funny. She hasn't the same name as me. I have the same name as her. And Tony, scrawled on the permission slip in a file at the hospital. His brown-stained finger thumping the signature as if it would drive us back to that time, so he could do things differently. But we can't go back to that or any other time. We can only deal with now and tomorrow and everything tomorrow will bring. That's what he really signed. Here was the man who scrawled his name next to mine, who said, 'I'll take care of it.'

The intensity of his words moved me and I wondered at his strength and his weakness.

The Cathedral was less than a third full the day we got married. Martha sang a solo. She still has a voice. Anna sat close to my mother all through the Mass. The huge pillars and the vaulted ceiling towered over us. The priest, a trendy boy with wavy black hair and a beauty spot low on his left cheek, joked with us at the altar. Tony's right leg quivered all the way through the ceremony, as if he would burst into a run out of the big doors, which seemed to be a mile behind us. But his hand was steady when he signed the register. Anthony Bradley. A narrow 'A'. A rounded 'B', both leaning forward. My own letters tidy and upright beside his.

When I finally made myself glance at the file at the hospital meeting I was shocked by Tony's signature. Here the letters were cramped, tiny and bent away from the line of writing, as if afraid to go on. Did the loss of Teresa do that to him? We weren't the sort of people who signed lots of documents. We don't do autographs. More cheques now I suppose. He probably has agreements and contracts to sign. I have letters, memos and reports.

I told my mother none of this as we shared the cheesecake, following the one-on-one at the hospital. A silence grew between us when she realised I wasn't going to argue with her. Maybe the fact that I didn't defend Tony felt like a victory to her.

'Will you be all right, Donna?' she finally asked.

I said, 'Let's have another piece.'

Lemon, like the one wee Babygro I've always kept from my wanderings and shopping trips. Lemon with little green florets. An item of baby clothes for the first three months. White snappers along the legs to get a nappy on and off. And up the back so you wouldn't have to pull it over a delicate head. Teresa never needed it and the Babygro was never used to clothe a baby. It was simply a fire blanket for my burning self. Wrapped in light tissue paper whereon I'd written Teresa Bradley – her name, Tony's name, my name – in fragile letters that hardly dared to be seen.

Myself and my mother had another slice of the cheesecake each and fresh cups of tea. The light moved away from the window and my mother switched on a standard lamp. We sat in its glow for another while and she listened to me and was quiet, as if she had resigned herself to the second funeral, confident that I would be all right and that, even if she didn't like Tony, she'd have to go along with whatever we put in place.

Martha phoned me later that evening and I told her.

'Don't worry,' she said. 'I'll let Anna know.'

'Nothing will happen immediately. There's a fair bit of sorting out to be done yet.'

'Well, whatever you need, Donna, just ask us. Long as you're okay, Donna.'

'I should be okay. It feels like yesterday.'

'We'll have to tell the kids something. What do you think?'

'We'll figure something out. Give me a wee while.'

It's never ending. The fine threads that link us all together spread out, link up, entangle and spread out some more. I would have to find a way to tell my nephew and nieces. I would have to find a way to tell people at work.

I practised on Amra. Email is our lifeline. I have a hotmail account solely for keeping in contact with her. She's better at giving news. She even sends photos of her children and her husband. Fine sturdy children dressed in Sunday best. He's a tall man with a full smile, in a dark suit standing beside a car, readying for a family drive. A clay and wattle wall in the background. A mango tree leaning to offer shade.

Amra's emails are full of news of work, developments at Lagos City Council, plans for waste management programmes, new initiatives she is heading up. She always asks about my mother and about Martha and Anna and their children. She even asks about Tony. Sometimes she asks about other men.

'There must be one who can interest you,' she wrote. 'If not, come here to me. My husband has a brother. He is a teacher and a non-drinker. Still lively. Maybe he can interest you. If not you can come anyway. I will show you everything. Even where we dump the waste from Europe.'

She always invites me and that invitation, even if I never take it up, leads me into the future. When I reply I promise to make a trip and when I told her about the meeting at the hospital and the organs they had retained, I mentioned Gerry.

I did go with Gerry to see the bluebells, though they were almost finished. Clumps of them on slopes under the trees at the riverside edge of the park, exactly as he said. You could peer between the bushes and the trees and catch glimpses of the river on the other side of the railway line. And beyond that the grey steel and glass block of our office building.

'Anyone still at it on our floor?' Gerry asked.

'Still a couple of lights burning,' I noted.

It was a grey evening, quite dark for half five in May. There might be rain later. Under the trees the light softened even more, so that the blue of the flowers was close to mauve and the green of the foliage around them was so dark it drew what light there was to them and held it. I told Amra all this and how Gerry had passed my desk earlier that day and said, 'Last Chance Saloon, Donna. The bluebells'll be gone in the next few days.'

I said I'd meet him at the cars. Then I followed him over the bridge and into the park. Ours were the only two cars there. I had my wellingtons in the boot of the car – I always do – and I wore them as we strode off together down the path beside the hockey and football pitches. Was it an indication of how well we got on that we didn't speak? Shyness or easiness? I couldn't say. Down we walked in the direction of the river, taking a right fork in the path where the trees and bushes thin out and bank away, giving a full view across the water to the oil storage tanks and the chapel with the onion-shaped dome. A grey sky rested on the city and a traffic hum came across the river. There was an end of day, home-time feel in the air. I felt a small pang of guilt to be alone with Gerry like that, almost as if I should explain to Tony. I smiled to myself, thinking that whatever I said to Tony, this was none of his business.

'A penny for them,' Gerry finally spoke.

'Oh, nothing. Just, well, I was wondering what I would tell Tony. My ex-husband.'

'You sure he's your ex-husband?' Gerry said, feigning worry.

'Oh, I'm sure. Just I think, no, I know, this is my first date since I was married to Tony.'

'Nice of you to see it like that. Just a walk in the park as a date. But we'll have to get a move on if we want to make the most of it.' Perhaps he saw a flicker of anxiety cross my face, because he added, 'Get a move on ... with the walk, I mean. Before it gets fully dark.'

So we turned away from the darkening river and walked down the slope to the swings and roundabouts, my Wellington boots squelching on the spongy underlay put there to break children's falls. Children always fall. And old people. Martha and Anna regularly have stories about scraped knees or bumped heads. We're all waiting for our mother to fall. Anna is sure of it.

'She'll fall in Brooke Park one day, I'm telling you. We always ask her to phone us and we'll pick her up in the car, but she insists on walking. "What's the use of going in a car? Shur you meet no-one that way." Traipsing back up with her bag of goods like a widow with no family. She'll end up on the flat of her back one day.'

It was wet grass that did for me that evening with Gerry. We passed the swings and the roundabouts and began to climb the grassy slope to the upper path. Gerry was a stride or two ahead of me. I could feel my tights stretching and slipping in my boots.

I should have pulled on my work socks, too. I usually did, but haste or maybe vanity, meant I didn't this time. Gerry puffed as he reached the top of the slope and looked around, then down at me, sensed I was struggling and reached his hand to me just as my left boot slipped and I went down on one knee.

'Oops-a-daisy,' he laughed, as he pattered down to me, took my left arm firmly in his right, offered me his left and hauled me on to the path beside him. That's twice I'd let him help me and twice I'd felt okay about it. Winded a little, I checked the knee of my trousers.

'That's clean dirt,' he said. 'You all right to go on another bit? Just over along there and then down to the river. That's where the bluebells are.'

We set off again on a path between brambles and stunted oaks that grew up from the railway cutting, a wide path undulating gently like my breath. I settled into an easy rhythm, until an involuntary gasp escaped me.

'Fox,' Gerry hissed.

There she was – I'm convinced it was a she – right on the path in front of us, more red than brown, her tail a rowan bush she sailed under rather than pulled. We stood still for a heartbeat or an eternity, until a gull called and the fox turned her head slowly and in two lopes made it into the brambles above the railway line.

'There's a gift, now,' Gerry said.

He was right. A gift for us. In time to come, we could say, 'Mind the time we saw the fox.'

Maybe it was the heightened atmosphere or the way the evening crept around us, but I felt it was Halloween time, instead of late May. That it was autumn, on the verge of winter, and that spirits were about and among them was Teresa. The proof of it had passed before us. The fox was Teresa's familiar. We could wonder had we really seen it at all.

When we came to the place where the fox had been, there was not a trace of her. No mark in the tufted grass or in the tangled brambles she had passed through. Gerry peered over the fence and looked down to the railway line.

'She caught the late express to Belfast,' he quipped and I grinned. We walked down the bluebell slope to the lowest section of the path, the bramble sparse now, giving us a clear view of the river and our workplace on the opposite bank. The last nodding bluebells, held in the green grasp of their foliage, caught what light they could before sunset.

'I always like it here,' said Gerry. 'Specially at this time of year. With the bluebells.'

He paused.

'I'm a bit of late starter. Going out like this.'

It was a date. The fox and the special place made it so. Gerry showed me something of himself and I was glad of it.

Martha congratulated me when I phoned her.

'Now there's something positive to be said about going to work. Donna started a job and got a fella.'

She must have texted Anna, because she phoned me later and asked me if Gerry had tried anything.

'You know, down in the woods, like. Did he try to kiss you or anything?'

'You're reading too many romances, Anna,' I said.

'I bet he asked you to go for a drink or something,' she fished some more.

In fact, he didn't. We finished the circuit of the park, round past the running track and the allotments and then back to the car park.

'See you tomorrow,' he said as he climbed into his car. I was a wee bit disappointed he didn't say anything else, but then again, neither did I. I wasn't really worried. I knew there'd be other times. Martha was right. The job and the man somehow went together.

Anna was certain of it.

'You need to make sure you have clean knickers. New ones. For when he asks you again.'

I told Amra all about the walk and the fox in an email. How I felt that the fox being there meant that Teresa was there, too. I knew Amra would understand. For her, Teresa and her dead boy are always with us. I told her about the quiet but warm way Gerry had with him and when she replied she joked that her husband's brother would have to look elsewhere.

CHAPTER TWENTY-THREE

SET AGENDAS

The meeting I typed up, during the anti-incinerator campaign, and signed the agenda for, at Olivia's insistence, pushed my confidence hard. A stack of photocopied letters with my name on the bottom. Envelopes I addressed and stuffed. People would get this letter, read it and put a date in their diaries. Some of them would read my name and wonder, 'Donna? Which one is she? Oh, aye, the young one. She's quiet, isn't she?'

The biggest benefit I got from being involved in the anti-incinerator campaign was that it trained me for the job I'm in now. Of course all the stuff I did at the Tech and at university, that all helps, too. But I wouldn't have gone on to do any of that without the anti-incinerator campaign. I'm indebted to it, to the people in the office, to the people who came to the meetings and to the thousands of people at the rallies and protests. When I go into my office now I feel confident and capable. The campaign built that in me.

No-one ever gave me any formal training, though Olivia acted as my mentor. I remember she gave me a line to use on the phone.

'It's not the house, Donna, so you'll need a bit more than just hello.'

It was one of our edgy days, when she was really busy and I wondered if I was any use. I felt I was getting in the way. I felt like that most of the time in fact. In my own house, with my mother and my sisters. In the town even. Feeling like I was hemmed in by people in shops. Feeling like I'd better move, go somewhere else. It was nothing that Olivia or the rest of them did. It was simply me.

'Lift the phone and say Derry Development Education Centre. Anti-Incinerator Campaign. Then say hello.'

It was a bit of a mouthful and changing Olivia's words to suit myself, while still doing what she asked, helped me face the challenge.

'Hello. Anti-Incinerator Campaign at the DDEC. Can I help you?'

I heard myself putting on an accent, half-English, half-Dublin. All television. Most of the time people simply asked if Jack was there or was Frances in. If they weren't in, I was stuck and quickened into television/hotel-receptionist mode.

'No, I'm terribly sorry. Jack's not here at the present. Would you like to leave your name and number and he'll return your call?'

Someone must have said something to Olivia.

'That new wee girl, the one who answers the phone? She's very nice, but a bit formal. I thought I'd phoned the wrong number and got through to the Hilton.'

That's what I was then. A nice wee girl. Out of the confusion of my depression I was rebuilding myself from the bottom up. It was as if I was on a placement from secondary school, learning all the time, soaking everything up. The people in the campaign office were ultra-busy, creative, positive, dynamic and funny. I miss some of that now. The council office is hectic in a more humdrum kind of way. Less sparky. But the campaign office trained me for it.

After Olivia's nudge, I started saying, 'Hello. Anti-incinerator Campaign, DDEC. Can I help you?' more upbeat, brisk and bright.

And when the caller said, 'Is Bill there?' I said, 'No, he's not here at the minute. Do you want to leave a message?'

More often than not they said, 'Naw, that's grand,' or 'Tell him Melanie phoned.'

I started the phone-message book. It took me a couple of goes to get the layout right, but eventually I ruled the pages of a black hardback A4 notebook into five columns headed Date, Time, Who for? Who from? Message. There were merely scraps of paper before that. Olivia, your ma phoned: Jack, the *Irish Times* wants an interview; Frances, Lenny at the council confirms the four o'clock meeting on Tuesday.

Olivia said I should tell everybody about the phone-message book at the following office meeting. It was the only way to get them all using it she said.

It seems trivial now when I look back on it. Nothing more than red biro lines on pages in a cheap hardback office notebook. My handwritten words printed schoolgirl style across pages and pages of blank columns. Yet, by taking such timid and small steps, I came to be where I am today: Waste Management Officer, working under the Environmental Manager, in the City Engineer's Office of the Council.

There was a campaign office meeting every week. I used to make the tea for it and then sit at the edge of the circle, hugging my mug and hunching myself into a tight ball in case someone might ask me a question. Every time I did that, whoever was nearest to me would say, 'Here, push round there, open out the circle a wee bit and let Donna in. Pull in there, Donna. Pull in.' That was my salvation. People asking me to pull in.

So I did, but I'd still sit hunched into myself while the others talked about meetings, setbacks, progress, money, costs and plans in a flurry of paper, pens, diaries and notebooks.

My first words at those meetings were: 'Does anybody want more tea?' in a muted version of my television/hotel-receptionist voice. There was a chorus of: 'Aye, dead on, Donna;' 'I'll have one;' and 'Here, I'll give you a hand.' I was carving out a role for myself.

'You tell them about the message book,' Olivia advised. 'I'll make sure it's on the agenda.'

It was and I did, in a quiet, creaky voice that sounded like a girl's and made me feel awful.

'It's only a book where we can write in the messages. So if we're looking for a message we know it's in the book. Or somebody's name or something.'

'We all have to use the book. Not just Donna,' Olivia chipped in her support.

I can laugh at myself now, looking back at that meeting. I had moved from domestic (making tea) to secretarial/administrative, yes, at a very junior level, but I was developing roles. I was acting. Just as the street performers did on Saturdays in the town centre.

I saw one of them appear as Richard Needham, the British Government minister pushing the incinerator idea. Another actor gathered a crowd to ask the 'minister' questions. A third went around the square telling people that Richard Needham was outside Wellworth's and that if they wanted to ask him questions about the incinerator they could. People did. They asked questions and made points to the actor playing the minister – he wore a silly khaki trench coat and a dented trilby hat and pinned to his chest was a cardboard sign, written in red marker: Richard Needham, Minister for Incineration.

People took those clowns seriously.

'Why don't you build it in Belfast?'

'You think we're thick round here? We don't want the country's toxic waste in Derry.'

'You should be cutting down on it, not expanding it.'

'How would you like it if your kids were getting poisoned?'

The bottom line. We don't want it here, not for our children. In the campaign we took the line 'we don't want incineration anywhere'. Now, in my job, I'm not so sure I can say that any more. It's on the agenda again. Maybe it never went off the agenda. Incineration. Burning. It has another name now: Energy Recovery. It's a term that could describe me. I was learning how to recover my energy. Take the waste I had produced – become, even – and convert it into energy. Fine in theory, in practice I'm not so sure. It'll take more than simply ruling columns in a hard-backed office notebook.

* *

Let me record the day Frances came up to me and said, 'Donna, can we have a chat? Are you busy now? Maybe after lunch? How would that be?'

I had been involved in the campaign for about six months.

She always talked like that. Like she was very busy – and she was – and that she always assumed you were busy, too. I never thought that about myself. I got on with what I was doing and if someone else asked me to do something, I did that and then went back to what I'd been doing before. Usually stuffing envelopes!

Keeping to the agenda was one of Frances' strongest points. I agree with her. Wandering off the agenda is used by people to take over meetings. But when Frances asked me to chair the big meeting at the office, to keep us on the agenda, I nearly collapsed. I see now that she was right. That she was playing a long game. Like a chess grandmaster, she was always two or three moves ahead.

'Thanks for making the time to see me, Donna,' she began. 'It's just the campaign meeting coming up. You did the agenda last week?'

She meant I'd typed it up, signed it and posted it out. She and the others had decided what was on it. And that was fine by me. I was learning that, too. How I fitted in as a person in a big political event. I was no longer the woman to whom things happened. I was making things happen myself.

'I was wondering if, you know, because you handled the agenda, if you wouldn't mind chairing the meeting? Just take us through it, item by item. Someone'll take notes, Olivia or Jack, whichever one of them can make it.'

It was on my mind to say that she always chaired the meetings. Or Bill or Jack. Olivia usually took notes. She said she was the only one who could read her handwriting, so she'd do up the notes, type and circulate them. There I'd be, stuffing the envelopes, as usual. Now it seemed Frances and the rest of them wanted me to do more.

Since that day I've learned that there are always multiple reasons why people do things. Frances, no more than anybody else, has an agenda. She wanted to be free, not confined by the position of chairperson, so she could get what she wanted from the meeting. That's what I learned in the campaign. That, in the end it's the people that matter and how we think and feel and how we make things happen. How we ensure things go the way we want them to go. I was learning about power. I see that now. I'm glad of it. I'm not saying I'm suspicious of everybody. I'm not saying you can't trust anyone. I'm not saying that. That's not what I learned. I'm just saying that everybody has an agenda, even, and maybe especially, the people who say they haven't.

'I'm ... do ... you mean, you want me to run the meeting?' I stammered.

'We'll all be there. Olivia could sit beside you if you wanted. Just take us through the meeting, step by step. You'd be good at that.'

She saw something in me I didn't know I had. It suited her, but she was willing to take a risk with me. There was no guarantee I could bring it off.

Olivia was surprised when I told her what Frances had asked.

'Well, I suppose it makes sense. Sort of training you up, too. I can see that. Jack'll be there, of course, and he'll help you if you have any bother.'

I almost went back to Frances to say I'd changed my mind when I heard that. If Olivia couldn't be there, I'd be lost. I needed Olivia beside me. I liked Jack and he would support me, but I needed Olivia.

I didn't back out. I won't say I was brave. I'll say I was orchestrated by Frances. By events. Agendas. By people. No. Orchestrated is too strong a word. I was required and I began to exert my power. No longer was I a girl who went from one task to another as people bid me. I was doing things because I wanted to do them and because I could. I had my own agenda and that agenda was me.

Tony sensed something was up.

'You're a bit jumpy these past few days. You still taking them tablets?' he asked.

I must have been, but maybe their effects were wearing off. 'Course I am,' I replied. 'I might be on them for the rest of my life.' 'No, you won't,' he said. 'You're getting better, Donna. Stronger. You're becoming a new woman. I might have to start taking some of those tablets myself.'

He smiled a weak smile. He sensed something all right. A shift in power. First inside me. Then with people close. Then in the wider world. And all because I chaired a meeting, so that people stopped calling me 'a nice wee girl'.

I put copies of the agenda on every chair, in case people forgot to bring the one I'd sent out. I did them on vanilla-coloured paper. They looked professional, sharp. We were using the big room upstairs because so many people were expected. It was always like that with the campaign. It grew and grew, bringing in more and more people. This meeting, if I remember correctly, was for representatives from all the active groups across the City Council area and Inishowen. Anyone affected by Du Pont's plans to build a toxic-waste incinerator.

'Just say your name and which group you're from. And if you're not from a group, just say your name.'

My first words came out slightly funny and managed to break the ice. Olivia said tell them we'd have a cup of tea and biscuits at the end. She told me that if we had tea and biscuits at the beginning the meeting would never get started. She'd briefed me fully, but I was still shaking. My fingers clutched my copy of the agenda. I had written notes in red biro alongside the typed words. I read 'introduce self' and managed to say, 'I'm Donna. Donna Bradley. I help out with the campaign and I'm chairing this meeting.'

There was a shuffling as people settled, called greetings to one another, made remarks about the weather and the difficulties of parking, picked up the agenda on their seats and sat down. Twenty-four people, all waiting for me. Frances, Jack and Bill, from the office, were there. All the other people were from groups across the city and region. Shantallow, Culmore, Greencastle-Moville, Strathfoyle and many more. I knew some of the people and they nodded at me.

'We'll make a start, then.'

The water boiler rumbled in the corner of the room as it reached the set temperature and then clicked off.

'First item on the agenda is the next rally in the Guildhall Square. And the delegation to the council, that's the second item, though the two are connected. We'll take the rally part first.'

When I recall this now, I find it unbelievable. Did those words come out of my mouth? People glanced at their agendas and Bill spoke.

'Donna, if I could offer a few pieces of information?'

And we were away. Plain sailing until I realised Olivia wasn't there and I began to panic. Who was going to take notes? I looked at my sheet, full of my own notes and directions, exhortations to myself. Speak slowly and clearly. Say name. Say hello. I think I missed that one.

Jack twigged, signed to me with his pen and his notebook and then spoke. 'Sorry, Bill. Just to say, I'll take notes from the meeting. Just the main points and the agreed actions.'

I smiled at him and he smiled back and Bill continued and the first steps in my recovery from the loss of Teresa took a huge stride forward. I am still taking such steps, sometimes timidly, sometimes with great assurance. I am recovering from grief and loss, noting the 'main points and the agreed actions' in these pages, building a dossier of recovery in my personal life and in my life in the world.

The discussion about the rally went well. Plans fell into place. Everyone knew where they stood and what they were doing. Bill had the practical details in hand. The meeting grew awkward when we got to the second item, the delegation to meet the council. Deciding who should be on the delegation was tricky. It was about power and people bidding for it, so we could then negotiate with Power.

One man said, 'What do we need a delegation for? We'll all go to the council meeting. Or at least any of us who can make it.' There were murmurs of agreement with that, but also voices saying that wouldn't work.

Lizzie from Shantallow said, 'There's no way the council will allow that. We wanted a big group of women from our area to meet them to give off about the closing of the wee nursery, but they said we could only bring a maximum of four.'

'What are we going to talk to the council about anyway? It's Du Pont we need to be hitting. That's who's looking to build the incinerator,' a man from Culmore added.

'And the British Government up in Belfast. Not to mention the Irish one in Dublin. They all want the incinerator here in Derry, matter a damn what we think.'

'I think we should all just go and tell the councillors to get their act together and stop pussyfooting around and tell Du Pont to shove the incinerator where the monkey shoved the nuts.'

The laugh that followed these remarks allowed Frances in. She was waiting for this moment. It seems underhand when I write it like this and I don't mean it to be. She was – still is I'm sure – a very fine and honest woman. The thing is, maybe more than anyone else in the room, she had an agenda, not typed up on vanilla-coloured paper, but deeply ingrained in her heart and soul. That agenda meant she would do everything in her considerable power to stop Du Pont's plans to build a toxic-waste incinerator in our city and the primary means she would use was 'us'.

'If I could just come in here, Donna ...'

That's what she said, choosing her moment. A light comes on in my brain every time I recall that intervention. A switch is flipped and a way forward is illuminated. Choose your moment. Then grab it.

Everyone waited. The laughter subsided. Frances had our full attention.

'Lizzie's right. They'll only allow us a small number. I think they said five. Isn't that right, Jack?'

Jack nodded and scribbled a note.

Frances played us like a stringed instrument. Plucking here. Strumming there.

'The key thing is to ask what we want from the delegation and organise ourselves so we get just that.'

Amen to that, I echo now. There was a reassurance building from the sense that she had it worked out. Whereas most
of us turned up ready to do what the meeting bid, Frances was
already looking beyond the delegation to the council. Maybe
even beyond this campaign, to a wider, bigger picture I had no
inkling of at that time. I was being introduced to politics and I
reverted to the only knowledge I had of that world. What I saw
on television.

'At the end of the day, we all want the same thing,' I inter-
jected with one of the great TV soundbites of our time. In the
final analysis, based on the bottom line, at this moment in time
– I had them all. Was I really so naïve a young woman? Is that
truly me, the child chairing the meeting? Who let such a child
take the chair? Frances, the virtuoso. She played a few fine notes
on us then.

'If we could get a small group together, a working party, we
could gather ideas and put them in summary form, highlighting
our demands and our experiences to date. We've been working
hard at the campaign for half a year now, more even, and we've
learned a lot. So if we had that summarised, along with our aims
and objectives, that could be the basis of the demands we put in
front of the council.'

And the working party would be handpicked by Frances. And
from that the delegation would emerge naturally. Small moves
happen in all our lives, personal and professional. Nobody taught
me these processes at the Tech or the university, but I learned
them during the campaign.

The man who'd made the crack about the monkey came back.

'I'm only saying we should go in hard when we meet the council. There's thousands of us out on the streets, most of us paying
rates. We voted for them didn't we? It's time we got them to do
something to earn the big wages they're on.'

Tommy Dunne you called him. I haven't seen him since, though
at the time he was one of the most active people on the campaign.
Always on the rallies. Good at getting people out. Smart, too.
It was Tommy who came up with the idea of hanging a banner
over the city Walls welcoming visitors to 'Toxic City'. He was a

leading light in the cavalcade of cars that drove to the plant at Maydown and blocked the entrance for an hour. Some people were uncomfortable with that. Frances wasn't. She liked Tommy and what he did. She simply had strong ideas about where and when he did it.

'I couldn't join that working party you're on about, Frances. We have enough going on in our group at the minute,' Lizzie said, and a bump was nudged over. We'd agreed to Frances' proposal without really discussing it. I should have stepped in then and noted that. What could I do? I was the 'nice wee girl' who answered the phone. Do I remember wobbling then? I don't think so. I can speculate now that I sensed the foundations of the meeting tremble and shift, but I had been so skilfully positioned by Frances that any tremors I felt were mild. Perhaps I gripped more tightly on my copy of the agenda, even as power ebbed and flowed about me. Frances came back in.

'No, that's fair enough, Lizzie. We're all very busy with our groups and the campaign. I know you're tied up with the rally and getting the lorry and the PA sorted out, Tommy—'

Tommy spluttered, 'Well, I just think ... as long as we get stuck into them.'

Frances drove on. 'This working party is a short-term thing. I mean, I'll pull it together and we can circulate everyone so we get all views on board. Just two more people would do it.'

There wasn't a row or a debate. A woman from Culmore said she'd be okay to work on it. A man from the Bogside said he could call into the office any day next week because he was on night shift. Then a third person was added – a woman from Muff – to make sure Inishowen's concerns were included. And that was it. Frances plus three. A neat package.

'We can have a quick chat at the end of the meeting over the tea and arrange a get-together,' Frances wrapped things up. 'Shouldn't take long. When the document is completed we can finalise the date for the meeting with the council. And the delegation can deliver it on the campaign's behalf.'

Frances smiled at me and I tied the bow.

'Next item. Fundraising.'

There was a collective groan, but no-one went back to the delegation question. Frances kept smiling at me. I returned her smile, pleased to be on her team.

I can honestly say that Frances was one of the biggest influences in my life. Did I model myself on her? Become what I thought she was? Or would want me to be? I certainly learned from her, especially about how to be a powerful woman with an agenda.

She complimented me on my running of the meeting a few days later.

'You did a great job the other night, Donna. Really handled the meeting well. You should consider doing more. Maybe more of the community sessions.'

Always moving things along. Always nudging people in the way she wanted them to go. Moving pieces on the board. Playing variations on a theme she'd composed.

'That's if you have time, Donna. I know you're very busy.'

All the time in the world, Frances. All the time in the world. At the end of the day we all want the same thing don't we?

I bring Frances' influence into my work now. We're currently canvassing for modifications to the council's waste management plan. Targets for the EU are increasing. There's going to be a big shake-up of local government soon. No-one knows exactly when, but we expect to be heading up a new super-council, amalgamating two or three around us. Having Frances' influence inside me is really important, because my agenda has incineration right at the top of it. Incineration and how to stop it. Recovery will be part of the plan to stop it. My recovery and the city's.

I never socialised with Frances. Never went out for a drink or to the pictures. Of course, I was just 'the wee girl in the office' for a long time, but even later on, after I'd done community meetings on my own and met City Council officials and drafted campaign press releases, even then, there was no way I could have gone socialising with Frances. Bill, Jack and Olivia did. They asked me a few times but I said no. Truth is I didn't know how to work that with Tony. He was never happy to see me depressed; he never wished that on me. But the person I became as I emerged out of depression confused him, as if I'd gone underwater on a deep-sea dive and when I resurfaced I was someone else. Becoming a woman who chaired meetings, not being a 'wee girl' in the campaign, was a major step. Thinking about doing courses at the Tech was another. The real tragedy is that it took the loss of Teresa for me to grow into my power. I'll always feel bad about that.

I don't think I model myself on Frances any more. I think I'm my own woman now, at least in that work way. I still have a long way to go with men. I do more fantasising these days. Dreamy, romantic, misty-eyed fantasies, which I suppose are healthy enough, though they make me feel silly.

I can write about these things because I've lived through them. The cursor blinks on the computer screen in front of me, waiting. I have a glass of red wine beside me. Half-full? Half-empty? Half-full, I think. It's not there to fight fire with fire any more. It's merely a relaxer at the end of the day. I feel the wine freshen and warm me as I live a life more ordinary every day. I'm walking a hard and long road, yes, but I'm walking.

CHAPTER TWENTY-FOUR

LOVE

Tony is walking a long, hard road, too. I've only recently been able to say that to myself. In a sense I've always known it, but it took me a long time to accept it. That's down to me, but also down to him, too.

Let me look back now and try to find the day I fell in love with Tony. Maybe there isn't one single day labelled 'that's when it happened, that's when I found him and he found me, so that we fell in love and got married'. Yet he is the man I spent most of my adult life with, courted, married and divorced.

Once, in the near past, when we were planning what to do about Teresa's organs, I said he could come round to the house, that I would make him some tea.

'I'll be making something for myself,' I said.

There was silence on the other end of the phone. Eventually, I had to say his name.

'Tony?'

'Sorry, Donna. Just thinking there for a minute. I haven't been back in the house, your house, in what ... I don't know ... all those years ... I ...'

Not since the day you moved out, carrying two black plastic waste disposal bags to journey on your own long and hard road. How easily you left everything we'd built up together! The furniture, the cups, the plates, the television. The bed. Two black plastic bags and a man walking down a narrow street at dusk. Nobody else on the street but him. Walking away from me and Teresa. That's what I thought then. My mother still thinks it.

Now I'm not so sure. What was he doing or where was he going? We both struck out on roads that lead us back to each other, to junctions where we meet in the name of Teresa.

'I don't think that would be a good idea, Teresa ... I mean, Donna.'

'I shouldn't have asked. Be awkward for Mary and the kids.'

'It's not about Mary, Donna. I know you've never been happy with all of that, but Mary's fine. She's not the problem. I am. See the way I called you Teresa?'

I don't know what I feel about Mary. Jealousy must be in there. Pain, too. I don't think I was heartbroken. My mother reckons Tony got into it too fast, but I know he wanted a family and I couldn't hold him back from that. I know he's a good father to their children. I've come to know and accept that he's a good father to our Teresa.

'The house is full of Teresa,' he said. 'And, well, I couldn't face that.'

I wasn't going to argue with him, but I wanted to say, 'No, Tony. The house is full of me, your ex-wife. Our daughter is not here. She's up in the City Cemetery. Or at least some of her is. And we're going to put the rest there soon.'

'I didn't mean anything by that, Donna,' he continued. 'I know she's not there. It's your house and, well, I'd be happier if we just met like before. Over a drink or something.'

Tony wanted – needed? – to keep things between us as 'business'. Something you did over lunch. Over a drink. Maybe over dinner, but that could be tricky, too. But certainly not in our own homes. So we arranged to meet over a sandwich and we faced into another stretch of the long hard roads we both travel on.

There was no single day when I fell in love with Tony. No single period in my life when that love grew between us. I love him now. I always will. A muted, echo-love, quietly sounding deep inside me, more flicker than flame, more pool than torrent, permanent as regret, steadfast as grief. He's the man I went with when I was a girl. He's the man I became a woman with. And I don't only mean sex. I mean growing up and feeling responsible and important in myself and in my family. When I say I love him now I don't mean I yearn for him. There is a well of feeling inside me for him. The well is deep but not very full now. He's the only man I loved, and I've never been unfaithful to him. That's a crazy thing to write and me divorced from him.

I did fall head over heels in love, during my science course at university. Charles Dillon was my target. Totally the opposite of Tony he was. Tall and fair-haired, he cycled across the border from Donegal every day. He was finishing his PhD and he supervised lab sessions and ran seminars for second and third years. 'Paul Newman on wheels, just like in the film,' a third year called him. He wasn't that good looking, but when he smiled, he drew you in. I was a fish he caught without even trying. Aching tight inside since losing Teresa, battered by the ending of my marriage, running to stand still on a science course I loved but struggled to keep on top of, I wriggled on the end of Charles Dillon's line and he never even knew I was there.

'Do you ever wonder why it is you do what you do?' I asked him once.

'You think too much, Donna,' he replied, laughing.

'I don't think enough,' I said.

He was helping me with an experiment involving mass spectroscopy for metals. We had a spectrograph set up in the darkroom and I was calibrating it before looking at vanadium. It's come back into my life these days, vanadium. One of our major problems in waste management. Can't be landfilled. Same as asbestos, oils, paints and solvents, our TV sets and computer monitors. We need special, highly regulated processes to deal with them all.

'I mean your PhD is on the stars isn't it? Metals in the stars?'

'Just one star, Donna. Just one metal. I can only handle them one at a time.'

'Well, if you're going to tackle them all, you'd better get a move on. There's a fair crowd of them up there.'

I was relaxed with him, but infatuated. I had a crush on his lanky, loping walk, his soft Donegal drawl, his easy way with everything.

'One of them will do me. If I get to the bottom of how much beryllium is in Fifty-One Pegasi, I'll be doing well. There's enough going on there to keep any man happy. Enough excitement. Enough beauty.'

Is it any wonder I fell for him?

'Have you that thing calibrated yet?' he asked.

He had calibrated my heart, set my measures against his standard, so that for those moments in the lab, I was primed and ready. It gave me an inkling of the feelings I now have at work. Of being in the right place at the right time. I felt protected by him, strange because he was practically my age, maybe a year older. But I was back in secondary school in my uniform and my pulled-back ponytail and he was the science master, in his shirt and tie and tweed jacket with leather elbow patches.

He was nothing like that. He wore blue jeans and tee shirts with science logos or cartoons on them. There was one showing Einstein's flowing white locks and an error in the famous equation in a speech bubble. It said: '$e=md^2$' with the line 'I told you I was dyslexic'.

I wasn't sure if you could joke about things like that. I was still in awe of myself as a science student doing a second-year Environmental Science module: Heavy Metals, Their Uses and Environmental Impact. I was in a place far removed from my life experience, from my family's experience, from Tony's experience. Who could I talk to about this excitement and beauty? Only Charles Dillon.

When you diffract or split the light emitted from a metallic source, maybe from the heart of a star, maybe from a beam under stress, the light is separated into its constituent colours and you can tell what metals the source is made from. That's what I was doing. Diffracting and splitting light so I could analyse it.

'Do you never go home?' Charles asked me.

Why would I? To an empty cold house, because I still would not light a fire. To no-one but myself, staring into the fridge, the light playing on the side of my face in a darkened kitchen, wondering how I'd make yesterday's leftovers edible. I stayed in the labs for excitement. And beauty.

'I'll go home all right, but not for a while yet. I'll switch off everything and pull the door behind me.'

'You trying to do me out of a job?' he laughed. 'Here, let's get this thing set up so you can come in tomorrow and finish the experiment.'

I was looking for vanadium. Putting light through and receiving light from various materials and sources. Diffracting it with parallel slits or splitting it with prisms, then taking a photograph of the spectrum, a spectrograph, so I could compare it with standardised samples and identify vanadium, if it was present. I had a notebook under a desk lamp next to me, ruled off in columns for my own records, which I later transferred to a computer. I'm a big fan of ruled columns!

Charles Dillon humoured me. I think that's it. I never knew if he had anyone, a wife or a partner. He always seemed singular. Like me. Of course, I can imagine him now, in Sweden, where he went to do postdoctoral research at the University of Lundt. I can imagine he stayed there and worked his way into a teaching and research post, a lectureship. That he is now married to a Nordic beauty who cycles to the crèche she runs with their own blond baby boy bouncing in the cart she pulls behind her. They have a white and gold pine-built house on the edge of a lake. Even when he is at home, Charles can look at the stars, because he has set up a telescope on a wooden jetty. There is a small boat tied to the jetty and in the northern dusk, Charles Dillon rows it out to the centre of the lake where he can fix his mind on one star, before rowing back to shore, seeing his wife – Irina, I name her, though she looks like a blond version of me! – at the window of their kitchen, the last rays of the evening sun burnishing the glass around her.

I am as prone to dreaming, imagining, speculating as anybody else. There's a comfort in it. A sort of pained longing I can control. It's a technique I have developed. Create a fantasy to stifle a memory. I never see Tony in imaginings like that. He's in my life in a real way. But Charles Dillon is that part of me where yearning goes.

'Do you think you'll ever know everything there is to know about Fifty-One Pegasi?' I asked him.

'No. In fact, I hope not. What would I do then?'

Of course, I looked it up and found that 51 Pegasi is a star like our sun and that it has a planet beside it called Bellerophon, after the Greek hero who killed the fire-breathing monster, Chimera. Such food for my fantasies!

'You're looking for vanadium, aren't you?' Charles asked.

He always brought conversations back to work. Easier to deal with. Or maybe he was so interested in the science that he didn't need anything else. For a while I thought I could be like that, too. I had a fantasy of being a research student. In the labs for the rest of my life. But he was in pure science and I'm in applied. I prefer it that way. I like the stars and the elements, the gaseous masses and nebulae, but I want the rivers and the lakes, the mountains and the wind and I want them toxin free. Clean and white like the floors in the house where I imagine Charles Dillon steps barefoot towards his loving wife. The Nordic blond version of me.

That night I set up the vanadium spectrum experiment with his help I lined up light sources. I selected prisms. He suggested I use a diffraction grating to give me a comparison. I took his advice and that was probably what got me a distinction for the assessment of the module. I'd shown initiative and experimental flair.

All I wanted was for someone like Charles Dillon to put their arms around me and hold me close. I wanted to be in his constellation of Pegasus, to be his Bellerophon, the Greek hero held in his orbit. The system he studied and analysed intently. Is that what I want from love? To be an object of such attention? How frail I was! How needy! I'm sure he sensed that and it exerted a forceful push away from me. There was never anything going to happen, except my adolescent fluttering.

I had coffee with him once, after which I experienced a mixture of elation, at the pleasure of capturing a slice of his time for myself, and dismay, at the fear that it would go no further. I was sitting in the Students' Union café with two other women from the course. They were younger than me and they tolerated me as an eccentric mature student who didn't know how to kick back and have a laugh. They rushed off in a flurry of hurried remarks.

'I have to get that lab report written before midday.'

'Ach, Donna, have you handed that in already?'

'Do you never sleep?'

I smiled and said no, and they weren't sure I was joking. I wasn't. They left as Charles Dillon arrived.

'Any of you seen Mick? Mick Loughlin? He let that electromagnetism experiment run too long. I had to turn it off.'

Mick was in our class. We all said we hadn't seen him. I hardly saw anybody, moving through the days at my own pace, not attached to anyone or anything except my own schedule. Twenty-three people in my class, nearly a hundred in Second-Year Science. All round me, in the way tropical fish swim in a tank. Multicoloured, visible, active, but not seen by one another. Feeding and procreating, active and busy. But ultimately alone or in small packs of two or three.

'I may as well have a coffee, then,' Charles said.

I was on the point of returning to the library, but I added milk to my cup and said, 'Aye, you may as well wait here. Mick'll turn up.'

I hear myself flirting with Charles, like an overly familiar schoolgirl. What notions or plans I had I can hardly bring myself to remember, because when I do they make me cringe hard.

I told him I got a distinction in the Metallurgy module.

'The practical side pulled me up because it was weighted more than the written assignment,' I said.

'Well, you certainly put in the hours in the lab.'

'It's no bother to me. I've nothing else to be doing.'

Ask me out, please! Just for a drink, I silently begged him.

'And what are you on to now?'

'I'm kind of up-to-date. I've written up my lab reports and handed them in. That's what has those two diving. I'm thinking about revision for the exams.'

'Fair play to you,' he said as he stirred his coffee. 'Have you any plans for when you qualify?'

'I was thinking about research maybe. But there's still another while to go.'

'That won't be long passing. I can't believe I'll have over four years done on this PhD when I wrap it up in August.'

'And will you be back here after the summer?'

'Probably not. There's no jobs coming up here as far as I can make out. So I reckon I'll be hitting the road.'

He put a bit of a Yankee twang into the end of that sentence.

Take me with you, Charles Dillon, I almost blurted out. Take me with you, on our own Route 66, across the wide plains, the searing deserts, the fabulous Badlands and on to the vineyards of our very own Cal-i-for-ni-ah!

That was one of my lowest years. As far as everyone else saw things, I was flying. I'd whizzed through the GCSEs, the STEM Access Course at the Tech and the university's Science Foundation Programme. Miss Jennings said that if I wasn't careful I'd win the Nobel Prize for Chemistry. I had made the transition to university without a hitch and sailed through the first year with good grades.

Martha was ecstatic.

'You're the first person in our family to go to university, Donna. I'll be hammering that into my weans, I can tell you. Look at your Auntie Donna. If she can do it, you can do it.'

She bit her tongue just in time and added, 'I didn't mean it like that, Donna. You deserve it. You work hard. But, I just ... you know. Look at where you've come from.'

I didn't have to look. It was always in front of me. I came from the bottomless pit that was Teresa's grave. I was never far from the lip of it. In that second year when the strain of pushing to get that far began to take its toll, when some of the newness of my life had worn off, when the lack of deep personal resources began to be felt, I reached for the stars and Charles Dillon. But neither they, nor he, ever knew.

'I'll take a run to the States in the summer first,' he said. 'Do a bit of cycling. I've work lined up on a camp for gifted kids at the University of Chicago. I'll be applying for research jobs for the autumn. See what happens.'

He was lost to me and found his own Valhalla in Sweden. I hope he's well, living the life I dream for him. I reached for the stars, yes, but I finally chose the debris of all our lives, the detritus of the whole city. It swirled before me in the sandwich sauces on the plates between Tony and me when we met to plan the second funeral. There is no way for me to dream my life away from that. I could work and plan, but always the waste I made my first moves away from would swallow me up.

It didn't take me long to cool down on Charles Dillon when I got back to the university. I went straight to the labs, where I felt the heart of the course was. The senior lab technician told me.

'We lost Charles, Donna. We'll have to get ourselves a new pin-up boy. He's away to Sweden, if you don't mind. But shur he'll miss us, won't he, Donna? Lots of cold sleepless nights ahead of our Charles in the far north, eh, Donna? You have a good break?'

I wasn't surprised. I wasn't even disappointed not to have heard from him directly. For all my fantasising, I wasn't a fool. Besides, losing Teresa prepared me for all the other losses I would face. The really big one is going to be my mother. Sometimes me and Martha talk about it. I'd never have a chat like that with Anna. She's more caught up in her own life. I think Martha is more comfortable talking about such matters. In dark moments I wished my mother wasn't around to see us bury Teresa's organs and tissues. I don't wish that now and I'm more prepared for what may come. I'm not sure Martha is.

'I hope she has no pain, Donna,' she said. 'Like, whatever happens to her, that she has no pain. That she goes quickly.'

'Wise up, Martha. She's in top form. She's not going anywhere.'

'I know, Donna. But we have to think about the future.'

Martha, like everybody else, is scared about the future. She's worried about what will happen. I'm not. I'm worried about the past – about what did happen – and about how it rears up on me again and again.

CHAPTER TWENTY-FIVE

THE BIG WHEEL

A pattern developed in the meetings about a second funeral. Tony would text me a possible venue and time. I would text back and agree. Whoever got there first ordered the sandwiches and a pot of tea for two. Oh, happy domesticity! I never kidded myself about that. I never fantasised about getting back with Tony. I'm not saying we couldn't have made a go of things, if we hadn't had Teresa. But I do wonder. If we could be so completely blown off course like that how could we have survived other challenges that might have come? Now we faced another one.

'I'm scared, Donna,' Tony said. 'Really scared. You must be scared, too.'

'Course I'm scared. But there's no way we're backing out of this. Just tell me where we're at now.'

I was treating it like a work meeting, which in a sense it was. Burying Teresa for the second time was one of my major projects then. That and the roll-out of the new recycling blue bins across the city. Plus making sense of the EU's Vanadium Directive and how it applied to us. And liaising with Waste Management Officers in other council areas to work up our regional waste management plan. I had a list of projects and if it helped me to see the burying of Teresa's organs and tissues as one more on the list then that's how I was going to approach it.

'I have Bradley and McLaughlin lined up to handle it. The undertaker I spoke to was very helpful. Knew what I was dealing with. He said they'd done other ones. He went over the options, but we knew them from the hospital and he said that if we wanted to have a funeral, that they could handle it no problem.'

Fair play to them; if they could handle it, 'no problem'. I admire that. People who wouldn't flinch to face the hard days, who could walk to the lips of the graves and not be scared. We'd need people like that, me and Tony.

'And do you think they can handle it? Do you think they know what they're doing?'

Tony nodded and it rushed through me that we could simply give it all over to them. Let the professionals deal with it. We'd be busy dealing with ourselves.

'Well, then, tell them we want them to do it. Talk to the Pathology Department and all. Tell the undertakers we want to keep it simple. Nothing fancy. And we want whatever the hospital gives them to go down with Teresa.'

And my father. We never even discussed that. We were dealing with unfinished business, something we should never have had to deal with, so the best we could do was keep a rope around it, keep it corralled into the times far past.

Everything is then and now. Everything is happening all the time.

If I knew anything about myself and the journey I was making in the world, I knew it was essential that I didn't go back to being a victim. I was slowly carving out a life for myself, burrowing like an earthworm in the compost piling upon me.

If I could survive this heap, I could survive long-term, by making something of my life. This second burial could not be allowed to knock me backwards. But I wasn't prepared for the possibility that it might do that to Tony.

'I know what you mean, Donna, but it's not going to be simple. I spoke to the undertaker. They have to open the grave again.'

'I know that, Tony.'

'And we'll all be standing around and there'll be prayers. It'll be just like a funeral, Donna.'

Of course it fucking will. What did you expect?

I didn't actually shout the words. They simply bellowed inside me. My hand shook as I lifted the teacup and voices around me rose to a throbbing hum. Family matters, work cares, television highlights, love, lore, football musings. I'm glad I didn't let the roar out of me. Was I getting stronger then, because I didn't cry out?

Tony continued. 'I'm scared I won't be able to carry it off. When it comes to it, I won't be able to ... stand there.'

Beside his new family. In front of my mother, scowling at him. In front of the rest of our families and some of his friends. In the midst of the gravestones that rise up the slope of Creggan Hill and overlook the sweep and bend of the river Foyle.

It's always windy up there, even on a summer's day. How can you pick a good day for a funeral? A good day to reopen your daughter's grave?

'You stood there before, Tony, and you'll stand there this time.' I took a deep breath. 'We both will.'

He smiled and reached his hand across to pat mine, resting on the paper napkin beside my plate. It was a diffident, awkward gesture and he pulled his hand back quickly and coughed.

'I'll just go out and ...'

He gestured with his other hand to let me know he needed a cigarette. My fires were internal and dampening down. Tony's were all about him and flaring.

I never really grew out of Tony. I don't think I ever will.

When Tony came back after the cigarette, I offered him more tea, but he said he'd had enough.

'I was just laughing to myself, Donna, standing out there with the fag. I was remembering the time we went to Barry's Amusements in Portrush.'

'What brought that into your head?'

'I don't know. We had some good *craic*, Donna, didn't we?'

'Don't go all sentimental on me now, Tony,' I said lightly, but I meant it.

'No fear of that. You were all excited going up on the train. There was a gang of us. It was before we were married. Just a day out in the sun. You said there was no way you were going up on the Big Wheel.'

I smiled at him, doing my best to hide my puzzlement. I had absolutely no memory of ever being in Barry's Amusements in Portrush. And definitely not on a big wheel. I couldn't see myself on a swing in the park, never mind on the Big Wheel.

Tony grew animated.

'I was slagging you and saying, "Come on, Donna, you're not scared, are you?" Oh, I was the big fellow. I remember running on ahead. I must have been seventeen or eighteen. We all ran from the train station. Old fellas and old wans had to jump out of our way, nearly dropping their ice-creams all over the street.'

He paused then, letting the memories crease a smile across his face. He pulled his seat closer to the table and his voice grew hushed, intense.

'When we got to the Big Wheel and joined the queue, you were still nervous, giggling a bit, pushing along with the rest of us until our turn came and we scrambled into the moving seat. You remember that, Donna? The wheel never stopped. It kept going and you had no choice but to jump on. Your sandal caught and fell off but the fella running the machine threw it in after us and, Jesus, we were laughing. You were busy trying to get your sandal back on and I was telling you to sit back so we could pull the safety bar into our stomachs. You had no time to be scared then. You just closed your eyes and pulled the bar right back when you got your sandal on. The wheel rose up and our little seat swung on its pivots. Well greased they were. I remember that. Up we went and then backwards until we reached the highest point at the very top of the wheel. They do it to everyone, not just us, but when our seat stopped and started swaying up there, I thought it was a mistake. I was sure something had gone badly wrong. "Mammy," I called out in a wee boy's voice that didn't sound like me. You opened your eyes and laughed. I looked over your head and there was only the sea and the sky and no clouds and nothing. Just nothing as far as I could see. The thing juddered and I said, "Ah naw!" and I thought I was going to be sick, throw up the cans I drank on the train. You put out your hand and grabbed mine and we started moving again, backwards and down and I was all right. While the wheel did a few more loops, backwards and forwards, you held my hand. And you never even squealed.'

I smiled and nodded, pretending to see myself there, but all I had were his pictures. I had no memories of my own. Does that mean it never happened? Or that it did, and Tony was with someone else? I don't think so. I don't think he went with anybody else at that time.

'I always remember that, Donna. The way you never squealed. I mean the way you never told the rest of them what I shouted out.'

The way he looked into my eyes that lunchtime told me. I might not be able to identify the moment or the period when I fell in love with Tony, but he had revealed exactly when he fell in love with me. Like the turning of a flock of swans, moving forward across the sky, an instance of recognition occurred and the chevrons realigned, as the great V-shape of them banked and they moved on, stronger, clearer.

I couldn't remember the incident or the day, so perhaps I never did actually fall in love with Tony. It was more a seeping than a falling. More acquiescence than assertion. I'm not going to blame him for that. I've written that I still love him and I know that's true. It's the feeling the petal has for the stalk, the leaf for the twig. Bound to one another forever, maybe existing only because we have each other and at the heart of that existence is a grave, one we were about to claw open with the bare hands we used to clasp about each other.

'No need to be scared, Tony. We'll be sad, but not scared. Whenever it comes, the two of us will be standing there and whatever you do or say, I won't squeal.'

I let him take care of it. He said he would. I was clearing the ground for him to have a closer run in. From the positive way I'd seen him at the one-to-one meeting, I picked up a sense that this was his time. That he needed to take the burden of putting the second funeral together. I was right beside him, but well out of his way. I saw us at the lip of the grave again, like the first time, only the wheel had turned many times since then. Me and

Tony are still in our little swinging seat, the safety bar still tight across our laps, with the sea and the sky and the nothing going on forever around us.

CHAPTER TWENTY-SIX

REMELLURI

A s soon as I got the job at the council I bought my little Fiat. Had to, though as an Environmental Scientist, the irony of running a car, even a small one, while trying to cut down on waste, hits me every day. I try to walk to work as often as I can, but most days I need the car for work visits. It's good to walk, now that the riverside path has opened right in front of the council offices. There are always people on it, enjoying the ease the river brings and the lift you get from seeing a shag skim over the surface or gulls dip and flock together. Sometimes, there are even swans.

I often get a bit of shopping at the end of the river walk at Sainsbury's. Something nice for the tea and I keep my wine stock up. A glass a day is good for the health they say. It seems Miss Jennings has the same idea. I met her at the wine shelves during the period when Tony and I were planning Teresa's second funeral.

'You supping with Bacchus now, Donna?' she said, coming up behind me.

Her sister – I recognised her from the meeting in the hotel – was beside her, pushing a trolley of goods. I had a basket, with a few items. Sliced ham. Cheese; cheddar and feta. A lettuce. Three tomatoes. I do a full shop about once a month, usually with Martha and Anna. We amble down the aisles, with our big trolleys, consult lists, keep tabs on the children, select, pick and add to the trolleys, all the while keeping up the banter and the gossip. Anna calls it 'therapy for sisters'.

But that day I was on my lunchtime walk along the river, to grab a few items in the supermarket – essentials like Rioja!

'If Bacchus wants wine, he'll have to buy his own,' I quipped at Miss Jennings and she smiled. Her sister smiled, too, or rather her smile brightened slightly and never actually switched off.

'Dinah and I like a little glass with our dinner every now and then. Medicinal, of course. Don't we, Dinah?'

And the smile beamed brightly.

Miss Jennings continued. 'This is Dinah, my sister.' Then she raised and slowed her voice. 'This is Donna. She was one of my best students at the college. She's gone on to be a scientist herself.' And to me, she added, 'Dinah and I watch all the science programmes on television, especially the nature ones.'

Still the smile shone, lighting up Dinah's face. She was younger than Miss Jennings, sixty to her sixty-five perhaps. Her unlined face and glad eyes made her seem childlike. Miss Jennings is her carer, looking after the sister who is capable enough, but ever so slightly vulnerable. It shames me to write that I wished Teresa had been given to me like that. I could have cared for her, even if all she had was a radiant smile.

I took Dinah's hand and we shook briefly. Her hand was cool and slim and felt like a refreshing cream had been caressed into it.

'A glass of wine with the dinner is always a good idea. Gets me through the day,' I said.

'Dinah, will you get us two bottles of that flavoured water? The one you like. It's around that aisle there,' Miss Jennings said, pointing.

Dinah hesitated and the smile darkened slightly until Miss Jennings continued, 'That's it. Take the trolley. I'll wait here with Donna. Two bottles, now, mind.'

The smile returned as Dinah pushed the trolley between us and moved away.

'She can do most things herself. Just needs a little bit of encouragement every now and again. It's good for her to do things on her own,' Miss Jennings explained, and then she asked, 'Did you and your ... did you have a meeting with the hospital?'

'We did.'

I let out a long sigh.

'It was, well, a bit traumatic, but Tony, my ex, he was very good. Stronger than me, really. We got through it.'

'I'm not sure I did. We had the one-to-one meeting they offered. I didn't bring Dinah to that one. I shouldn't have brought her to the public meeting in the Everglades. But Colin was her brother, too. She picks up everything, you know.'

I remembered the baleful gaze on Dinah's face as she looked up at Miss Jennings, standing to ask the hard questions we all wanted answered.

'And what did you decide to do?' I asked.

'Oh, we've done it. It all happened so fast. I agreed we'd take the organs back. Adairs handled it for us. The Reverend Hamilton was wonderful. Everyone at the church. It was all, you know, so ... fast.'

'I'm sorry. I ...'

'I only hope Dinah goes before me. I couldn't have her deal with ... I allow myself dark thoughts, Donna, as if I could play God, may the Almighty pardon me, but I can't believe he would want things this way.'

I know from my own pain that you can never tell when it's going to surface in your day. At work, hanging clothes on the line, watching a soap on TV. Here, by the wine shelves in the supermarket, Sting on the Muzak, not many shoppers around on a quiet Tuesday lunchtime. Miss Jennings was shaking, struggling to control herself as she said, 'I hope you'll be all right, Donna, whatever you decide to do.'

'We've decided on another funeral. We want to do what's right for Teresa.'

'You're very brave, Donna. Very brave. So is your ...'

'Tony.'

'Tony. Yes. Tony. Sorry about that.'

She paused once more and began rustling in her handbag, slung like a satchel on a long strap over her shoulder.

'I thought I was brave. I even thought I was over it. But burying him again, it was just wrong. It made me think I had wasted my entire life. Working and being busy. I should have paid more attention. Should have paid more attention.'

I didn't expect such a show of weakness, so much vulnerability, as we faced the wine labels: Rioja Gran Reserva La Sabrosita; Old Vine Garnacha, Calatyud; Rioja Reserva Remelluri; Berberana Reserva. The supermarket exploded silently around me and opened into a great bazaar where I prowled about in sunshine laced with hail showers, seeking sustenance and succour. The simple act of holding a bottle of red wine took on the weight of centuries, centuries of toil, of grubbing in the earth, fretting over weather and disease, of yearning for ripeness and a harvest. I believe that's all we want. A harvest in our lives. A harvest in our world. Fruition, even though that fruition, as the story of Jack and the Nut told me, brings death.

Teresa did not die at birth because I did not give attention. I was young, but I was fit and able and the mite that stole into my womb, the blemish that came into my daughter and spoiled my harvest, came from far away in time. The real far past. Lurked about me until it found a way to cleave itself to my egg, maybe to all my eggs, to deprive my daughter of sufficient life to smile or push a shopping trolley round an aisle to search for bottles of flavoured water. Tony and me trod the bazaar and filled our hampers and our bags. The dealers were ourselves and each other. Our hopes were the same. Could we replenish our larders for comfort and the future? Or would we prowl barren onwards?

'I'm not brave, Miss Jennings,' I said, echoing Tony. 'I'm scared I won't do it right. Scared I'll let Teresa down, like I did before. You're right. We have to give attention. All of us.'

Miss Jennings found her handkerchief and dabbed her eyes. When it seemed like she'd composed herself, she began to blub fully.

'That bridge is so high, Donna. So high. How long must it take a man to reach the water? Our Colin, he never ... we never ...'

The tears fell from her, her cheeks glistened and I didn't know what to do. What words could I say? What gesture could I make?

Dinah saved us. She came back via the aisles behind us, from the opposite direction she'd gone, her smile more radiant than ever, surprising and delighting us.

'Oh, Dinah!' gasped Miss Jennings. 'You went the long way round. Oh, and you got the Pepsi, too, I see.'

Dinah creased her brow and lifted the two bottles of fruit-flavoured water, showing them to her older sister.

'Perfect. Apple and blackberry. What's that one? Citrus rush. Sounds wonderful. Okay, we'll take the Pepsi, too. What teeth we have can suffer in silence.'

Let's not do that, a voice inside me bellowed. Let's not suffer in silence. Perhaps it was the tension of the time, but I remember, a number of different occasions, exhorting or chastising myself, hearing a voice inside. A demon or an angel, I was never sure.

'That lemon looks good,' I said to Dinah. 'I might get one myself. I always liked lemon.'

'I'll take this Gran Reserva. It'll give us a break from the Pepsi,' Miss Jennings said.

I had a glimpse of their lives then. Two nearly elderly sisters, one caring for the other. Two vegetable lattices from the oven. Potatoes and broccoli for the older. Pasta and tinned corn for the younger. Two comfortable armchairs with sturdy side tables attached and glasses of Rioja (large) and Pepsi (small) side by side like acolytes. In front of them the bushy-eyebrowed David Attenborough detailing the mating habits of stick insects, while the subjects themselves contorted and elaborated their limbs into slow-motion Meccano sculptures.

'Could you come, Miss Jennings? I'd like you to come,' I blurted out. I almost added 'for old time's sake'. What I really meant was 'for the sake of the science'.

In case I confused her I added, 'When we have the day for Teresa.'

'I'll come, Donna. If you want me to.'

I nodded hard as she rummaged in her handbag again to find pen and paper to give me her phone number. I have that number pinned on the cork board beside me in my little study, her name, Edith Jennings, underneath it, in a pristine hand.

'Better get back to the shopping, Donna. Come on, Dinah. We're only halfway down this list,' and she flapped a white sheet of paper in front of her, a flag of surrender to the necessity of shopping in the face of the awfulness of life, her sister smiling as she eased their trolley past me.

I stood there and thought once more about weakness and strength. Miss Jennings was a rock and a tower of strength to me when I was at the Tech. When the portals of science were cracking open, she stood beside me and pointed the way. I will always be in her debt for that. Seeing her frailty brought me even closer to her. She ceased to be the distant goddess who had set me on the path of knowledge and righteousness that led me away from the grave of my daughter only to find myself back there once more, scared but determined not to be beaten down or alone.

I chose the Remelluri. Pricey but necessary. I'd need the heat of Spain's vineyards coursing in my blood before I walked with Teresa again. I put the bottle into my basket, feeling its reassuring weight draw my arm down and I made my way to the checkouts. I saw Miss Jennings and Dinah in the cereal aisle passing boxes into their trolley. I was well ahead of them and knew I would be clear of the supermarket before they approached the tills.

I don't sit in front of nature programmes on television. I sit upstairs alone in my little study. Or in the sun-roofed extension to my downstairs room, reading science books and magazines. The rain patters on my roof as I sip the sunshine of Spain. And I rest.

As I walked back to the office, my bag-for-life swinging easily in my hand, my thoughts were full of Miss Jennings and her sister, Dinah. I wished them well and I vowed I would phone her when Tony got the details sorted, if only to break the rhythm of dark thoughts that might lead her to murder and to suicide.

CHAPTER TWENTY-SEVEN

BOSS MAN

The afternoon following my encounter with Miss Jennings and her sister, I couldn't settle. I brought up the document I'd been working on: *North West Regional Waste Management Group: Draft Modifications to the Waste Management Plan.* It needed an edit, not much, an hour's work perhaps. Fine-tuning, that's all. I couldn't get into the shimmering screens of bullet points, graphs and comment boxes. I had a hard copy on the desk beside me and I pulled out a drawer, took out a pencil sharpener, dragged my bin towards me with my foot and began sharpening a pencil. A hard read with notes in the margin is what I planned. I could do that much at least. I watched the slim curls of wood and lead limp off my yellow Faber-Castell 2H. Tiny slivers of wood and graphite that built into a little pile on the edge of an empty box that had contained stapler clips. A pile of pencil shards formed, each one clinging to another, on a precarious slope. One more landed and tipped the lot over the precipice of the edge of the small cardboard box and into the bottom of the waste bin. If Gerry hadn't turned up just then, I would have sharpened that pencil to a stub.

'Mr Robinson wants to see you. Your name came up in a meeting I was at this morning,' he said.

'You're talking about me behind my back now?' I answered.

'Only in a good way. Seems you're working wonders with the blue bin roll-out. He might be going to nominate you for Wheelie Bin Queen of the Year.'

'Just another award to go with the stacks I already have on the mantelpiece at home,' I quipped.

'You'll have to show me sometime.'

I let that hang, the phrase 'don't push it, Gerry' bubbling up inside me. He sensed it and moved past my desk saying, 'Robinson will probably send you an email. He's dead efficient.'

So he is. Paddy Robinson, the Environmental Manager, my boss and mentor. He's the man who took me under his wing during the sandwich year part of my university course. He's the one who told me there could be a job coming up in the unit and that I should keep an eye on the newspapers. He's the one who shook my hand when I started in that job, pointed me at my desk and said, 'Welcome back, Donna. It's good to have you on the team. Prepare yourself for a full frontal attack of work and then more work. Here's your desk, your little island of drudgery. Make it a fortress. Abandon all hope here.'

For an engineer, he has a great line in flowery language, full of military allusions. He brings a squash player's competitiveness to the job. Lean, fit and old school, he wants things done right and done right now. Some people find him difficult to work with, but I like the fact that he wants results and he'll always be the man who said to me, 'Donna, I'm glad you got this job. You're the right person for it. Never forget that, no matter what happens. Now, settle in, do your probation and get on with it. Don't lift your head above the parapet until it's time to collect the pension.'

Because he's my line manager, I see him at least once every day. I report to him, because it is my job to do what he needs done. I had that figured out from the sandwich year and when I got the Waste Management Officer's job, I simply pinched myself and got stuck in. Everybody in the City Engineer's Office welcomed me. I suppose they were delighted that 'the devil you know' got the job. But I was definitely 'Paddy's girl'. I knew a bit about how such offices work, from the anti-incinerator campaign. They make television programmes about it now and I'd read articles in glossy magazines in doctors' waiting rooms. 'Office politics' they call it. Paddy is brilliant at it and I'm a fast learner, so I watch him closely. I soak it all up, because if I'm going to survive – and that's what I bloody well intend to do – nothing is ever going to creep up behind me again.

Hence my wary reaction when I opened the email from Paddy that day: 'Donna, drop by this afternoon. I need to check something with you.'

It felt threatening and I suppose, like any junior in a big office, I panicked. I pulled out my diary to see if there was a meeting or deadline I'd missed. I'm meticulous with dates. Everything goes into the big A4 page-a-day hardback diary I lug around like an infant. I line off a column on each page and I put in dates and deadlines, using blue, black and red pens. People probably think it's childish, something a twelve-year-old schoolgirl would do until she finally realises that she's in secondary school and that the other girls are laughing at her. I keep to that system because a) it's all I know, given that I left school at sixteen; and b) it's a way of keeping on top of things. For someone who is permanently scared, that's important.

I wasn't scared of Paddy Robinson as such or of the roll-out of the blue bins. Or the consultation document on modifications to the regional waste management plan. I was scared of myself. So I ruled columns in my diary, with different coloured pens, I sharpened my pencils and lined them up in neat rows, I cocked the monitor of my computer at my favoured angle, checking each time I sat down to it. I wore the same type of trouser suit, dark blue, sometimes with a faint pin-stripe, shirts and blouses of a lighter blue. I wear blue because Anna says it's a good colour for me and I trust her on that. Everything I did, said, wore and thought was about being in charge, being in control. Of me.

That's what threw me about the unexpected command to call into Paddy's office that afternoon. We were due a regular weekly meeting the next morning. I thought of phoning Gerry to ask if anything had happened at the earlier meeting that might give me a clue. I could have emailed Paddy back asking if it was anything in particular, but the afternoon was moving on and there wouldn't be time for that. Besides it could seem like I was putting him off.

Tony rang as I was gathering my diary, setting my computer monitor at my desired angle, lining up my pencils and pocketing blue, black and red pens.

'Hello. Waste Management Unit,' I said.

'Donna, it's me. Tony.'

'Tony, yes. Look, I'm diving here.'

'Yeh. I ... just something has come up and we need to have a chat about it. If—'

'Tony, I'm going to have to phone you back. This isn't a good time.'

'I know, Donna. I just—'

'I'll phone you later. Tonight. On your mobile.'

I pushed him away. Yes, I can record that now. Maybe someday I'll have a real conversation with him. One where we don't talk about Teresa or funerals, but we talk about ourselves.

Even as I write, I sense that it will never happen. I can't go back and repair things. New physics may speculate that Time is circular or elliptical. That we live in zones of permanent present. That other zones of Time, past and future, nestle one inside another. There may be worlds out there, among the stars being observed by Charles Dillon and his colleagues, where the future is behind and the past before. But for my life, I can't go back, even to small moments like this brusque phone call with Tony. I can't go back and repair it. I didn't even think I would say 'sorry' later. I probably did, but how does that repair the moment?

Instead I carried the stress of his phone call into my boss' office. I'm not good when unknowns stack up around me. There's a fillet of salmon in the fridge downstairs now. I know I will cook that tomorrow. I want everything in my life to be like that pink salmon. Known. Present. Under control.

I tapped on Paddy's door and he called me in. He has his own office, one of the perks of middle management, at the end of the open-plan room the City Engineer's technicians, administrators and officers occupy. Other middle-management offices line a short corridor to the door marked City Engineer, where our head, Eddie Green, works.

Paddy's office has no view. Two high windows let in a grey light that falls on his desk, covered in waves of reports and documents. There is a computer workstation to one side and a colourful, whirling screen saver passing the time in mute display. There are charts on the wall, including a year planner Paddy amends and updates with great flourishes. But even he can't go back through time.

'Ah, Donna. Sit down. What do we know about Eptoron?'

He might as well have asked me what I knew about the gaseous composition of the third star to the left of Ursa Major. He sped on as he usually does.

'We had the monthly City Engineer's meeting this morning. Top brass and a squad of civilians. Routine enough. Blue wheelie bins going well. Our paper warmly received, by the way.'

He has a way of saying 'we' and 'our' when it was really 'I' and 'me'. The wheelie-bins paper was all my work, but he presented it as ours. I stayed shtoom, knowing he would go on again, feeling like I'd been caught out somehow.

'I tried googling them, but that turned up nothing. I might have the wrong spelling. I'm not even sure I picked it up properly. Lots of static in the room and I only managed to get one ear tuned in.'

I could picture the scene. The meeting breaking up. Councillors, managers and officials moving into pairs and threes, little caucuses, wherein banter and trivia could be enjoyed, snippets of information could be shared and overheard.

'They run incinerators apparently and they're moving to set one up here. A commercial deal, though Coleraine Borough Council may have an angle on it. I only heard half of it. A couple of councillors were talking about it. Do we know anything?'

I was still paddling furiously under the waterline, a duck in an oil slick.

'I couldn't say—'

'When was the last Regional Waste Management Group meeting?'

Paddy knew exactly. Such dates shine out of his year planner, like beacons on the foggy Foyle. I fumbled backwards in my diary.

'You were at it. Last Tuesday, wasn't it? No-one said anything about an incinerator for Coleraine?' he continued.

I found the meeting entry in my diary. Nothing exceptional there. Notes towards a new draft of the consultation document I was working on. A date for a follow-up meeting. Nothing about an incinerator being built by a neighbouring council, fifty kilometres up the road.

'Make a few inquiries will you? Nice and discreet. Need-to-know level. We don't want to be blind-sided by something like this, especially with the reorganisation of councils coming up.'

Paddy's concerns are always political. How to position himself as the moves and changes come, so he can survive and prosper. He loves the intrigue, the tiny chinks of light that slip out of the box of tricks we're all looking into.

For me, the possibility of an incinerator up the coast rang alarm bells. I know it's always on the agenda, as the thin man in the café correctly said. But I didn't, like him, think I'd need a gun. Not just then. I'd need a spade and a searchlight to dig out what I could.

'Give me what you have,' I said. 'I'll get back to you. Might be tomorrow, now.'

The duck in the oil slick, paddling furiously, but coming across calm and in control. I sat with my black pen poised over my diary and wrote as Paddy recounted what he knew. I made notes and said, 'Leave it with me.'

I was getting good at it. Not quite intrigue, but certainly masking. Acting. Paddy saw the efficient, organised assistant, who would clarify a query and provide him with the information, the ammunition, to carry on the battles he was fighting. I was like jelly inside, caught by not knowing and by the proximity of incineration. If Coleraine could build one, why not us? We're the biggest, most populous council in the region. The one with the most waste. If an incinerator could be seen as a necessary, even a prestige, piece of infrastructure, why shouldn't we have it? I felt I was being tossed back to the dark days of the far past. Maybe I couldn't turn back time, but someone could. It wasn't that I couldn't go back to earlier times. I wouldn't have to. The far past – Teresa, the burning waste, the funerals and the in-cinerator – was welling up around me again. Flames I thought I'd doused were licking round my ankles. A pyre was building under me once more. All I could do was act like I knew what I was doing, get out of my boss' office and plunge myself into some cooling unguent. Where would I find that? Instead of unguent, I went for coffee.

I was sitting at a window seat in the canteen when Gerry came along.

'Can I join you?'

He sat as I nodded.

'Three swans went up there this morning,' he said.

I looked at the river, grey as school knitwear, corrugating in the breeze. I looked at him, turned to the window, showing me his fine profile.

'You don't often see three,' he continued, then laughed lightly. 'I wouldn't want you to think I do nothing but look out of the window and study passing birds.'

'You could do worse,' I said.

There is no salve but time. No balm but living. No unguent but the press of days and being in them. Alive. But while it's happening, living is relentless.

I had barely returned to my desk and focussed on my breathing, tweaked the angle of my computer monitor, when the phone rang. It was Tony again.

'I know it's a bad time, but the receptionist said you were in the office, so look, can I ask you a quick question?'

I took two further deep breaths.

'Go on.'

There was pause and then Tony asked, 'Do you want a priest?'

The deep breaths burst out of me and I laughed so hard people at other desks looked over, some frowning, most smiling. I put up my hand in apology and to acknowledge that I hadn't cracked up, as Tony continued.

'What? Donna? You okay? What was that?'

'I'm grand, Tony. I'm grand. Just a bit off balance.'

I shouldn't use that phrase. Tony's not as bad as my mother and my sisters, but like them he wonders if I'm tottering on an edge all the time. A pile of pencil sharpenings waiting for one final shard to knock me back into the abyss.

'Off balance?'

'Caught on the hop. The boss pulled me in and brought up something I maybe should have known about.'

'Just tell him he'll have to pay more for miracles. He can't expect you to have everything at your fingertips. You're not in the job six months yet.'

And I wasn't. I was still on probation then. I could still have lost the job. Lost everything. In trying to be helpful, Tony was in danger of making things worse.

'Don't let him screw you, Donna.'

I got my hand across my mouth just in time, before I let out another burst of laughing. Tony was on a roll, sweeping from religion to sex without missing a beat.

'Nobody's going to screw me, Tony,' I managed to say. 'And I'm not going to screw anybody. More's the pity.'

Tony got it and stuttered, 'Sorry, Donna. I didn't mean—'

'And I don't want a priest. It's only an issue at work.'

'It's not for you, Donna, or your work. It's for Teresa. For the funeral.'

It was my turn to stutter.

'Tony, I can't … this is not—'

'Only I remember talking to you one time about God and that and you said you were gone off it.'

At what point in those days would I feel that things had become too much? I suppose the fact that I never went back on the tablets tells me that I didn't get too low. I haven't had any since I started the Tech. The odd powder for a cold, that's all. I replaced medication with education, my drug of choice.

Tony was giving me a choice. I guessed what way he'd go, especially with Mary and their children. And I thought of my mother and of Martha and Anna and their families. We were doing this for all of them. Unfinished business, that's how I saw it, forced upon me by medical science. I was going to see it through, even though I knew it would take more direct rituals, ones that didn't require the mediation of priests, for me to find rest.

'Of course we'll have a priest. But we don't have to have a Mass, do we?'

'No, just prayers. Prayers at the graveside.'

Where else would we have them? The right place for them. At the graveside, with the wind rushing up from the river Foyle and chasing our coats about us, even on a June day, in the early summer sun, swifts and swallows swooping above the gravestones, joyful on their return from Africa, finding their summer homes once more.

When I got back from work that evening, I was weary. I was weary at the end of many days in that period. I bought my dinner from the local chip shop and I opened a Remelluri, took a deep draught first off, even before I'd kicked off my shoes, then a slower glass with the chips and battered cod. I guess I slept well after that, though most nights I didn't. Most nights, I stand at the lip of the grave, muttering the old prayers.

CHAPTER TWENTY-EIGHT

THE DEL

Tony made all the arrangements for the second funeral, as he said he would. I sent him a card afterwards, thanking him. I sent it to Carpet Deals, where his brother, Larry, and himself are based. I marked the envelope 'personal'. He phoned to thank me.

'You didn't have to do that.'

'I know. I just wanted to. I mean, I can say thanks to you—'

'You did. At the Del, after, when we were having the soup and all.'

'I just wanted to write something down. You know, I put it in my diary: Send Tony a thank-you card. I put every bloody thing in that diary. I even have two marks for the wheelie bins; a black one and a blue one. Every Friday has either a black or a blue X on it.'

'You're better organised than me. I have everything in my phone. If I lost that I ... I don't know. Larry lost his last week and it was like we'd have to reinvent the wheel all over again. Right back to scratch. Back to rubbing two sticks together for fire.'

'Did he find it?'

'Course he did. He sort of loses it – the phone I mean – about once a fortnight. It was under the seat in his car. Along with a skip full of other stuff. Anyway, I just phoned to say thanks for the card. I was glad to get it.'

He deserved it. A simple card with a simple lemony buttercup on the front cover, 'Thank You' in lacy writing on the soft, white paper. It took me two or three goes to compose the message inside. I almost abandoned it. I wasn't sure if I should send it. I didn't want to foul things up with Mary, his wife. I'm awkward around her. I prefer not to meet her. It's not anything she's done. It's all me.

She came up to me at the Del, on the day we buried Teresa's organs, after the lunch. Tony organised that, too. Hearty vegetable soup, sausage rolls, wheaten bread, tea, coffee, orange juice for the children, all laid on. Some people bought drinks. We had the function room at the back, away from the main bar and the restaurant area. It started quiet enough, but soon developed a lively buzz. The younger children climbed on and off the little stage. The older ones sat quietly on the dance floor, playing computer games. The adults sat around in small groups chatting, keeping an eye on the young children. I was with Martha and my mother. Anna and her family were at the next table. When I went to get a coffee refill, Mary, Tony's wife, approached me.

'Thanks for the lunch and for inviting me and the children, Donna. Howya doing at all?'

I nodded and managed to say, 'Tony arranged everything.'

'Oh, he's been very busy all right,' as if he'd been neglecting things at home. Then she caught herself. 'But only right. Only right. Yeez both have done a great job. Handled it very well.'

She put her cup under the flask of coffee and pressed the button. A gush of coffee came out, filling her cup, and then the flask spluttered.

'Must be empty. Was it coffee you wanted, Donna? Sorry, I didn't mean to take—'

'You didn't,' I said. 'You didn't.'

Lines of a deep frown pressed on her eyes. Frustration? Embarrassment? Grief? All I felt was awkwardness. A member of staff came up, a woman in a white shirt, black waistcoat and a name badge. Teresa. I remember her as small and a little stout, with a stud glistening in her nose.

'More coffee, is it?'

She lifted the flasks to try them, took two away saying, 'I'll get fresh ones. Give me a minute.'

Would Mary and I be able to stand there another minute? It could have gone either way. Broken up in fumbled separation, or continued in a frozen panic of what to say next.

Her daughter Sinéad came up to her and tugged at her dress. Mary put her hand down and touched her head. The child didn't want anything, simply to be with her mother, who was talking to the woman she'd seen standing next to her daddy at the grave. Then Teresa returned with two full flasks.

'Here you go. Everything else all right for ye?'

I should have answered, but I couldn't find the words. Mary lifted a fresh cup and said, 'You wanted coffee, wasn't it, Donna? We're grand, I think. Everything was lovely. Thank you, Teresa.'

'No problem, Mary. Just give me a shout if you need anything else.'

Mary handed me the coffee she'd poured and said, 'All the best, Donna. All the best.'

Then she took little Sinéad by the hand and led her across the dance floor, shushing her all the while, the wee girl leaning into her and I imagined her asking, 'Who's that lady, Mammy? Why doesn't she talk?' Mary saying, 'She's just sad, Sinéad. Just sad, that's all. She'll be better in a minute.'

As they reached their table, Mary stumbled as Sinéad got under her feet. She managed to hold the cup and saucer she was carrying, then spoke sharply to the child. Sinéad huffed away from her and flounced into a chair facing towards me, crossed her arms and glared.

I looked at my coffee and decided I'd had enough. Enough of the day. Enough of the child glaring at me. Enough of being me. I was as angry as Sinéad. I went briskly to Martha and had a word in her ear. When she made to turn and dissuade me, I put my hand on her shoulder and held her in her seat.

'Just say I've gone to the toilet.'

I picked up my handbag and made sure not to catch my mother's eye. I didn't look back as I headed for the exit. I felt Sinéad's glare following me, though I hoped someone or something might distract her. I walked through the foyer, past the toilets, and straight out into the car park. The cool June sunlight bounced off the windscreens and a light breeze ruffled the neighbouring house's hedge.

That must be the end of it, I thought. It must be over and by all my efforts I would make it be over.

Then I saw Teresa, the barwoman. She had a clipboard and stood with a man in a driver's uniform, beside a large red lorry. His colleague was passing flasks down to him, which he was arranging on the ground beside stacks of soft-drinks trays. They were bantering and joking. Teresa signed a delivery receipt, took her copy and laid the clipboard on the floor of the trailer.

Small and a little stout, with a stud glistening in her nose. In full control of everything she did. Teresa. Not in bits and pieces in a hole in the ground where we'd left her two hours earlier.

Tony made all the arrangements but I paid my share of the costs. Half. I was clear with him on that. From the very start. Partly due to the way I have become meticulous. I didn't fully appreciate that until I started writing here. I have become my own experimental subject and these are my lab notes.

Money was the final thing we talked about on the day Tony remembered calling out on the big wheel at Portrush.

'Fifty-fifty,' I said. 'I want to cover my half …'

'Don't worry about it. I have ple—'

'I know you have plenty, Tony. I know you do.'

He lives in one of the big houses built on a field bought from St Columb's College. Maybe he and his brother were the developers. They're part of the new changes in Derry. Maybe, cruelly, as in my case, losing Teresa was a good thing for Tony. It's a view you could take if you saw him talking on his Blackberry, sitting in his Audi saloon, wearing a smart green jacket over a cream shirt. I've never seen a tie on him, except on the day we got married. He looks exactly like what he is. A successful local entrepreneur who got in at the start as the ceasefires came on and the peace process bedded down. Costs would not be a problem.

'There won't be too much to cover. I mean, there won't be a big crowd. The Del said they'd stand soup and sandwiches for us, so I let it go at that. No point in having a sit-down meal.'

'Make sure you thank them for me.'

'Absolutely, Donna. Absolutely.'

Tony connected in the town. Tony's local bar and restaurant standing us lunch. A valued customer and associate. I imagined Tony there, with Larry, his brother, nursing pints at the end of another day, before they went home to their families, where they would be fed, entertained and loved. There's a bitterness in me about that. Perhaps an aftertaste of what I feel about my father, the boy who never grew up. I couldn't say that about Tony. He lives in a real adult world where your business friends pull you out, where a punt on a horse at the Curragh with your brother is the only risk you'll take all day, where handling the arrangements for your daughter's second funeral is another turn of an old wheel. At least you have a wife to cling to, even if you can no longer call out for your mammy.

'It's basically the priest, the undertakers, a couple of cars. We won't need a hearse. I'll take care of that.'

My mother and me travelled in one of the hired cars. Mary and her children travelled in another. Tony brought the small white casket on the passenger seat of his dark green Audi saloon, the seatbelt strapped across it. No. Not yet. I'm not going to write that yet.

The money. I gave him a cheque. Pay Tony Bradley. I phoned and got a figure off him, after some pushing. He didn't want it.

'Give it to the Hospice,' he said. '*Trócaire* or somebody.'

'I'm giving it to you,' I insisted, implying that if he wanted to pass it to a charity, that was his business. This was ours.

'You in town tomorrow?' I asked.

'All day, on and off.'

'Meet me in Fiorentini's for a quick coffee at quarter past nine. I have to be in Coleraine at half eleven.'

When we met in the quiet café, two black coffees in front of us, I pushed a white Manila envelope towards him, the cheque inside. Pay Tony Bradley. At least a part of it. That's what I was doing. I had certain debts, most of them I could never repay, so it became essential for me to pay the ones I could.

Tony pocketed the envelope without a word. He wanted to be past this part. I was with him on that, but not so sure about how we'd manage it. We sipped coffee in silence until Tony finally said, 'You're off to Coleraine, then?'

'Aye. I've a meeting there at half eleven and I want to catch a few other people. Easier to go up there and do it all face-to-face rather than by phone or email.'

'Over the mountain road, what, forty minutes?'

'Something like that. Maybe an hour for me, taking it handy.'

He shifted in his seat then, coughed into his hand and came out with something that had been with me for weeks.

'This could be the end of it, Donna. Could be. I mean, the end of you and me meeting like this.'

It was too serious to make a joke about, but I still managed half of one.

'The gossipers will have to find something else to go on about, though you and me having breakfast in Fiorentini's is providing a late flurry of material.'

Staff settling in. Three men in clay-covered boots and hi-viz jackets tucking into full fries and mugs of tea. Sonny Fiorentini whistling *Finiculì, Finiculà* as he prepared the deep-fat fryers for the day's fish and chips. No-one was interested in a man and a woman quietly stirring coffee, a brother and a sister perhaps, taking a chance to face mutual concerns. An elderly parent wandering into Alzheimer's. A sibling who needed financial help. A house deal gone belly up. Me and Tony could be facing all or none of these at the same time.

We had escaped from the grave of our daughter for the second time and though it was he who said it, I was thinking it, too. This meeting could mark the end of us. Maybe that's why I sent him the card and wrote the lines I did.

Tony, you made all the arrangements and I thanked you. But I never really thanked you. I never really said that I'm glad it was you who sorted things out for us. For Teresa.

She's always ours, Tony. We made her and she made us. When you carried her, you carried me, Tony, and I'll never forget it.

Good luck to you and Mary and the kids.

Good luck, Tony.

Donna.

Like I was signing off forever. Waving goodbye from the deck of a grand liner. Saying *bon voyage!* as the cruise ship pulled away from the dock. Like I was sailing to Italy, to Naples and Rome, resplendent in the pictures on the wall of Fiorentini's.

'You're right, Tony. This could be the end. But we won't know that.'

'I suppose not.'

We are living through the great unforeseen, in swathes of Time. We are passing through the events of our lives to create the histories we never guessed we'd have.

He shifted in his chair once more. Something was bugging him and I didn't know how to help him get at it, so I stayed silent. Eventually he managed to stammer it out.

'Were you happy with the way things went on the day? I ... you know if ... I ... I did my best.'

'You did, Tony. Always.'

'Only, you left all of a sudden. From the Del, I mean. I saw you talking to Mary and Sinéad and then you were gone. Mary said you seemed all right. Quiet, like. But I told Mary you were always that. Quiet.'

CHAPTER TWENTY-NINE

KEENING

I drove my car into the traffic and turned left, away from the city, leaving the funeral lunch behind me. Let them figure it out I thought. Let Martha protect me. For one brief moment I considered going back to work but I'd booked a day's leave, so I was clear. I'd told no-one what was happening. I'm sure people knew. We live in a small city and word gets around, especially about something as unusual as a second funeral. I know that, in general, people are sensitive and that a code of quiet operates for such delicate matters. People talk, yes, but quietly and not in the presence of the victim. Curiously concerned though they were, I wasn't giving anything away.

The traffic thinned as I left the city. The last of the new round-abouts negotiated, I crossed the border into Donegal and another country. No markings at the crossing. A monument to dead soldiers and civilians at the old British army checkpoint. A run-down customs post on the Irish side. The hills and countryside opening out to become Inishowen.

This journey is for now and for all time. It is a journey I frequently make. In time to come I may bring other people but since that first day with my mother, I go there on my own. The view I was heading for is the one captured in the photo on my desk at work. The little harbour. The white surf. Yellow furze dabbed on the hillside. An open sea and maybe on a clear day a hint of the Scottish Isles. A far land.

I did consider swinging round to the back roads, maybe stopping at *An Grianán* hill fort to catch my breath on my way home. But an ancient pull dragged me along as I caught glimpses of Lough Swilly on my left, where I saw little boats moving among inshore oyster beds and the purple hills, above Rathmullan, on the other side, resting one upon another, climbing away from me.

My homing instinct was drawing me to the other, eastern, side of the peninsula, so I cut inland, heading northeast into the open wilderness of bog and mountain that echoed my life on that day. Of course I was running away. Running away from the people in the Del Bar and Restaurant. Running away from the soup and consolation. Running away from the grave.

The route I chose took me through the isolated hills and glens of the Illies, under Slieve Snacht, where small patches of snow high up as late as April told its name. This was a cold June day as if summer was hesitating. I climbed out of the glen, looking back at the dammed lake, my little Fiat chugging up and down the gears, not even a tractor to trouble us as we rose to the high ground that gave the view that always gladdens my heart: the sea, the island of Inishtrahull and the headlands at Culdaff and Glengad, basking in a dappled sea light. My mother's home place.

There was one other car in the car park behind the dunes, but I saw no-one. I struck out up the path through the marram grass and caught my first glimpse of the beach where oyster catchers flitted to and fro at the edge of the running wavelets. I regretted not bringing my warm coat from the car, as the sharp breeze caught me. It's a place that never lets you forget that it rests upon the north Atlantic. It's a place that brings me solace.

I concentrated on my footing, bracing myself into the cold breeze. I arrived at the *caldragh* and saw the kneeling figure, so suddenly there that I stumbled and let the air out of me in a muted 'oof'. A man in a heavy black overcoat knelt for a moment or two more on the flat grass in the clearing among the rocks and then gingerly raised himself off his knees, blessed himself and pocketed his rosary beads in one practised movement.

He had a newspaper folded on the ground where he knelt and he reached down for it, tucked it under his arm before turning to face the sea. I saw his dog collar then and recognised he was a priest.

'You must have forgot your coat. That day'll skin you, my child,' he said.

It skins me all right, that day and every day, but the writing of it is a kind of easing lotion. The 'my child' confirmed he was a priest, in his seventies, with a tanned face and grey hair slicked back from his forehead.

'I had to borrow this coat from Father Donaghey in Bocan. He's going round in his shirtsleeves. I can't get heated. Blood must be thinning. Too long in Los Angeles, Father Donaghey says. He wants me to retire back here. I haven't told him yet, but there's as much chance of that as of Donegal winning another All-Ireland. Were you at the funeral? I didn't see you. We gave her a great send-off. Ninety-four and not a blemish on her soul. How many of us could say that, even in this place? Flock of sinners in my parish at home. Good people every one of them. Not easy to get the head around that at times. Do you want the coat? Here, I'll give you the coat for a minute. You must be perished.'

'No, I'm grand,' I said. 'I'll not be stopping long.'

'I'm sorry if I disturbed your visit. I … well, I come here whenever I get home. It's holy ground you know. Maybe not consecrated or blessed, but holy all the same. I'm not sure Father Donaghey would approve of me saying that, but even if you tell him he'll just tut-tut and raise his eyes to Heaven.'

'I won't tell Father Donaghey. I don't even know him. I'm not from here. I have a great-aunt buried here.'

'You have my child. You have,' he said in a gentle affirmation that warmed me. He asked me no questions about what I told him, because in the instant of our meeting in that place we went beyond details. He had just buried his mother. I had reburied my daughter. We would never meet again.

No doubt he's dead now, deep in a plot in the sunshine of southern California, tended by Mexican women who lovingly remember their Irish priest.

'A place like this could tell some stories,' he continued, echoing my mother. 'But then again, every place could, I suppose. It's mad to think we're all special, unique as they say, and yet we're all the same really. Not easy to get the head round that either. Ach, we only think we know the world. Did you ever hear tell of the Selkie?'

And then he told me the story of the seal and the young girl. He said it was his mother's favourite, because it had a Scottish connection and it was handed down in her family, the McFaddens. We stood in the green clearing with the breeze cutting through us. When the images of the seal diving in the sea were spoken, I felt icy water run in my veins as the heaving tide of loss and grief.

This is the story I remember the priest telling that day. He told it for his dead mother. And for Teresa.

The Story of the Seal Woman

A fisherman called McFadden lived in a thatched cottage on the headland above the small harbour. One day, he was out with his nets and he knew by the weight of them that he'd made a good catch, but he was surprised to find it was not mackerel he had, but a seal, with long, flowing, fair hair that reached to her slim waist where a line of fish scales began the single fin tail she swam by. He got her settled in the boat and calmed her crying until he brought her ashore and up to his cottage, where he removed her tail and hid it high in the thatch so that she took legs and human form. She lived with McFadden as his wife and they had a lovely child, a girl, whom they both cherished. And their lives were happy, though each evening, as the sun set in the hills behind them and threw red flames across the metallic sheen of the water, the woman would sit on a rock and tears would fill her eyes as sea creatures called to her on the wind from beyond the breaking waves.

The girl grew strong and hardy and by her sixth year she was running and climbing everywhere on the headland and down in the harbour. She kept asking McFadden when he would take her out to sea with him, because she said she loved the sea and longed to go out there. He told her he would take her but not yet and he made her promise she would always stay with her mother whenever he went out fishing.

The girl filled with energy and curiosity. She delighted to see her father's boat pull out of the harbour and move past the rocks to the open sea where he would cast the nets, so she decided to climb to the ridge of the thatched roof to get a better view. And what a view she had! Her father in his little boat, cresting the waves at the mouth of the bay and moving into the open sea that rolled on and on forever.

She stood up then to get a better view as the little boat dipped behind some rocks and the thatch gave way underneath her. She slipped down and down, sliding along the straw of the roof, dragging her mother's tail clear of its hiding place to land hard on the packed clay of the yard. Her cries brought her mother running. She took her in her arms to console her, all the while staring at the tail her daughter's fall had returned to her.

When the child was quiet, the woman took her inside the cottage and laid her on her bed. With gentle fingers she stroked her daughter's hair until the child fell asleep. Then she took the tail and walked to the little harbour where she put it on and changed her form once more and returned to the sea.

When McFadden came home in the evening he found his daughter still asleep. The track of her slide in the thatch and the pieces of straw strewn about the yard told their own story.

The girl woke up and looked for her mother and when McFadden said she was gone she was distraught and began wailing. Almost at once the sea creatures called back, a heartfelt keening rising from the bay below them.

McFadden lifted his daughter and carried her down to his little boat, where she calmed. He rowed them out of the bay, cresting the swelling tide as he rounded the rocks to reach the open sea. There, on flat rocks, a group of seals called to them and the lead one flapped forward and called joyously. McFadden paused the boat and his daughter stood tall in the prow, calm now, watching and listening to the seals, who dived off the rocks and swam towards the boat. Around the boat they swam, underneath and behind, a streak of fair light flying behind the lead one as she cruised under the boat before surfacing and calling one last time. The girl reached out her hands and McFadden thought she would plunge into the water. But she stood resolute and the seal flipped over, her black form knifing the water as she dived and dived and dived.

From that day forward, whenever McFadden went to sea, he returned with full nets, so that himself and his daughter never went hungry.

The oyster catchers flew off when the priest finished the story. Clouds banked over Dunmore Head and the breeze freshened.

'Looks like the rain's coming,' he said. 'You get a touch of it nearly every day round here. In LA, now, we hardly ever get it and when we do it's a kind of grey sludge that might run off a ditch at the end of blighted potato field.'

'The mother never came back?' I asked.

'I guess not. She never forgot them though. Never forgot the wee girl. Always nourished her.'

Like I nourish Teresa. At least my memory of her, like the girl in the story, part human, part fish out of the waters that grew and swirled inside me for nine months.

'I'd better be getting back before Father Donaghey sends out a search party. If you're the praying kind, say one for me. If not, all the best anyway.'

I certainly wasn't going to pray there and then. The wind cut through my cotton blouse and tore at my skin. I'm not sure if I'm ever going to pray again. This priest with his wondering and his stories might have drawn me to it, but I doubt if he had the enthusiasm required for saving souls. Perhaps his host, Father Donaghey – who seemed to be made of sterner, local stuff – might have a go at it. Or even the pinched face younger man who laid Teresa to her second rest.

He was the one who'd come to me when my mother had asked that a priest visit during my depression. He's the one, sleek-cheeked and innocent then, who I'd frightened with my impression of female biology gone wrong, whose blush lit up the room as I darted past him to the toilet and whose embarrassment confused and scared my mother even more. If I remember him now it is because of the priest on the dunes, the storyteller in the *caldragh*. I can't yet write about the image of the priest droning at a shallow grave. But I will. I must, if I am going to make this what I want it to be. A full telling. The complete story.

The Los Angeles priest moved off, tucking his newspaper tightly under his left arm. He didn't look back but strode across the top of the dunes like a hooded crow. He stopped and faced out to the sea, then descended the dunes inland to the car park and out of sight. The wind was strong enough to cover the sounds of his car departing. Strong enough to make me waver on my feet. I wouldn't stay there long. Just long enough to acknowledge my great-aunt Eileen buried there and to focus on the briny, cold solace the place brought into the deepest part of me, so that, despite the bitterness of the wind, a tepid comfort grew in my stomach, like one sod of turf glowing on a bed of ashes, determined to give heat even as it burned out.

When I got back to my car, I turned the heater on full blast and sat for ages listening to my teeth chattering above the whirring of the fan. In those days I spun from great heat to great cold, and all with one cause, one effect. Teresa.

My phone rang on the passenger seat beside me. Martha checking up on me.

'You all right?'

'Freezing, but fine.'

'I'm in the car park at the Del here. It's breaking up. Just a few stragglers.'

'Good.'

'Anna's got Mam. I have to take Aoife to dancing. I told Mam you went home to sleep it off. You did, didn't you?'

'Yeh,' I lied. 'I went home.'

Like the seal woman. Back to the sea where I felt at home, away from my human form and my human family, back among my own kind, the singular ones with the half-human, half-fish children they never forget, but continue to nourish even from the deep crevasses of the floor of the ocean of grief they inhabit.

I told Tony I was happy with everything, the day I passed him the cheque. And I agreed with him.

'Yes, Tony, that's right. I'm always quiet.'

I could have added, 'But if you listen carefully you can hear me crying, a low keening you'd hear at an old funeral, a noise the wind would make, coming far across choppy seas, to sound itself amidst the caves and flat rocks of an island shore.'

CHAPTER THIRTY

THE ICE WALL

From this vantage point in my life it's easy for me to be wise. I can lay events on a timeline, infused with the wisdom – and I'm not sure wisdom is the right word – of hindsight. So many crises and pressures ran in my life at the time of the second funeral. I space them out, one before, one after, the other. The view I have of them is through an ice storm. Sheets of dangling ice hanging from the air freezing me and blurring my vision.

Paddy asked me to investigate what our neighbouring council was planning with incineration and that struck right at the heart of my own moves. I know that linking my personal recovery with waste recovery is irrational at the core, but when was I ever rational in this? What I do know is that recovery, my own and the city's, is central to everything.

The cold infused me at that time, an ice block in my stomach, another behind my eyes. My fingers and toes turned blue and brittle. I took hot baths when I came home from work, immersing myself in water that came scalding from the tap, but that soon grew tepid when it met the ice floe of my body and my mind. There were days when I wondered if I'd need to go back on medication, this time some form of rub like the Deep Heat my father used to plaster on his calves, sore after playing football. I put a blob on my hand once and rubbed my palms together.

The burning heat pierced them like nails. By the time I got out of those evening baths, blue-toed and blue-nailed, goose-bumped and pimply, I needed Deep Heat all over.

The press of the working day kept me going. I remember I went to the Borough Council offices in Coleraine after meeting with Tony and handing over the cheque. I got the information Paddy Robinson, my boss, wanted and I gave him a briefing.

'It's Estoron, not Eptoron, like you said. Big incinerator company, head office near Brussels. A couple of Coleraine councillors were at an EU thing over there, met Estoron and have come back all fired up about it.'

'No worries, Donna. I will pardon the pun,' Paddy cracked.

I let it go.

'They tasked some of their waste management people to work up a paper. Feasibility, location, economic impact, environmental impact.'

'Political impact?'

'I'm not sure if they're covering that.'

'The Waste Management Officers mightn't be, but you can be sure the councillors are. Did you get a sense of the views of different parties in the council? What does their mayor think?'

'She's Ulster Unionist, keeping her powder dry at present, apparently. As are all the rest of them.'

'Typical.'

'Understandable. Anything that might mean jobs and comes under the banner of 'development' is not going to be easy to oppose. We saw that here with Du Pont.'

'How long have you been in this job now, Donna?'

'Just six months. Six months next week, in fact.'

'Well, this clinches it. I'll be writing your 'end-of-probation report' and it'll be on Eddie Green's desk by the end of next week. It'll say: Hold on to this woman, retire from the field of action and clasp your pension to your ample bosom, Eddie, because she'll be looking for my job – and yours – very soon.'

I must have at least smiled. Why wouldn't I? It's what I wanted. I couldn't say it was what I always wanted. I never knew that. I don't know if I had a vision like that, something I always wanted. I know I had no sense of my desires in the days before Teresa. I can't remember being on the Ferris wheel with Tony, a memory that is vivid for him because it's what propelled him to marry me. But I can say I am where I want to be in terms of work. Perhaps there are other areas of life I want things from. But having my boss confirm that I had successfully completed my probationary period must have, at least, made me smile. Perhaps it didn't, because I remember my boss changed gear and got out of his chair, as if action was needed in the face of my coolness.

'Yes, well. Back to the Coleraine thing,' Paddy said, striding round his desk to stand in front of his year planner. 'Let's see if we can put this in the bigger picture. Mustn't ever forget the bigger picture.'

It's one of his stock phrases. That, and 'in the real world'. He uses them all the time. I must have stock phrases, too, verbal tics that identify me. Maybe I haven't been at this game long enough to develop any.

I picture Paddy at the annual conference of Environmental Managers in the bar of a hotel, at the end of the afternoon session. Delegates are boisterous and loud, delighted to be able to speak after being lectured for two hours on the topic of *The Waste Management Team in the Local Government Setting: Challenges and Opportunities.*

'In the real world, and you fellows know what I'm talking about,' Paddy offers to the clutch of colleagues gathered round him, drinks in hand, 'the key figure – figures, if you happen to be big enough to a have a couple of them, like yourself, Ian' – drawing a laugh from his mates – 'but no, we all know that the key person is the Waste Management Officer. The very centre of all our operations and stratagems. Now, take the woman in my office, Donna. She's a bit of a cold fish at times. Pleasant enough, but she's not going to light up the room. But, I tell you, if she gets her teeth into something she really goes for it. In detail. Lets me focus on the bigger picture. Which is what we're about. Right? When's dinner?'

Murmurs of assent, wrists flicked to check watches, one or two catching a call on a mobile phone, a nod to the barman who comes to take an order and Paddy Robinson at the heart of it. As I picture him like that, there's no way I'm looking for his job. But I have made enquiries with the Chartered Institute of Waste Management and I might go about membership. Take a few professional diplomas. Paint my own bigger picture. That day I stayed with Paddy's.

'There's two ways this could go. Maybe more. Coleraine, already on the offensive, cracks it. Brings in Estoron, EU money, swings the local population. Cross-border money, too, because the South needs this sorted, too. I presume we're talking toxic waste here?' he asked.

'Yes.'

'And location?'

'Nothing confirmed yet, but a coastal site is being considered. The mouth of the Bann river maybe.'

'Which gives us the second way it could go. Scuppered. The yachting fraternity'll never buy that. Which might work in our favour.'

His office is small, but he managed to pace. Three steps to the left towards the door, then a swivel and back three steps to the edge of the desk in front of his year planner.

'We're better placed to do it. And, politically, we're probably in a stronger position than they are.'

'But we don't want an incinerator here, Paddy,' I almost shrieked.

'We certainly don't want an incinerator in Coleraine. If they manage to steal a march on us with this one, it'll make it tough when the rejigging of local government comes up. As it most certainly will, sometime in the next five to seven years. Eddie Green might be on his pension by then, but I won't be.'

What Paddy didn't appreciate that day was the powerful urge inside me never to have incineration in our area. Never to have it anywhere. The frozen core of me echoed the molten lava of my heart when we first buried Teresa. I would push away anything that would take me back there. I was an Alpine climber on an ice wall, a hell-hole of fire and flames below me, looking for a grip, seeking purchase, slamming my ice picks home, scrabbling for a

235

handhold I could secure in order to pull myself clear. 'I am not letting go,' was my vow. Probably still is. And I know that what drove me up that ice wall was anger. A potent mix in my life, anger and grief. There was enough anger to steady my nerve, to fasten my resolve to the day-to-day of a working life. I could never bring Teresa back, but I could do my damnedest to ensure 'they' never brought incineration back.

'They', a mythical body of people, many in white coats, lab and medical, who knew more than me and presumed to know what was good for me. I'd just completed six months probation to become one of 'they'. A professional. An expert.

My sisters and my mother talk about 'they' as if about another, more exotic, species.

'I see they've opened the roundabout on the Buncrana Road. About time, too.'

'First they told us it would be free. Now they're telling us we'll have to pay. It's not on.'

'Sheila, up in the post office, said they're changing the pension book to a card thing, like a credit card. What do I want with a credit card? The book'll do me fine, but they won't have it.'

'They'. Faceless and powerful. On the inside.

The urge I felt as Paddy pondered the bigger picture was to take control of this situation. It's always about control with me. Here was a threat I could see off. Or at least do my utmost to stall. Never again would I be caught out. I knew things and I was not going to be ignored.

'Leave it with me, Paddy. I'll draw up a paper. Put what we know about Estoron and Coleraine's plan on a couple of sides of A-Four. Meanwhile, you can have a mull about it and we can review and plan a strategy.'

He liked that. Me doing the beavering. Him doing the thinking. I was still only learning, probation just completed, but I was wise enough to know that when something is coming straight at you, it's often best to go round the side of it. To outflank it.

I've said before that beginnings are always difficult to pin down, but I sense now that the meeting with Paddy was the beginning of something. One handhold secured, another one, higher up the ice wall, identified. Enough confidence to raise my head to gaze up the sheer cliff ahead of me, flames still licking my heels and a view, in glimpses, often no more than a hint, of the light of a day that might see me stand unfettered from my past.

CHAPTER THIRTY-ONE

THE SECOND TIME

'Dust thou art and to dust thou will return,' I remember the priest intoned.

I will attempt to write about Teresa's second burial now. I've put it off, for good reasons. There are glacial cliffs before me. And torrents of fire below me. But I'm committed to telling the story in full. The second burial is a crucial hand-hold on my climb out of the ice cave. I draw strength from it even now.

I was nervous on the morning of the day, anxious and fretting because I'd let Tony handle all the arrangements. We were to meet at the cemetery at two o'clock and by midday I was pacing the floor. Why couldn't it be done now? Or earlier, at ten o'clock? At half one I went to my mother's house, two streets away and waited with her.

She had her hair done, tight curls framing her head, a light mauve wash through them. Her eyes beamed, not sure whether to sparkle or to cry.

'What time is that car coming?'

'Don't panic, Ma. They'll be here.'

'There was no need for a car. Haven't you got a car?'

She had a point, but I wasn't going to argue it with her right then.

'Have you an umbrella? You'll need one up there. You'll need something to break the wind.'

'I have an umbrella,' I said and she started tittering, hiding her mouth behind her hand.

'Listen to me. Something to break the wind. Your father would have enjoyed that one. He could break wind, I'm telling you. No matter where he was, even up in the cemetery.'

By now she was giggling, cupping her hand over her mouth. Suddenly she stopped, sharp as a tap being turned off tight.

'Anyway, he is up in the cemetery. With Teresa. And it'll be windy up there, so we'd better hap up.'

I wore a new trouser suit, with a dark blue wool overcoat, even though it was June, and a matching bag. I looked like someone's spinster aunt, which, of course, I was. To Martha's two – Aoife and Claire – and to Anna's three – Tomás, Fiona and Eithne.

Working out what to tell them was difficult. My mother wasn't for having them there at all.

'What's the point in taking them off school anyway? No point in them missing a day at school,' she argued.

'A half-day,' Martha said. 'We're not meeting up until two o'clock.'

'That's another thing. Why are we having it at that time of day anyway? Must suit Tony and his business buddies.'

'Suits everybody,' I said. 'Suits the priest.'

'Dust thou art and to dust thou will return,' he said as the wind ruffled his curls.

That's not what we said to my nephew and nieces. I imagined Martha and Anna would come up with a line involving Heaven, angels and Teresa, their cousin, dead at birth and looking down on them with benevolent regard. Maybe one of the children would ask the hard question.

'How can you be born and die at exactly the same time?'

'No place for children anyway, the cemetery. Especially like this. Will he have his children there?' my mother asked.

'Yes.'

'Course he will,' my mother snarled. 'Doing the big man, the big family man with his wife and weans and his cars and his lunches, like he was shoving it down our throats.'

'Mother,' Anna said, 'Donna has worked it all out with Tony. It's up to us to support Donna in whatever way she wants to handle this. My three'll be there, for Teresa, their cousin. And for their Auntie Donna.'

I could have hugged her. I could have hugged all of them, even my mother with her bitter words.

'All our children will be there,' Anna continued. 'As well as our husbands. The whole family. If there's anybody else Donna wants to ask, they'll be there, too. All proud of our Donna, even though it's a sad day. We're just doing right by her and Teresa.'

Martha began a slow hand clap and called out, 'Fair play to you, Anna. Fair play to you. Up our house!'

'Go away out of it, will ya?' my mother said, but she was smiling then. The lemon sucked out, she smiled her sweetest face, enjoying her daughters and not really put out by not getting her way.

'I reared ye too soft, that's where I went wrong and ye have me up in a heap all the time.'

She bustled out to the kitchen and the three of us looked at one another until Martha nodded and Anna got up and followed our mother.

I've just remembered the time when I started courting Tony. One night, we were clinched together like limpets and pasted up against Mrs Peoples' wall, when car headlights caught us. We took no notice, but when I got into the house, Martha and Anna were waiting to read me the riot act.

'Are you mad, wee girl?'

'Have you no sense?'

'Who the hell do you think you are, snogging the head off that fella? Who is he?'

Their questions came rapid-fire, rattling like a machine gun.

I remember I was cool.

'Tony you call him. Tony Bradley. He's a fitter.'

'It would be fitter for you to be in the house and not giving Mammy a headache.'

'Mammy's in bed.'

'Yeh. With a headache.'

'I didn't give it to her.'

Anna got to the core of it.

'You'll give her some headache when you get pregnant. And don't tell me you can't get pregnant doing it standing.'

'We weren't *doing it*. We were only snogging.'

'Snogging, yeh. And his hand up your jumper.'

'Are you jealous?'

'You're right I am. Has he a big brother?'

And then Anna laughed. So did Martha. Warm, sisterly laughs. After which, they told me the facts of life. The full facts.

The full facts of the second funeral for Teresa's cousins needed to be worked out.

'What do you want us to tell the children, Donna?' Martha asked.

'I don't know, Martha. You and Anna know them best. What do I know about children?'

'More than most people in one way.'

Then she paused and added, 'We'll tell the bigger ones, we'll tell them a little bit about, well, the medical side. They're big enough. The wee ones we'll say we're going with Auntie Donna to say a prayer for Teresa and, you know, give her a little present.'

A present. A gift. A gift of organs and parts and slices of herself. I don't feel so angry now, but back then I was seething. Angry at myself for bungling even a stillbirth. Angry at the medical authorities who deceived me and Tony. Why should I have to sit with my sisters and my mother, trying to figure out how to explain all this to children, when I couldn't explain it to myself?

Dust thou art. Dust I am. And dust occludes my eyes so I can't see clearly. My fingers are poised over the computer keyboard. A robin rests briefly on the whirligig clothesline in my garden. A dog barks aimlessly three houses up. He only stops when he's feeding or sleeping. I see him sometimes at my neighbour's fence and I fantasise about sighting down a rifle and sending a silver bullet into his gullet to silence him forever.

The day I went to my mother's house and she made the joke about breaking wind as we waited for the funeral car, I wasn't playing the delicate one. I was refusing. My position was if they're going to do this to me, they're going to get minimum co-operation. I didn't mean Tony and my family. I meant 'they'.

When the car arrived, I said to my mother, 'Okay?' and she stood for a beat, so I added, 'You're doing this for me. Don't question or fret about it. Don't worry. You look fine.'

She smoothed her coat and we went out to the car. She didn't look about her as we drove down the narrow street. If I had trouble figuring out what to tell my nephew and nieces, she was squirming on what to tell the neighbours. I was no help to her. I was solid dumb, by that stage, my gullet filling with the dust of the grave.

'To dust you will return,' the priest said to the knot of people gathered around him in the weak summer sunlight. As if we didn't know. We were ranged about him following the end of the procession from the cemetery gates, a procession that had gathered long before that really. A procession that was forming all day and every day since the beginning of Time. Tony manoeuvred his dark green Audi saloon to the front. The two hired cars followed, me and my mother in the first, Mary and her children in the second. The priest's car then and maybe five others. Tony's brother. My sisters. A small sliver of humanity. A tiny sample, no more than a couple of angstroms wide. Not a nation, a clan or a tribe. Simply a family, with a modern kink. Put us under the microscope and take a look at the dust that forms us.

Up the hill we crawled. I heard my mother mumbling a rosary under her breath, her fingers telling the beads deftly. The headstones swung round beside us on the cemetery slope. Below us and to the left the tepid sunlight soaked into the green mat of the football stadium and glinted thinly off the metal grandstand. Then the river appeared, curling away into the green fields of Tyrone and Donegal.

Up and up we crawled until we turned in at the Republican plot, the flagpoles empty, the bowed head of *Cú Chulainn* resting on his chest. We're lucky we lost nobody in the war. My mother used to say she thanked God she had no sons because she'd hate to have to walk behind one of them shot dead.

Our procession drove on until Tony's car stopped. Then I helped my mother out of our car and we stood as other people got out of theirs. For a long time, there was no movement from Tony's car. I could see the back of his head and his left arm stretched across the passenger seat.

I knew he was crying. Maybe we all did, so we gave him a moment, but when he didn't move, I left my mother, saying 'wait here', and I walked to the front of the procession and tapped on the passenger window. The face that turned to me that morning was not a man's, but a boy's. The face of a boy you would see scared out of his wits at the highest point of a Ferris Wheel ride, lost and calling for his mammy.

The window whirred down and I looked into Tony's eyes. I was avoiding the casket on the seat beside him.

'You okay?'

He blubbed a sound at me, a gasp rumbling up from an ancient hole in his life, rancid coal tar slurping there.

'Unlock the door.'

I grabbed the handle and pulled it. Smooth as a bank vault it came to me and the special whiteness of a child's casket filled my view. I had no sense then of the cars or the people waiting for us. It was me, Tony and the white casket. Teresa. A simple thing. A family, with a modern kink.

I can be wise sometimes. Evenings I sit at this desk and look out of my window into the tiny yards of my neighbours and I see the pigeons fly and flock together which draws an insight into my mind about community or life or time. Or a shape in the clouds, tinged russet by the setting sun, reveals to me a note about beauty or permanence or hope. In all of these moments, there is a core wisdom and it is this: every move I make in life, every positive step I take, comes from weakness.

I drew on my weakness then, the car-door handle cool in my

palm. Tony'd said he'd look after all the arrangements. And he had, right up to this point and here he'd stopped. What thoughts ran in his mind at that moment? Was he dropping Teresa off at school? At dancing? At football? Would she unbuckle her seat belt and say, 'Bye, Daddy, catch you later,' in a singsong TV voice? And he'd answer, 'All right, love, take it easy, your ma'll pick you up after.'

That much was true. Her ma, a young woman, old before her time, bent forward in a blue funeral coat, unclicked the seat belt and released it, then lifted the white casket – oh, weightless box – into her shaking arms.

'Take a minute. It's okay, Tony. I have her.'

I'd stepped out from behind the wall I'd erected in front of myself and it felt, not good, but at least right. Tony snuffled and got out of the car, shrugged into his suit jacket and nodded at me. It was my time to lead the procession. I turned left up a rising side path. Out of the corner of my eye I saw other people in groups, my mother surrounded by Martha and Anna and their younger children, their husbands and the older ones immediately behind.

Tony fell in at my right shoulder and we climbed towards the grave. He was with me, but slightly behind me. I liked that. As if he was saying 'you lead us, Donna, you handle this bit'. Still my arms shook and my breath rasped in my nose, as I turned once more along a line of graves until we came to my father's, the baker and the footballer, the *Tír na nÓg* man, who smelled of fresh baps and made bad jokes like: 'Weans, yeez know who's the richest man in Derry? Eh? Do yeez not know that? Eh?'

Martha and Anna knew the answer. It was one of his old favourites. They let me, the youngest, answer him. Was I six?

'You tell us, Daddy. You tell us.'

'Your da is the richest man in Derry and not because he has all that dough. But because he has ye three beauties.'

Then he cheered. We all cheered.

Now here I was at his grave, opened for a second time since it was opened for him.

Here's another beauty for you, Daddy. Here's more of the granddaughter you never saw. We never really saw her either.

Sorry for disturbing you again. It's only Teresa. Sorry for going back into it like this.

Such a small hole, maybe two feet deep, but big enough for the shoe box I held in my aching arms. Two gravediggers stood to one side, blessing themselves as I arrived.

Here she is, lads. She'll be no trouble to you. A simple dig. A spade, a fork, a few strikes of the pickaxe in the brown clay. A handy number for an afternoon.

And the new stone we'd got. Teresa's own stone now, her details blanked out on my father's gravestone. Tony had arranged this. A simple, small, rounded granite stone, neat as a milestone on a country road. Her name. Teresa Bradley. Her birth and death date. And the line we agreed. Born sleeping.

There was a hesitation then as people gathered around me, until the priest, sensing we were settled, began.

'Dust thou art and to dust thou will return.'

Tony was composed by now. My sisters were crying, holding each other's hands. My mother, close to me, saying another rosary. And away off, so only I could see her, a girl of eleven in a tracksuit, a lissom girl with her hair pulled back in a ponytail and a sports bag over her shoulder, joining her grandfather at football training. 'She's good' he'd say, 'better than all the young fellas in the street. A natural. Where's she get that from? Eh?' A spring in her step as she passed between the headstones in the city of the dead.

'To enjoy for evermore her life as an angel of the Lord.'

My cue. The priest nodded. My mother touched my elbow. People waited. I looked at Tony and he blessed himself. Consolation at the graveside. But not for me. I could have run then, even from so small a hole. No consolation. No solace yet. Not then, not now. Not ever? I took the three small steps that brought me to the breach in eternity and I laid the white box – a wedding cake for the angels, a gift for Teresa – in the shallow grave.

Sometimes, since that day, I've wished I could have climbed in after it. A foolish thought I know. I've a bit of living to do yet, I hope. But I do know that the sense of a frozen cavern opening inside me grew at that moment. I barely registered the priest's closing prayers, the labourer's ease with which the gravediggers slid the lid of false green grass across the grave, the way the children – Teresa's five cousins and half-brother and sister – came forward and placed little knots of flowers – roses, gardenias, wallflowers, lilies – on the green lid, the invitation extended by the priest on behalf of 'Tony and his family' to join us at the Del for light refreshments.

My mother had words to say about that later on, I can tell you. But as Martha said, 'There's always something wrong at funerals. Same as at weddings. Something about the arrangements, about who got into what car, something the priest did or didn't do. Never worry about it, Mammy, we'll make sure we get your one right.' That shut her up.

I found myself alone at the graveside as people drifted back to the cars. Alone, staring at the clutch of roses, the bunch of lilies, an unseasonably Arctic wind coursing through my veins. Martha led my mother back to the car, with a, 'Come on, Mam, you'll freeze out here.'

Miss Jennings came up to me then. I hadn't seen her earlier. She wore a long black coat and her face peered out from under a small black hat pressed close upon her head. Her hand, clad in a black leather glove, brushed a strand of grey hair from her face.

'I knew you were brave, Donna,' she said.

I took her hand and we stood in silence.

What was there to say? Joined at a discontinuity in Time, a cold wind from beyond the far galaxies whistling through us, I took comfort from her presence. She manifests the dialogue I am having with the world, the humane science that may be my path to recovery. Two scientists attentive to the pull of earth at a graveside. I stood with Miss Jennings, as I stand with her always. Frail, cold and yet hopeful in the face of the dark unknown. Around us, people returning to their lives amidst memorials to the dead.

I saw Tony and his brother two rows up and off to the side, at their parents' grave. I didn't see Teresa. Gone to football in *Tír na nÓg*. With her grandfather. Forever.

Would anything ever heat me up again? I tried Tony's soup at the Del. Good country vegetable broth, with barley in it, which went some way to appeasing my mother. I got her back to my place in the hired car and then we went straight to the lunch in my own little Fiat. My own Latin 'let it be done'.

As it was done for the second time at Teresa's grave. Of course, I've been there many times since. But never yet to open it again. The next time we do that will be for my mother. Dust to dust. For all of us. At the end of the day, so much landfill.

CHAPTER THIRTY-TWO

LANDFILL

We won't be able to landfill for much longer. Even the ceme-
teries are filling up. I saw a letter in the paper today saying
we need a crematorium here. What kind of city will we be when
we can't bury our dead? So a crematorium. More incineration.
Space is at a premium. Seems to be needed for apartments. Maybe Tony and his brother are at fault. I don't know who's living in
them or where we're going to bury them when they die. Of course,
it's not all my responsibility, but I have taken it on, professionally
speaking.

'We're the night-soil minders, Donna,' I remember Colm, the
supervisor at the city's Culmore Landfill saying. 'You know what
that means, Donna? We take the stuff the city doesn't want and
we stash it for them out of sight as much as we can and only we
know how much of it is piling up and covering everything. You
see them posts down there?' he said, pointing.

We were standing on a platform at the weighbridge. There
was a gap in the arrival of lorries, so Colm could lecture me.
Only sparrows could be heard, twittering as they flitted among
the brambles behind us. And from the distance a sighing sound
as the tide rolled in, filling up the muddy crevices and the creeks
lined with reeds.

'For God's sake, look. Look. There, where the heron is coming in.'

I saw a speck, dark against the grey sky. It flapped, like a plastic bin-liner, then crossed the far end of the dump, where the green fields began and dipped out of sight behind a stand of reeds, so distant I couldn't tell if they were swaying.

'There's a wee stream, only a *shugh*, flows into the Foyle at that point. That was the end of the dump when I started here first. Now look at it. It's coming all the way down here in front of us.' His right arm swept across his body in a wide arc. Then he repeated the arc with his left arm, in the opposite direction. 'Then it swings round behind us. The way it works, Donna, the more things people have, the more things people throw away. And the night-soil minders, that's us, we end up with it. Now, I don't need any professor at university to tell me that.'

He was always slagging off the university. I didn't mind. He was good to me when I worked with him for two weeks in his little office beside the weighbridge as part of my sandwich year. Colm was my very friendly uncle, able to talk about things no-one else could go near.

'You married?' he asked the first day.

'Divorced,' I said.

It was not hard to divorce me and Tony. We were barely married. The house was sorted out easy enough. I remember Tony being so reasonable that a hint of resentment bubbled up in me. I was sure he had someone else, but he didn't. He met Mary after we divorced. I couldn't resent him really, because, after all, I had someone new myself. Colm.

'Fair play to you. I never believed in that make-your-bed-and-lie-in-it stuff. Easy enough to say if the bed's cosy and warm. Not so easy if there's rocks in it. No sugar, you said.'

He handed me a mug of tea.

'See next time, get yourself an auld fella. Now, a fit one, like. But an auld fella, with a bit of money about him. Don't bother looking at me. Shur herself'd never let me go and run off with a young one, after thirty years now. But there's plenty of fellas out there with a spring in their steps and a full wallet. Do right by yourself next time. Do you have any weans?'

'No,' I mumbled and a flare lit up inside. Not even Colm could get me to go there. Anyway, that was the bare truth. I bit my lip and swallowed hard to quench the flare. I'm not sure he even noticed.

'That tea too strong?'

'No,' I gagged. Too hot. Roasting. Just keep talking, Colm, and let me cool down and, if you can manage it, talk about something else.

My mother knows him. 'That fella! He'd talk the legs off a chair and you sitting on it.'

She was right. He could talk about everything and anything, but his big topics were his family and the way the dump was going to swamp the city if we didn't do something about it.

'Here's another lorry coming now,' he said that day he pointed to the boundary posts. 'Have a guess. Remember, now, metric tonnes. None of your imperial rubbish here. Have a look at the back wheels. How well down is she? Gauge it that way.'

He had me guessing the weight of the lorries coming in, writing them on my clipboard, then comparing it to the proper weight on the digital display. It was pointless and fun, but it felt like work and enough like the experiments I had done in the Tech and the university to be manageable. It was also terribly childish – why guess when the weighbridge gave the actual weight? – but there's got to be some fun at work. And for Colm, having what he called a 'wee girl' with him for a fortnight gave him a chance to play Granda at work.

'Now, you've really cracked it if, as well as getting the weight right – I'll give you a ten per cent margin of error – you can say what run they were on. That's a more sophisticated analysis. Different folk make different waste. And it all comes here,' he concluded as the lorry eased to a halt in front of us.

I wrote down a guess: 8.9 metric tonnes. The display lit up: 12.2 metric tonnes.

'You're way off, wee girl. Way off. You must have forgotten to include the three Telly Tubbies in the cab,' Colm laughed.

The men in the cab waved as they drove off and me and Colm returned to his office, where the computer recording the weights whirred in greeting and Colm went straight to his tea corner and topped up his mug as he continued his disquisition.

According to Colm, there'll come a day when the whole city will be nothing but a grand dump stretching up the hills on either side of the river. 'You'll be around to see it. I'll be up in the cemetery by then, talking to myself under six feet of clay, but you'll still be here. You'll see. It'll be Dump City.'

He knows he's exaggerating, certainly about his age. He's still working down there, with at least two years to go to retirement. I've seen him grow more adamant over the years.

'You're going into this full time when you qualify? Well, see if you do, you'll never want for work. Never. If there's one thing we're good at, it's making rubbish and not knowing where to put it. Oh, we've always been good at it, right back to the day Adam and Eve were thrown out of the Garden of Eden. And you know why that happened? God was mad enough with them eating the apple, but when He saw what Adam did with the core of it, He went ballistic. Adam only tossed it in behind a lovely rhododendron bush and sauntered on. Well, if he did, God tapped him on the shoulder and said, "Here, youse two, clear off outta here and don't be littering my lovely Garden of Eden." So He chucked them out and they started tossing and throwing their rubbish everywhere and we're continuing that tradition to this very day. Only now there's millions of us – billions of us, when you include all the Chinese – and we have more than apple cores to be tossing away.'

I couldn't get the words out of my mouth to ask him a question or to make a point. The best I could do was mumble a remark, a half-phrase that formed somewhere in the back of my brain, struggled to the tip of my tongue and limped into the air between us.

'We have better systems now,' I said.

'Better systems? Better systems? Now, that's a laugh. Matter a damn what systems we have if we keep over-producing the stuff. Sup up there, Donna. Here's another lorry. Have a guess, now. Go on. You have to do better than last time.'

And I did. Each day I got a little better, closer to the real weight.

Colm was relentless. More lecture than conversation, more rant than argument, Colm's speeches ranged far and wide. The bottom line was his grandchildren's future. How those two girls would inhabit a future world swamped by refuse drove all his concerns. I could picture them as adult women, with children of their own, twenty years into the future and I could ask myself Colm's question: will those girls be able to live in this city or will they have to zoom off to live on another planet?

Colm was a full-on eco-warrior. The tide of rhetoric and colourful debate he produced swept over me, often too rich for me to swim in. I don't think he wanted me to argue with him. Or even to agree with him. As far as he was concerned, he was stating self-evident facts. But that wasn't enough for me.

Late in the second week, I asked, timidly, 'What are we going to do about it?'

That opened the floodgates.

'What are we going to do about it? What are we going to do about it? I'll tell you what we're going to do about it.' And he paused, licked his lips and delivered his punch line with relish.

'Nothing. Absolutely sweet FA. Big nothing. Zero.'

Before I could get in again with a comment or a question, he continued, 'And do you know why? I'll tell you why.'

Another pause then, underlined by hitching up his trousers and reinforced by the steady wag of a crooked finger.

'Because there's no votes in it. And there's no votes in it because there's no money in it. If there was money to be made, we'd have sorted it out years ago. In fact, there's so much money to be made producing things we can throw away that there's nothing we can do about it.'

I don't know if I would apply the word 'hopeless' to Colm's thoughts at that time. I don't even know if the word 'hope' was in my vocabulary then. It would be hard to see how it could have been.

I remember the day the solicitor phoned me and said, 'That's it, Donna. I have the papers here. Call in and we can wrap things up so you can get on with the rest of your life.'

Wrap things up and dispose of them, Colm might have added, grinning madly. No matter how upbeat the solicitor played it, the conclusion of the divorce felt more like an ending than a beginning. I teetered on the brink of despair rather than on the threshold of hope.

Where does hope come from? I honestly haven't a clue. I'm not sure if I have a capacity for it. I try not to think too much about the future, my own or the world's. Every time I do, I feel scared. And that makes me feel angry. If I can't bring hope to bear, then the best I can do is go forward in anger, take that flame with me as I burn my way into the future.

By the end of the fortnight with Colm at the landfill, I was livid with anger and returned to continue my sandwich year in the City Council's office, resolved to confront Colm's prediction of waves of rubbish and waste overwhelming the city. But I got swept up in daily tasks and never settled to really thinking and planning it out. When I went back for the final year of the Environmental Science degree, all my energy went into experiments, essays and exams. And the piles in the landfill mounted higher.

I know now that the anger Colm fired in me feeds my own recovery and my own theses about money and votes as I fuse them with the city's recovery, my job and my own teeth-gritted climb out of the landfill of my past.

CHAPTER THIRTY-THREE

BLUE BINS

Two days after the second funeral, Paddy Robinson called me into his office. He must have heard something.

'You need a couple of days off? You can have a couple of days' compassionate leave – a bit of R and R – if you want. I'll approve it.'

'Thanks, Paddy,' I said. 'I'm better off at work.' That's how I dealt with the icicles draped inside me, the block of ice in my chest, the hollow cavern, frozen to its deepest point, at the front of my head.

He paused, doubtful.

'You any further forward on that incinerator thing? We need to get our artillery lined up. No point in letting the Coleraine ones dominate the field.'

I should ask Paddy about his military allusions. Is he one of those fellows who has lines of miniature soldiers arranged against each other on papier-mâché battlefields, re-enacting great battles of the past? Waterloo, the Boyne, the Somme. So many rivers! Here I am on the Foyle, fighting my own battles.

'There's a council sub-committee meeting coming up,' he continued, walking to his year planner and tapping a red pin. 'Two weeks from today. Think you'll have some kind of strategy for us by then?'

'Yes,' I lied. Everything's a deadline in this job. Soon as you hit one, there's another one looming. It doesn't daunt me anymore. I live to work and I work to live. So, if there are extra hours to be done, I just do them. Anna thinks I'm crazy. Martha has a different view. She thinks I'm civic-minded.

'If more of them down in that City Council office took their jobs as seriously as our Donna, the town wouldn't be in the mess it is.'

'Looks like you'll be working again this weekend, Donna,' Anna hit back, sounding like Paddy. 'Martha has you leading the charge from the front.'

I never mind working the weekend if I have to. It's quiet. There's always a few people in, but you don't have to be as formal. I might do a few hours, catch a bit of shopping at Sainsbury's and get home to watch a DVD in the early evening. I always feel better being on top of things, rather than sensing they're on top of me.

I know Martha is protecting me when she says, 'Fair play to Donna for doing her bit. Maybe more of us should follow her example.'

I know what she's really saying and what I can read behind Anna's tight-lipped smile. 'She has no kids, no family, no Sunday dinner to cook. No homework to supervise, no lawn to mow and no man to barge because he won't do it, lounging on the sofa watching football.'

Maybe I'm being harsh. Anna might let her thoughts run like that, then cross herself, saying, 'God forgive me,' before launching into the next item on her lengthy 'to do' list. Martha wouldn't think like that. I'm guessing her line is that I'm more to be pitied than castigated. I'm guessing she takes the view that I'm still recovering and that it's not her place – or Anna's – to criticise. Martha, perhaps because she's the eldest, will always consider me delicate, spoiled somehow; treated unfairly by life and love and thus somebody to be, as our mother would say, 'minded'.

I threw myself into responding to the news that Coleraine, our adjacent council, was considering an incinerator, with all the energy and enthusiasm of a single woman with no children, no

255

lovers, no hobbies, no friends and nothing else going on in her life except making sure the past never caught up with her again.

Things had changed considerably in the years since my placement and my fortnight with Colm at the landfill. Now I was a full-time WMO, Waste Management Officer, following a successful probationary period. Colm had been right about one thing. The tide of waste had grown over the years, but the concept of recycling had come in from the margins and was now a central part of the council's strategy and a daily occurrence for most people in the city.

I was so proud of the roll-out of the blue recycling bins. They were already in a pilot phase when I started the job, but Paddy had me supervise their release in a staged manner all across the city. I still get a buzz of personal pride when I see a row of them at the end of my back lane. Clean and neat they look, full or empty. My little project. My offspring, almost. But, without getting carried away, what they do say to me is that I am holding back the tide. Even Colm acknowledged that.

'The blue bins? What? The blue bins? Should have been done years ago. Obvious now, isn't it? But wasn't I going on about it for years? Did anybody listen? What? Re-cy-cling! We had it when I was a boy. You never threw out anything. Someone'd use it. Now it's fashionable. But the tide's rising. The blue bins tell you that the flood is coming up the side of the good ship *Earth* and we'll need more than blue bins to bail us out.'

He's good on descriptions and illustrations is Colm. Diagnosis, even. He's not so good on solutions. That's my job. Coming up with solutions. So I worked hard during the week, monitoring the blue-bin programme, collating the statistics we gathered on a weekly basis and I did two weekends on a response to the Coleraine plan. Paddy needed a solution and I came up with a belter. A conjunction of my own life processes and the city's. A grand blue-sky programme that would sweep us onward towards the light, onwards to a new age of recovery. But only if we faced the dark, the eternal dark.

CHAPTER THIRTY-FOUR

TUMBLING

There is a coloured photograph of a women's football team in the paper today. A dozen players, six kneeling at the front, six standing at the back, tall ones, with long hair pulled back in ponytails. They all wear the red-and-white-striped shirts, black shorts and white socks of Derry City Football Club. The trainer – a paunchy, prematurely balding man – stands at the end in a black tracksuit with the club crest on his chest. They are announcing the start of a new season, training sessions getting under way. Second from the left, at the back, is Teresa.

A shudder started in my heart, then boomed all through my body when I saw her. Slim, tall, a dirty-fair ponytail pulled tight off her face, a small smile, more serious than frivolous, and a joyful glint in her eyes. Most of the players were aged between sixteen and maybe twenty-two. Teresa looked no more than fourteen. That's the age I usually see her at now, especially when I dream about her. I don't do it often. Amra says it's a good thing to think about the dead and to have them visit you in your dreams. It means you are comfortable with them. Happy for them in some way.

This Teresa as footballer is the strongest image I have in my dreams. The girl crossing the cemetery with a sports bag on her shoulder.

I remember seeing her one Halloween. That's probably what fixed the image in my head. In the Guildhall Square, in the midst of the carnival crowd, all dressed up and going mad. We make a great celebration in Derry at Halloween, the feast of the dead. We revel in the dark and the fire, the masquerade and the booze. We hug our children to us, dressed in the most ghoulish costumes, and present them to the night of the dead.

Anna's children are at the *Bunscoil*, getting educated through Irish, and I learned from them that Halloween is the night the dead come back and have a party with the living. *Oíche Shamhna* they called it, the night before winter begins. So we all dress up and the City Council puts on bands in the Guildhall Square and fireworks on the river. Ghosts, devils, monsters, skeletons, they're all there, but every kind of costume is on show, the madder the better.

The night I saw Teresa I was with Anna and her three. Tomás was dressed as a pirate with a hook for an arm, a sabre to slice the air, a skull-and-crossbones bandanna, an eye patch and a fake scar across his cheek. Fiona was a witch with a long cloak and a conical hat and a broomstick that kept losing rushes so that by the end of the evening it had lost all its besom and was simply a stick. Wee Eithne was a fairy princess, her costume, left over from a school show, fluffed out like a meringue. Anna wore a witch's hat and wig, some scary green false fingers and a slash of red face-paint diagonally across her nose. I feigned terror as I got into the back seat of her car next to Eithne, who immediately said, 'Mammy, Auntie Donna has nothing. She's not anything.'

'Don't worry, love. I'll give her a loan of my witch's hat.'

'Then you'll be nothing.'

'I'll give her a couple of my witch's fingers, then.'

I could see Anna's fingers, gnarled and green, clasped around the steering wheel and I joked, 'Is it legal to drive with them on?'

Anna laughed and said, 'No worries. Half the cops we'll see tonight are wee boys and wee girls from up our way.'

We saw plenty of them. Teenagers in police and army uniforms. Young fellas in Richard Gere *An Officer and a Gentleman* suits. Packs of Saddam Husseins and George Bushes. Girls in St Trinian's outfits, shivering in their short skirts and torn blouses. Slasher doctors. Pregnant nuns. Drunken nurses with hairy men's legs.

I wasn't anything. But at least I was there and I was glad.

I got Anna's car into the City Council car park. That's why I was with her. I don't know if I wanted to be there, but I remember the delight on Anna's face when I said I could use my pass to get us into the office car park. I would not be looking at the fireworks out of the corner of my bedroom window, glimpses of the lights to my left above the river. I wouldn't be anything, but I would be at the festivities.

Crowds of people massed along the riverbank, between the council offices and the Guildhall. In the middle of the river sat a low barge. We could see dark figures moving about and then points of light – head torches? – criss-crossing each other. The evening was cold, the first hint of winter in the air on the last day of October. I pulled my coat around me and watched the fancy-dress crowd mill about. Draculas and Frankensteins, Telly Tubbies and werewolves, Clark Gable and Marilyn Monroe arm-in-arm. So many Elvises it was like a convention in Las Vegas. Men in fishnet stockings, short skirts and suspenders. Anna joked that they weren't really in costume. They dressed like that at home all the time, she said.

The first boom from the barge drew an 'ooh!' from the crowd. We were pressed against the railings so the children could see. A purple ball exploded in the sky, then a series of thumps came from the barge and a great shattering of gold light broke above our heads. We strained our necks to stare. Orchestral music came out of the speakers further up the river, slightly out of sync and raspy, as if the leads weren't plugged in properly.

Tomás and Fiona loved it, pointing and calling.

'Look, Ma, there's the dangly ones.'

'I hope there's more of them big bangs.'

'There's the rockets. Neyaw! Neyaw! Neyaw!'

Colour and noise filled the air. The water flashed bronze and zinc when the fireworks exploded. Across the river, the dark outline of the trees of St Columb's Park made a suitably sombre background, the bluebells huddling in the cooling earth.

Eithne grew quiet and pressed into Anna, pushing past Tomás and Fiona. Anna put an arm on her shoulder and pulled her to her.

'Look,' Anna said. 'They're sparkling like your tiara.'

At the end of the display, the crowd broke into cheering and applause, the music ran on a little more until someone switched it off with a squeal. People moved away, some going home, others looking to continue the night's festivities.

'Did you enjoy that?' Anna asked.

Tomás and Fiona were enthusiastic. Eithne lowered her head and nodded slowly. So much light and noise. So many people. Anna made a face at me, saying she'd be all right and then brightened Eithne up by saying, 'Will we go up and see the bands and then get chips?'

When Eithne said she wanted a battered sausage we knew she was fine. We walked along the river, admiring the costumes around us. A King Kong, a shoal of tropical fish, a headless coachman. More soldiers, this time chatting with Arabs. The tone of the revelries changing from 'family' to 'teenager', from street to pub, from fireworks to fire-water.

By the time we got to the Guildhall Square, the band was in full swing. Zoot suits, rock and roll. The crowd swaying and dancing. Baby witches on daddies' shoulders. Family groups in circles, adults taking children's hands and dancing.

Groups of teenagers milled through the crowd, all in costume, some already drunk, calling to each other.

'Wait for me, Chantelle. Wait for me. You have me vodka.'

'Where we going? Where we going, hey?'

'We're going up the Walls. Dino's up the Walls.'

'Don't step on my blue suede shoes, mucker.'

A group of three teenage girls stopped beside us. They were dressed in football shirts. Manchester United, Liverpool and the one that caught my eye and struck me dumb was in the red-and-white stripes of Derry City. They formed an arc and struck a set of football poses in a frozen tableau. People around them stopped to watch. Then, as if life were breathed into them, they sprang into action in a routine of acrobatics and ball-juggling. The star of the show was Teresa, in the red-and-white stripes. Keeping the ball up. Rolling it behind her head and across her shoulders. Tossing it up, catching it and swirling it under her thighs. Spinning and moving all the time.

It was Teresa as I'd seen her cross the cemetery on the day of the second funeral. As she comes to me in my dreams, on and off – less so in recent months – and as she is in the photograph in the paper beside me on this desk today. I do not know this girl – these girls? – only that I know she comes to me as Teresa. Some combination of the time, the place and my mood conjures her up, sometimes in an image, sometimes in a dream and occasionally, as on the night of the dead, Halloween, as a real person, a living, breathing girl brought before me. For consolation perhaps?

We stood transfixed by the performance. I looked down and saw Eithne's face brighten. Teresa focussed on her and rolled the ball to her. Eithne kicked it back and Teresa performed a wild dive, scoop and lift as if saving a mighty penalty kick in the World Cup Final.

Then Eithne waved her fairy-princess wand and Teresa and her colleagues froze. Teresa was right in front of Eithne, the ball held out to the child. The other girls framed her, frozen as bookends behind her. Time stopped for that instant and my hands moved in my pockets. I would reach out and touch Teresa's hair. I would lay my hand on her head, stroke her tightly pulled-back ponytail, take her arm and draw her to me. I would roll back the years to that hospital bed and the death I gave birth to and claim the vibrant life in front of me.

Eithne took a half-step forward, just out of Anna's reach, waved her wand once more and with a big sweeping gesture touched the top of Teresa's head. Instantly, she sprang into life, somersaulted backwards between her two friends, who spun away, tossing the ball across to each other. When Teresa landed on her feet facing us with the ball under her arm, people 'oohed' and 'aahed' and began to clap. I burst out laughing. Laughing. Laughing so hard and long that Anna looked across at me, frowning slightly. We all joined in the applause. The footballers formed a line and took a bow, then swung to the right, one putting an arm on the shoulder of the one in front and pranced off to perform their stunts in another part of the square.

'That was cool, Mammy,' said Eithne. 'Can we go after them?' I would have gone after them. Anything to enjoy that laugh again. Anything to see that tumbling Teresa, tumbling in the air as she had ceased tumbling in my womb.

The band leader announced their last number. 'Let's get you shaking out there. Rattle them bones, all you skeletons at the back!' The ghosts and fairies, skeletons, witches, Elvises and pop stars, cross-dressers and Draculas danced to the music. Anna bypassed Eithne's question and said, 'We'll get chips in Frankie Ramsey's and head back to the car. A sausage for you, Eithne.'

'A battered one,' the child corrected.

A battered one. Like her aunt. Battered but still smiling in the afterglow of the laughing guffaw brought on by Teresa's back flip.

I could have asked the festival people at the City Council for details of the street performers, because that is what they must have been, but I never did. The council paid for a number of them: jugglers, acrobats, stilt-walkers. Why would I enquire about them? What use would that be to me? I know it wasn't Teresa, though I feel it was. A funny line for a scientist to write. Where's my rationality now? Where's my evidence? In that laugh she drew out of me. That laugh I remember as a warming draught that coursed through my body on a sharp October night. *Oíche Shamhna.* The night of the dead.

We got chips and battered sausages. Eithne grew tired and it was a slow walk back to the car. I took her wand under my arm as she negotiated her food. Anna and I shared a bag of chips. Tomás and Fiona had their own. We made our way out of the city centre along the Strand Road as more and more people came towards us, heading for the pubs and the City Walls and the late-night revelries. A bottle smashed on the ground. Two men pissed against the wall of a supermarket. Police vehicles moved into place and police officers, in real uniforms, not fancy dress, got out. More broken glass underfoot. A tangled witch's hat. A feather boa, straggled and strung out.

I would wave Eithne's magic wand and remove it all, but it will take more than magic to do that. Grand powers will have to come into play to respond to all this waste. I knew my colleagues would be working in the early-morning light, armed with their brushes and their machines – Colm's night-soil minders – sweeping and mopping up after our festivities.

Could I wave Eithne's magic wand and take all this waste, all this rubbish, litter, glass, time and human energy and turn it into something good? If I had such grand powers, I would touch Teresa with my wand, with every yearning of my heart, and turn her from waste into life, from loss and grief into laughter, from the past into the future. But that is not to be. I have no grand powers to overtake the Laws of Thermodynamics, which say that Time's arrow goes in one direction and that disorder and waste increase as time goes on.

That affronts me, both as a scientist and as a person. Perhaps the only recourse I have is to laugh, as I did at the tumbling Teresa, the acrobatic footballer, who performed at Halloween, the night of the dead. Laugh heartily at myself for thinking I'd seen my stillborn daughter there, though I knew in my deepest core that I had buried her twice.

CHAPTER THIRTY-FIVE

POWER POINT

For all the images of the dead I carry inside me, all the consuming flames of anger, all the freezing ice blocks of grief, it is images of life that will save me. I try to create them in my daily life. I try to make them flourish in my work. But it's a battle.

It's not called 'PowerPoint' for nothing. Simple screens of text in bullet points only – sharp and killing – that run in sequences on the big screen at the head of a darkened room, where a woman with a pointer and a laptop – me! – holds a City Council sub-committee in thrall. Paddy Robinson as commander, me as leader of the line in the battle for recovery.

'You present it,' Paddy said when I showed him my proposed response to Coleraine's incineration plans. 'I'll be there, introduce it and then hand over to you. Any questions, you take them. Anything tricky you bounce it off to me. Two-pronged attack.'

'Defence, you mean,' I said.

'Not at all. Not at all. You did all the work. It's basically your proposal. You pitch it at them. Fire the first salvo, see where that gets us. Don't worry, I'll be there if there's any counterattacks.'

PowerPoint is what it was. Paddy playing the power game. A bold move, pushing his queen up the board. If she gets toppled, he can always say she was reckless, inexperienced, foolhardy, it's only a draft, let me take it away and sort it out. If they get heavy with him, he can apologise, in a manly way. 'Sorry, my fault entirely, took my eye off the ball slightly. Should have kept her on a tighter leash. Will do so from now on, I can tell you.'

Of course, if it went well he could glory in it, don the laurel of victory, celebrate, accept the pats on the back and ride off into the sunset to enjoy further triumphs in the days ahead.

Paddy was playing PowerPoint with me. When I showed him the outline of my ideas before I committed them to a final version, he got excited.

'You're right, Donna. We have to come up with something strong. A full-frontal attack. We are the biggest council in the region and if we want to be top gun, we have to be bold. This is good. Your targets make sense in terms of the EU directives. And the job-creation dimension is excellent. What I really like about this' – as he flapped my pages in front of him – 'is the way it will work in the media. Oh, they'll go for this all right.'

Meaning the politicians. The members of the City Council's Environmental Sub-Committee. I remember they were all in attendance on the day of the presentation. Maybe Paddy had wired them off. Every party represented. No apologies. No absentees.

I wasn't nervous in the ordinary sense of that word. I was tense, ready, prepared. I'd done the work. Just one phrase could cause me grief: Zero Emissions Site. That was the one to get across. Now that I'm on the inside of the waste management problem, if I want to see off incineration I've got to box clever. I've got to prove other options and I've got to prove them against two further tests. They've got to make money and they've got to win votes.

Paddy introduced me, saying, 'Thank you all for being here this morning. We'll take ordinary committee business after the break, but for the first thirty minutes or so, I'm putting you in the capable hands of Donna Bradley, our Waste Management Officer, who has completed her six-month probationary period. Successfully, I might add. She'll take you through some ideas she has and I ask you to give her your full attention. Donna.'

He played it cleverly, distancing himself sufficiently from the proposal – 'some ideas she has' – while at the same time being generous himself and inviting the councillors to be indulgent; tolerant, even.

I started lightly. The first slide in my PowerPoint presentation showed an image of a rolling Californian landscape, with golden sunlight on vineyards and fluffy white clouds in the distance hinting at the azure Pacific beyond. Under the image, I added the text: *A Regional Waste Management Proposal – Getting to a Sunshine State.*

I spoke clearly and directly, drawing on my experience of the anti-incinerator campaign meetings. No breeze-block walls of a community centre here, but the comfortable surroundings of a conference room in the City Council's modern offices. Not a rickety video player and a portable TV set on plastic chairs, but a state-of-the-art laptop computer and a screen. Not a girl, but a woman. An expert. A scientist.

'This is an artist's impression of what the Culmore Landfill site will look like when this proposal is fully realised,' I said in a light tone.

Being flippant, even slightly, is risky. Some people may not get it. Some people may get it, but think you're wasting their time when there are very serious matters to be dealt with. Would I come across too frivolous? Too girlie?

In the semi-dark, the faces of the councillors were hard to see clearly, but enough light fell on them to know that my opening hadn't totally bombed. There were some grins and smiles, a muttered 'if only', a couple of frowns and two or three shuffles in seats. It was time to drive the point home. After all, we were dealing with the Second Law of Thermodynamics.

It's what I've been dealing with all along. Certain physical truths about the world mean that we move forward, strapped to Time's relentless arrow. The Second Law of Thermodynamics is the closest I get to belief in a religious tenet. I learned it in my final year at university, the physics module, always the hard one for me. Too much Maths. When I was faced with the Laws of

Thermodynamics, I was floored. We all were. Now they are daily truths for me. Everything I do, the way in which my life plays out, is an irreversible process. If I want to turn things back, reverse them, then it's going to take work. There are some things I won't be able to turn back. Recognising them is the trick. Identifying them and living with them is the big challenge. It's the only way to cope with the Second Law of Thermodynamics and its favoured constant, entropy.

The shattered jug is the best image I have for it, that time when I organised the tea party for Amra. That time when Teresa appeared to me and I got such a shock that I let the jug of juice slip out of my hands. In slow motion it fell. Time lapsed so that I can picture it fall, level by level, under the pull of one of the great physical forces, gravity, until it hit the floor and shattered into pieces. Disordered. The jug I'd held in my hand was an ordered object. An event happened and the jug that splayed in shards across the floor was a disordered object so we can say that its entropy, a measure of disorder, had increased. My business, my professional challenge, is to slow down and, if possible, cap entropy. For entropy is a measure of my lack of knowledge. My knowledge has increased, so my entropy has gone down. But life is more complex than that. It isn't that I have managed to reverse my process. I am still moving towards Teresa and equilibrium. Towards death. But I am, paradoxically, also moving away from her at the same time. The full structure of my life is richer than my language can describe and my brain can comprehend, even as I live it day by day.

The second slide I hit the councillors with was an image of Derry flooded by waste. I showed an iconic image of the city Walls, the Guildhall, the river and St Columb's Park behind it, that, with my crude but serviceable knowledge of Photoshop, I had doctored, adding mounds of domestic waste, barrels of chemical and hazardous waste, dumper-truck loads of white and electronic goods, until only the tops of the trees in the park were visible, facing the barrel of a cannon peeking out from the Walls. Above the festering heap, the clock on the Guildhall clasped its hands together at midnight. I even had a sound effect which chimed twelve bells in a deep, sonorous tone.

I cut the bells off at seven. The text I'd written to accompany that image was *Likely future if we don't act now*, to which I added, in a hushed voice, 'This is probably where we're headed.'

I continued in a sober tone, paraphrasing the Second Law of Thermodynamics when I said, 'There'll always be waste. By-products. Heat generated that we can't use, no matter what the human process. The question is: what do we do about it?'

'Tell us something we don't know' was written large across the faces of the councillors in front of me, in the gloomy light from the screen.

There were two women on the council sub-committee, one from Sinn Féin and another from the Ulster Unionist Party. They seemed to be nodding at me. The four men's faces were harder to read, but I was confident I had their attention. All of them, men and women, nationalist and unionist, seemed to be urging me on. So I took the plunge and showed them a slide paraphrasing a text from my central thesis: *Waste Management Means Saving Resources, Making Money and Creating Employment.*

For politicians like the six in front of me, 'creating employment' in our district-council area equates with one of my key points: winning votes.

I spoke my lines clearly, breathing easily, an expert in charge of the material and of the event.

'I'm going to take you through ten more slides in this presentation. A hard-copy is in front of each of you, but I'd ask you to please follow the slides on the screen for now. Also, there's a link to a paper on our website, which expands on the presentation, giving fuller details, with international case studies and academic support. You can have a look at that at your leisure.'

There was a suppressed laugh, a muted guffaw, from one of the men. Paddy Robinson shifted in his seat beside me and raised his eyebrows at the councillors as if to say, 'Give her a chance. She's not long in the job.'

I knew I was in danger of losing them so I went up a gear and presented the key slide of my proposal, which carried the text:

From Landfill to Recovery
From Waste to Jobs
From the Past to the Future
The Foyle Resource Recovery Park

I was bent on turning back the tide.

My target was a hugely reduced waste output from the city in terms of household, municipal, commercial and industrial waste, to be achieved by targeted reductions in each sector. I then presented a range of facilities and programmes for sorting, recycling, re-manufacture, education and publicity. I connected our unemployment statistics with job-creation possibilities, including incubator units for new technologies, supported by research and development. I drew in my old Department of Environmental Science at the university, advocating an expansion. More jobs! I sold the city and region as an exemplar of waste management, one that other cities and regions would flock to in order to witness our successes and then return home to emulate. I housed all this in a business model that was sustainable and inclusive of commercial and community enterprises in partnership with us, the City Council, under the management of a stand-alone body including all the groupings and stakeholders and supported by the two governments, British and Irish. I gave them the full range of phrases that buzzed about the modern waste-management world: *creating new partnerships, joined-up thinking, advancing economic development and job creation, viewing waste as a resource, warding off threats from EU infraction proceedings.* I even arranged to use the phrase *holistic paradigm shift*, but moved along swiftly after that one. That was even more 'Californian' than my Sunshine-State vineyards at the start.

In summary I presented charts, graphs and diagrams adding, 'Don't forget, all of this is in the handout in front of you and in more detail in the paper on our website, accessible by the link given.'

I presented my vision of a thriving eco-industrial park where the city's minimised waste was managed largely by conversion and re-manufacture into useful goods. I gave a timetable aiming at a Zero Emissions Site and I projected up to 500 new jobs. It was music to my audience's ears.

I left them with a final slide showing the rolling Californian vineyards where, nestled on a hillock, was the Guildhall clock and our walled city, like some medieval Camelot under which I had the text:

Foyle Waste Recovery Park:
A Realistic Approach to a Modern Challenge

And I added my own remarks: 'This presentation – and, as I said, everyone has a copy in front of them – is an outline of the full proposal on the website. It offers a realistic approach to a vexed modern problem and' – the line Paddy liked most – 'positions Derry City Council as the lead local-government authority tackling waste management creatively in a manner that develops the economy and delivers jobs. Thank you.'

Paddy used a remote control to bring up the room lights. Right on cue, the door opened at the back of the room and one of the council catering staff rolled in a refreshments trolley. A waft of coffee glided up the room and the restive shuffling in seats quickened among my audience. I wonder if Paddy had a second remote control by which he summoned the tea and coffee.

'Ah, perfect timing! Just what the troops need. Fresh rations! Thanks, Majella,' he said as the catering worker parked the trolley and left. 'I don't think we need to worry about waste when it comes to that coffee and those scones. I doubt there'll be much residue there.'

A small ripple of laughter travelled around the room and I heard two muted 'hear, hears'.

'But I think we could restrain ourselves for just a few more minutes to allow some quick comments, some initial responses, a question or two, perhaps. Can I, on behalf of us all, congratulate and thank Donna on some challenging, innovative and realistic ideas?'

Paddy using the word 'realistic' was important. It meant he was getting behind the notion, albeit obliquely. Putting the word on my last slide had been my attempt to disarm any criticism that might come.

The first speaker was the woman from Sinn Féin.

'Thank you, Donna. At the end of the day, we have to face into the future with new ideas like this. The EU won't let us bury it in the ground or blow it up a chimney for ever. So, and of course we should look at this nationally and make sure the Dublin Government plays its part, so our party is not ruling anything in or we're not ruling anything out at this stage, but I can say there's definitely possibilities going forward here.'

She waved her copy of my presentation in cautious welcome. The committee chairperson, a senior Democratic Unionist, raised his finger at that point and began to speak.

'No doubt this was an impressive presentation, but we're going to have to see some of the meat on the bone before we make any commitments.'

He continued before I could direct him to the full proposal on the website.

'I've been speaking with party colleagues in Coleraine and they tell me they are considering a proposal to build a large-scale incinerator on the north coast. Some of us are here long enough to remember the bother we had when Du Pont put out such an idea. No doubt the technology has improved since then. We have to be realistic in facing the issues of dealing with hazardous and toxic waste.'

He flicked through his hard-copy of my presentation and added, 'I picked up ... ah, here it is ... your slide nine. You say this will be a Zero Emissions Site. How realistic is that?'

The mention of the Coleraine proposal stirred Paddy. But before he could speak, I was on my feet again. 'The councillor is correct to ask for more details and I direct him, and all of us, to slide fourteen of the presentation, where the link to the full proposal is found. There is a very enlightening report from the town of Kamikatsu, in Japan, where zero waste is a daily reality. You'll see that a transition period is envisaged involving a move to clean production. All industries locally can commit to that and advance their own timetables to achieve it while modifying current practices within the framework we lay out here. There will be EU financial and other support for such modifications.'

The councillor came back at me.

'I can't wait to check this website. You've plugged it plenty. All I can say at this point is that we need more details and that we're going to have to be rigorous. There are targets for waste reduction, recycling and reuse coming out of Westminster and Brussels now that will hit us hard if we don't meet them. No-one around this table wants to preside over further rates rises, especially if they're to cover fines.'

A chill hit the room and councillors were momentarily stilled. Then an SDLP member, a young man building his political career, took up the point.

'No-one would disagree with that. I think we can all accept that Donna's ideas offer, at the very least, the basis of an approach we can take into the future. These waste-recovery parks are all over the States and we could see if we could partner up with one of them as a way of accessing inward investment.'

Paddy beamed. *Inward investment* is another one of the key phrases. Emboldened by the generally positive response to my presentation, I pushed the point. 'No doubt there are investment possibilities. The new Shamrock Fund, which American friends of the peace process are putting together, specifically lists waste management as a targeted area. More details on that are in the full proposal, which you can access via ...'

'Our website!' was called in a chorus of laughter by all the councillors. There then followed a more concerted shuffling of papers and shifting in seats and Paddy rose to close this section of the meeting and to invite us to get stuck into the coffee and scones, but I didn't want it to end there. I didn't want my proposal to be merely one more good idea on a shelf somewhere. I wanted to drive it forward.

'There's a full council meeting in a fortnight's time. Might I be so bold as to suggest that this committee consider tabling the draft proposal at that meeting?'

I was pushing matters faster than they were supposed to go at local-government level. Paddy, spluttering beside me, confirmed that. I remember sensing sweat on my palms and a flutter in my stomach, but a memory of Frances in action came to me as Paddy found his voice.

'Donna, it's not ... well, you have some ... I wonder when ...'

'If I could just come in here ...'

It was as if I'd pulled hard on the handbrake of my little Fiat, like I remember doing when a dog ran out in front of me. My heart bounced in my chest that day and it somersaulted once more as the meeting, the very room, shuddered to a halt, and it took a few beats before I eased the handbrake off and gave a tweak to the accelerator.

'That's going to be a very busy meeting with the debate starting on the new rate,' the senior Democratic Unionist chair of the committee said.

'If I could just come in here,' I repeated, echoing Frances. 'This proposal offers us, in the medium and long terms, a way of bringing down the rates. And of warding off EU fines. Which will surely be relevant to the discussion of the budget and the new rate.'

Another chill descended on the room when I said that. Once more, the meeting stalled, this time in need of an early-morning cold start.

'There's no point discussing this proposal unless we action it in some way. We're all agreed – let us say – that there are ideas worth considering here?' the Sinn Féin woman, who had spoken first, asked her colleagues and a general murmur of assent travelled round the room, so she continued.

'Then I propose we table it at the full council meeting. I'm looking for a seconder here.'

The chairperson came back in at that point.

'I've already said this. I think we need to see some meat on the bone.'

'But you're not objecting to it?' the Sinn Féin woman cut in.

'No. I'm not objecting to it, but—'

It was my turn to cut in as the chairperson began to reply. I don't know where I got the courage to do that. I was cutting across a councillor with over twenty years' experience, someone who led politics in the city and who represented the city in

273

Belfast and London. I was only in the job seven months. But I was desperate – I think that's where my courage comes from – desperate to push my ideas forward. I have my own agenda and I wanted this on it. I was desperate for recovery, for the city and for myself.

'I can certainly beef up this outline in time for the full council meeting. I can look at any specific gaps and omissions councillors would like to see dealt with. I wouldn't presume a full debate on the proposal at the next meeting, but I suggest that this council can show it is responding to a major waste-management challenge by offering this proposal for initial consideration by bringing it up for mention as an opportunity to reduce waste, reduce costs, attract inward investment and create employment.'

It was as close to a political speech as a council official could go. My knees were shaking as I said it.

The Sinn Féin councillor said, 'I'm still waiting for a seconder.'

The young SDLP man added, 'If Donna agrees to work up a number of the points – and I suggest we get our own comments and queries to her within the week after we've read the full proposal – then I'll second the proposal that we present for mention a revised version of this outline proposal.'

He took his hard-copy of my presentation and waved it in front of him. If any more of them did that, it would look like a victory parade.

'I'll certainly take comments and queries with a view to putting meat on the bone, as it were. And committee members would have sight of the revised version of the outline before it went to full council,' I concluded, nodding directly at the chairperson.

He gathered his papers, taking full control of the meeting. I knew he was going to draw the discussion to a close.

'It's a tight schedule. We have to put a strict timetable on this. Comments and questions on this draft outline must be with the Waste Management Officer no later than the fifteenth. Then we'll need to see a worked-up new version by the seventeenth. Subject to that being satisfactory, we'll get it on the full council meeting agenda for mention only.'

I could have jumped out of my skin. It was clear. His tone was positive.

The Sinn Féin woman spoke again. 'I'll propose it on that basis. For the third time.'

The SDLP man said, 'With the chair's timetable in place, I'll second it.'

I don't know who started it – Paddy probably – but a round of light applause began. I couldn't believe it. Unanimous cross-party support. No objections. Everybody rose from their seats and moved to the end of the room where the refreshments trolley waited. I was ready for coffee and scones myself.

Paddy leaned into me and whispered, 'Congratulations, Donna. Well done. You've cracked it. We're over the battlements. A new beginning for the council, I can tell you that.'

He was as effusive as I'd ever seen him. I was more low key. I'd given the committee a jolt, a charge of energy that propelled it faster than it usually travels, but there was enough inertia in the system for it to grind to a halt again.

We waste-management scientists work, at our best, to the 'proximity principle', which says that waste should be dealt with close to where it is produced. I operate my life on the same principle. I wonder now if that is why I never went for counselling. I have no objection to it, but it seems I relied on my family and on myself, people near me and the source of the waste.

If I had a success with the council, surprising Paddy, other officers and the councillors themselves, then it was only because I cannot live 'on the outside', as if I were a spectator of nature. I am a macroscopic being, embedded in the physical world. These pages record the everyday dialogue I write between myself and the world.

CHAPTER THIRTY-SIX

THE SHINING SPADE

It has been a while since I wrote here. A new beginning? There are many 'new beginnings' and nothing comes to an end. I know that. But there was something about what I did this morning, about the way I went about it, something that said to me: 'Donna, you have doused the flames. Donna, you have stilled the fires and you have climbed out of the ice cave.' I consciously brought Gerry. He's wise enough not to read too much into such moves. And calm enough to feel good around. I told him I was going to the beach and taking my mother.

I remember her hesitating on the phone.

'Ach, I don't know, Donna. The hip is not great at the minute.'

'I'll give you a hand,' I said. 'And Gerry will be with us.'

That swung it. She likes Gerry. Actually, that's maybe over-stating things. She doesn't mind him. She's more tolerant, perhaps. Or just desperate for me to meet someone!

When I picked her up, Gerry was already in the back seat of my car. As I helped her into the passenger seat, she said, 'Ach, Gerry. You're here, too. Did you leave your car at Donna's then?'

He grinned at her, knowing full well that she was fishing. So he said, 'Good to see you again, Mrs McDaid. No, Donna called at my own house first.'

'Oh ...' said my mother, making it sound like she was surprised and a little disappointed.

I caught Gerry's eyes in the rear-view mirror as I settled myself behind the steering wheel. He winked at me. I knew then that there would come a time when Gerry would stay at my house and I would stay at his. I felt that for the first time. As we drove off, a plan formed. Something about me and Gerry going away for a weekend together. Yes, I could see that happening. I liked the way Gerry kept things clear. I liked the way he didn't presume.

We drove to the beach without speaking. There was no need. So early on a Saturday morning, the roads were empty. Light traffic was driving towards the city. We were going in the opposite direction. That felt right. Sitting here now, writing this, I realise I have been trying to find my own direction for years. Trying to find a way for myself out of the smoke and the flames and into the light.

When we got to the beach and I parked the car, my mother said she'd stay where she was, but I insisted she get out. I know she's frail, but I also know she enjoys the fresh air. Gerry helped her and she let him take her arm.

'Only as far as the sand, then. I'm not going out on the Point. Only to where I can see the water.'

We were wrapped up in coats against the brisk wind. Clouds dashed across the sky and I grew excited as I smelled the sea on the wind. I wanted to get on with it. Gerry could sense this and he nodded to me. He leaned into my mother and said, 'Come on, Mrs McDaid. Let Donna sort the car out. We'll make a start.'

My mother let herself be led on, saying, 'Okay, Gerry. But you needn't think you're getting me into that water.'

I heard Gerry laugh and say, 'Ach, we might risk an auld paddle.'

I went to the boot of the car and opened it. Inside, the new spade I'd bought lay shining and efficient. Beside it, a little clump of baby clothes rested cosy and shy.

A simple thing. A Babygro. Lemon. With little green florets round the neck and cuffs and ankles. Such a delicate green!

Such tiny feet! Such a slim garment! You could hardly imagine anything as vital as a baby filling it out. When I took it from the drawer earlier this morning and slowly removed the tissue paper, of course, I cried. It was the one item in that drawer, centred and alone. Small and huge at the same time. I feared I'd tear the tissue paper, that it would all dissolve in my hand. But it held firm and I unfolded it to release the tiny garment. I pressed it to my face, sucking the memories and the years out of it and then slowly, gently, as if bathing an infant, I dried my own tears with it.

As my mother and Gerry made their way to the end of the car park, pointing at tracks on the dune, I lifted the Babygro and rubbed it against my cheek. Then I reached for the spade, the sun glinting on its bright blade, its weight swinging the blade easily under my arm as I slammed the boot closed and walked in the direction of the *caldragh*.

I walked to the edge of the car park and climbed slightly, the sand soft beneath my shoes until I crested the dune to see the beach below me. Then I turned away from the car park and Gerry and my mother and, without looking back, I crossed the top of the dunes, keeping the sea on my right side until the dunes gave way to the craggy point where the *caldragh* was. The sun spangled on the open faces of the rocks there and the grass had a more settled, almost domestic feel in the flat space among them as compared with the wilder swaying of the marram along the dunes.

I paused to catch my breath and let my mind come to rest with the peace of the place. I had no doubts about my plan. I laid the lemon Babygro on the largest, flattest rock and I thrust my spade into the ground beneath my feet. It skipped and twisted, jarring my wrists. I moved slightly and tried again. Three times I moved and tried. Each time, the rocks below me wouldn't yield. I smiled to myself and moved once more. A gust of wind tossed my hair across my face. I looked up to see gulls gathering above me, calling gently as they rested easily in the onshore breeze. I plunged the spade into the ground once more and this time it gave enough for me to turn a sod and then another until I'd cleared a space so I could dig a small hole, a small hole big enough to take the Babygro and all I could leave with it.

Then I took the garment that would have been Teresa's and kissed it to my lips. Once more, my tears bathed it and I used the Babygro to dry my eyes. The gulls screeched above my head as I folded it, caressing the florets and the smooth folds of the fabric. Down on one knee, I placed the Babygro in the hole and with my hands turned the sods back over it until it was covered. Buried in the *caldragh* with my great-aunt Eileen and all the other children.

As I stood there, my new spade in my hand, the broken earth now stamped with the imprint of my feet, I sensed that I could renew myself, arise refreshed and ready, set to travel wherever Time's arrow drew me.

I looked back to see Gerry and my mother standing side by side on the dune behind me. They were laughing. The wind swept the sound away so I couldn't hear them, but I could see by the way they held themselves and the way they threw their heads back, how they scrunched their shoulders, that they were laughing. I turned my face to the sea once more. There, on the flat plain of grass among the dead, I gazed upon the waves rolling in to meet me. Resolute. Earnest. Unceasing. And I laughed quickly to myself. A gentle laugh of thanks. For myself. My mother. My father. My great-aunt Eileen. My sisters. For Gerry. For Miss Jennings. I remember how she clasped my hand after we'd buried Teresa for the second time, staring into my eyes. The immeasurable depths of our hearts sounded to each other as black holes sound to one another mirthlessly.

I laughed for Tony, too. A warm laugh. And, most especially, I laughed for Teresa.

Then I walked towards Gerry and my mother. The gulls followed me overhead, coasting on the wind. The three of us stood side by side and my mother asked what was I doing with the spade. Gerry smiled encouragingly. I said I would tell her later. I might even show her this book some day.

The gulls swung away from us and flew in a curve away and over the *caldragh*, where they hovered briefly before sweeping back in front of us, descending in a gentle swoop to land along the front of the waves, where they ran and jigged in and out of the surf like children on a summer's day, lit by a sudden burst of sun.

I will show my mother this book. It has become a story, just as she wanted. And just as I want it, too.

CHAPTER THIRTY-SEVEN

HOLLY

I don't write here so much now. I have gone into the past, the far past and the near past. I have set it before myself on these pages. They are a cherished possession.

It is December. I buy a branch of holly and put it in a vase. It leans to one side, and after trying to right it two or three times, I just let it lean. I arrange it so that most of the blood-red berries are to the front. The leaves curl in on themselves, prickles reaching for one another.

At the end of the day, I'm dealing with the Second Law of Thermodynamics. Change, always change. Irreversible change. I don't know enough about this really, about the way a system – my life – initially simple and easy to know in detail, eventually became so complex, starting with the chaos of Teresa's birth and death. I wrestle with the living of it. But I won't give up. That seems to be just the way I am. I am an evolving thermodynamic system. Changing, stretching and folding into the future. Moving from one equilibrium state to another, through a series of more or less huge crises. Losing Teresa was the biggest, the most devastating. I won't say I've grown stronger over the years. I still feel a jangling frailty nestled inside me, delicate stalactites of ice hanging within me. But thawing, too, from solid to liquid with an increase in entropy. Disorder.

I'm reading more and more about chaos. And how chaos produces complexity. I subscribe to *New Scientist* and I look forward to receiving it every week. I've continued to read science books because I still see that's where I'll learn what I need to know.

I am – we all are – sensitive to initial conditions. If Teresa hadn't been stillborn, my life would have taken a different trajectory. But simple questions often have complex answers, so when I ask myself 'why me?' – two little words and a question mark – I open up a range of possible answers that are far beyond my capacity for statistical analysis. The mathematics was always the hardest part for me. I took a GCSE repeat. Maybe I need to do another course. The Statistics of Complex Dynamical Systems or something like that. I can't see Paddy Robinson at the council paying for that, no matter how much of an ally and a confidant I have become for him.

'A new beginning,' he trumpeted my success at the Environmental Sub-Committee meeting. He was soon referring to it as 'our' success. He oversaw my revised outline, based on comments councillors sent in. All six sent in something, which Paddy said was a record. Under his direction, I made a two-page bullet-point revision of it, amended the main proposal on the website and emailed it back to the committee members. The Democratic Unionist chair emailed it back, saying it was clearer, meatier. He said he would forward it for mention on the agenda of the full council meeting.

Paddy presented it as 'our' proposal. The chair of our committee asked formally that councillors note it, adding that the committee would do further work on it with a view to bringing it forward for full discussion later in the year. The young SDLP man repeated his confidence that the proposal could trigger inward investment. The Sinn Féin woman said that the proposal offered a genuine way forward and thanked me by name. All eyes turned to me. I was blushing like a schoolgirl.

'The council needs to acknowledge the hard work of this young woman and congratulate her on successfully completing her probationary period with this very relevant proposal. At the end of the day, a waste-recovery park is our best option for the future.'

Paddy was right. A new beginning. I am not waste. I am an expert on waste. A new set of initial conditions for my life and for the future. It will never be a smooth curve. Chaos makes sure of that, but the fractals, the apparently irregular, complex shapes and trajectories generated in the chaotic geometry of my life, will be mine. And they will be beautiful.

I prop the Christmas card Amra sent me against the vase with the holly.

'It is special, coming from a Muslim,' she wrote. She included a number of photographs of Lekki beach, showing herself and her family and a view of the beach with nobody else in sight. The long stretch of golden sand caressed by the curling white waves makes me yearn to pack my bags and fly away. I know from other photos she has sent me that many beaches in Nigeria are not so beautiful, especially in the Niger Delta, where the oil wells are.

I resolve that I will see them all, that I will pack my bags and visit Amra and see Nigeria, the fine beaches and the devastated Delta. My mother and my sisters will rush to protect me – 'are you sure you could manage that, Donna?' – but I will insist. Tony will wish me well. Gerry may get a little nervous – jealous, even – but I'll tell him I'm visiting Amra and that I'll bring him back a present.

That I need a holiday before I start again.

ACKNOWLEDGEMENTS

This is a work of imagination, though it includes real events, organisations and institutions. All errors of fact are entirely my own.

My heartfelt thanks to: Alistair Wilson for the tour of Culmore Landfill; Michael Canny, priest, and Joe Carlin, Bradley and McLaughlin Undertakers, for information on funerals; Conor Maher-McWilliams, physicist, for relevant texts; James King and Jan Vaclav Caspers, my colleagues in Toxic Theatre; Bernie Webster, health visitor, for medical information; Garbhán Downey, writer, and Lisa Fitzpatrick, theatre academic, for notes on drafts; the Arts Council of Northern Ireland; everyone at Guildhall Press for their professionalism; all the staff at Altnagelvin Hospital, especially at Ward 3 and the Intensive Care Unit, for survival.

Brian and Fiona for love and support.

And my deepest gratitude and love to Diane Traynor for breathing the life of it.